Feathered
Serpent

蛇

Feathered Serpent

A Novel

XU XIAOBIN

Translated by John Howard-Gibbon and Joanne Wang

ATRIA INTERNATIONAL

NEW YORK   LONDON   TORONTO   SYDNEY

ATRIA INTERNATIONAL
A Division of Simon & Schuster, Inc.
1230 Avenue of the Americas
New York, NY 10020

First Atria International hardcover edition February 2009

ATRIA INTERNATIONAL and colophon are trademarks of Simon & Schuster, Inc.

For information about special discounts for bulk purchases, please contact Simon & Schuster Special Sales at 1-800-456-6798 or business@simonandschuster.com.

Designed by Dana Sloan

Manufactured in the United States of America

10 9 8 7 6 5 4 3 2 1

Library of Congress Cataloging-in-Publication Data
Xu, Xiaobin.
   [Yushe. English]
   Feathered serpent : a novel / By Xu Xiaobin ; [translated by John Howard-Gibbon and Joanne Wang]
      p. cm.
1. Xu, Xiaobin, date—Translations into English.   I. Howard-Gibbon, John.
II. Wang, Joanne III. Title.
PL2862.U15627Y9813 2009
895.1'352—dc22   2008015396

ISBN-13: 978-1-4165-8380-6
ISBN-10:   1-4165-8380-7

CONTENTS

ACKNOWLEDGMENTS

My profound thanks go out to:

Atria Books of Simon & Schuster for their wisdom and strength of judgment.

Judith Curr, my publisher, for her passion for international literature.

Johanna Castillo and Amy Tannenbaum, my editors, for their diligent work.

First translator, John Howard-Gibbon, for his unsurpassed power of insight and devotion, and his hard work over a period of more than a year in translating *Feathered Serpent*.

Professor Jan Walls who suggested the project to Mr. Howard-Gibbon.

Overseas Chinese Canadians Zhang Mai and his wife, He Na, who encouraged John along the way.

My dearest friend Mr. Wang who introduced *Feathered Serpent* to Miss Joanne Wang.

Mr. Grant Barnes and Professor Lawrence Sullivan for their invaluable editorial insights for the translation.

And my very deepest and heartfelt thanks must go to Joanne Wang herself, the book's agent and support translator. Like a scholar already long ago won over, she immediately grasped the spirit of *Feathered Serpent*; and like a high-spirited and courageous commanding officer, she laid out a well-planned strategy for the timely publication of the book. In our working together on *Feathered Serpent*, we have become like sisters.

Dear readers, I hope you enjoy and understand *Feathered Serpent*, and I also hope that the book shall belong not just to China, but to the entire world.

After meandering around mainland China for more than a decade, *Feathered Serpent* is at last venturing abroad in the form of an English language edition! Once I realized this was happening, I couldn't get these lines from one of my favorite songs out of my head: "There's naught that can *be* done / To quash your passion for *free*dom"—now these words flood my eyes with warm tears. For God knows how many years, our hearts have been unceasingly soaring toward freedom, but at a price greater than that for life itself—*Feathered Serpent*, in one sense, was written with blood.

We were unfortunate: We were born and raised in a nursery where we were all pruned to the same height to ensure uniformity, with no chance to stand gracefully and erect as individual blossoms. What was most painful to bear was that any out-of-the-ordinary blossoms were all doomed to be uprooted, even though their shoots were rich in fresh blood. Any that were fortunate enough to survive and become a new class of blossoms had their bright colors eaten away by pollution, to ultimately become commonplace.

But we were also fortunate: In today's world, in what other country have people in our age bracket had the rich experience that we have had? As little children, we were unhappy; as youngsters, we were lacking in elementary education; as youth, we were unaware of love; in middle age, we were lacking in vitality; in maturity, we lacked a spiritual home to return to . . . In a different world, people who had affection for one another never heard of Big Character Posters, Self-Denunciation Meetings, and arbitrary Arrest Orders; while, like a revolving lamp, all of these things spun past our eyes. Even though the Chinese people have the ability to for-get, all of these things that have happened are deeply carved into the mem-ory of the heroine of this book, and into the minds of countless people of the same generation.

Feathers that have left their wings can only drift, they cannot fly, because their fate is in the hands of the wind.

So in concluding these introductory words, I feel compelled to add that we live in a society that has lost its conscience, and where we have lost our spiritual convictions.

Beijing, February 8, 2008

Feathered
Serpent

蛇

| # A CLUSTERING OF QUEENS

 Late one evening, with an autumn breeze rustling out-side, I picked up a pen normally used for signing documents and began casually setting down some rather odd-looking lines on a sheet of imitation antique paper. Assessing my creation, my ten-year-old son said, "It looks like a snake that's growing some feathers."

Actually, it was a girl. Her hands were exaggeratedly long, so long, in fact, that they looked more like the branches of a tree—withered and silent, but beautiful; or like the great horns of a spotted sika deer, jutting out from the top of her head, entangled with the dark silken strands of her hair. The growing profusion of lines stirred the mind and touched the soul as they, one after another, took form on the paper, set against the girl's motionless face with its air of total indifference. I pointedly planted a mole between her eyebrows and used a great quantity of black ink to fill in her lips, giving them a rich and sultry allure. Hanging from the tree were her breasts, which of course were its fruit, while the lines of her waist formed quickly only to vanish in her navel; and her lower extremities bore the neatness of the patterns of the skin of a python, their curves slowly exuding a quiet beauty.

But as I sketched in some jewelry on her arms, a drop of ink spread out on the paper, destroying the drawing's feel of unity, so I had little choice but to turn the spilled ink into feathers. Only many years later did I learn that "*Yushe*," or "Feathered Serpent," was one of the names used by some primitive peoples to refer to the sun.

My sun was born under my pen, its birth as fortuitous as that, and there was nothing I could do about it.

But, in fact, Yushe is the name of one of the girls in our family clan. I spent several years researching our history. The way I see things, our blood ties carry a deep bit of mystery, especially on the maternal side. In order to better understand how our clan was formed, imagine a huge international chess board with a queen placed on its central square, from which she cannot move, while the pawns from any starting point on the perimeter of the board are permitted to move completely at random, as aimlessly even as a drunk, in any of the board's four directions, the direction of each step chosen from four equal probabilities. When a pawn gets to the very last square, which abuts against the base of the original queen, the pawn itself becomes the new queen and can no longer move. In the end a cluster of queens in the form of a treelike aggregation of branches, not at all like a net, gradually takes shape. In contemporary physics, such a wonderful pattern of branches is known as a "Witten-Sander DLA (Diffusion Limited Aggregation) Cluster."

Blood ties form just such a striking pattern of branches.

The patterns of blood ties allow us to fully appreciate the beauty of contemporary fractal art. Blood ties are a tree that can produce intricate, complicated forms that leave us baffled but allow us to appreciate the deep and subtle relationships between them and the real world. After many years of research I at last understand the treelike diagram of the structure of our family on the maternal side; or to put it another way, our cluster of queens.

On this treelike diagram, Yushe was the frailest but most resilient of branches. She started off with the wavering steps of a drunk, only to die prematurely, before becoming a queen.

But Yushe's early death had no influence on any of the other women in our clan. Jinwu, Ruomu, Xuanming—all of them—were the suns and oceans of earlier generations. They all came with life and coexisted with this part of the earth.

CHAPTER I | # TWILIGHT IN GOD'S COUNTRY

1

At three fifteen in the afternoon on a late spring day in the closing years of the century, when the bright green and red swatches of winter clothing had not yet completely disappeared from downtown streets, the doors to the operating ward of the city's most well-known hospital for brain surgery swung slowly open. As quietly as a boat rowed over calm waters, a gurney emerged. A nurse headed the procession, holding up an intravenous bottle, and in the usual order following the gurney were the head nurse, an intern, an assisting physician, and the surgeon in charge.

Although the young woman, whose name was Yushe, had obviously not yet emerged from a full general anesthesia, with the help of the rays of the afternoon sun you could make out her pale face with its bluish yellow blotches. Her head was largely swathed in bandages, giving her face with its bluish yellow tinges a bit of a ghostly air. It was not a beautiful face, its only redeeming feature being her extremely long eyelashes. Right now, with her eyes closed, the lashes completely cover her dark eye sockets, reaching right down to her cheeks with their tint of greenish yellow.

3

She was one of those women whose age doesn't show, this being especially true in the dim light of the afternoon. Like reflections in a soft golden pool of pleasantly cool water, her completely blurred facial features changed at will, shrinking or expanding in size, gathering together or drifting apart.

Of course, she had nothing to do with *Yushe*, my feathered serpent painting, with which she shared her name.

At that moment, some people who had been sitting on a sofa came to the gurney, but the dim light of the afternoon rendered them featureless; while my attention was drawn to an apparently young, blond-haired, blue-eyed male foreigner who was standing quietly in the corner.

The first of the people to go over to the gurney was the lady named Ruomu. Seventy-five years old, she was wearing a silk-floss-quilted black vest with cloud patterns embroidered in gold. The fragrance she exuded, as delicate and exquisite as an ethereal grove of bamboo, made the young women around her seem foul by comparison. It was a kind of aristocratic fragrance so deeply embedded in her being that no one could take it from her.

Ruomu's snow-white skin was unusual, something associated with women of the 1940s or even a bit earlier. Today such truly snowy whiteness, which was a result of the skin never being directly exposed to the sun, has largely become a thing of the past. So when the head nurse first saw her she felt a bit overwhelmed. There were no wrinkles on Ruomu's face, but, quite out of keeping with this, there were big bags hanging below her eyes like two chilly, burnished pendants. Her nose was reminiscent of the hooked beak of a raptor, and her lips, shaped like the leaf of the peach tree, were daubed with crimson lipstick, giving them a rich red luminescence. These, too, were some of the marks of a declining aristocracy. There is no way that a later age can carry on the strengths of a previous generation. In the past Ruomu had the kind of beauty that could overturn cities or topple empires. The lines of her face were delicate yet firm, a perfect contrast to the fuzzy lines of Yushe's face. Even though she was over seventy, the power of her beauty was overwhelming. Despite the fact that there were no wrinkles in her old face, it remained, nonetheless, a bit frightening.

With a very obvious look of gratitude in her eyes, Ruomu raised her intertwined hands to block the progress of the oldest of the doctors. The moment she did this, it gave the doctor a bit of a fright, as to him those hands appeared to be a set of beautifully preserved white bones.

The operation was a success—an unprecedented success. The chief surgeon had performed a frontal lobotomy, skillfully removing the germinal layer of the patient's brain. In guiding his precision scalpel through the complex network of nerves as tangled as unkempt hair, the surgeon had not damaged a single one. The decision to operate was made as a result of intense pressure from the female head of the patient's family. Her reasoning went this way: she wanted to have the germinal layer of her daughter's brain removed in order to preserve the girl's mental health and allow her to live out the rest of her life as a normal person.

Now her wish had been realized.

This beautiful seventy-five-year-old woman was none other than Yushe's mother. Right now her attention is riveted on her daughter, who is still under the anesthetic. Slowly, the loving mother's tears begin to ooze forth, as warm as spring waters bubbling up beneath a snowy sky.

2

In the early years of the 1960s, this now famous scenic area had not yet been recognized as such. Quite to the contrary, it was seen as a barren and desolate retreat for some of those who didn't fit in with the society of that time. Rising up fairy tale–fashion in the middle of this copse of tall deciduous trees was a small log cabin. Beyond the eye-catching golden glitter of leaves, an intense blue corner of the heavens exuded an inexplicable aura of tranquility.

There are mysteries in life that are beyond our ability to control. All we can do is yield to their power to carry us to those ancient visions floating about in the heavens. But those old stories, worn away as they have been by the wind and rain, can never fulfill us. What I want to describe is the fantastic changes in the scenes of my story that make it different. We must adapt to such changes ceaselessly.

In the twilight, these forests, with their great trees ablaze with a mysterious golden radiance, made the rest of nature seem like a lifeless graveyard.

There is also a lake. Fundamentally, in this story of ours, we should have eschewed such seemingly fairyland scenes. They are obviously not that realistic. This is especially true of the lake in front of the log cabin. Seemingly born out of the blue, the lake took form before the backdrop of the forest. The water of the lake was as blue as a translucent piece of crystal. Looking rather like coral, the weeds on its bottom sprouted countless beautiful tendrils. In the early 1960s, when Ruomu accompanied her husband when he was banished to this place, under absolutely no circumstances would she put her hands into that water. She was afraid that it contained a blue dye that could poison people, and that if she were to put her hands in it, the dye would get into her joints and she would never get rid of it. It was only after her little daughter stuck her hands into the water in play that Ruomu finally overcame this taboo. The little girl's name was Yu, or "feather," which she carried right from birth. It was only because she was born in the year of *She*, the "snake" or "serpent," that, pushing things a bit far, I threw the two words—"feather" and "serpent," or feathered serpent—together. Of course, there were also some other reasons, which you'll have to look for carefully as the rest of the story unfolds. Yushe's birth was a great disappointment for Ruomu, who had been hoping for a son. And the little girl was a long way from sharing in the kind of beauty her mother could have expected. Aside from the amazing eyelashes, there was simply nothing exceptional about her. But when those eyelashes fluttered, they made you think of the opening and closing of a black feather fan. That's what led Ruomu's mother, Xuanming, to give her the name Yu.

The names of Yu's two older sisters, on the other hand, were Ruomu's concoctions: at the time of the birth of her first daughter, silks and satins held a special interest for Ruomu, hence she named her Ling, a kind of delicate satin; when her second daughter was born, Ruomu had taken up playing the *xiao*, or vertical bamboo flute, hence that daughter's name was Xiao. At Yu's birth both her sisters were attending school in a large city a long way from the family's log cabin in the desolate retreat.

At that time, Ruomu's mother, Xuanming, had just entered her sixties.

She was born around the close of the nineteenth century, and her entire body gave off the melancholy gloom of that era. When Xuanming was alive, Ruomu would always sit in the wicker chair in front of the window and slowly clean her ears using a special solid gold ear spoon. Yu could not remember Ruomu ever going into the kitchen. Whenever it was time to cook, Ruomu would take up that solid gold ear spoon, while Xuanming would jump to her tiny feet and disappear into the kitchen. Those tiny bound feet were exquisite beyond compare.

As Yu remembered, Xuanming's feet were singularly special, and Yu had a passion for anything and everything out of the ordinary. In the evenings, when Xuanming had taken off her shoes, tiny little Yu, lifting up her grandma's feet in both hands, would kiss them. Every time she did this, Xuanming's dignified face would brim over with affectionate amusement. "Smell bad?" she would ask. "Bad," Yu would reply. "Are they sour?" "Sour." This indispensable little daily ritual of theirs always pleased Xuanming. Relegated to a lonely corner, those black satin shoes were reminiscent of the little folded paper boats that Yu liked to make. Their toes turned slightly upward, just like the bow of a real ship, and each featured a diamond-shaped piece of green jade.

For Yu, everything connected with Xuanming was both enigmatic and alluring. She had a very large chest made of a fine variety of rosewood called *jin hua li*. One of the most revered materials used in home finishing in the 1990s, proclaimed to be "worth more than its weight in gold," it was the finest material for hardwood floors. The cabinet had twenty-two drawers of various sizes, the keys to which Xuanming would clutch tightly in her hand. She could very quickly and accurately pick out the right key for each and every one of those drawers. Later on when she had lost her sight in both eyes, she could still do this. The moment she ran the tips of her fingers over those cold bits of metal, she could determine precisely which one was which. Xuanming was very precise in everything she did. There were countless sums planted in her head. After she had gone blind, many of the seemingly symbolic sort regularly traversed the lacquer-black darkness before those sightless eyes. Like little fireflies those numbers gave off a dull silver glow, bringing light to the remaining years of Xuanming's life.

One evening around dusk (many of the scenes in this story of ours are set at this time), Yu had squirreled in under the bed to play with her cloth doll. Yu liked playing under the bed, where she would stay for hours, feeling a kind of security in the shadow she found there. From under the bed she would see that pair of black satin shoes set with diamond-shaped jades come into the room and stop in front of the rosewood chest. Holding her breath, Yu would watch as, one by one, her grandmother opened its twenty-two drawers. In each of the drawers, there was a violet blossom shaped from pieces of violet-colored quartz. The twilight glow gave an unusual ethereal aura to these violet-colored blossoms. Xuanming would link the translucent, glasslike flowers together in sequence, to form a lamp—an absolutely gorgeous lamp, in the shape of a Chinese wisteria arbor. Just as with the keys, from the very outset Xuanming had worked out the coded sequence of these blossoms. These flowers all looked the same, but Xuanming knew they weren't and that if even one of them was out of sequence the lamp could not be put together.

Yu was simply enchanted. With riveted attention she watched her grandma's little game. In front of the twilight-filled window, the lamp revealed a beauty all its own. It was a dream—a dream played out before the restrained luxuriance of green leaves outside the twilight-filled window. Yu could not experience that dream, but her fingers could clearly feel a kind of glassy chill in the air.

In the twilight is a lamp made of violet-colored quartz. Its strings of blossoms give off a sound like wind chimes. Yu knows it is an expensive sound.

Facing the lamp, Xuanming may steep a fragrant cup of tea, but under the light of the lamp it will slowly cool.

3

For a long time now I have not been much for talking. Because I was very late in starting to talk, my father mistakenly thought I had been born mute. But I was quite aware that the reason I didn't like talking was that grown-ups never believed me. I saw things differently than they did. This was a major problem that reared its head again and again and was ultimately the root cause of all the misfortunes in my life. For example, were I to look out the window at night at some clothes that had been hung out to dry as they fluttered in the wind, I might just think it was a bunch of amputees dancing; or were I to hear the rustle of wind through the rosebushes, I might get so scared I'd start to cry, convinced that the house was surrounded by slithering snakes. In the lake across from the entrance to the house, with its water so clear you could see the bottom, on some twilit evenings (impossible to say precisely which ones), I would catch sight of a huge freshwater mussel. Sometimes the dark shell would reveal a long fissure as it started to open. The first time I saw this mussel, I cried out in terror, but eventually I got used to seeing it. On those occasions, I would simply go and get either my father or my mother, and taking him or her by the hand and holding it firmly while rooted to the spot, I would use my other tiny hand to point into the lake while shouting, "There! . . . There!" But it didn't matter which of them it was, I would be taken unceremoniously by the arm and told, "It's time to go home and eat!"

I also often heard sounds that resembled whispering, but just as often they were obscure and indistinct. Occasionally I would be able to make out some words, but couldn't altogether understand them. Nonetheless, to me, these whispers seemed like heavenly decrees. Frequently, I would act according to their obscure instructions. As a result, the things I did usually left the people around me feeling puzzled. Because I was so small, my actions didn't draw all that much attention, and when they finally did, a lot of time had already passed.

Back then, I still couldn't talk, and by the time I could, I had no desire to discuss those things. Oftentimes at twilight, I would stand staring out over the lake in a trancelike state, when in the dim light of dusk the many species of strange flowers along its shores would be quietly closing their petals. In those moments when sunset and moonrise shared the evening sky, these blossoms would take on darker tones, their petals becoming as translucent and fragile as glass. To my ears, when squeezed between the fingers, they would emit a chaotic, tinkling sound. At such times I might also see that huge mussel lying quiet and absolutely still on the bottom of the lake. One evening when there was a thunder-and-lightning storm, slipping out of the house unnoticed, I went down to the beach with my hair dancing in the wind like smoke, my face alternately obscure or lit up by lightning flashes. That evening, with no moon or stars, the lake was a blanket of darkness. Just as I was making my way through those huddles of strange flowers, a huge bolt of lightning lit up the whole lake, and I saw that huge mussel start slowly opening. It was empty; there was absolutely nothing inside. I bent down to get a closer look, my hair floating in the water like a pale green jellyfish. At that moment, in concert, the rolling thunder, lightning flashes, and pouring rain crushed down upon my little six-year-old girl's body. At that time, I still didn't know what fear of thunder and lightning was. All I felt was a kind of excitement, as if something was about to happen.

But after a while, the gleaming rays of a flashlight were added to the flashes of lightning. This mixture of light sources broke the images of both myself and the lake surface into myriad facets, reminiscent of the rococo stained-glass windows of European cathedrals. At the same time, I began to hear my grandmother's hoarse and exhausted cries.

A lamp was slowly approaching and I could smell the fragrance of tea leaves.

4

In an album of photos that Ruomu put together, there is an image of Xuanming when she was very young. It was taken near the end of the reign of the Qing Dynasty emperor Guangxu. Although Xuanming was only nine years old at the time, she was already astonishingly gorgeous. Everything about her indicated that she was destined to become a beauty with a heavenly allure the entire nation could admire. But the political upheaval at the end of the century downgraded that destiny. Her beauty was eclipsed by the turmoil of those times. Or else you could say it was changed, replaced with an unfortunate, chilly gloom. In that photograph, it was the girl standing behind Xuanming that gave it a special value. Looking fat and shapeless draped in a palace gown, with big eyes in a round face and a meticulously painted mouth, she was obviously totally lacking in vitality. She could not in any way be regarded as beautiful. But serving as a vivid symbol of sacrifice, that girl's name has been recorded in the annals of history. She was Zhenfei, Emperor Guangxu's favorite consort, and one of Xuanming's paternal aunts.

That was a midsummer day in the twenty-fifth year of Guangxu's reign and also the last summer in Zhenfei's life. There are many different accounts of how she died. The most common versions started with Zhenfei meddling in state politics, for which she was roundly condemned by the scheming Empress Dowager Cixi, then locked up on nothing but a basic sustenance diet. Finally, following Cixi's issuance of an Imperial edict, she was thrown by a eunuch named Cui Yugui down a well, where she died. But Xuanming insisted that that was definitely not Cixi's intention.

Xuanming said that Cui threw Zhenfei down the well without waiting for any order from Cixi. If this had not been the case, there was no way that Cixi would have been afraid of seeing Eunuch Cui afterward, nor would she have had him removed from his position of authority and dismissed from the palace as soon as she could arrange it. Having Xuanming and her aunt Zhenfei photographed together was a special favor for Cixi that she arranged. In the sunset years of her life, the old dowager enjoyed the beauty in small things, the kind of beauty that could be cuddled. For Cixi, with her failing old cataract-ridden eyes, little Xuanming's striking beauty made her think of her own teenage years. Then she sniffed the odor of bottle gourd blossoms, and the raw silk fragrance of the delicate folding fan that waved in her hand. She invited little Xuanming to come and sit on her lap, but by this point in Cixi's life her limbs had become as thin as sticks of kindling. Xuanming very carefully curled up her own legs, afraid that those withered old bones beneath her might suddenly snap.

Over the next several decades, this event became a regular and unchanging theme in Xuanming's conversation. It would always start out like this: In the twenty-fifth year of Guangxu's reign, Empress Dowager Cixi cuddled me closely in her arms . . . In the decades that followed, this theme was to develop into a most unusual tale: Xuanming was one of the most beautiful

Manchu girls in the waning years of the Qing Dynasty, and the most doted upon of all of Cixi's great-granddaughters. Cixi had on many occasions summoned her to enter the palace, and intended to have her installed as a young princess. But the death of the old empress dowager turned all such plans into empty illusions . . .

Time always turns history into fairy tales.

Her mother's talk convinced Ruomu that she was the descendant of a Manchu princess. As a result, in everything Ruomu did, she always demanded of herself the standards of a princess. Even during wartime disruption, Ruomu always combed her hair meticulously, using a hair pomade popular among older women of the time, made by soaking paulownia wood shavings in water. Ruomu would arrange her rich and abundant hair in a very heavy coil. On one occasion only, after the air-raid sirens during the war with Japan had sounded three times, her hairdo was knocked askew in the jam-packed air-raid shelter, the coil tumbling down like a black waterfall, leaving her feeling as painfully embarrassed as if she had been stripped naked in front of a crowd. Following the custom of people of the Manchu ethnic group, Ruomu walked without moving her body from the waist up, a practice she stuck to throughout her entire life. Even into her seventies, with her face as pale as snow, she still wore russet-colored traditional Chinese dresses made from gambiered Guangdong gauze and walked with her body as rigid as a ramrod, leaving in her wake the traditional fragrance of jasmine and lavender.

In actual fact, however, Ruomu's family on her mother's side had absolutely no ties with the Manchu ethnic group. Ruomu's maternal grandfather and grandmother were both full-blooded Han Chinese, but the family held office under the Manchus and accepted the Manchu political banner system. Yet, there was not, indeed, a drop of aristocratic Manchu blood in Ruomu's veins.

5

Yu had a high fever that persisted for seven full days, scaring her mother out of her wits. Xuanming came up with the idea of getting some white whiskey and giving Yu a rubdown. When Xuanming's decrepit old fingers contacted Yu's skin, it had a chilly feeling, like a piece of pottery. It was as delicate and lustrous as if she were the descendant of some aquatic creature—so delicate that if you touched it, it would shatter. But despite this, Xuanming carried on her massage. With her large hands, she vigorously rubbed every inch of her granddaughter's little body, a body so feeble it didn't seem to have any bones. Xuanming was getting so tired that she gasped for breath. With the two pieces of jade on her black satin shoes jiggling because she couldn't hold herself steady, she kept chattering away as she rubbed. She said this child must be the reincarnation of a snake; otherwise, how could she be so cold, so cold?!

When Yu awoke she saw Ruomu in front of the twilit window cleaning her ears, her gold-colored ear spoon a waving spot of golden light. For a long time Yu couldn't figure out where she was. Watching her in the golden rays of twilight, Yu noticed a strange protuberance in her mother's abdomen, a protuberance that spoiled her charming and graceful figure. Her mother was wearing an ocher-colored cotton cheongsam printed with black flowers, actually black chrysanthemums. Yu could imagine that in the natural world a genuinely black chrysanthemum would without a doubt be frighteningly beautiful.

Her father, who seldom came home, showed up one weekend. The first thing he said when he saw Yu was: how come this kid is so thin? He was the only one in the family to pay any attention to Yu's weight. Before Yu had a chance to think of a response to her father's question, the door to Ruomu's room opened. The room had a cold, gloomy atmosphere, but the father braved its chilly breath and entered, his face swathed in an attitude of unavoidable martyrdom. Then Yu heard the sound of suppressed voices and the heavy sighs of her father. She waited outside with persistence, hoping to get a chance to have a private chat with him, but he didn't come out.

Yu realized very early in life that her mother and maternal grandmother didn't really like her. Whenever her grandmother saw her she babbled out, "Our family will decline now a demon has been born . . ." Her mother swung her head around and stared at Yu. Those absolutely empty eyes filled the little girl with fear. Nothing could have been more frightening than that absolute emptiness. It made her think of that huge freshwater mussel and the time when the shell opened to reveal there was nothing inside, bringing an abrupt end to all her fantasies about it. That kind of emptiness filled her with fear, a fear that made her sick.

She didn't want to admit it, but, in fact, she enjoyed being sick, because when she was, her mother and grandmother were a bit nicer to her. Her grandmother would make her a bowl of wonton, then sit beside the bed watching her eat and recalling the good times of the past. Her grandmother might tell her about the pastries shaped like ram horns that oozed honey as soon as you bit into them, and which were sold in the company store during the family's years on the Gansu-Shanghai railroad. Just hearing about them made Yu's mouth water. She loved to eat, but in her time, when there were no pastries, she had to settle for a bit of watery wine or wontons with mushroom stuffing made by her grandmother. There were always plenty of mushrooms in the woods around their home.

Forever dissatisfied with the realities of life, Yu's grandmother Xuanming lived entirely in her world of memories. Her eyes would light up whenever she indulged in her reveries, but then reality would intrude, disillusionment would blanket her face, and she would mutter and pout. And whenever Father encountered such moaning he would drown it with his own. Very obviously, he disapproved of Grandma's attitude. Father and Grandma were always at odds in Yu's family, and everybody in the family knew this.

After Yu had recovered from her illness, she enrolled in elementary school. The school was located in the nearby forest. Her two elder sisters, however, went to school in the large city located a long way from their home. Their father had said that even if it had been farther away, they definitely could not hold back the girls' education. Yu also knew that the name of the lady looking after her sisters' education was Jinwu. But Yu could not see that her mother expressed any gratitude toward Jinwu. For a time Yu's curiosity and interest in Jinwu completely dominated her life. In her mind, she dreamed up many images of Jinwu, but she couldn't find a single trace of Jinwu in the family's eight fat photo albums.

6

The snowfall that day was so heavy that the entire world was white—the kind of absolute white that admits of no lacunae.

Languidly and without cease, it floated softly earthward, the flakes so large they frightened you. When she was very small, Yushe had already discovered the wonderful variety of hexagonal shapes that can be seen in a kaleidoscope. In order to pick those beautiful hexagonal flowers, she broke open the kaleidoscope. The result was total disappointment. She found it was nothing more than a tube made of thick paper, with three long slips of glass and some broken bits of colored glass inside, and not a single hexagonal blossom.

Through the open window, Yu caught some snowflakes in her tiny hands to bring them inside. As she looked at the hexagonal ice crystals, their exquisite beauty was something beyond man's doing, they quickly melted. Yu tried futilely to think of some way to preserve these six-pointed wonders, but eventually she did come up with the perfect solution.

In her art class at school one day, her teacher told the students to paint something they liked, the thing in life they liked the best, to give to the person they liked the best. Using poster paint, Yu completely covered a large, white piece of paper in an exquisite blue. When the blue had dried, using a deep, rich, snowy white, she covered the paper with a series of hexagonal snowflake designs, each of them unique unto itself, each revealing through the unsophisticated simplicity of a child's hand a unique kind of beauty. The blue and white she chose were so gorgeous they dazzled the eye of the viewer. From her own desk, as if suddenly compelled by something to do so, the teacher went over and planted herself beside Yu, where she remained until the painting was finished. As soon as Yu put down her brush, the teacher picked up the painting and went up to the dais. She asked for the class's attention and told them to look at Yu's work. She said she wanted to hang it in the classroom and that the students should learn from Yu, should emulate her, because she painted so beautifully. Then she said no, that she wouldn't hang it in the classroom because she wanted to enter it in exhibitions, exhibitions for the work of young artists. Then she said no, no, not just painting exhibitions; she wanted to enter it in international painting competitions for youth and children; she hoped her student could win a prize in an international competition . . . Deeply moved as she was, the teacher had so much to say that she was taken completely off guard when Yu bounced up to the front of the room and without a hint of hesitation took back her painting. This happened so quickly it took everyone by surprise, leaving the teacher and all of Yu's classmates completely dumbfounded. Just as Yu turned to leave, the bell rang, signaling the end of class.

Without so much as a glance behind her, Yu left the classroom. When she got to the reception office at the school's front gate, with one hand she held the painting against the wall while with the other she wrote, "For my mother and father," in lopsided characters in the bottom right-hand corner. At that time in her life, her hands were still so small that more than once she almost dropped it. So she had to take extra care not to dirty its gorgeous shades of blue and white. As she was finishing her little inscription, the parents who were arriving to pick up their little charges began milling around at the school entrance. Just as she always did, Yu had climbed on a high stone terrace to wait. She looked a bit more lively than usual; but, although she was still the same tiny little thing, she had, quite amusingly, assumed an adult air. Solemnly clutching the rolled-up painting, she focused her gaze on the horizon. The clothes she was wearing that day were made out of one of her mother's old outfits. Originally, it had been green, but after so many times in the washtub mixed with other colors, it had acquired the tone of an ancient bronze artifact. So from a distance, and totally out of keeping with who and what she was, Yu looked like a tiny bronze statue.

In dribs and drabs eventually her classmates had all gone, but no one had come to pick up Yu. With the painting getting heavier and heavier, she started a countdown, but the numbers just kept mounting up. After a while, the school yard was empty. As more time passed, it started to snow, the heavy flakes fluttering slowly earthward, huge in size and falling one by one. Yu tucked her painting under her clothing and stood there in the snow, taking no heed of the shouts of the old grandpa in the reception office. Standing at the window, he called out, "Which class are you from? Quick! Come on in and warm yourself in front of the stove. You look frozen!"

Yu had been standing there so long that the melting flakes had soaked through her clothes and then frozen solid again to clad her in icy armor. From the outside, it looked like a white, gleaming layer of frosty snow, but it wasn't soft—it was frozen solid. Just at that time, a bicycle came wobbling along and stopped at the school gate. Yu saw that it was old man Li, who looked after the public telephone. As he raised his arm to rub his nose, which was a frozen rosy red, the arm that had been wounded on the battlefield in the war to assist Korea in the struggle against American aggression, he gave a squinting smile and said, "Let's get you home right away. Your mom has just given birth to a little brother for you!" Yu stared at him blankly, apparently not understanding what he had said. With his good arm, Old Li quickly picked her up and set her on the backseat of the bicycle, smiling as he said, "Your father is busy looking after your mother, and he asked me to come and fetch you. Oh . . . who wouldn't want to have a son! Your mother is almost forty, she's really blessed to have a son at this late age!"

Yu sat quietly on the bicycle's backseat. Because they were cold, she brought her hands to her mouth and blew on them, the pale, whitish mist of her breath dissipating quickly in the passing currents of air. At that point in time, she had no idea what had happened nor of the significant part it would play in her life.

7

When Yu got home, she saw her mother was in bed, looking very relaxed and comfortable, with a tiny little fellow lying beside her. The tiny little fellow was asleep. He had a skinny face, as wrinkled as the shell of a walnut, and only a few sparse strands of blondish rather than nice black hair. The little fellow was truly not the least bit good-looking—you wouldn't even say he was lovable. He was not in the least like Yu imagined a little baby would be. But what Yu felt really strange about was how the family could be so solemn about the little fellow's arrival, and where, in fact, he had come from. It all seemed so strange to Yu that she reached out and pressed on its wrinkly little nose. That's all she did, but it was enough to elicit a little cry, rather feeble at first, but it quickly turned into a storm.

Yu's heart gave a tremendous thump and she jumped back, overwhelmed with fear. She was totally flabbergasted that such a tiny creature could without notice produce such a loud noise, and that his face, like that of a little old man, was so expressive; a face that, with its ever-changing patterns of wrinkles, was reminiscent of the lovely textures of a slowly opening chrysanthemum blossom. While she was still caught up in this startling wonder, she suddenly felt a heavy blow on her cheek, a blow so hard that it was beyond the ability of a six-year-old girl to bear, and she toppled to the floor. As she fell, she knocked over the tea tray beside her and four porcelain teacups with gold-rimmed phoenix-head covers shattered as they hit the floor.

Still in a dazed state, Yu saw her mother's distorted face so close to her own that she could clearly make out the dilated, dull yellow pupils of her eyes. Yu knew that they looked like this only when she was extremely angry.

Before Yu had fully recovered from the first blow, she was struck again on the other cheek. Even Yu herself could never remember how many times her mother hit her that day. She didn't even have time to cry. All she knew was fear. She had no idea why her mother's behavior changed so radically that day. All she had done was softly tap that little nose—it wasn't really anything at all!

After crawling out from under the dark green satin quilt, the mother had put on a light-colored wool-and-cotton-mix blouse-and-trouser outfit. On her tiny feet, the grandmother also came stumbling into the room. As soon as Yu's mother saw her own mother, she started to cry, as if she, not her daughter Yu, had been the one to suffer a beating. The sounds of her mother's crying, talking, and mumbling all penetrated into the very marrow of Yu's bones. "Poor me, for a whole day and a night, I haven't been able to close my eyes," said the mother. "It's hard to know what to do. That little brat just waited for a moment when I wasn't looking and pinched shut my little baby's nose. If I hadn't noticed this right away the poor little fellow could have died!" In her heart, Yu was shouting out that her mother was lying, that it wasn't true; but except for her bitter crying, not a sound came from her, Yu's outpouring of tears stifling her heart.

The old grandmother's face dropped as she listened to her daughter's words. She responded by saying that very early on she had realized there was nothing good about this selfish little granddaughter, and asking Ruomu if she had forgotten that when Yu had just been born, old man Li had read her fortune and said that she was destined to hinder the birth of male heirs, and that, in fact, in Ruomu's two subsequent miscarriages, the fetuses were already male in both cases. Thinking about it for a while, the mother agreed, adding that this was precisely what had happened and that if she hadn't been reminded by her own mother, she would not have remembered it. She also spoke self-pityingly of how much suffering those two miscarriages had brought her, and of the fact that both her hands were still numb and that she couldn't clench her fists. It seemed that the more she thought about it, the more wronged she felt, and she started wailing again—mumbling, sobbing, talking.

The pain in Yu's head made her think it had exploded. In the midst of this chorus of mumbling, the grandmother turned to Yu and in a loud voice said, "From now on you must never again strike this little guy. Understand? He is your little brother, a boy. He is going to carry your family line, and is more important than you are. Understand? Your mother can't have any more babies. Understand?!" Yu could see that the usual cool beauty of her grandma's eyes had been replaced with raging flames. Yu knew that her uncle—Grandma's only son—had died in the turbulent years of fighting and that after her husband died, she had to move in with her daughter because she had no place else to go, which had led to endless bickering between the two. Yu had heard all the nasty things her grandma said behind her mother's back: "Shameless bitch! Can't live without a man? Heartless bitch! Poor me—for the sake of the likes of her, I sacrificed my wonderful son! That rotten . . . ! That stinking . . . ! That good-for-nothing . . . !" And Mother was no slouch in this line either: "You old widow, if you're so good at this, so good at that, how come when Father was still around he preferred sleeping with showgirls, not you!"

Her mother and grandmother's heated exchanges often left Yu gaping dumbstruck with fear. But now, suddenly, they had joined hands to deal with her, the focus of their alliance being the little guy on the bed with that face as wrinkled as the skin of a walnut.

On the other hand, when there was none of the foul language, the grand-mother and her daughter were usually refined in manner. The grandmother had little in the way of education other than a few years in a traditional old private tutorial school, but when it came to paying a bill, even the sales clerks couldn't outdo her on the abacus. As far back as Yu could remember, her mother never went into the kitchen. Whenever mealtime approached, the mother would sit in that wicker chair in front of the window and clean her ears using her solid gold ear spoon, which, of course, had been a gift from her own mother.

Yu deeply admired her mother for this. At that time, in her dreams, a beautiful middle-aged woman often put in an appearance, always dressed in a cream-colored traditional silk jacket, buttoned down the right side, her hair combed in waves, skin white as snow, and lips sporting a dark shade of lipstick. Yu was fully aware of her own longing to grow up, to become just this kind of woman. Yu's fantasies then were quite straightforward. She longed to dwell in a fantasy-filled dream, a dream like an indestruc-tible kaleidoscope, with its endlessly intriguing colorful patterns. What Yu liked more than anything else was sleeping. Sometimes she was so eager to get to sleep that she even forgot to do her homework. Then dreams came to her in endless strings, to the point that she had trouble distinguishing dream from reality. If she encountered something upsetting in her dreams, recognizing it as part of the dream, she would usually manage to prod her-self awake. Painfully shy, she would go as far as feigning crudity or blind stubbornness to hide such feelings. She was so afraid of people that often, when the family had guests, she would slip out at the first opportunity and not come back until the middle of the night. If she didn't get a chance to slip out, she would lock herself in the bathroom, then crawl out through the little window and use the branches of the mulberry tree in the backyard to climb over the wall. Fortunately, at that time the family still lived in the little log house, so none of the walls were very high. Because of her fear of meeting people, Yu could go without meals or sleep. She didn't really know what it was in her life that frightened her, but at this time, with both her mother and her grandmother unexpectedly turning hostile toward her, she suddenly felt that this thing that she had so blindly feared for so long was suddenly close to revelation.

8

From the very depths of my heart I loved my father, despite the fact that he seldom came home and was always so cold and serious. I remember one occasion when we still lived in that big city, just when Mother was about to bawl me out for something, Father suddenly pulled out a theater ticket and, waving it about, told me to leave right away, that if I didn't, I would miss the beginning of the show! I quickly stuffed the ticket in my pocket and took off like a shot for the local theater—I was a dyed-in-the-wool movie maniac.

The lights had already been turned off when I entered the theater. I started on my way into a row of seats and as I stumbled and bumped my way along, the people in the row behind me rebuked me, calling out things like: "Hey, kid! Sit down!" In a confused panic, I almost sat on someone's legs. At that moment a hand delicate and smooth as a piece of jade took hold of me and gently and patiently guided me into an empty seat. I tried to get a better look at the person who owned that hand, but it was so dark I couldn't see a thing.

The film's opening music was still playing, its strangely bizarre style totally new to me. I found it a bit unnerving, and without thinking about it, I moved closer to that person beside me and once again that gentle hand very lightly grasped my arm, easing my tension. Just then I saw a woman's hand appear on the screen. It was precisely that hand just as I had imagined it, that hand as delicate and smooth as a piece of jade that had made me feel secure. The girl was doing the nails of that hand, using a red nail polish. The scene was shot from behind her. She was dressed in rags but had a beautiful figure and long brown hair that reached her waist. At this point a very pleasing baritone voice queried, "Zhuo Ma?" The girl turned around and a close-up revealed a pair of brown eyes set behind long eyelashes. The radiant luster in those eyes filled my own heart with light. At this point the audience's gaze was transferred to the fastidiously dressed baritone who had just walked on-screen, but I didn't like his flashy green and gold outfit. I felt that in his golden threads, he fell far short of the radiance of the girl in her dilapidated duds. The story's development proved my instinct was right. The man was a headman. His love for the girl ended in her having a baby. After that he invented endless excuses to avoid seeing her, leaving her to swallow disappointment, until finally, with her own eyes, she saw him making love with another woman. Her revenge was frightful: with her own hands, she strangled their child—that innocent child who was the product of their love. The moment she killed the child, the theater echoed with incessant cries of horror.

When I saw that beautiful pair of hands reaching out for the child, I suddenly slipped out of my seat and for the longest time didn't dare raise my head, until finally that hand as delicate and smooth as a piece of jade helped me up. I was totally awestruck: to my utter surprise, the young woman sitting beside me had turned out to be the actress in the movie! At this point, my eyes had already been adjusted to the light level in the theater for a long time. I could see very clearly the unusual radiance of her brown eyes.

When the movie's closing music started, the screen was filled with the white of falling snow and a back view of the girl with the beautiful figure, dressed in rags, staggering off into the distance. I watched in amazement as the entire screen was filled with fluttering snowflakes. The close-up of snowflakes was exceedingly beautiful: the beautiful snow blanketed everything—both the beautiful and the ugly.

As we were leaving the theater, I heard the people around me discussing whether the girl would put an end to her life or not, but that didn't worry me in the least. I persistently kept my eyes on the back of the young woman ahead of me who had been sitting beside me. She kept disappearing then reappearing in the crowd. But my mind was definitely made up: to catch up to her, talk to her, even just one sentence! I actually did catch up to her once, but just as I got close enough to touch her, I hesitated, and right at that moment the crowd pressed between us again. My heart was in my throat the entire time. I truly didn't care whether that woman in the movie lived or died. What concerned me was this living young woman with her radiant brown eyes and lovely hands.

9

We have already mentioned that Yu knew very early in her life that her mother didn't really like her. But the mother said this was because Yu "was not likable."

Yu very much wanted to be a likable child, but it was beyond her ability. When she was very small she discovered that if you wanted to be a likable child, you had to say things you didn't mean. But she would sooner have killed herself than done that. Falsehoods aside, she even found it hard to say things that were true, because she had discovered that when the things in your heart were turned into words they lost much of their special value, and that whether a lot or just a little, whatever you put into words was bound to contain some element of falsehood. Because of this, she very seldom said anything. The result of this reluctance to speak was her "being unlikable," and there was nothing that could be done to change this. But today, for the first time in her life, Yu hated her stupid mouth and lack of courage. She thought that if she was a little girl who "was likable," she would have been able to smile sweetly at that young woman and, taking her by the hand, invite her home. Things would have been going smoothly, definitely not as they were at that point, with her throat seemingly sealed with a coat of lacquer, a muffled thunder pounding in her heart, and not even the slightest sign of bold action on her part.

Once she had passed through that rather barren little wood, she could see the front door of their home. Her heart was filled with despair, so when that long brown hair suddenly appeared among the scrub, for the longest time Yu couldn't believe her eyes.

"You and your father are not the least bit alike."

The young woman smiled, her brown eyes flashing brightly in the evening glow.

The long brown hair floated on, while Yu stood rooted to the spot, her throat still sealed shut: "She knew I was following her; for sure she knew!" thought Yu, her face suddenly turning crimson. "But it's hard to believe she suddenly turned up in this woods like a fairy just to say something like that!

For sure, she's a fairy!" When Yu thought of this word, her mind became a blank. Memory and illusion were inseparable. Every time she recalled that event, the young woman, whose name was Jinwu, always made her entrance in the form of a fairy, a fairy who suddenly appeared in a mysterious forest. Dressed in pale pink satin and enshrouded in her long brown hair, she would suddenly disappear then reappear like a pink cloud against the background of an evening sky. That incomparably lustrous evening glow seemed to represent some kind of irresistible force. Facing that force, Yu's kaleidoscopic little heart was deeply touched, breaking into countless translucent fragments. While she was caught in that kind of controlling pressure, the fairy would whisper to her, "You and your father are not the least bit alike."

Although that whisper was very soft, it was terribly unnerving, since at that moment the sky was reverberating with background music. Yu's memory was clogged with countless examples of just that kind of intimidating background music, so what she heard was a kind of magnified whisper—a terrifying unearthly gibberish.

Only a long time after the event did Yu finally tell her mother her tale about the fairy. The mother raised those exquisite eyebrows arching out on either side of her nose as she said, "What fairy? That was one of your father's students. She's a mixed-blooded whore who's had parts in a couple of movies."

10

Yu didn't eat supper. With her nose dripping blood, she went into her room and bolted the door. After a while she smashed everything around her to bits, leaving her room looking like the inside of that kaleidoscope. In complete contrast with her gentle appearance, Yu had a fiery temper. She used the pieces of a smashed vase to mutilate her own body, spilling her own fresh blood. Following her own childish yet determined way of thinking, she repeatedly told herself that what she was doing was real, that only this was real. Yu felt that only through her own physical suffering could she ease her mental pain. Mother doesn't love me, she told herself, Mother doesn't love me—to this six-year-old girl this was the fatal fact, and it smashed her heart to smithereens.

The mother and grandmother in turn banged on the door to Yu's room, calling softly, then loudly. The sound of her mother's mumbled crying penetrated straight into her brain. What was strange was that the mother always made herself out to be one who suffered. When Yu had reached the point where her pain had crushed her desire to live, it was surprisingly her mother who would receive others' compassion. When Yu withdrew into her room, she could see a corner of the sky through her window. Her attention always wandered back to this corner of clear blue sky, which was gradually shrouded in darkness. Yu felt that she was able to see beyond the surface layer of the sky to something much deeper—a kind of color that inspired terror. When she looked at it, she recalled the whispers of that young woman. They were the gloomy sky's bedtime prayers, which had a kind of frightening power that was very difficult to convey in words.

The sounds outside her room gradually faded away. It was already impossible to distinguish the colors she had seen in the sky. She heard the front door open and apparently someone came in. Yes, the sound of those footsteps was very familiar. It was her father. Then she heard the sound of suppressed voices and her father's heavy sighs.

The darkness reverberated with the whispery sound of her mother's voice.

Her mother was saying that she thought that brat Yu had something frightening about her. The look in Yu's eyes made people think she had cannibalistic tendencies, and that they had better not let her too near the baby.

Father sighed and said, "Please don't complicate things. Okay? They're organizing another political movement out there, so I've already got more than enough on my plate."

But mother continued on as if she hadn't heard him: "Anyway, she'll soon be on winter vacation, so the best thing to do is send her to stay with your big sister for a while."

Yu knew that the big sister she referred to was her father's elder sister. This aunt, who had never married, had a vicious demeanor and Yu had always been afraid of her.

This suppressed conversation continued without pause, stopping only when the fragrance of fresh tea wafted out of the grandmother's room. Yu was standing absolutely still in the hallway, which was so black that as her eyes bored into the depths of the darkness, the darkness became for her a kingdom of quietude. But now the stillness was shattered by a kind of terrifying whispering. Just at that moment Yu could clearly see Xuanming standing in the corner dressed in black. Unable to suppress her fear, Yu let out a loud cry as she barged into her parents' room. But an even greater fright awaited her: she saw her normally rather sanctimonious parents locked in each other's arms, the yellow and white of their naked bodies clearly twined together in the darkness. As she stood there not knowing what to do, through the darkness she heard her mother shrieking angrily, "Get out! Get out! You brat! You brazen bitch! Get out of my sight!"

In a panic, Yu flew to her own room. The grandmother, who had fallen into a deep sleep, was snoring loudly in company with the roaring thunder outside. Little Yu felt that there was no place for her to flee to. Those three words—"you brazen bitch"—burnt like a branding iron into her heart. Many years later, when she recalled that scene, she still felt that searing pain in her heart. Shame totally blanketed the six-year-old girl's life, a totally unjustified shame that had no connection with her, but she still had to bear it. This condemnation made her feel that she was the one at fault. From that day forward, she always felt that she was always in the wrong. In everything that she attempted, even before she started, she would have overwhelming premonitions of defeat. In the end she really was defeated, soundly defeated by all those around her.

Her father came out and spoke to her. She felt that she couldn't bear his indifference, but she couldn't explain things to him—not for her entire life. When her father was talking, she didn't take in a thing that he said. Her attitude incensed him, and he flicked his sleeve in anger and turned to leave, but suddenly he heard a small voice mutter something and he stopped and said, "What is it?" She looked up at him, and as soon as he saw that pair of eyes, easily hurt and as soft and sensitive as water, he relented. In a gentle tone he said, "What did you say, Yu?" Her reply was very clear: "Is Jinwu pretty?" When she said this her face turned deathly pale, as if preparing herself for a vicious slap in the face. Caught off guard for a moment, her father eyed her warily as he asked, "My little girl, what leads you to ask me such a thing?!"

From that day on, Yu knew that there were some things a child should never ask, let alone do. But there wasn't a soul who could stop her from thinking such things. She shut herself in her own world. An idea had firmly taken root in her brain: she was determined to meet Jinwu face-to-face.

When Yu discovered that where she had seen Xuanming standing there was a clothes rack with black clothing hanging on it, she told Xuanming about it. When she heard this Xuanming said nothing. Several days later, talking to herself, Xuanming said, "I'm not going to live that much longer. My soul has been scared away by that little demon!" From that day on Xuanming and Ruomu called Yu "that little demon" behind her back. Xuanming would say, "The family will decline now that a demon has been born into it." But Xuanming, in fact, was to live a very long life, almost becoming a centenarian. The evening before she passed away, she still managed to play her wonderful "threading the lamp" game, but didn't have enough time to dismantle it, so the lamp just hung there in all its startling beauty. Ruomu had taken it away to sell it, but no one wanted to buy it. It seemed it was the kind of rare treasure that could only belong to one person, and that person had died before she could pass on the secret of its construction. It was only after the passage of several generations that the lamp was finally presented to the country's most well-known museum—by Yun'er, the daughter of Yushe's older sister, Ling. Only after the comrade in charge in the museum had done a lot of research did they finally decide to accept the unusual lamp. But it was displayed in an inconspicuous corner, with no explanatory material identifying the dynasty and reign to which this cultural relic had belonged.

11

Yu shut herself in her room and didn't eat for several days. Gnashing their teeth, her parents and grandmother kept reminding one another to ignore her. None of them considered that the eccentric behavior of this young girl was worthy of their attention. All of them clustered around the little baby

with a tiny penis. All their hopes rested on him. His every cry and smile elic-
ited an eager reaction. He was going to be the genuine uniting force in this
family, with its plethora of *yin* and paucity of *yang*.

It was apparently four days later, at three o'clock in the morning, when a
muffled sound, like something heavy hitting the ground, rudely awoke Yu's
parents. The mother sat up quickly, saying, "Yu, it's Yu," as her entire body
began shaking violently. Without uttering a word, the father shot outside,
with the mother right on his heels, but she didn't forget to put on her quilted
satin jacket and trousers. Sometimes the mother liked to go for theatrical
effects. If Yu had been just a bit older, she could have understood why her
mother frequently indulged in the misconception of seeing herself as a young
thespian longing for the season of love. But Yu was too small. She was only
six years old; and, like any six-year-old girl, she longed to keep her mother to
herself, to be the pampered child nestled in her bosom. But her mother had
forsaken her, and to Yu, an introverted and sensitive six-year-old girl, this
was like having the heavens collapse.

Actually, all Yu had done was open her window and throw a chair outside.
As Yu's father and mother rushed outside, a real drama was taking place—
perhaps the very drama that the mother had been hoping for. Like a specter
from the netherworld, Yu slowly made her way to her parents' bedroom. She
knew that there was a tiny cradle lying there, like a fat silkworm cocoon,
shrouded in the warmth generated by the parents' bodies.

Stretched out beside the little cradle, Yu could see that the little fellow
still looked about the same, but in the moonlight that walnut-skinned face
looked a bit smoother, rendering the little guy a bit better looking. He was
sound asleep. As the changing light crossed his face, it would light up for
a moment, then disappear in shadow. Quite inopportunely, Yu at this moment thought of that movie she had seen. When that pair of beautiful hands
reached out toward that innocent child, it suddenly started to wail. It seemed
like this wailing was signaling someone that this little something was alive.
But the way it was wailing distorted the child's face: suffused with crimson,
it seemed to have taken on a savage expression.

But in the shadow of this dark night, Yu had not noticed her little brother's expression. At that moment, the window was lit up by a slanted shaft of dim moonlight. Yu thought the window looked like a gargantuan snowflake. Snowflakes are supposed to be beautiful, but this one, because it was so huge, looked absolutely sinister.

The grandmother's snoring stopped for a moment, then quickly resumed. Yu thought that the sound was a kind of hidden hint, rather like that inconceivably unsettling whispering, and that it had an irresistible power.

12

That huge snowstorm was recorded in the historical annals of the region. When the snow finally stopped, both the sky and the lake took on a deep shade of blue that had never been seen before, and the trees stood erect in a swatch of dark green. There were reports that this part of the nation's north had had disastrous snowstorms before, so the people who live in the area should pay special attention to the weather report. On that occasion the weather report was: tomorrow afternoon will be cloudy, then will clear; the wind will be from the north, then will shift to the south; winds will range from force two to force three; temperature high will be three degrees Celsius . . .

On that day, a lot of people were out shoveling snow. Lots of things got buried in the snow. The strangest thing that turned up was a painting shrouded in a frozen layer of snow. The one corner that wasn't covered clearly revealed that it was a painting of snowflakes against a blue background. The flakes, both big and beautiful, breathed a kind of childlike simplicity. The people who saw it all whooped in wonder, but it eventually ended up in the garbage can along with all the other pickings.

Like a magnified whisper, the sounds of the weather report resounded among the people sweeping snow: "There is a high-level trough in the country's northwestern region."

CHAPTER 2

TRIAL IN ABSENTIA

1

Ruomu was among the students who graduated from university in the 1940s. One of the marks of that decade was destitute students crowding around the hearth eating food paid for from their meager student loans. Pea sprouts had become the symbol of Guizhou, a province rendered destitute in the war against Japan, and they were the staple of the students' diet throughout those times. But memory can add color to everything. Several decades down the road, the same second-rate verse the students used to recite while warming themselves around the stove was looked back upon as something utterly romantic: "Standing round the fire eating boiled greens, / Our empty lives seemed full of beans. . . . Congee was always our staple means." Once into the 1950s, that kind of congee, with a thick layer of rice oil floating on top, was not to be seen again. Perhaps because Ruomu's diet included no regular fare, that kind of thick rice fragrance had seeped straight into her internal organs. With her innards pickled in that kind of odor, Ruomu's original aristocratic bouquet was essentially masked over. But her inner drive was exceedingly strong, and even though she was steeped in that smell, she never lost sight of her original goal in attending university—to find herself a suitable, university-educated husband.

Already twenty-nine years old at that time, Ruomu was the oldest member of her class. To be not yet betrothed at that age was almost unheard-of in those days. Even the handicapped, let alone the poorest, the ugliest women, would almost never find themselves in such a situation. Quite the opposite of such women, Ruomu was from a rich and influential family, and possessed a serenely beautiful face and fair and delicate skin, along with a superbly sound mind and body. That Ruomu, at twenty-nine, was still not married was entirely her mother's doing. Xuanming, whose observant eyes never missed a thing, strictly policed her daughter's contacts with the opposite sex.

When Ruomu was seventeen, a new family, with the surname Qian, moved in next door. Four transport trucks arrived loaded to the gunwales with the family's furniture and a wide array of valuable possessions. The Qians had no daughters, just two sons—Qian Feng and Qian Run. Ruomu remembers Xuanming bumbling around on her tiny feet that morning, her face suffused with a seldom-seen elation. Xuanming said that the two Qian boys looked like they might just as well have stepped down out of some painting. Like a branding iron, that pronouncement seared its way into Ruomu's heart. Xuanming's only daughter, Ruomu had experienced none of the passions of youth or innocent love. Her tall and slender body showed none of the usual signs of sexual development. Lacking the usual humps and hollows, it was not the least bit curvaceous. What attracted people's attention was her snow-white skin. If she were to stand stark-naked in front of a freshly white-washed wall, the only thing you would see would be her hair and her eyes, and if she wasn't wearing lipstick, her lips would be pretty much invisible as well. Very few people have skin like that, with the entire body an absolutely uniform white color, as if it were dyed, and completely free of blemishes, wrinkles, or discolorations, although you definitely couldn't say it was glowingly beautiful or translucent. If you took her away from the wall out into the sunlight, you would clearly see that her skin had the kind of sickly dull white of the finely ground glutinous rice flour used to make chewy New Year cakes. Xuanming had no idea what kinds of things filled her daughter's mind, nor did she have the time to contemplate such matters. The events of Xuanming's days were organized very tightly, and after the evening meal she always set aside time for gambling games like cards or mahjong, usually starting around midnight. From when her daughter Ruomu was very small, Xuanming had accepted her reluctance to communicate. She figured that Ruomu was taciturn and reserved by nature, that this was an innate aspect of being a girl, and she heartily approved of this.

One midsummer evening when the fragrance of honeysuckle filled the air, Ruomu was sauntering to and fro under the grape trellis outside the front door, as she was often wont to do. Every time she did this, the Song Dynasty poems her mother taught her to recite when she was a little girl would pop into her head—like Li Qingzhao's *Double-Ninth Festival,* set to the lyric tune *Drunk in the Flowers' Shade*:

> *Thin mists and thick clouds clot the saddened day,*
> *As the golden censer's camphor burns away,*
> *And the festive Double-Ninth seems less than gay.*
> *Now my silken chamber and pillow of jade*
> *Turn bitter cold in midnight's darkened shade.*
>
> *As by the eastern hedge I sip late wine,*
> *Its subtle fragrance filled with old lang syne,*
> *I cannot say my love is in decline.*
> *As my curtain lifts in the cold west wind,*
> *It reveals a figure still flowery thin.*

Or Li Yu's *In Captivity,* set to the lyric tune *Shifting Dunes*:

> *Outside my curtain the sound of rain*
> *Announces spring is on the wane;*
> *The predawn chill seeps through my silken quilt,*

While in my dream of pleasure without guilt,
I quite forget that I am but a guest.

Beside this railing I should not stand
To gaze upon this endless land;
Endings are easy, beginnings tough
Whether in heaven or on earth
Flowing water and falling petals mark spring's death.

That evening the lovely light of the moon gave the grape leaves a bright translucence, as Ruomu's snow-white skin wended its ghostlike way in the shadows of the trellis. On this occasion, she suddenly felt there was an unfamiliar gaze penetrating the shadows like a sword, cutting the beautiful leaves from the vines one by one. Hesitantly turning around, she suddenly froze in her tracks. A handsome boy was standing behind her. There was no need for her to ask anything; she knew immediately who it was. It's Qian Run, she thought, no doubt about it.

It was indeed Qian Run, the second son in the Qian household. When they are little, good-looking male children always have a few feminine features. Perhaps because in their dress girlish elements may be favored, they sometimes look convincingly like beautiful girls. Qian Run's mannerisms were also effeminate: he didn't much like to talk, and when he did, he stuttered and was bashful and incoherent, and inept at conveying his meaning. Ruomu, too, as a result of her mother's severity, was often at a loss over how to conduct herself when in front of others; and she had the same problem when she was with Qian Run. But behind others' backs her behavior was a totally different story. She could be cold and calculating, sly and savage, her heart hard as steel. Because of Qian Run's softness, she felt that she had immediately gained a new strength. Ruomu wanted to lord it over others, and not be denied. And Qian Run made the perfect target. As a result, it was pretty much love at first sight for the two of them. Although he behaved like a girl in front of others, when he was alone, his mind was often filled with the profane curiosities of a pervert.

One day when Xuanming had gone out to play mahjong, Qian Run sneaked into the house, and underneath the large oak dinner table he undid his trousers and pulled out his little penis. In tense excitement, he queried, "Do you have one of these things? Do you?"—sweat dripping from his forehead. Ruomu's pale face twitched with an icy brightness, and without uttering a word she quietly stripped from the waist down. Choking with curiosity, Qian Run leaned close to get a better look. In this way, in Ruomu's simply decorated but spotlessly clean quarters, the second young master of the Qian household brought to fruition the curious longing that had been haunting his dreams day and night. He thought that the pink thing hidden between Ruomu's white thighs like a peach stone must be that special secret of womankind. He just couldn't stop staring at and exploring it from every angle. But, finally, white-faced, he did up his trousers. With her eyes like a surveillance camera, Ruomu's relentless stare had left him helplessly frightened. That kind of behavior was just out of the question in front of a surveillance camera, especially for a young lad whose lust was being crushed by his cowardice.

But this little performance was to be continued. Because Xuanming and her husband didn't enjoy each other's company, she was spending more and more of her evenings going out to play cards and mahjong. All Ruomu had to do was go to the storage room and knock lightly on the wall three times, and Qian Run would come rolling over like a breath of evening breeze. As time went by, he was less and less satisfied with just looking at and visually examining that peach stone–shaped protuberance. Then one evening he took a gold German Parker ballpoint pen out of his pocket and used it to lightly probe the center of that bump. He felt that his own little tool wasn't much thicker than that Parker pen. But just at that point, the wind chime hanging at the front door started to jangle. Qian Run's blood mounted in a sudden flood to his pale face. Like a couple of thieves caught in the act, the two of them hurriedly began pulling their clothes on. Xuanming had come home to get some more money after losing everything at the gambling table. If the young couple had just been able to keep their cool a bit, they needn't have startled this woman whose every thought was still on the gaming. But the noises they were making amid their fright shattered Xuanming's train of thought. She turned toward the source of the sounds, and like a blast of wind burst the door open and entered the room. Deathly pale, her daughter clung to the wall of her white-as-a-snow-cave boudoir. Next to her feet, a mound of sapphire-blue clothing was shaking uncontrollably.

That magnificent sapphire blue stabbed directly into Xuanming's eyes. She raised one foot and kicked the heap of clothing. Like an awl, the incontestably gorgeous little pointed foot found its way to the person underneath. When she yanked the young boy to his feet, he was like a just-gutted fish with its tail still flapping, and as he arose his trousers slid down, revealing the stage prop he had used so many times in his performances.

Xuanming's shouting reverberated through all the buildings in the compound. The young female attendants, old nurses, kitchen staff, and all the other servants were kneeling neatly in a dense mass in the courtyard. As the young Qian Run pulled up his trousers and fled, he was on the verge of collapsing. None of the servants kneeling outside had even the slightest inkling of what had happened. When Xuanming came out, she locked the inner courtyard gate from the inside. The servants saw that the dark, heavy drapes of the daughter's boudoir had all been drawn so that nothing could be seen.

Ruomu's snow-cave-white boudoir was now a black cave. As punishment for what she had done, she was forced to kneel, and no limit was set on the duration of her sentence. So there she knelt, motionless, in her black cave. She had nothing to eat or drink, or say. There was only silence. Only in the lacquered blackness of the depth of night could she hear the faint sound of her mother's snoring and the distant chirping of katydids.

2

One evening at twilight, Mrs. Peng, the oldest servant for Xuanming, cautiously asked Xuanming, "Mistress, how come we haven't seen your daughter these last few days?" While continuing to dig for some little fishbone stuck between her teeth, taking her time, Xuanming unhurriedly said, "Don't ask about things you shouldn't ask about." Taking the bull by the horns, Peng continued, "Even if your daughter acted improperly, she is, after all, a youngster, and, on top of that, she is your own flesh and blood." This last comment made Xuanming raise her brows and respond, "If I should decide to keep her kneeling until she dies, I would kill anyone who tried to intervene."

Shocked and deeply disturbed, Peng went to look for the daughter's personal servant, Meihua. Qin Heshou, Xuanming's husband, had not been home for a couple of weeks. Rumor had it that he had bought a house on the outskirts of the city, where he kept a couple of actresses; but given the size of the city, it would be difficult to find him. The obvious solution would be to go to the Gansu-Shanghai Railway Office, which he headed. To do this would incur his wrath, but in this life-on-the-line situation, not to notify him would be equally as disastrous. Caught between the husband and wife, it was hard to decide what to do.

But Meihua had her own way of doing things. She was the prettiest servant in the Qin household. She knew how to get things done and had a clever tongue. Everyone in the household, except Ruomu, liked her. Meihua was born into the Qin family. Right from when she was just a child, Xuanming had given her the job of attending Ruomu. Although she was several years younger than Ruomu, she understood the rules of decorum and the principles of good behavior, as well as being morally upright and skilled at reading people's intentions. If they were to be seen walking together, it would be difficult to determine which one was the mistress and which one the servant. On a number of occasions, Ruomu hoped to get rid of Meihua, but couldn't find anything to fault her with; so there wasn't much she could do other than assign her to the servants' quarters to do needlework and not require her personal services most of the time. She sought, instead, an opportunity to speak to her mother, when she said, "Mother, Meihua is of age; it's time to arrange for her marriage. I think that younger brother's servant Shu'er is a bit simple; but, on top of that, my brother is away from home studying, so he has no need for her services, so the best thing to do would be to give her to me." Xuanming heard all this, but chose not to answer.

Meihua, of course, understood Ruomu's attitude toward her; but she had long ago already set her sights clearly on the man she wanted in her life. That man was none other than the only son in the Qin household—Ruomu's younger brother, Tiancheng. At this time, Tiancheng was going to school away from home. It was his father's intention that he would eventually major in railroad management, following the custom of the son following in the father's footsteps. Neither in appearance nor temperament did Tiancheng have the characteristics of the Qin clan, but there was no doubt that he was the flesh-and-blood son of Qin Heshou and Xuanming. He was truly as dignified and handsome in appearance as the descriptions found in traditional Chinese thread-bound books of men as good-looking as the jade ornament on an official's hat. But Tiancheng's brow was always knitted in gloom. Even when he smiled, the clouds of worry could not be chased away.

From when they were babies, both Tiancheng and Ruomu were brought up surrounded by the endless quarreling of their parents; but their responses to this and its influence on them were not the least bit similar. From very early on Ruomu recognized but ignored it. Even if, right in front of her, the father confronted the mother brandishing a stool, you'd be wrong to think it would raise a wrinkle on the girl's forehead. But things like this would truly and deeply disturb Tiancheng. Even at the age of four, he had figured out that by crawling over to his father on his knees and putting his arms around those legs, he could better beseech him not to hit his mother. But, in fact, tiny little Tiancheng did not know that his father was a paper tiger, and that the really formidable one was his mother. Looking back on those times today, Tiancheng's mother, Xuanming, was clearly in the front lines of the women's liberation movement. Xuanming's will to live and to struggle were unmatched. She could curse and pound on that rosewood table from dawn till dark. Her every word was a gem, every sentence priceless, resounding with irrefutable reason. Heshou detested being trapped in such a net of words, but his own way with words was limited and below the mark. So all he could do was create a storm by grabbing and brandishing that stool like a smoking gun to try to gain a little prestige and save a bit of face in front of his son and daughter and the family's servants.

But all these doings deeply hurt Tiancheng's kind, gentle, and sensitive heart. Once, when his mother wasn't home, with his own eyes he saw his father, dressed up in Western clothes with a bow tie, facing two women sitting on the sofa while he beat out the rhythm for them as they sang opera arias. Little Tiancheng didn't know that one of the two women was the understudy of Cheng Yanqiu, one of the four famous players of female roles in Peking opera. When compared with Xuanming, neither of the two women were the least bit good-looking, but their humble submissiveness and slyly winsome and inviting smiles meant more to men than did genuine beauty. Throughout her life, Xuanming never cottoned onto this, and as a result she spent her entire life immersed in quarreling.

There were also odd times when Xuanming would show restraint. Tiancheng was consistently a top student. His grounding in Chinese cultural studies was especially good. An essay he wrote in his third year of elementary school was singled out by the school as a model essay. But when Xuanming, bubbling over with joy, bounced into the principal's office on her tiny feet, she was awestruck by the downcast expression in the eyes of the principal, the dean of instruction, and the teachers. To her the title of that essay was worse than just a thunderbolt—the title was "A Broken Home."

After all the important members of the school's faculty and administration had confirmed the outstanding quality of Tiancheng's natural endowments, an abrupt silence filled the room. After a long time the principal hesitantly probed, "Mrs. Qin, please forgive my prying, but how was your son able, at so young an age, to write such an essay. Of course, it is very well written, but . . ."

That evening Xuanming shed tears. It seemed as if she suddenly thought that aside from all the romantic antics of Qin Heshou and his actresses, there were countless other shenanigans going on without cease in this world. Her son and daughter were no longer babies. Their eyes could already read the world around them; their ears understood the quarrels of adults. This was a terribly dangerous, frightening, and also woeful situation!

In the darkness of that night, for the first time in many, many years Xuanming took the trouble to sort out her thoughts. She suddenly realized that the things she was really interested in were already far back in the distant past.

Xuanming was indeed the youngest daughter in a very large clan. Her father had put together an extremely wealthy family, but hadn't taken on a single concubine. Her father and mother raised a family of seventeen children. She was the smallest—"Little Seventeen." Right from when she was a little girl, Little Seventeen was good at mathematics and household affairs, and was skilled in managing finances. Her grandfather had been a widely known businessman in the financial world of Hunan and Hubei provinces. It was precisely in her father's generation that the family's financial situation surged to new heights. Of all his children, the father's favorite was Little Seventeen. When she was fifteen years old she took over the family's iron abacus. Her female siblings would practice their skills in needlework in one room, accompanied by the background music of Little Seventeen's calculations on her abacus.

From the time she was a little girl, Xuanming had been afraid of no one, but from that evening on, she was afraid of her son.

3

Later on, during the turbulent years of the war with Japan, Xuanming's son contracted typhus fever and passed away. Only twenty-two years old and just graduated from university, he died in the prime of life. Xuanming insisted that if at that time she had not been ignoring her son because her attention was focused on Ruomu, Tiancheng definitely would not have died. This was to create an eternal rift between mother and daughter. Ruomu, having been made aware of the importance of having a son through the experience of her mother, was determined that she herself would bear one. Her wish finally bore fruit when she was forty years old. She gave birth to a son. Even though the little fellow was born prematurely and turned out to be ugly, small, and weak, he was, nonetheless, a son, a son who could carry on the name of the family and the worship of its past generations of ancestors. Thank heavens, she at last had a son.

After she graduated from university, Ruomu worked for only four years. After Ruomu gave birth to Xiao, her second daughter, Xuanming told her that she was not to go back to work, that Lu Chen, Ruomu's husband, had been made associate professor and earned enough to support the family. By that time, Xuanming's husband, Heshou, had already passed away, and Xuanming turned the focus of her attention to helping her daughter run her home. But Ruomu treated her mother like she treated everyone else—with suspicion and jealousy. She wouldn't let Xuanming have a finger in the family's finances, but at the same time she herself did not want to do the family grocery shopping. So mother and daughter worked out a system of keeping track of bills for reimbursement. It was not for nothing that Ruomu had studied financial management, and she would not let even a single penny go unaccounted for. Xuanming, born into and used to administrating a rich and powerful family, very often found it impossible to bear these little humiliations, and would roundly fling abuse upon her daughter's doings.

Through all this, Yu gradually got to know the history of her family. Yu knew that she had had an uncle who was the much beloved son of her maternal grandmother, but while fleeing the hardships of the war, in her concern to look after Yu's mother, the grandma neglected and lost her beloved son. Xuanming retold this story so many times that her originally sympathetic listeners eventually got bored with it. After venting her spleen, following her usual practice, she would stumble off on her tiny feet with a shopping basket on her arm to buy groceries, then return home and, as always, skillfully whip together a delicious meal, serve it up, and call everyone to the table. But everything that appeared on that table had to be paid for. At the dinner table of the Lu family, which was still considered well off, they all had to listen to Xuanming as she rattled on about what she had had to pay for everything. But in front of Lu Chen, Ruomu didn't dare utter a word. All she could do was bow her head and silently scoop in her rice, like a long-suffering little daughter-in-law. But, of course, in his judgment, Lu Chen was naturally bound to have a bias; and with the passage of time, he and Xuanming eventually behaved like personal enemies, each with no time or patience for the other.

This went on until a genuine and priceless new cohesive force made its appearance in this endlessly squabbling family, in the form of the birth of a male heir. Xuanming immediately told Ruomu to write a letter to Xiangqin, the daughter of their former longtime servant Mrs. Peng, and also to Ruomu's personal servant Shu'er. Ruomu's daughters Ling and Xiao were both cared for from childhood to adulthood by these two women. Now that they had a little son to carry on the ancestral line, there, of course, were not enough hands to look after him. But if just one of these former servants were to answer the call, it would be enough to solve the problem. Aside from this, Xuanming stubbornly advocated that the boy take the surname Qin, and be taken as the adopted son of her deceased son, Tiancheng, which would make him Xuanming's legitimate grandson. Of course, Lu Chen would not agree to this. The Lu family had for a number of generations struggled hard to produce just a single male heir. How could they now give their only begotten son to the Qin clan?!

But while the unrelenting argument was going on as to whether he should be named Lu or Qin, the child was no more, his life prematurely terminated. He was choked to death. That evening, the Lu family's world fell to pieces. The crying of that little fellow with his thin and wrinkled face no longer came from that tiny cradle that looked like a silkworm cocoon. His face and body a greenish purple, he laid there without a sound or breath.

After her initial uncontrollable tears and howling had eased up, Ruomu parted her tear-soaked hair and, through her grimly clenched teeth, shrieked, "It was her! It was third daughter!"

His face turning an ashen gray, Lu Chen saw what appeared to be a pair of unusually bright, demonic eyes flash through the darkness, then quickly disappear. The eyes were those of his little daughter.

4

It was on a clear spring morning with a gentle breeze caressing her face that Yushe located Jinwu. It was in the city's first multistory apartment building. After she had pressed the doorbell for the third time, a woman opened the door and stuck her head out. Yu's eyes brightened—it was, indeed, that fairy woman, that brown-eyed movie star that Yu had been yearning for years to meet.

"Gorgeous" would be a fitting word to describe Jinwu's face and clothing. With her long brown hair combed back and coiled in a large bun at the nape of her neck, and her radiant and full forehead, she looked very much like a Western beauty. The apricot shade of her lipstick heightened the contrast in color between her lips and her skin. Yu noted that Jinwu's skin was as beautifully delicate and as lustrous and rich in color as a baby's. In comparison, Yu's skin much too early in life showed signs of withering and dying. Jinwu was a woman who appeared to be in the flower of youth, while Yushe was a slovenly child who paid no attention to her appearance.

Age is a strange measure of things. It is not tied to how black or white the hair is, or the number of wrinkles one has. Changeable elements, or software, like the skin, hair, and even one's overall appearance are not the final arbiters of age. Age is governed by hardware. Since ancient times, because of their fear of age, countless numbers of beautiful women have devised myriads of ways to keep themselves beautiful. But ultimately not a single one of them escaped failure. From the earliest forms of red mineral powders to today's top-of-the-line Chanel rouge, all of these beauties, for the sake of masking age, have worked to devise means of self-deception. But no matter how intelligent these women may be, without remorse or regret, they all end up cheating themselves just as in the past.

It is best that no one unveil the real situation, because this world basically is a form of chaos, a river of gray; it is best that no one break the already established pattern, because this pattern is the naturally formed result of thousands of years of cyclic change. If this pattern should be broken, people will have to pay for it with their lives, without the slightest benefit therefrom. In real life, on occasion the truth is turned into a joke. If you honestly tell a woman how old and ugly she is, her hatred for you will penetrate your bones and she will, when you think that she has forgotten your comments and when you least expect her retaliation, deliver the fatal blow. Also, there could be many others you never considered who suddenly one evening become your enemies. For example, a beautician who had earned a lot of money from her, or business owners who had made their fortunes in cosmetics. They unceasingly exhausted their brains thinking of ways to advance the lie of beauty, while you in one sentence try to put an end to their lies . . . their means of livelihood and their rice bowl.

In this world, those who deceive themselves as well as others can be a trap that is dangerous but beautiful, and therefore best avoided.

On that occasion, Yu took note of the blue silk pajamas Jinwu was wearing. They were an especially gorgeous turquoise-tinted blue that immediately made Yu think of that limpid lake in front of her home. In those days, she would sit by the side of the lake every evening at twilight, always hoping for some little discovery. Sometimes she would see that huge freshwater mussel quietly opening its shell. She was never able to clearly discern what was tucked away inside, until one day she suddenly had the feeling that, in fact, it was not a mussel at all; instead, it was a number of black feathers stuck on a metal frame shaped like a mussel. It was like a scene from a play: it was a woman's cloak. The woman secreted inside was a genuine backstage hand, who had of her own choice locked herself away in a feathery prison. It was a kind of isolation, a kind of protection.

She was a lot like this lady before her.

5

At that time, Jinwu was already a well-known movie star in that city. She had already appeared in three films. Two of them were about national minorities, but in the other one she played the part of a female secret agent or spy from the United States. Her role as a spy brought her instant fame. As a result, within the world of performing arts she acquired the nickname "The Spy Lady." Jinwu was born with an innate kind of warmth. As a woman, she was always charming and gracious—never too young, never too old.

Jinwu was ageless.

She belonged to the moment, always to the present moment.

It is said that she had a countless string of illicit lovers. In this city, she had at least half as much influence as the mayor, perhaps even more than that.

So when Jinwu personally went to bat to find a school for Yu, everything went very smoothly. On a damp and rainy day, she was directed to a classroom where the language and literature teacher was reciting Lu Xun's short story "A Small Matter" aloud to his class. Yu summoned up enough nerve to glance around at her classmates, but said nothing. The teacher, partly out of concern and partly out of irritation, said, "If you would take that empty seat over there, the class representatives for your different subjects will issue you your textbooks shortly."

When Yu went to her seat, she noted that the student sharing the desk with her was a foreigner, and that he was, in fact, very handsome. But this, she felt, was of no significance. His good looks had absolutely nothing to do with her. She didn't even think to give him a second glance. But the foreigner shot her a smile, his suntanned face revealing two rows of dazzling white teeth.

In the past, this school often had foreign students. There was nothing particularly unusual about this. What was unusual was that this foreigner sitting beside Yu was the son of a famous leader of the left-wing movement in the United States.

The boy, whose name was Michael, always seemed to be in a good mood, with a smile on his face, but he didn't talk very much; and whenever he did come out with a word or two, nobody could understand what he was talking about. He was totally inept in language studies—the exact opposite of his little sister, Joan, who was in a different class. Michael wore the white shirt and gray trousers that were the common attire of male students in China at that time. Joan, on the other hand, was a bit special: she did her hair up in coils and wore long print dresses in Persian patterns. Both of them had pale blue eyes and were thickly freckled, even on the backs of their hands. Joan's skin had a whitish tinge to it, but although she wasn't particularly good-looking, she impressed people with her natural liveliness.

Jinwu got to know Michael through Yu. She heard that there was a boy in Yu's class whose father was a leftist leader in America, and out of curiosity urged Yu to invite him home. For a long time, Yu didn't respond, but eventually suggested that Jinwu write him a note, as she never talked to the boy.

Jinwu was quite used to this kind of response from Yu. Yu was afraid of people. Every time guests arrived in her home, she would flee at the first opportunity. She would miss meals and sleep to avoid meeting people; and, as a result, even when she was very young, her eye sockets were dark and her bones were as thin as sticks of kindling. Jinwu always felt that Yu had some secret in her heart that blinded her to the truth, some apparently frightening secret.

Because of this, Jinwu was unusually indulgent with Yu—because of Yu's sad habit of confining herself indoors, her unfortunate loneliness, her lack of affection and respect from others; because of her frightening secret, and even more so because of Yu's inability to hide her real feelings.

Because of Yu's eternally revealing face.

6

Jinwu was giving Yu a bath in a large bathing pool filled with freshly plucked flowers. Yu's body was just as Jinwu had imagined it to be—soft and lustrous; delicate, lovely, and slender. Her bosom was totally flat, her pale white nipples strangely lacking any hint of pink. She did not have even a single strand of body hair, and her skin was cool and slick to the touch, as if she were the descendant of some aquatic creature.

Hoping to turn Yushe into a perfect young beauty by imparting some of their fresh scent into her body, Jinwu used both hands to scoop up the flower petals and begin rubbing them into Yu's skin. Encrusted with a layer of blossoms, the water of the bathing pool took on the color of the pink juice of the crushed petals of the touch-me-nots, carnations, and China roses. While the flower-tinged water and the steaming bathing pool had turned Jinwu's face totally pink, Yu's face remained its usual pale white, as if her body had been completely drained of its blood.

All of a sudden, after watching her for a long time, Jinwu got the feeling that Yu's body had at the same time both a cautiously delicate beauty and a bold exuberance, like a delicate stroke of the writing brush or a drowning plunge into song. Her blood vessels, like flower stems in winter or riverbeds gone dry, could only render her beautiful in the warmth of love; but now, like a bolt of summer silk tucked away on a high shelf for winter, she could do nothing but hibernate.

Jinwu decided to awaken her.

Jinwu took off her nightgown. Yu's gaze fell on Jinwu's ample bosom, but only for a moment—as if she was very shy, as if Jinwu made her feel bashful and even a bit frightened. Bewitched by Yu's expression, Jinwu reached out with her hands and pulled Yu toward her. In the water, Yu's arms took on the translucence of two entangled stems of milk-white coral. Supported by the water's buoyancy, the two of them floated on the surface of the pool. Jinwu gently drew Yu close to her and began to slowly caress her. Yu's long hair covered her face, obscuring her expression, as Jinwu's caresses became more and more pronounced, stroking every inch of Yu's body, seemingly without regard for what was actually being touched. Afterward, she lay there waiting for Yu to kiss her. Yu looked at Jinwu's luxuriant pubic hair waving back and forth on the water's surface like seaweed. A bit hesitant at first, she was quickly overcome with passion, becoming more excited even than Jinwu. The pair of them flapped around in the bathing pool filled with blossoms like a couple of crazy fish engaged in battle, their long hair waving, gasping for breath, spurting bodily juices; until finally, totally exhausted, like a pair of corpses, they floated quietly on the water's surface.

From seemingly out of nowhere, also floating on the water, there was a dark-colored flower—a black tulip. Yu took hold of it and gently inserted it in Jinwu's eager vagina. With a strange expression on her face, Yu eyed her masterwork.

7

Yu tossed the handwritten invitation to her desk mate Michael. From Yu's point of view, he was no different from any of the other idiots around her. Yu simply could not understand Jinwu's obsession with the name United States of America. That's certainly all it was—the name *Mei Guo,* or Beautiful Country—two characters in Chinese. Yu figured that if it wasn't for those two characters, Jinwu would not have stooped to writing such an invitation.

Jinwu's subsequent action made Yu even angrier. She had gone to the downtown market and bought a huge heap of things, including a tapestry hanging, little flower baskets, plaited wicker ornaments, and all kinds of tasty edibles. She had heard that Michael liked to eat Chinese dumplings, so she had also bought a variety of prepared fillings and had personally spent the entire afternoon kneading the dough, rolling out the little skins, and wrapping the dumplings. Yu sat to one side crocheting a handbag, never raising so much as an eyelid. After a while, Jinwu pressed Yu into helping her wrap the dumplings, but Yu's dumplings laid flat and lifeless on the cutting board, while Jinwu's, on the other hand, as beautiful as Jinwu herself, looked full of life, their wings spread ready to fly.

By the time Michael arrived, almost all the dumplings had been wrapped. But this was the first time he had witnessed the process, and he insisted on having a try. Since Jinwu was busy boiling dumplings, she asked Yu to show him how to do the wrapping. An unenthused Yu responded, "I shouldn't be the one teaching him; my dumplings are all hospital cases." With a little snort of laughter, Jinwu recognized the utter truth in Yu's words, then responded, "You little bitch, if you're always this stubborn and unyielding, who'll dare to have anything to do with you down the road?" With a quick and wide-eyed glare, Yu responded, "Down the road none other than you yourself will dare!"

Taken completely by surprise, Jinwu was both touched and tormented, thinking that this was no time for such games.

With the dumpling skins serving as nothing more than a kind of intermediary, Jinwu's snow-white and Michael's sunburned fingers intertwined. Jinwu noted that Michael kept his fingernails very long, and that he wore a splendid ivory ring on the middle finger of his left hand. At that time, Michael could already speak a bit of odd-sounding, awkwardly expressed Chinese. He knew how to express a polite thank-you and to quickly ingratiate himself with the opposite sex, although his ability to do this was limited to a single expression: "You're truly as endearing as a fledgling dove."

When the steaming dumplings were served up, Michael, hard-pressed to find words to convey his delight, spouted his rather inappropriate fledgling-dove line as he looked at the little stuffed-pastry creations. Jinwu thought he was praising Yu, while Yu thought he was referring to the dumplings, although neither of them responded to his comment. Michael had never at any time had much faith in his ability to speak Chinese. Now, looking at the expressions on their faces, what little confidence he had was even further eroded. To try to save a bit of face, he quickly swallowed a dumpling; then, holding up one of his long-nailed thumbs, he said, "Wow—they're terrific."

In truth, at that point Michael was not yet actually aware of the taste of the dumplings.

Women like to make judgments based on precisely identified details. But these two gals, in making a judgment based on the act of eating dumplings, came up with totally different conclusions. Yu concluded that Michael was a total idiot; while Jinwu, on the other hand, felt that he was absolutely adorable. Michael was precisely the kind of male that Jinwu had always been looking for: an unadorned innocent blessed with a pure simplicity. Jinwu had a passion for enlightening others.

8

I have a sandalwood fan with an exquisite, delicate fragrance very much like that of budding bottle gourd blossoms. I also like wearing clothes made of silk. Even when I was just a little girl, I loved going to the silk shop with my adoptive mother. The bolts of tightly rolled silk would spill down from the gentle fingers of the proprietress in bright and dark shades, some as soothingly cool as water, some as sleek and soft as moonlight. In company with the emission of that special sound of silk being torn, from within the layers of silk there emerged beautifully valleyed mountains and cloud masses. Those swirling patterns filling the heavens, like grape leaves, like birds, like silver foil, possessed a kind of inimitable beauty that was all their own. During my girlhood I wouldn't dare to touch those silks. I was afraid that they were not real, and that if I were to touch them they would vanish.

My first silk outfit was given to me by my adoptive mother. It was an old silk cheongsam. That evening, under the bright glow of the lamp, when she fetched it out from the bottom of her clothes chest, the big flowers worked into the silk in gold and colored thread gradually filled the entire room with the scent of camphor as they were unfolded one by one. Under the curious eyes of my adoptive mother, I put on the dress. In the mirror, I could clearly see that I had been changed into an ancient dreamlike character whose beauty exuded a kind of archaic charm. The coiling golden flowers had the ocher tone of old photographs. Although I was only fourteen at the time and not yet fully developed physically, the dress did not look too big on me; in fact, aside from being too long, it fit perfectly. It was easy to imagine that its original owner had had a very slender figure, but I thought that my adoptive mother could not possibly have been the owner of that figure.

With a gentle smile, she said, "Jinwu, my child, you sure look like her."

I responded, "Like who? Who do you think I look like?"

She smiled again. "Not really that much like her. You have to take into account that she was twenty when she wore that dress. When you're twenty, it might no longer fit you. She was tall and slim, not thin—gracefully slender. Today's women are either fat like pigs or all bones. They simply don't understand what slim means. Put it like this: her waistline was as tiny in proportion as the mouth of a bottle, but not a single bone showed through her skin. When I was young, I also had a nice figure; but when she came on the scene, it was my time to disappear, or be ignored. Anyone who hadn't seen her walk couldn't possibly understand the phrase 'swaying like willows in the wind.' That kind of attractiveness, to say nothing of its effect on men, truly drew my most tender love."

With a laugh I said, "Aunty, you're unfair to yourself. What woman would venture to compete with you in this respect?"

Almost snared by my ploy, she hastily began looking for that photograph, but suddenly, as if awaking to what she was about to do, she sat down. Swallowing a mouthful of cold tea, she unhurriedly said, "There is no point in your being impatient; eventually the day will come when you will find out who she is."

During the war against Japan, my adoptive mother, Luo Bing, was a well-known female commander and my adoptive father was under her jurisdiction. From as far back as I can remember, she had had health problems. She was always undergoing treatment in various kinds of sanatoriums. She suffered from a variety of chronic illnesses and also could not bear children, but I always felt that she was one of the few genuinely beautiful women in the world. Should disasters and hardships dry up such women's bodily fluids, leaving them nothing but skeletons, then their bones will still resound with a truly extraordinary beautiful music. Luo Bing possessed just such a morbid beauty. I found it difficult to imagine that anyone as sickly in appearance as she would be able to direct massive military forces on the field of battle. But this fact was attested to countless times by my adoptive father. His greatest passion in life was to glorify the merits and achievements of his wife. Luo Bing was the very first feminist I was to encounter in my life. The respect and admiration for her that graced the faces of every ilk of men who entered our doors was not demanded of them, but came genuinely from their hearts. This made me feel very proud.

For a period of time I had called Luo Bing mother, because at that time I needed someone I could call my mother. But Luo Bing was dead-set against me using this word. She insisted that I call her aunty. She said to me, "You have a mother. Wait until you're a bit older and I will tell you her story."

But she didn't realize how intelligent her adoptive daughter was.

One day when my adoptive father was yet again lauding his wife's merits and achievements, he pulled out an old photograph that already possessed the faded tones of an ancient oil painting, but one look was enough to let me see that the young woman dressed in the uniform of the Communist Eighth Route Army was my adoptive mother. With one arm extended, she was talking to some men in front of her. Standing beside her was a woman wearing a cheongsam. Although the picture was a poorly taken angle shot, you could still see that she was a beautiful woman, apparently much more beautiful than Luo Bing. I immediately pointed at her and asked who she was. Quickly, as if he had been burnt, my adoptive father reclaimed the photograph, saying that they had nothing to do with this woman and that her appearance in the photograph was sheer chance.

But I didn't believe a word he had said.

Some years later, during the biggest political storm, I, just like all young people at that time, charged boldly into that new and unfamiliar world.

That thick and mysterious curtain unyieldingly blocking my view of what lay ahead generated in me an irresistible urge to tear it open. Using rooting out the "four olds"—traditional ideas, culture, customs, and habits—as my excuse, I started rummaging through everything in the house. What would have been ordinary objects took on a new value because they had been covered in dust for such a long time, just like an ancient jewelry box might increase in value with its increasing age. Some years later in the SeaWorld park in the United States, I saw just such a box. It was on a huge pirate ship. All the treasures were wrapped in cobwebs. Some delicate undersea animals were attacking them in vain and without regret.

Finally, there came a day when, tucked behind a poster titled "Chairman Mao Tours Our Great Motherland," I discovered an answer to the mystery in the form of a large, old photograph of exceedingly fine resolution that was much better than the other one. It was of a woman with her hair done up in a bun, wearing a vest worked with embroidered outlines of flowers. She was like a tiny flower bud not yet fully opened but already revealing an extraordinary beauty. It was a shot of the woman in the cheongsam in the other photo, but taken when she was very young.

Just at that moment, I heard a voice behind me saying, "Yes, indeed. That's your mother. You've found her at last. But I have to tell you she was a traitor to the revolution."

I turned around and saw my adoptive mother standing in the dim evening light. I couldn't see her facial expression.

9

It was at that precise moment that Jinwu grew up. It was very frightening for her to find out at the same time as discovering her natural mother that she was a traitor to the revolution. But in Jinwu's heart that beautiful, tiny little flower bud and the word "traitor" had absolutely no connection. Jinwu did not sleep that entire night. She worked out in her head all the countless possibilities someone of her age might be capable of conceiving, including thinking that her adoptive mother might have said this because she and Jinwu's mother were both in love with the same man at the same time. But she immediately rejected this idea: a Smiling Buddha–like image of her adoptive father appeared before her, and there was no way she could associate him with that beautiful little flower bud.

From the time that photograph appeared, Jinwu's adoptive parents were relegated to a very remote corner of her heart, while her mother—that hallucinatory incarnation of unparalleled beauty—after so many years came to her at last out of a distant past. The appearance of her mother made history suddenly blossom into something with a clear message—from some dull and commonplace tune into a stirring and magnificent melody.

She felt that the "hat" of traitor did not, from any point of view, fit her mother, that such an accusation was unfair, and that her mother was being tried in absentia.

10

Now we should go back in space and time to Yan'an, in northern Shaanxi Province, as it was thirty years ago. In those days, Yan'an was reminiscent of the highly detailed realistic paintings of the Song Dynasty. It was situated in a mountain pass at the confluence of two small rivers, with precipitous cliffs soaring up on both sides. On the west side, the city wall with gun embrasures snaked its way up the mountain ridge to a lookout tower on the top. The city itself was located in the center of the mountain valley, with its eastern wall reaching the riverbank, and on the mountains rising up from the river there were the tumbledown ruins of temples and pagodas. The river, of course, was the famous Yan River. There were a number of women washing clothes along its banks, but its waters, clogged with the soil of the Loess Plateau, were by no means clear.

The lengthy city walls were built in the Song Dynasty, at the time when Yan'an marked the dynasty's outermost base of defense in the struggle with the northern barbarians.

Now Yan'an's famous Chinese People's Anti-Japanese Military-Political Academy had been set up in a temple complex. The walls were festooned with repulsive caricatures—all of them, naturally, of Japanese.

In the spring of 1943, a young woman arrived here riding a camel, its head draped in vermilion flowers as if it were delivering a new bride; but what really drew people's attention was the young woman herself. She was decked out in a red cloak, with riding trousers and boots. The red cloak fluttered and sparkled with the soft brilliance of the morningstar lily. It goes without saying, the young woman was Shen Mengtang, the mother that Jinwu was to spend so many years of her life looking for. But at that time she was still just a young woman of twenty-five. When she was twenty-one, she had joined the Communist New Fourth Army, where she worked exclusively in intelligence gathering, and indeed was nothing less than a genuine "spy." (Obviously, Jinwu's nickname, Spy, had deep-seated roots that reached back a long way.) After the New Fourth Army Incident took place in southern Anhui Province in 1941, when the KMT forces, Chiang Kai-shek's Nationalist army, betrayed the trust of the Communists while they were fighting together against the Japanese, Shen Mengtang's work was exposed. After experiencing a number of setbacks, she finally got on the road to the revolution's most sacred place— Yan'an. Of course, even in her wildest dreams, she did not have an inkling of the magnificent drama that awaited her, and she threw herself so totally into it that it almost cost her her life.

But during that spring she was overwhelmed with happiness and deep feelings. Seemingly as if to welcome her to Yan'an, on that very evening, a special performance was staged in the auditorium of the Northern Shaanxi Public School, and the usual weekend dance party was canceled. Everybody contributed twenty cents in local currency, raising a total of two hundred yuan to stage a very creditable outdoor banquet. This was the first time in her life that Mengtang ate fresh lamb. Everything here was fresh. On this very freshest of days, Shen Mengtang met a young graduate student from the Military-Political Academy. Dressed in military garb and with a determined look on his face, he stood out sharply from the bustling crowd.

That evening she was put up in an old but simple and spotless cave dwelling. A very thin girl had already heated water for her bath. The thin girl was none other than Luo Bing. Right off the bat, Shen and Luo were like old buddies who never tired of each other's company. That night they talked together until the cocks crowed. Mengtang liked Luo Bing's frank straightforwardness and chivalrous sense of honor and fair play, and Luo Bing was attracted by Mengtang's intelligence and charm. It was from Luo Bing's lips that Mengtang first heard the phrase "Rectification Campaign." Luo Bing said that the part of the Rectification Campaign that dealt with the examination of cadres' family backgrounds, work experience, and social connections was undertaken in 1942 and reached a peak in the fall of that year, and that now a second wave of this aspect of the campaign was about to get under way.

Mengtang, who had come from the KMT-controlled "White Areas," didn't have the slightest interest in this burgeoning campaign. She was much more concerned about anything and everything to do with the life of her new friend Luo Bing. Luo openly admitted that she already had a boyfriend, and that he had just graduated from the Military-Political Academy and was leaving for the battle front in just a few days. She herself had graduated two years earlier and was now teaching in the Northern Shaanxi Public School. It was only when she started talking about her boyfriend that her face took on the expression of a young girl. Mengtang found this expression very moving. "Can you bear having him go to the front?" Biting her lip, Luo smiled, saying, "What could be unbearable about it? When you come here you devote your everything to the revolution."

The very next day Mengtang met Luo Bing's boyfriend, only to discover that he was that Military-Political Academy student with the determined look on his face. The moment she saw him, she thought what a terrible thing it was that she and her newfound friend were in love with the same man.

But Mengtang didn't feel the least bit guilty. From the time she was a child, she had received a Western-style education. Her father, Shen Xuanjian, had gone to France to study as a young man. Her mother was the daughter of an Imperial Qing Dynasty envoy stationed in France and was also a well-known disciple of the famous dancer Isadora Duncan. The mother was a prominent figure in contemporary dance in China, and, not surprisingly, Mengtang was influenced by her in some ways. Not only was Mengtang an excellent dancer, she was also proficient in both English and French, and could play the piano as well. But dancing and piano were not things she could devote her entire life to. According to her mother, there was something bold and dark buried deep in her mind. Even as a little girl, Mengtang liked to do risky things: the more dangerous they were, the more they would stimulate her cleverness and creativity. Totally unlike her seven older brothers and sisters, she chose the route of revolution, which was, in fact, the choice of a dangerous life-time career. She was extremely proficient in her intelligence gathering in the KMT-controlled White Areas, receiving a number of citations for her work. Every time she had made use of her talent and ability to complete another assignment, she would be rewarded with a deep sense of satisfaction.

When she first arrived in Yan'an, because of the changes in her surroundings and position, she was truly and totally filled with a new kind of enthusiasm. But after three months, the only remaining interest she had was in Luo Bing's boyfriend, Wujin, and eventually he did become her boyfriend.

11

It is reasonable for us to assume that Jinwu never fully accepted her adoptive parents' accounts of her mother. Jinwu thought that whatever they said was always one-sided, and she was determined to go and find her mother herself.

Of course, her adoptive father was not Wujin. Wujin had given up his life in battle. Jinwu firmly believed that it was her mother that Wujin had loved. Men's preference in love is for beautiful women who are intelligent and lively and also very feminine. But her adoptive mother had a kind of sexless beauty. To her surprise, Jinwu discovered that after she found out about her real mother, she had erected a protective screen between herself and her adoptive mother. In her imagination, she always saw her mother as the image of perfection. When she envisaged herself as being in some ways like her mother and in others like her father, her adoptive mother in hateful tones told her that her father was a foreigner from the United States, adding, "It was because of him that your mother turned her back on the revolution." On the sidelines, her adoptive father heaved a sigh as he added, "My child, honestly, our emotional ties with your mother run very deep. We like and respect her. Back in those days, she was unusually beautiful, and she spoke three languages fluently, played the piano, and was marvelously accomplished in modern dance. Among the women in the Yan'an area, there were none who could vie with her. But she was lacking in revolutionary will and could not stand being condemned or misunderstood. Eventually she fled the area with the guy from the States. That was just too big of a blow for us. Through all those years, we could never forgive her . . . but our strong feelings for her were never severed. Your aunty and your mother were like blood sisters, so there was never any question about us looking after you as your mother had wished . . ."

Jinwu was surprised to see her adoptive mother, who never cried, shedding tears that looked as big as pearls—tears that seemed as heavy as history itself.

After this, Jinwu would spend hours in front of the mirror. Standing there, she would think at great length about things like the fairness of her skin, her large brown eyes, her long, curved eyelashes, and everything else involved in being of a "different country and a different race," including how the blood of two different races could intermix, and how just one drop of male sperm and one female ovum could tie together two totally different individuals, countries, races, and cultures to give life to something absolutely new and different. Some years later, Jinwu was to learn a new phrase—"international integration." But on one occasion standing in front of the mirror back in those days, smiling coldly, she picked up an apricot-colored lipstick and slowly smeared it over her entire face. Looking into the mirror, this apricoted lady declared: Bastard. A very clear declaration.

It took Jinwu all of two years to finally get a record of her mother's past pieced together. From the series of accounts she gleaned from her adoptive parents, she eventually understood that her mother had been branded as a "top suspect" in the Rectification Campaign that dealt with cadres. It was only to be expected at that time that a person who had done espionage work in the KMT White Areas for a long time and was fluent in three different languages would be branded as a top suspect. But what had set the whole process off was really quite insignificant. "Your mother hadn't been in Yan'an two months when she was already fed up with conditions there," said her adoptive mother, pulling fiercely on her cigarette, again on the verge of tears. "It wasn't that she was afraid of hardship; it was just that she felt that cultural life there was too empty. There was no music, no poetry, no fiction, and no movies. All there was were a few ancient plays, some political dramas, and some clapper tales and tongue-twister cross-talks. The Yan'an Bookstore was the only place you could see newspapers from outside, but they were always a month out of date and soon of no interest. Intellectuals faced continual brainwashing and anyone with an education had to learn from the illiterate and semi-literate . . . Of course, all this was your mother's biased view of things, picked up when she was in the White Areas, where she fostered her incipient capitalistic tastes. We did everything we could to help her change her view of things . . . It didn't occur to any of us that your mother would write a formal report concerning all the things we tried to do for her. You think about it, given the situation at that time, who could have saved her?"

An unbroken string of ideas raced through Jinwu's mind. She envisioned her beautiful mother in the fall of that year locked away in a dark and tiny little room, subjected to unending bouts of interrogation. The autumn winds and yellow leaves outside her window were bleak and forlorn. At that time Shen Mengtang had to have been trapped in the throes of despair, because everybody, on the same morning, openly and clearly drew a line of distinction between themselves and her, including her deeply beloved Wujin. The only person to visit her after that was Luo Bing, who went to see her twice. On the second occasion she brought a man who Mengtang didn't know with her. Luo Bing brought along many dishes she had prepared, but Mengtang didn't eat a thing. Luo Bing pointed at the fat stranger, introducing him as Commissioner Lin of the Yan'an area. Jinwu realized that Commissioner Lin was none other than her present adoptive father.

The last time Wujin visited Mengtang before leaving for the battle front served as the closing ceremony of their short-lived romance. Just how things went that day it is now impossible to say. But Luo Bing insisted that Wujin was extremely distressed and that as the moment of his departure drew near, all he could manage to say was, "Look after her for me." This sentence turned out to be his dying words, as three months later he was killed on the front lines; but he did not die a hero, because his death was the result of the accidental discharge of the rifle of one of his own comrades.

For a long time after that, Shen Mengtang was ignored by people in the area. Then, one year later, when the Yan'an area received its first delegation of foreign reporters, one of the local authorities was incensed over the lack of adequate translation services. Only at that point in time did people recall that holed up somewhere in the area doing nothing, there was this woman translator who was fully fluent in three of the world's national languages. Like a bunch of archaeologists scouring the earth for cultural relics, they began their hunt for Mengtang; and eventually they located her in a darkened cave dwelling where she had been holed up for a very long time. The first time Luo Bing saw her old friend she was truly shocked. She saw that that natural beauty, that lively and lovable creature, was nothing more than a withered stump of her old self enshrouded in a pall of loess dust. She found it hard to imagine that a year and a half's time could wreak that much damage. Three days earlier she had received instructions from the top brass requesting that she get Shen Mengtang back to normal in the shortest time possible. They told her she could ask for anything she felt she required.

In that dilapidated, old, but clean and neat cave dwelling, just as she had done the first time they met, Luo Bing quietly went about heating up some bathwater. While using a clean towel to help Mengtang scrub herself, Luo discovered that her old friend was as frail as a little baby and found it hard to breathe in the hot water and steam, but that she had an incomparable will to live. That evening Luo Bing used specially supplied ingredients to cook up a sumptuous dinner for Mengtang. Mengtang ate very slowly, but Luo Bing was surprised to find that with each mouthful of food a tiny bit of color would work its way back into her friend's cheeks, and her eyes were slowly brightening. Like a slowly inflating balloon, Mengtang was gradually filling out. To her surprise, after all the dust had been washed away from that face, Luo Bing discovered that it was really more like a layer of some special kind of greasepaint, and that the face encased within it, aside from being much thinner than before, had not changed at all.

A very important press conference was held in the auditorium of the Northern Shaanxi Public School. The female translator Shen Mengtang broke out of the old trends. Only when the foreign journalists realized that there were still extremely talented and beautiful people like this in the Yan'an areas did their fear of the "Red Bandits" begin to dissipate significantly. During those days, Shen Mengtang more or less served as a bridge connecting the Yan'an area with the outside world. After having shut herself away for a year and seven months, she once again became involved in life. Almost under the very eyes of Luo Bing, who was keeping her under close surveillance, she eventually started an affair with a young journalist from America named Smith. Jinwu was nothing less than the product of their passion.

Jinwu felt that no matter what people said, her mother definitely had her reasons for what she did. She felt that she clearly had to find her mother. She could not tolerate the thought of others trying her mother in absentia.

But the trials in absentia were to continue. Now they involved her adoptive parents. The old couple who had been loyal to the Communist Party their entire lives could not avoid getting caught in this new campaign's "trials in absentia." Their dubious connection with a "traitor" cost them their name and also cost them their clean life record.

| *YIN LINES*

1

In the *I Ching*, or *Book of Changes*, *yin* and *yang* stand for hardness and softness. Yang symbolizes masculinity and *yin* femininity. Odd numbers are classified as *yang* and even numbers as *yin*.

So, of the six line positions of a hexagram, always built upward from the bottom, the first, or base, and the third and fifth positions are *yang* positions, while the second, fourth and final, or sixth, places are *yin* positions. All of these lines and positions can be in positive, or correct, relationships or in negative relationships.

The inner and outer, or lower and upper, three-line trigrams that are combined to form the hexagrams all have appropriate defined interrelationships. Only a masculine and feminine line, with their mutual sexual attraction, can work together in positive harmony. If the two lines are of the same sexual orientation, they will oppose rather than complement each other.

In addition to the creation of trigrams using *yin* and *yang* lines, there is another way of structuring them called "changing lines."

Blue Arch Strings

Violin 1
* Karen Seigel
Ann Alcorn
Pam Bazinet
Kailey Moore

Viola
* Emily Janz
Clive McGowan
Janice Schneider

Violin 2
* Judy Wark
Jihad Charanek
Richard Armand

Cello
* Mona Chappellaz
Barb Bamber
Lynn McLean

* Denotes section leaders

Many thanks to our special guests, Carmen Ashmead, Matt Heller and Margot Scullen.

Blue Arch Strings (formerly *Baroque & Buskin' Strings)* is a community string orchestra that was started in Calgary in 1988 by Elisa Sereno-Janz. In *Blue Arch Strings,* we believe that making music with others is a fundamental part of the human experience and we support a fun social and noncompetitive atmosphere. We accept new members each term, and are always looking for enthusiastic string players who love to make music with others.

To contact us, or for more information on rehearsals and audition requirements, please check out our website: www.bluearchstrings.com

Spring Concert
Blue Arch Strings

Directed by

Elisa Sereno-Janz

Sunday, May 6, 2012

3:00 pm

Scandinavian Centre, 739- 20th Ave. NW

2

Of course, Yushe didn't know how hard her grandmother, Xuanming, had been on her mother, Ruomu, that year. If Yu had known, perhaps she wouldn't have been so easily upset by her mother.

That was the year that Ruomu's personal servant, Meihua, came to her mistress's rescue.

The helping hand Meihua sought was Tiancheng.

She delegated Old Zhang, the servant of the master of the house, to go to Tiancheng's school to find him. She said it was very important, that if he didn't find Tiancheng and fetch him home, Ruomu was doomed.

One evening at twilight, the big brass ring on the front gate of the courtyard reverberated with the soft metallic sound of Tiancheng's fading but persistent knocking. The family's servants all recognized it as the knock of the house's young master. Nineteen-year-old Tiancheng was already a tall, slender, and refined-looking young man with a spare but resolute and awe-inspiring face that set him apart from the other members of the family. That evening, together with Old Zhang, Tiancheng, bearing the banyan tree scent of a different small city, opened the courtyard gate. Perhaps as a result of the delicate evening light, the young lad was sure that the body of the young woman kneeling there in front of him was totally translucent, as if she had been cut out of white paper. It was a soft and fragile light; it seemed as if all you had to do was reach out and touch the light and the shape of the kneeling figure would instantly disappear.

Tiancheng felt like he was on the verge of tears. He bent down to offer his sister a helping hand, only to encounter an unexpected resistance. The young paper-cut woman remained absolutely motionless. Tiancheng said, "Sister, it was Mother who insisted I come. She asked me to take you to see her." Off to one side, Old Zhang added that she should get up right away, the old mistress had told the cook to make stewed chicken with wolfberries especially for her, to strengthen her body, but only if she would admit her shortcomings to her. But Ruomu, the young woman who looked like she was cut out of a piece of white paper, remained silent; and because of her drooping, downcast eyelids, there was no way for Tiancheng or Old Zhang to measure her expression. With fear slowly but steadily piercing its way into his bones, eventually Tiancheng could no longer bear it and screamed out, "Mother! Mother! Come quickly. Look at sister. What's wrong with her?"

Xuanming, who, all along, had been furtively listening outside the door, came stumbling into the room on her tiny feet.

That night, Xuanming did something that she would deeply regret for the rest of her life. She prostrated herself before her own daughter. Her initial thundering fury gave way to a mildness as gentle as a spring breeze or summer shower, and ultimately to her kneeling in total capitulation in front of her own daughter. Not until Xuanming was kneeling in front of her did the young woman cut out of white paper finally collapse. In the confusion, no one noticed the hint of a smile that appeared on the young woman's lips. On that pale face, that smile was frighteningly sinister.

3

Nearly all beautiful women live ill-fated lives. Our story is no different. Meihua's luck did not take a turn for the better just because she had rescued her young mistress. Quite the opposite; everything in her life took a turn for the worse as a result of this affair. This was something that Meihua, with her limited intelligence, could not possibly have foreseen.

Ruomu's entire life was enshrouded in a dark mental haze. From that night on, in the darkness, this young woman with the appearance of a white paper cut would frequently harbor a hideous sneer. She remained as taciturn as ever, unrelentingly playing the part of a young princess. The lines of her face were as exquisite as they had always been, without the slightest trace of hurt. The only thing different was the amount of time she idled away doing nothing, and the pitiful amount of food she ate. She would sit staring endlessly at the grape trellis outside the window, slowly cleaning her ears with an ear spoon. The ear spoon, made of pure gold, had been given to Ruomu at that time by her mother. Xuanming was sure her daughter would be wildly delighted, but she accepted it without the slightest sign of gratitude and started digging the crud out of her ears. Ruomu's cool haughtiness as she probed repeatedly into her ears so unsettled Xuanming that she tottered out of the room on her tiny feet, bumping into the wind chimes hanging in the entrance patio on her way. But the usually clear and crisp tinkle of the chimes sounded muffled and moldy. It was the middle of the rainy season, when everything got moldy, and that included the first love of this young woman with the appearance of a white paper cut.

Meihua was the only one who could get close to Ruomu. Every night before going to sleep, Ruomu would read a few pages from a book she had. Although Meihua was not totally illiterate, the print in the book Ruomu was reading looked like strange little tadpoles to Meihua's eyes. Among the tadpole-shaped words swam some illustrations that truly made Meihua tremble with fear. One of them depicted a woman in a long dress that left her breasts and her back completely bare. She had big, mournful eyes and startlingly long eyelashes. With his arms wrapped around her, a man was cuddling her ample breasts against his chest. Of course, Meihua had no way of knowing the book her mistress was reading was an original edition of the classic French novel *Manon Lescaut* by Abbé Prévost. With her heart pounding and her ears burning, Meihua felt that some part of her body was sending her a strange signal that was completely new to her. She turned away and headed for her own otherwise barren little room, which she had brightened up with all kinds of perfumed sachets that she had embroidered herself. Once in her own room, Meihua buried her blushing face in a heap of these beautiful fragrant sachets. She felt so stiflingly hot she had to unbutton her floral, light green traditional jacket. The two meaty mounds of her bosom protruded from under her red satin *doudu*, a diamond-shaped traditional biblike undergarment worn by young girls, like just-ripened plump, beautiful, and fragrant melons. As she patted them gently, a delicate sensitivity pervaded her entire body, while even the embroidered sachets around her began to quiver delicately, emitting an enchanting aroma of gardenias and lavender.

The following afternoon, equally as enchanting, Meihua walked into Tiancheng's room just as the young master awakened from his midday nap. Ruomu had sent Meihua to dust her younger brother's room, as she always felt the room was dusty and in need of cleaning. The moment Meihua entered Tiancheng's room her eyes brimmed over with a brightness like the glitter of tears. Her enchanting appearance totally unnerving him, Tiancheng felt like his heart was being smashed to bits with a hammer, instantly overwhelming him with a dull pain that immediately began spreading its tentacles throughout his entire body. With the rise of his youthful male passion, Tiancheng's entire face, including even his eye sockets, turned red, giving him a look of pure simplicity, the kind of look that belonged to young men only.

Many years later Meihua would still remember the scene. Just at that moment a sudden gust of wind had blown the window open, and a flurry of silky white willow catkins drifted in, with one of them landing on Tiancheng's shoulder. Instinctively, Meihua went over to him and flicked it away. She saw the young master's handsome yet somewhat stiff face suddenly brim with vitality. Rather than letting her hand go immediately, he cradled it gently in his own for a while, and Meihua could feel a bright crystalline fluid running through her arm and into her body. But this lasted only a moment, with the young master quickly releasing her hand. She noticed the faint beating of the bluish veins in his forehead and could see his gaze slipping hesitantly toward her only to be involuntarily withdrawn. It was the perfect kind of gaze to create an air of bashfulness. Seeing it kindled a fire in Meihua's heart, and its flames immediately began to spread. She knew that her own face must be a bright crimson, but that there was nothing she could do to quell the flames. She felt like every single cell in her body had suddenly become extremely sensitive. She was afraid that if the young master's hand were to touch her again, she would not be able to prevent herself from crying out. Yet she yearned uncontrollably for his touch. She longed for his hands to caress her, to arouse her just like the April breeze outside the window. Silently she raised her head, her eyes shining as brightly as falling stars. The young master was clearly overwhelmed by those shining eyes. Feeling like he had lost his voice, he stood there silently without uttering a single word.

Precisely at that moment, the sound of Ruomu's voice calling for Meihua wafted into the room.

4

At midnight, as she always did, Meihua took Ruomu a mug of scented tea. She could clearly see Ruomu grinning at her ominously from the darkness under the grape trellis. That sinister grin, etched on Ruomu's pale face, scared the wits out of Meihua.

Slowly sipping her tea, Ruomu walked back to her room and motioned to Meihua to close the door. As soon as Meihua had done so, Ruomu sat down in the chair in the center of the room and, picking up her pure gold ear spoon, began casually poking at the wax in her ears. Meihua couldn't make out whether the softly thumping sound that could be heard in that ever-so-quiet room came from the clock pendulum or the beating of her own heart. Meihua had no idea how much time had passed before her honorable mistress finally said to her with an endearing smile, "Meihua, get down on your knees. I have something to sound you out on."

Already scared out of her wits, Meihua dropped slowly to her knees with a soft thud. She was too young, so much so that without giving it a second thought she classified her inner passions as something evil. Her entire face flushed crimson as if she had truly done something to feel guilty about. Once again a faint smile graced Ruomu's face as her gaze came to rest on Meihua's heaving bosom. She said, "Meihua, you're truly getting more and more beautiful. You really should be getting married."

These words, like a vicious clap of thunder out of a blue sky, left Meihua, with her luscious, delicate figure, looking like a rigid wooden pillar. As the flow of blood in her veins seemingly slowed to a halt, her arms and legs became cold as ice. Without the slightest sign of hesitation, she began bashing her beautiful forehead against the concrete floor, crying out, "Mistress, I'd sooner die than get married. I want to serve you my entire life!"

Ruomu picked up that pure gold ear spoon again and recommenced her slow scraping for earwax, the French edition of *Manon Lescaut* lying open beside her. No question about it, Ruomu was truly the aristocratic daughter of a family of high social standing, with no interest in bad habits such as playing mahjong or smoking opium. Like smoke or clouds, her brief fascination with the second young master of the Qian family had also soon dissipated. And now, the young mistress Ruomu was as tranquil as still water, her life consisting of nothing more than three meals a day, reading, drinking scented tea, and meditation. Ruomu's reputation was as solid and impressive as that pure gold ear spoon. In the presence of such a sophisticated and mature young mistress, who was both well-read and well schooled in the courtesies of life, all Meihua could do was look up in awe at the towering mountain before her. But at this moment Ruomu's painted lips parted slightly to issue only two words: "False talk." Like twin bullets these two words struck Meihua, a beautiful and affectionate servant girl, a mortal blow.

Still scooping away at her ears, Ruomu casually added, "There's no need to get upset. I'll only do what's in your best interests. I think you and the master's servant Old Zhang would make an excellent match . . ."

Meihua felt like her body was being smashed to bits, and the excruciating pain made her tears pour down like rain. The blood from her battered and bleeding forehead was clotting her bangs into little clumps. With her eyes wide open and her face totally drenched in sweat and tears, she said, "Mistress, you mustn't forget that time I came to your rescue!"

What Meihua would never know was that it was precisely these words that crushed her last hope. Her life as a young girl ended abruptly at that point. She saw her mistress's brow furrow for a moment before she pulled the servants' bell cord. A few minutes later, Old Zhang, the forty-six-year-old servant of the master of the house, entered the young mistress's boudoir.

Meihua sobbed and screamed hysterically, and in her last struggles shouted out the young master's name—"Tiancheng!" Her determined resistance served only to intensify Ruomu's loathing. Ruomu never truly loved anyone in her entire life. And, of course, there were even limits on how much love she felt for her younger brother. But she understood the differences between social classes and the need to protect one's family's honor. She had absolutely no doubt that her younger brother was destined to marry a rare beauty of divine fragrance from some noble family, definitely not this base servant girl, Meihua, groveling before her. Any shred of compassion that Ruomu still might have felt for Meihua and her younger brother was tossed out when she saw them making eyes at each other. The moment that her relationship with the second young master of the Qian family had been severed, Ruomu's heart had turned to stone, and this left her feeling very proud.

Two muscular and powerful male servants dragged Meihua off to Old Zhang's tiny little room. In the fierce struggle, some of her clothes were torn away and one of her breasts popped out from under that triangular-shaped red *doudu* she wore next to her skin. That fresh and plump young breast was seized tightly by the big, coarse, grubby hand of the old male servant. Meihua knew that any further resistance on her part would be futile. What was most overwhelming was that even though both her mind and body were being ripped apart, she still felt intensely aroused. Like a fresh fruit that had been sliced open, she couldn't stop her bodily juices from overflowing. Her youthful passion kept pouring out in orgasm after orgasm, sending the forty-plus-year-old bachelor into mad ecstasies.

In a single night, Meihua's orgasmic juices were sucked dry, leaving her instantly withered.

5

Though Tiancheng was to come home again, he never saw Meihua again, and the melancholy look in his eyes became sadder and sadder. When Shu'er observed Tiancheng opening the window to let swarm after swarm of willow catkins flutter into his room, she went over and closed it, drawing a condemning curse from Tiancheng: "Bloody fool! Bloody fool!" Shu'er knew the young master never cursed anyone. When he lost his temper like this, it could only be because his heart had been irreparably broken. The young master had come home for the spring holiday, but without any explanation, he left after staying for just a few days. Following that departure, he never returned home again.

Tiancheng died the year before Japan surrendered. That year, the university Tiancheng was attending moved to the south. While they were en route, Tiancheng came down with a serious case of typhoid fever. By the time Xuanming and Ruomu had heard the news and rushed off to the hospital, Tiancheng was already in his death throes. Ruomu was stunned to see her brother's fair-skinned face had become black as charcoal. In her bewilderment, she thought it was someone else, not her brother. It was the first time for Ruomu to experience what dying could do to a person's appearance. Tiancheng's dying wish was to eat a tangerine. Because of the phlegm clogging his throat, his pronunciation was totally unrecognizable, but from reading his lips Ruomu was able to figure out that what he longed to eat was a tangerine. So she ran as quickly as she could down to the street to buy some; but, despite her anxiety, she didn't forget to haggle with the vendor over the price.

When she returned to the ward, Ruomu could hear Xuanming's despairing sobs. Tiancheng had stopped breathing but his eyes were still open. Xuanming had tried to close his eyes several times but to no avail. Only when Ruomu put a shimmering little golden tangerine into his widely opened mouth did Tiancheng's eyelids finally close. Xuanming started crying bitterly again: "Poor child. None of us can ever know how much you suffered! A bite of tangerine was all you wanted. Every year from now on Momma will buy you tangerines! . . . How pitiful, how unfair!" Ruomu, too, was weeping quietly, but she knew her tears were shed for others to see, and that even her mother's tears were mostly for show. Ruomu felt her mother's tears were her way of venting her indignation. At that time, it was already four years since the families that worked for the Gansu-Shanghai Railway Company had been told to relocate because of the war. Heshou and Xuanming took advantage of the national turmoil to end their marriage. Although they didn't go through any legal procedures, they lived many miles apart. Xuanming took her children to the south, while Heshou, in full agreement, sent them on their way, thus gaining his own freedom. He could freely bring his showgirls to his own home, indulging in the company of beautiful and affectionate young blossoms in rich and luxurious surroundings. Only he forgot the rich and luxurious surroundings were an empty illusion that could all turn to dust the minute the Japanese bombs started to fly.

Tiancheng was buried on a small hill near his school. The night before the burial, Xuanming painstakingly embroidered a pair of insoles with golden tangerines. She kept saying that Tiancheng must take them with him, but for some unaccountable reason, she kept puncturing her fingers with the needle through the entire night. When Ruomu woke up, she saw her mother sitting under the lamp, holding up her hands spattered with flecks of blood. Her black hair had turned totally gray overnight and was not done up in a bun, but hanging loose. The night breeze blowing in through the window lifted her hair high over her head. Xuanming's sinister stare focused on Ruomu's not yet fully opened eyes, which were heavy with slumber.

Ruomu cried out in fright and buried herself beneath her quilt.

6

I decided to give Jinwu a present on her birthday. I knew what she liked best.

In my hand was my most treasured possession, something that belonged to a distant age.

One night, a long, long time ago, when my maternal grandma, Xuanming, was engaged in her usual pastime of taking apart or putting back together an ancient lamp, I awakened without a sound, and peeking through the mesh of my eyelashes, I could see the lamp. Reminiscent of the Chinese flowering crab apple, that magnificent lamp lit up my forehead. It was made of violet-colored quartz crystal, and I could even see clearly the speckles in it. They must have been there in the water originally to give the crystal its indescribable fragrance. It was an inviting labyrinth that left me feeling that myriads of spirits were floating therein, fighting their way out of gold or silver embryos to return to life.

I instantly determined that it was of great value.

Just at that moment the scent of tea drifted into the room, and Grandma disappeared. I knew that she would come back to sit beside the lamp and drink her tea. Under that decorative lamp the tea would gradually get cold. To me, all this seemed like a ceremonial ritual, an ancient and mysterious ritual that only Grandma understood.

By the time she returned, I had completed my clandestine little act without leaving a trace. Totally out of curiosity, I had removed a piece of crystal, a violet petal. I thought that given that luxuriant bouquet of violet blossoms, a lone purple petal would be too small to be noticed. It never dawned on me that precisely because that one tiny piece was missing, Grandma would not be able to put the lamp together again. Grandma's lamp had been made with the precision of a computer, so that even the slightest flaw could disrupt its function.

If on that occasion Grandma had been a little bit milder, calmer, a bit more personal, I might, perhaps, have opted for a different option. But Grandma, as she reacted to everything else in life, immediately flew into a rage. She jumped up as if her tiny feet were spring-loaded. As usual, whenever I encountered something like this, I always felt like everything around me had become unreal. The only things that remained real were the diamond-shaped green jades flopping around on Grandma's feet. Their unusual dull green color always caught my attention. When she barged into my parents' bedroom, shrieking and shouting, I quickly threw the "criminal evidence" out the window.

That evening had the undeniable air of a drama. As if gone mad, my parents charged into my room while still only partially dressed and pulled me out of my bed. It was also the first time I had ever seen my father in such a serious state. He asked me, "Grandma's thing, did you take it or not?" then continued, "Any daughter of mine must be honest." Just as I was about to open my mouth, Mother's whining started up again. There is simply no other sound quite like that whine of hers. It can penetrate your skull and pierce its way directly into your brain. I think that anyone confronted by that sound would have no choice but to give in. She started in whiningly: "This nasty little brat is really upsetting the family. Poor me! I worked like a slave all day and now the night is nearly over, and I still haven't had a proper sleep. Did I commit some kind of crime in my previous life? It's so unfair! Poor me!" As usual, Father could not bear the weight of such whining. When Father could no longer bear it, it meant it was time for my flesh to feel pain. All of this had long ago become a vicious cycle, but nonetheless, with every recurrence my pain remained as fresh and sharp as always, and the wounds in my heart bled constantly, never really healing.

Even though I had fully prepared my body, I still wasn't able to handle the first blow from Father's fist. I lost my balance and collapsed over the bed railing. Mother's voice could be heard again, only this time, no longer the usual mumble, it was cold and calculated: "Look at the brat, what a fake! Daddy didn't use a lot of force. You are your daddy's favorite daughter. How could he bear to hit you? What a show you put on for someone so young! What even worse things will you get up to when you are older? Will you deceive the entire world?"

To me, Mother's words were like a metal hammer that was smashing my heart to pieces. Unable to utter a single word, all I could do was cry. I was completely lacking in language skills and totally unaware that the main reason God had humans learn languages was for self-defense. I didn't know how to defend myself, but as I cried and cried, a voice next to my ear laughed grimly: "Go ahead, hit me, curse me. I've thrown away your treasure. I can't give it back to you."

That whisper stayed with me for a long, long time. It always gives me strength at critical moments. This strength, no matter whether it is righteous or evil, is the only God-sent power I hold in veneration.

Because there was no other way, Grandmother eventually substituted a piece of glass so she could put her lamp back together again.

7

Yu dislikes school more and more.

When Yu had just started school, several of her teachers liked her very much. But at that time Yu thought there was no way they would go on liking her forever. They would eventually, just like her parents and grandma, despise her. The reason Yu thought this way was that that voice, that terrible voice in her heart, told her so. Very often Yu could not distinguish between that voice and what was genuinely her own thinking. In fact, that voice and her own thinking had become one and the same thing, a kind of premonition. What was unfortunate was that these premonitions, one by one, turned out to be the truth.

The art of getting along with people is a major branch of learning. If you master this branch of learning, then life can be peaceful, ill luck transformed into good, and calamity into blessing. To shortchange this branch of learning is to bring trouble on oneself, change good fortune into ill, and to deny success for want of a little effort. What was so damning was that Yu had no idea at all that this branch of learning existed. Given this precondition, everything that is to follow in our story makes logical sense.

Now we know that Yu lived with Jinwu, attending school on a temporary basis in the city Jinwu called home. But Yu was not like any of those Cinderellas whose fate was changed when their prince came into their life. Quite to the contrary, she always managed to screw up things that had started out full of promise. It was always the same old story: in everything she did, even before she had started, she was sure she would fail. Yes, she could never get out from under the dark shadow of her mother. Whenever Yu was about to cheer up, her mother would tell her she was going to fail, that everything she did was destined to amount to no more than a zero—or even a negative figure. Before she had actually started anything, she was always already defeated. But we never knew and had no way of finding out what it was that defeated her.

With friendship, there are always prerequisites and limits. The math teacher grew to like Yu because she was intelligent, so intelligent, in fact, that he thought she was a genius. But at first, he took scant notice of this skinny creature of obscure background. Even though she was introduced by Jinwu, the famous movie star he idolized, it was only with reluctance that he accepted her in his class. But he very quickly discovered that this young woman who paid no attention to her appearance, time and again would work out the solutions to difficult math questions that he himself found challenging. Once to check out just how good she was, he had her try a difficult math problem that was well-known for being beyond the level of high school students. She quickly worked out the answer, using her own method, not the one given in textbooks. He dashed madly back to the head office of the math department and called together all his colleagues. His voice hoarse with excitement, he waved the exercise sheet in his hand as he said, "All of you take a look at this.

The solution was worked out by a junior high school student. No, in actual fact, strictly speaking she's still an elementary student. And, surprisingly, not only was she able to work out the answer, but she did it using a new method. I'd venture to say that this is a brand-new method that has never been used before." Following his words, the exercise paper was passed from hand to hand, eliciting a continuing chorus of glowing praise.

But Yu's rise in repute definitely did not bring anything good into her life. On the contrary, she received an unwarranted amount of attention and revealed her true inner nature too soon, and the teachers quickly began to dislike her for her arrogance, stubbornness, and rebellious streak. One time during a chemistry experiment, she was the first to finish. Noticing this, the teacher said to her, "Students who have finished their work should leave so as not to interfere with others." As if she hadn't heard him, Yu continued playing around with the chemical solutions on the lab table, until suddenly there was an explosion. On that day, the enraged teacher dragged her across the drill ground and shoved her into the principal's office. While she was being dragged across the drill ground, Yu suddenly recalled an occasion from her distant past when she tried desperately to shut herself off from others, like a silkworm in its cocoon, but her never-ending strands of silk kept pouring out. These secretions, as always, stirred up the resentment of others. Their gaze, which she feared like a deadly sword, pursued her endlessly to destroy her, from her previous life to this one, from this one to the next.

On that occasion, Jinwu paid a compensatory fee to bring the matter to a close and said nothing further about it. But when it was all over, Yu was more uncommunicative than she had ever been.

But Yu's silence could not save her. The teachers felt that this young girl was using her silence to express her disdain, that she was using her disdain to destroy this group of respected teachers. If they allowed this to go on unchecked, then anything could happen. So the teachers formed an alliance to deal with Yu and protect their dignity.

In this protracted struggle, Yu was doomed to be the victim. In her dreams, Yu still frequently revisited that gloomy little blue lake, the place where she was born. The freshwater mussel in the lake that would slowly open its shell must have been lonely, incurably lonely. But she, without a doubt, must have welcomed, treasured, and protected her loneliness. She had rejected her blood ties. She had nothing and was nothing. In her heart, there was a zero, an everlasting zero. It is precisely this zero that is in contention with our equally contentious world. It is doomed to be crushed. According to the explanations of the *yin* and *yang*, or male and female, lines that make up the trigrams and hexagrams of the *Book of Changes*, when a zero is crushed, it becomes an unbroken line —; and when a line is broken it looks like this --, which is the *yin* line of the *Book of Changes*. That is to say that all women are ultimately destined to be crushed, and all this reflects the great wisdom of our ancestors.

8

Yushe quietly opened the door and entered Jinwu's room. She had bought a box for that unusual birthday present. In the predawn hours of the morning, when everyone else was sound asleep, she had sneaked out and retrieved that violet-colored piece of crystal from the little flower garden in the front courtyard. Regarding it as a talisman or lucky charm, she tucked it away in an inside pocket next to her skin. Several years later, she carefully made it into a brooch. If presented as part of a large jewelry display, a brooch like this, made of a violet-colored piece of crystal in the shape of a flower petal, would immediately attract the attention of viewers, leaving them feeling there was no other choice.

Now she was about to give this brooch to her beloved friend. She felt Jinwu was the only person in this world whose beauty matched that of the brooch.

But the room was quiet.

This was a beautiful house. Yu adored it. Compared with the place she had lived in before, this was truly a paradise. Yu enclosed herself in this house from dawn until dark, cherishing every moment of life therein. It became her protective coloration, her armor, her cocoon.

The world outside, with its flamboyant and charming streets, was not part of her life. She had nothing in common with the people there in their vast array of shapes and shades. She understood neither the words nor actions of that world; but from among that vast sea of people she could single out her own ilk. She ignored the group, showing interest only in individuals.

Now we can see this thin girl pass through the living room heading for the bedroom. She is wearing an old shirt cut in a man's style. It is so large that there is absolutely no trace of her waistline. Even from far away her slovenly appearance is readily apparent. Not one of the lines of her figure is normal. They all make her look as if she had been stretched or distorted by some special computer program, or as if she had stepped down out of one of Picasso's paintings from his blue period—lanky and deformed, mystic and dark—an obscure soul floating about. But if we focus in on her, we will discover that this young woman is truly a one-off, a world unto herself. It seems like all the lines on her face could move about like water, and these moving lines meant her face was constantly undergoing changes. The only thing we can all remember clearly is her eyes. Usually those eyes were well hidden behind her eyelashes, but suddenly you would feel them approaching you, coming closer and closer. It seemed like there was a pair of soaring birds fluttering inside them, and the fresh floral scent of incense filled the air.

Yu stopped in front of a panel-screen. Just as if she were attending a shadow-puppet theater performance, clearly visible on the screen were the reflected images of two people—a man and a woman. They were moving in unison in a series of actions reminiscent of dancing, but much more intense and splendid. Yu saw some men's and women's clothing hanging on the screen. She recognized the floral, lake water–blue silk dress Jinwu had just changed into. She also saw a sunburned hand covered with freckles draping a woman's bra and panties over the screen. To one side, through the partially opened venetian blind, she caught a brief glimpse of the rich sprinkling of green leaves beyond the window. That brief moment was fixed forever in her memory.

At this point, we see the thin, ghostly girl turn and leave. In a flash, the pair of birds in her eyes flew off and the fragrance of fresh floral incense faded away, as if all of this had never existed. That pair of eyes was suddenly far, far away, having instantly separated themselves from those seeking to control them, escaping to a quiet and uninhabited mountain valley.

9

The young girl lay there in the deepening darkness, like a corpse.

Jinwu came in and turned on the light. The light fell on the girl's hair. Sitting down beside her and gently stroking her hair, Jinwu said, "Michael is going back to his country . . . It's true, we are in love. Falling in love is a normal thing. Of course, I am older than him, but love has nothing to do with age. The day will come when you'll understand this. Love has nothing to do with reality. It is the only thing the gods have given us . . . Aren't you happy for me?"

We can see that the young girl's oppressed and sunken little face is drenched with tears from her weeping. She was thinking that she loved Jinwu so much, so much, but that Jinwu clearly didn't love her. Jinwu, just like her own family in the past, like everyone else in her life, did not love her. Jinwu, whom she loved and admired so much, was about to forsake her for a man. Jinwu was in love with a man. That man occupied every corner of Jinwu's heart. To Jinwu, she was of no importance. She was of no importance to anyone. In the entire world, there was not a single person who truly loved her. Believing this left her engulfed in sorrow.

"My God, child, what's the matter? You're crying? Don't be so narrow-minded! . . . so foolish! You can rest assured that I shall love and care for you just as I have always done. Good heavens! How can you be so foolish?"

"Don't say any more. I know I can never be forgiven . . . They have told you everything, haven't they? Yes, I committed a crime. It was me who killed my baby brother. But . . . but I was only six years old at the time. I don't understand life at all . . . I . . . I really don't know how I might make amends for my crime. If only I knew how, even if I had to die a thousand times, I'd willingly do it! . . ." In her heart, Yu sobbed on: "Jinwu, Jinwu, don't leave me. Just as long as you don't leave me, I'll do anything you ask . . ."

Jinwu was totally stunned. At first, she thought Yu's words were childhood gibberish. But she quickly realized that Yu was telling the truth. No wonder Yu's parents had never cared for her the way they did for Ling and Xiao. All of Yu's living expenses were, in fact, borne by Jinwu, who didn't see this as a burden at all. In fact, Jinwu craved Yu's companionship. In Jinwu's eyes, Yu was much more lovable than her two older sisters. What Jinwu needed was a permanent female companion. She said to Yu, "Is there anyone who hasn't made a mistake at some point in life? Time erases all mistakes. Because you were too young to understand life, what you did cannot be viewed as a crime—only as a mistake."

Yu did not sleep that entire night. She kept thinking that Jinwu was lying to her, couldn't forgive her, that none of them could forgive her. With these kinds of thoughts, her tears overflowed and continued until the sky began to lighten. Soaked in her tears, she felt very light, as if she were floating aimlessly in a sea of sorrow. Then a voice whispered clearly in her ear: "At Xitan Mountain's Jinque Temple you can atone for your crime . . ." Frightened, she thought it was Jinwu's voice. She sat up quickly, only to find there was nobody there. But she felt a kind of calming atmosphere pressing down on her. Her heart was beating so quickly it unnerved her. Suddenly she recalled this was a familiar kind of feeling, a kind of restraining air, a childlike whisper appearing in a snow-filled, threatening sky.

Jinque Temple on Xitan Mountain: she remembered now that when she was a child her grandmother had once told her the story of the temple and the master tattoo artist, Fa Yan, who lived there.

10

A snowy day again.

Enormous snowflakes, one by one, created whiteness that nothing, not even the wind, could penetrate. Walking aimlessly in this depressing white world, Yushe looked terribly tiny.

Her sole purpose was to destroy herself. She hated her life, hated every inch of her own skin. Her skin had become meaningless and contemptible to her because no one touched it or showed interest in it. She thought her living in this world was truly a waste of time. But no one could ignore this kind of huge snowfall that was filling the heavens. One after another, the patterns of the huge flakes were reflected in the pupils of her eyes.

Those patterns were fragments of her childhood. Yu used to love those hexagonal snowflakes. She had once painted them on a sheet of white paper she had first given a wash of bright blue, to present to her mother and father as her most beautiful and valued treasure.

But her father and mother definitely did not love her.

Now, as she looked at the depressing whiteness, from some spot in her heart her blood spilled forth, flowing like a river. She feared that her blood would pour out uncontrollably onto the snow-covered ground, turning into fiery red flowers as uplifting and soul-stirring as Chinese winter plum blossoms. She thought the best thing for her would be to have the blood in her heart run dry one day; then she would never again feel pain.

Precisely at that moment, a grand temple came into view.

It was obviously a huge Buddhist temple. The white snow lightly and effortlessly marked the outlines of the temple. As twilight faded toward sunset (a continuation of twilight), the temple often made people think they were looking at a jade palace carved out of ice. At that time, Yu was still young, of course, and could still recall there was a word called hope. The moment she laid her eyes on the temple, a ray of hope penetrated her heart. With great difficulty, she climbed up the snow-clad stone stairs. Towering upward, the stone stairs were like a cloud stairway leading to heaven. She counted the stairs one by one. Suddenly, when she could no longer remember which stair she was on, everything before her seemed bathed in a magnificent golden light. The temple appeared to have changed into a sparklingly bright piece of embroidery of no weight and no value, about to melt into a sheet of pure gold—this was Yu's last impression before she lost consciousness.

Only a number of years later did I learn that Ruomu had eaten a lot of fish eyes from a certain type of poisonous fish while pregnant with Yu. Unaware that the fish was poisonous, Ruomu loved its delicious taste, especially the taste of the eyes. Ruomu had eaten this fish many times with no ill effects. But one day she, by chance, read a newspaper article that said the fish was poisonous. Ruomu immediately threw up the fish she had eaten that day. She threw up so much she almost lost consciousness, and she never ate that kind of fish again.

Yu was born before Ruomu read the newspaper article about the fish.

So Yu's eccentricities may perhaps have come from those poisonous fish eyes. They may have taken root behind her own eyes, giving her the ability to see deeply into things. Perhaps such an ability to see deeply into all things allowed Yu to understand the mixed-up feelings of the people in the world around her. Perhaps it was for this reason that Yu longed for the kind of love that came from heaven.

At twilight on that winter day, a goshawk passing across the heavens spotted a snake coiled up on the snow-covered ground. The snake was frozen stiff, but you could still see that it was once very beautiful. The shapeless jade hands of the mounting snow slowly covered the snake. You could see that the frozen snake would never again slither, never again be a representative of its species—a frozen coil left to endure the bitter cold of the wind and snow.

Perhaps this was the way for her to redeem herself. Perhaps she was longing for a transformation. No matter what, in that vast world of white snow she was insignificant and totally powerless.

| YUANGUANG

1

When Yushe awoke, she found herself lying in the temple. As her eyes adjusted to the shadows, she saw an old monk sitting nearby with his legs crossed. He had a white beard, clean and neatly trimmed, but Yu couldn't make out his expression in the dim light. "Why are you here?" he asked. "I'm looking for Master Fa Yan," she replied. The old monk's beard moved slightly. "Who sent you to look for him?" Yu said nothing. She felt the warmth of the room and gradually her frozen blood began to circulate. Like a fish that had just escaped from a frosty current, Yu opened her mouth, but she was so contentedly warm that no words emerged. Perhaps the monk was amused by her appearance or something else about her; he said nothing further. As he got up to leave, Yu noticed his robe made of handwoven cloth the color of honey locust, its broad sleeves so heavy that even in the wind they would not flutter.

Yu moved a little and found that she was sitting on an old and dirty mat made of colorful bits of cloth. No one could know how many people had sat on that mat, but Yu was strongly attracted to it. She even caressed it. But with just that one soft touch, a bit of the cloth fell into shreds.

Yu immediately withdrew her hands. Sitting with her arms tucked primly around her knees, she was staring straight at the temple's colorful hangings before her eyes, wondering if these seemingly splendid dust-covered hangings would also fall in shreds at a single touch.

Now a young man, specifically a young monk, entered. His face was impassive as he placed bowls of food before her—rice, soup, and stir-fried vegetables. Pieces of tofu, scallions, and small bits of shrimp were floating in the soup; as she raised the bowl to her lips, her face was enshrouded in fragrant steam.

Just as an oblique ray of the evening sun shone beneath the eaves, the young monk Yuanguang, on entering an adjacent hall, saw the blurred figure of a slender girl. Her body, reminiscent of snow and fog, seemed to be moving in and out of the rays of twilight. When she raised the bowl of soup to her lips, what seemed like melting snow and ice streamed slowly down from her forehead.

Yuanguang witnessed and took part in the entire process of tattooing the young girl. It was the first time for Yuanguang to participate in the holy ceremony conducted by Master Fa Yan. For Yuanguang it was no more than just that—a ceremony.

That winter night was extremely unusual. Because of the heavy snowfall, the sky that night had taken on the unsurpassable, ethereal splendor of an ice-chilled crown, casting its special glow on all blood that pulsed beneath it, whether clear or murky. On that winter night, the body of the girl or woman, known as Yushe, possessed a translucence that indicated the limpid clarity of her blood. Like a cloudy mist, her body had almost completely evaporated. Standing straight and tall like a fairy-tale figure, her fleshly body was draped in silvery moonlight, an undeniably beautiful image; but when seen beside the splendor of the heavens it was reduced to nothing more than an image of death.

This phantom image was doomed to die even before it was born.

2

Buddhist Great Master Fa Yan took out his complete set of tattooing needles, which he had not used for a full fifty years. In his hands they turned into living things. They tentatively probed into that totally unreal snowy mist of a body, which like some marine organism or body of plankton, completely lacking the special features of a woman, plied its unrealistic way through the ether.

In Great Master Fa Yan's eyes there was no sexual distinction between men and women. On a little table on one side of his room he had placed a bronze statue of Siva, the Hindu god of destruction and regeneration. This great dancing god of Brahmanism had a unique face—one half of it was male and the other half female; half male and half female, it was neither male nor female. But with the sexes brought together in this way, it was an absolutely perfect image of harmony.

A vast wilderness spread out before Yu's eyes. Carried in the gentle breeze blowing above the fresh yellow tones of the earth, vivid greens of the wild grasses, and bright blue of the lake water, one could eventually make out, mixed in with the odor of newts, a female figure sheltered in the mist-laden, rarefied damp air, with a bounty of beautiful grapes rolling over her cheeks and sheets of mica and fallen leaves shifting about beneath the water. After covering a great distance, a razor-sharp needle pierced her skin. The first drop of blood, because of its thick richness, was black in color.

The surface of the lake had been shattered into diamond fragments. Stagnant ponds gave off virgin fluids and pale white vapors. Yu felt that the fluids within her body, both the viscous and the watery, were about to squirt out in some form or other. She suspected it would be the tears she had swallowed, which had changed color because they had been pent up too long and now contained blood.

Perhaps blood and tears were inseparable from the very beginning.

Yu made no sound during the painful procedure. Yuanguang wondered if her body was real. Her endurance was moving, and he was tempted to test her stoicism with a sharp needle. But Fa Yan noticed a thin trickle of blood on her lip; she was biting it to suppress the pain. He glanced at Yuanguang, who knew what was on his master's mind and so avoided the elder's eyes.

"Young girl, I know you are in great pain," said Fa Yan firmly but warmly, "your skin is so tense that I cannot continue. Let this young man help you, it is the only way to get you to relax. Then I can create a beautiful tattoo."

Once again Fa Yan's glance fell on Yuanguang; this time it was a command. The young monk trembled. A man of strong will (you will find out just how strong as our story unfolds), he was frightened. Yes, he trembled with fear, as he knew he could not disobey Fa Yan, but the thought of what would come next made him shake with fear.

He gently rolled Yu under his muscular torso. He felt this young girl as light as a feather. Her obedience and endurance almost moved him to tears. He was hoping she could offer a little resistance so that he would be stimulated. But now he was placid, as his heart was filled with tender love for her.

When Fa Yan glanced at him for the third time, Yuanguang knew he must start. While concealing his tender feelings, he caressed her as gently as he could to reduce her pain. His eyes looked beyond her dimly visible body to linger in a faraway land. He was only mechanically doing what his master ordered. When he entered her body, she jerked violently, drawing back his attention. He saw fresh blood trickling out of her mouth as she bit down on her tongue, and a pool of blood gathered under her body. He did not expect to see so much blood, because he thought he had been extremely gentle.

Fa Yan's penetrating gaze had meanwhile observed a transformation in Yu's skin; the tension had gone, every pore had opened while the two bodies gently heaved and subsided like soft ocean waves. Directed by Fa Yan's eyes, Yuanguang tried different positions, still clasping the girl's body to his chest, finally standing upright with her against the central pillar of the grand hall. Now the whole of her naked back was exposed to Fa Yan, who at last glanced at Yuanguang with satisfaction.

The tattooing went on for two hours, the most unbearable two hours of Yuanguang's life. His sweat joined her blood while he wept silently in his heart. None of this escaped Yu. From the beginning she had observed the sympathy in his indifferent eyes. She had also seen that he was very handsome, even more handsome than Michael, the boy from America. Different from Michael, she was attracted to the young monk's good looks. Not merely a movie image, he was full of life, full of variations, and had a rich background. Yu sensed Yuanguang's background from the very beginning, and therefore accepted him.

Yuanguang was excited when he saw the finished tattoo on Yu's back. Wanting to do something of his own, he took up the tools himself but didn't know where to start. Yu turned over to look at him quietly and pointed to her breasts. "Come and leave a souvenir," she said. Moonlight streamed into the temple, giving her bosom the glow of cool porcelain. With total concentration, in thirty minutes Yuanguang added a tiny plum blossom to each of her breasts. Once again his sweat ran with her blood. The strong young man collapsed on the floor when he was done. Viewing his work, he sighed, "I will never be as good as the master."

Fa Yan closed his eyes in meditation and after a while said softly, "This is the most beautiful of all the tattoos I have ever made. I could never do it again. Young girl, you have shed a lot of blood, enough to redeem your sin. You may go now, the farther away the better, I don't want to see you ever again."

3

Once, a long time ago, Xuanming told Yushe the story of Master Fa Yan.

Earlier we mentioned that Xuanming was the seventeenth daughter in a large family. She had a precious old photo of her aunt Zhenfei. Not as beautiful as the rumors about Zhenfei suggested—she was chubby, with lackluster eyes. But Zhenfei is a celebrity, her name familiar to all Chinese. Could this have something to do with the circumstances of her unusual death? People always show love and care to the dead instead of the living. If the dead had a soul to know about this, they might regret having to depart from this world. But even when they do have an ability to return to this world, they once again fall into a trap of a hard life.

But Xuanming was a real beauty. The stories she told about Empress

Dowager Cixi were all true, with little in the way of exaggeration. There is only one story she would not tell: the origin of that mysterious lamp.

In addition to Aunt Zhenfei, Xuanming had many other relatives. One autumn day, another aunt, Yuxin, Lady Yang's older sister, arrived. Xuanming was still young at the time, but growing up in such a large family, she had seen a lot of people. But none were as comely as Aunt Yuxin. Even in her fifties, she had a transcendent beauty. She was fair-skinned, with elegantly formed cheeks and mouth, and her eyes, though often solemn, would light up a room. A small red mole was centered between her eyebrows. Her mother would always say Yuxin was born to be a good mother, but she never married. Her dexterity with needles was marvelous; every piece of embroidery she completed was of a quality fit for presentation at the imperial palace. But she would never part with any of her creations, preferring to treat them as an investment that would eventually benefit Xuanming's family. Once she said to Lady Yang, "I can never pay back what you have done for me. This may serve as a little dowry for your youngest daughter."

Yuxin would often stroll through the family garden with Xuanming as her companion. With the morning dew still on the ground they would pick bouquets from a large array of flowers as they came to bloom. Balsam, jasmine, and China pinks were among their favorites. Some of them they would separate and grind into powder, to be used in varying combinations in making rouge. The other women of the household prized these cosmetics and used them regularly.

4

Two years after she came to stay with the family Aunt Yuxin fell ill. Lady Yang warned her daughter that Yuxin might not recover. The news was devastating; for those she truly loved, Xuanming would do anything.

Xuanming stayed with Yuxin constantly, helping with small things, doing her best to bring good cheer to the sickroom. Always a commanding personality who enjoyed carrying the air of a young mistress, her devotion to her aunt was complete. For Xuanming, Yuxin not only represented an idealized womanly presence, but she also was a source of mystery. Why had she never married? Why was she usually deep in thought, sometimes even gloomy?

One afternoon Xuanming picked out some delicate snacks to take to her aunt, but found the purple drapes to the room were closed. After making sure that the girl was alone, Yuxin told her to come in. Xuanming was startled to find Yuxin dressed in full white funereal garb. She was busy assembling a violet-colored lamp. "Sit down," she said quietly, asking, "Is it hot outside?" Yuxin sent Ying'er, her maid, for tea. Xuanming did not have many hobbies, but tea—how it was fixed and served—happened to be one of them. Yuxin asked Ying'er to take out a special tea set, the pieces of which were apple green, the color of precious jade, with contrasting white bases. But on this occasion Xuanming did not focus her attention on the tea service. It was the beautiful lamp that captured her interest.

In the eyes of nine-year-old Xuanming, that lamp was not from this world. It had to be a luxurious gift from heaven. Those exquisite crystals were created by a magic power, mysteriously formed for the exclusive use of the Gods. When spread out they were like floral raindrops that had been deposited by the autumn breeze. She was entranced.

Xuanming became even more astonished as she continued to listen to Yuxin. Slowly, softly, she said, "Youngest daughter, my ills have long been with me. I may not have much time left, and I have been a burden to your family. But I worry about you. Who do you think I am? Now I wish I could write my story in a book. But I am in the twilight of life, exhausted, and without hope for myself. Today I will tell you some stories about my life. If they displease you, do not be overly concerned, just treat them as gusts of wind. If you like a story, take it as an amusing tale."

Then Yuxin took Xuanming's hand and asked, "Have you heard the story of the *Changmao*, the Long Hairs?" Xuanming stared and nodded. She recalled that her mother had mentioned using the *Changmao* story to scare her sisters into obedience. She knew it was another name for the famous Taiping Rebel Army, whose men wore their hair long and fought against the imperial forces of the Qing government. And that was all she knew.

"Do you think this is a pretty good lamp?" Yuxin smiled, pointing at the lamp.

"Aunt is too modest. It may be a crime to say this, but I have been to the palace a few times and I am sure that even the holy lamp there cannot compare with this object."

Yuxin smiled. "This is from the Palace of the Long Hairs. I spent three years there. It is my only souvenir from those days. You take this to Master Fa Yan at the Jinque Temple on Xitan Mountain. Do as your aunt wishes and from the nether world she will protect you from all manner of ill fortune and disaster."

Years went by, but Xuanming did not keep her promise; she kept the lamp. No one knows whether she tried and failed to find Master Fa Yan or never made any such effort. But she did commence a daily ritual: every day at dusk she put the crystal flower petals together. The system of assembly required many coded actions, as they were taught by her beloved aunt. But her whole life was filled with turbulence and tragedy, including the loss of her only son during wartime. Did her suffering stem from her failure to keep her promise? Now, as she was getting on in age, she realized she must tell Yu, her granddaughter, her stories in the hope of easing her burden of guilt.

5

In the mid-nineteenth century, a man named Hong Xiuquan established a capital called the Heavenly Kingdom of Great Peace in what is today the city of Nanjing and named himself Heavenly King. He appointed four commanders, calling them the Eastern, Western, Northern, and Southern kings. Each king had his own palace, with large, elaborately decorated portals, consisting of well-guarded inner and outer gates and doors. Paintings of dragons and tigers decorated these structures, and dozens of gongs were available for sending messages to various parts of each of the palaces. No male, only female servants were allowed within. The Heavenly King's own residence—the Heavenly Palace—stood in the northern part of the city. A ceremonial boulevard led up to a huge archway carved with golden dragons and then to the outer gate, which was prominently labeled "Glorious Gate," and to the inner, "Holy Heavenly Gate"; all these names and buildings were claimed to have been divinely inspired. The palace was of course surrounded by guarded walls; here and there were towers and pavilions, decorated with glazed tiles. The interior palace was extremely grand. Horizontal beams with more dragon carvings were decorated with gold leaf. Vividly painted dragons, lions, and tigers adorned the interior walls. To the east was a walled garden with a huge pond; centered in the pond was a gigantic bluestone ship. The Heavenly King often brought his concubines here for entertainment.

The Eastern King's residence was equally splendid, but ended up being burned to the ground after a clash between him and the Northern King. Afterward, the Eastern King's palace was rebuilt and called the Hall of the Nine Heavens. There were gardens in back and pavilions in front, with two Chinese prickly ash trees on each side. To the north were mounds of stone through which flowed natural spring waters; all about the palace there were gardens within gardens; kiosks and towers were hidden along winding paths. The luxury was beyond comparison.

There were thousands of women within the Heavenly Palace, mostly chosen for beauty, talent, or special skills that were needed in the self-contained enclave. The highest rank was the queen; below her, top rankings were given to only one or two women, with titles such as *pin niang*, court lady; *ai niang*, love lady; *xi niang*, fun lady; *chong niang*, darling lady; and *yu niang*, joy lady. Below these ranks, titles were given to young girls, such as *hao nü*, excellent girl; *miao nü*, fine girl; *jiao nü*, exquisite girl; *yan nü*, beautiful girl; *juan nü*, charming girl; *mei nü*, attractive girl; and *cha nü*, delicate girl.

Virgins were selected at age thirteen, although none would long maintain their innocence. The palace community was beset by conspiracy, jealousy, intrigue, and every kind of corruption known to human beings. One figure stands out among the many who vied for power: Meng De'en, who flattered and connived his way to gain the favor of the Heavenly King and his sister, Hong Xuanjiao, known as the Heavenly Sister. No one could escape from Meng De'en's traps.

Among the very few within the palace who maintained their integrity was Yang Bicheng, known as the "Needle Goddess" in the Embroidery Hall. She had been brought there at age thirteen. When she first arrived she did not eat or talk for three days. The Eastern King had a trusted female officer named Fu Shanxiang who was in charge of the Hall of Girls. Among the few trusted officers in the palace, Fu was kind and protective of the girls and appreciative of their talents. Under her patient care, Bicheng began to eat. She was young, intelligent, delicate, and beautiful. Fu was soon very fond of her. The two often exchanged poetry and became pen pals. The Heavenly Sister heard about Bicheng and summoned her. After getting to know the talented youngster, the Heavenly Sister did not want to let her go and proposed to adopt her. Bicheng had heard of the libertinism and debauchery at the center of court life and wanted no part of it, so she made excuses and contrived to postpone the adoption ceremony, not just once but several times. This offended the proud and arrogant Heavenly Sister; never on friendly terms with Fu Shanxiang, now Hong Xuanjiao blamed her for the delays and also began to find fault with Bicheng. The girl remained honest, loyal, and pure. And her needlework was first rate. Temporarily, the Heavenly Sister dropped the matter.

On the birthday of the Heavenly King, Meng De'en, the master conniver, arrived at the Embroidery Hall, to request Bicheng, the Needle Goddess, to make an elaborately embroidered dragon robe. It was customary for the Heavenly King to be given a golden satin dragon robe on his birthday; Bicheng's guard was down, and she readily consented to accompany Meng to the Heavenly Palace. But such was not his real intention; she was instead conveyed to a secret chamber of the Heavenly Sister.

6

By this time, as the story was unfolding, Xuanming had guessed that Bicheng was, in reality, her own dear aunt, Yang Yuxin—gracious and elegant, clear as ice, pure as jade. And that she had somehow escaped from the Palace of the Long Hairs. Given her limited worldly knowledge, Xuanming could not help trembling with fear at the thought.

After three years at the palace, Bicheng turned sixteen. By then she had become enamored of a young commander named Si Chen who served the

Eastern King, Yang Xiuqing. They were meant for each other. One day, Fu Shanxiang came to the Embroidery Hall and told Bicheng to make a robe for the Eastern King's young commander, Si Chen. Si had held an important post and had won many battles against the Qing army. Now it was his twenty-sixth birthday and the Eastern King arranged an elaborate party. A robe should be made featuring lions and tigers. Bicheng worked on it late into the night, until she fell asleep and had a dream. A young commander in a white robe, slender and handsome, smiled down at her from astride his horse. The lions and tigers on his robe came to life, roaring excitedly. Suddenly she was awakened by the voice of a servant girl who had come from the Eastern King's palace. Her sisters in the Hall helped her wash and dress for a trip in the black carriage, happily saying, "Sister is sure to receive rewards! This is the first time a carriage has been sent for such a purpose."

Most days, Bicheng did not wear makeup. When she did so, and it didn't take much, she was stunningly beautiful. The Eastern King took one look and fell into a trance. Seeing this, Shanxiang was annoyed. Forcing a smile, she said, "Your Honor sent for Bicheng so that she may be rewarded. Have you forgotten?"

At that point, the Eastern King sat back and, regaining his composure, said, "Bicheng's embroidery is so superior that she must be rewarded and given due recognition. From now on, only she shall make the robes for this king and his commanders!"

Then came the reward. It consisted of an embroidered sachet filled with huge pearls and pieces of jade. She was astonished and about to decline when Shanxiang got up and quietly walked to her side. "Bicheng, please accept this reward. The jewels are for you to eat. Follow the Heavenly King's method: two pearls and one piece of jade at breakfast. It improves the skin and extends life! The pearls should first be boiled inside a piece of bean curd for several hours. They will enlarge two to three times and will melt on the tip of your tongue. The jade must be braised with elm roots for a day and night, closely sealed. It will then be soft and delicious, with the addition of a little rock sugar."

Bicheng replied softly, "Please thank the Eastern King for his kind favor, but this humble servant cannot accept. Eastern King and Sister Shanxiang should keep them." Then she moved to one side, trying not to observe the discontent of the monarchs.

At that delicate moment, Bicheng noticed a man standing behind the Eastern King. He was slender and handsome; in fact, he was the man who had appeared in her dream and was wearing a white robe. And he was looking at her! His gaze conveyed admiration, approval, and good intentions. She suddenly blushed, embarrassed at having been observed reacting to his unflinching stare.

Had this been an ordinary day, the Eastern King might have been angered at this slender girl who had shown so little interest in the magnificent gift he had offered. But he was in a good mood; it was a happy day for his favorite commander, so he restrained himself and merely condemned the girl silently: a servant girl, talented and with a pretty face, all for nothing, stubborn like an elm root.

At this moment, Shanxiang took Bicheng to the adjacent hall to collect the silver that was part of her reward. "My little girl," she said, "you gave me a fright. You don't know his temper. He was offended. On a different day he might have had you executed. Let me counsel you as I would my little sister. You should remember this adage: 'Straight like a bowstring, death awaits; bent like a hook, noble titles will be rewarded.' You must make the best of your situation here, be aware of how your conduct will affect your future. Being too strong, too independent, will lead to a bad ending."

Bicheng just smiled. "I think they will have a bad ending. Eating pearls and jade, how extravagant and wasteful!"

Shanxiang stared blankly for a moment, then said in a serious tone, "I certainly know that, but when the sky is falling, who has the power to hold it up? I handle documents for the Eastern King daily. All the kings are building extravagantly and living sumptuously. The money is running out! Now the eldest princess wants to rebuild her palace, she thinks that what she has is not good enough. The last time I said something, the Eastern King lost his temper and put me in chains for a month! It was then that I got into the bad habit of using tobacco. Good sister, listen to me! Even in deciding upon making a change, even in retreat, you cannot show the slightest sign on your face. Otherwise you might ruin your entire life."

Bicheng was a smart girl who of course understood the weight of Shanxiang's advice. But things were happening so fast . . .

7

The day Meng De'en took Bicheng to the secret chamber of the Heavenly Sister, the whole Heavenly Palace announced a grand celebration that would last for several days. It would commemorate a great victory; Loufei, a smart and trusted officer of the Heavenly King, was put in charge. Two southern cities, Suzhou and Hangzhou, had been conquered. Commander Li Xiucheng had led the victorious army. He was a palace favorite and was known as Loyal Prince Li. For the opening ceremonies the queen and her entire court dressed in festive clothing and went to the grand hall for singing, dancing, and fireworks, and there was more of the same throughout the several palaces. Loufei told Fu Shanxiang to alert the girls at the Embroidery Hall. They must work hard to prepare the new robes for use that night.

Meng De'en's lust for Bicheng had begun when she first arrived at the court. Of all the women in the palace, young and old, she was the only one who did not flatter him, and this somehow added to her allure. Her beauty was beyond compare—cool and clear like ice, pure like jade, and somehow magnified by the strength of her character. Meng De'en had tired of women who were merely seductive. Now he was tempted by a new face and body that had proved immune to his power and blandishments. So he seized on the opportunity to lure her away from the protection afforded by Fu Shanxiang. Whether the Heavenly Sister was a conspirator, Bicheng would never know.

Meng never dreamed Bicheng could prove so resolute in her resistance to his attack. During the struggle, she moved to one side, grabbed his genitals, and while squeezing hard pulled and twisted with all the coiled-up strength she could muster. Meng immediately collapsed on the floor, wincing in agony, and watching with mounting outrage as the exquisite young woman walked out of his sight.

Bicheng walked furiously into the crowd during the height of the birthday celebration. The concubines immediately noticed her demeanor and drew a collective breath. Luckily the Heavenly King was giving full attention to one of the luxurious gifts that had just been presented, a chair festooned with pearls, agate, jade, jasper, and coral, complete with a canopy. From afar it looked like clouds blended with heavenly rays, dazzling all eyes; from nearby, one could sense the fragrance of ambergris and the real and unreal floral arrangements that decorated the scene, which was so surreal that one seemed to have journeyed through a forest of special treasures and arrived at a fairyland home. Everyone was singing praises to the Heavenly King, everyone except Bicheng, who, speechless and staring coldly, was sighing and shaking her head.

Elaborately made up and in a bright dress, Fu Shanxiang accompanied the Eastern King. Seeing Bicheng, she moved closer and whispered, "Foolish girl, today is a special day for the Heavenly King. Don't spoil it!"

Bicheng then told Shanxiang what had just happened. Clenching her teeth, she said, "Meng is worse than a dog! A true scumbag of the Heavenly Kingdom."

Shanxiang stood quietly for a moment, concentrating intensely. Then she said slowly, "This is bad. Go back to the Embroidery Hall immediately, fetch some clothes, then go to the Welcome Garden and hide behind the screen there. I'll tell Shun'er to help you." Seeing this, the Eastern King said, "Why are you joking around? Be careful, the Heavenly King might hit you with his silver scepter." Bicheng made her way through the crowd, trying to be inconspicuous; tears were welling up, tears as transparent as melting snow. Shanxiang was also on the verge of tears. She called Shun'er over and told her what to do: "Your sister Bicheng is one of the best people in our kingdom. If anything happens to her, I'll blame you."

Shanxiang had never spoken so strongly to a servant girl; most would be frightened if she did. But Shun'er was both courageous and trustworthy. She understood the urgency and left quickly. A practitioner of martial arts, she was also agile and would be able to move quickly, even in the dark. She was the perfect choice for what now must be done.

Late that night, as the sounds of the night watchmen echoed in the sky, the Heavenly King returned to the royal stage after touring the palace. The crowd was on all fours, kowtowing as the Heavenly King resumed his position on the throne. Suddenly he burst out laughing, saying to the concubines, "You are so loyal, just as mandated by heaven. This king will reward you!" Having said this, he ordered them to drink up and be merry.

Then, dressed elaborately for the party, the Heavenly Sister arrived in her carriage decorated like a phoenix. She ordered the concubines to present poems glorifying the kingdom, crying out, "Where is Meng? It is time to present the golden satin dragon robe to the Heavenly King, summon Meng De'en!"

Upon hearing Meng's name, Shanxiang began shaking with fear, as if a heavy hammer were pounding on her body. She wondered if all this had been planned beforehand and, if so, why the Heavenly Sister would choose this day to have a final showdown with her. She and the king were close; why would she want to ruin a good day for her brother? Before she could think more about the subject, Meng De'en came running in, a golden satin embroidered crown and dragon robe in his hand.

8

Historians differ in their explanations of Fu Shanxiang's sudden disappearance. But Xuanming insisted that the direct reason was her attachment to Aunt Yuxin—the Needle Goddess, Yang Bicheng. Yang Bicheng appears in all the unofficial histories of the Taiping rebellion. The records indicate that she was executed either by *lingchi* (death by slow slicing—also known as death by a thousand cuts) or *diantiandeng* (death by burning while hung upside down). In the latter scenario, the victim was first stripped, then wrapped in linen and soaked in oil overnight. The fire was started at the feet to make the torture last longer. In any case, even the most unsure historians all agree that she was executed. Some unofficial historians described the scene in great detail: when Meng De'en knelt before the Heavenly King, tearing open the supremely embroidered crown, bloodstains were exposed on the inside! Meng De'en banged his head on the ground until it was bleeding, then cried out tearfully, "It's my last duty to see that Yang Bicheng, this bold female demon, pays for her evil actions. She dared to stitch filthy vaginal secretions into the embroidery. This was revealed by witnesses and also by material evidence. Please, Heavenly King, issue a clear order."

Shanxiang remembered that the Heavenly King's smiling face suddenly froze, turning ashen, which was utterly frightening. He grabbed the crown, looked into it closely, and then threw it to the ground with all his might. Everyone froze. A few frightened concubines almost fainted. The Heavenly King soon calmed down and turned to the Eastern King to coldly say, "This monstrous crime cannot be tolerated. The laws of our Heavenly Kingdom decree that we must enforce the death penalty. Use *diantiandeng* for a public execution."

Looking sternly at Shanxiang, the Eastern King then repeated what the Heavenly King had just said. The Heavenly King then continued coldly, "Good. We ask that the Eastern King handle the case. Interrogation should be carried out before execution. The mastermind of this crime must be found!"

It was a while before Shanxiang thought of wiping the perspiration from her brow, only to realize she hadn't the strength to raise her arm. Then she heard Loufei's soft voice: "Heavenly King, please don't be angry. Today is a good day. No need for it to be ruined by these people. In my opinion, this can be handled later."

Normally the Heavenly King would be persuaded by mild-mannered Loufei. It was all the more likely that he would be persuaded this time, since it was she who had organized this grand celebration. And his new throne had made him very happy. But before she had finished speaking, the Heavenly King changed his expression. Suddenly he threw his scepter at Loufei. She tried to dodge, but it hit her right in the face. Blood streamed down her face and she screamed, then fainted.

In a flash, everyone assembled and knelt before the majestic Heavenly King.

The majesty of imperial rulers is often bewildering. What if no one knelt? Would the emperor himself be the last one to kneel? Of course that would be very unlikely, because among the "majority" there will always be some people who kneel first, followed by others. Only a small number would refuse to kneel, and they could easily be eliminated.

Those who are unwilling to kneel but want to protect their lives will no doubt have to rely on wisdom. Thus, in China there are always more strategists than warriors. This follows the rule that excellence wins and defects are sifted out.

That night of long ago, the horrible night for Bicheng, the Heavenly King's guards quickly surrounded the Embroidery Hall and arrested all the girls, sending them to prison at the Eastern King's residence. The Eastern King knew all too well that among these trembling girls, the only one missing was Yang Bicheng. He realized that Shanxiang was one step ahead of him.

Now Bicheng was walking away, dressed as a village woman and with a road pass that would allow her to travel hundreds of miles. She had found the Welcome Garden that night, where Shun'er was waiting. Behind the screen was a huge Western painting. Shun'er pushed the little mouth of the angel in the painting, which opened a door that led to a secret path. Moving quickly, she handed a bag to Bicheng, saying, "Sister Shanxiang asked me to give this to you. Take it in remembrance of your good friendship. She herself would like to leave. She asks that you take good care of yourself and marry into a nice family. The road pass is inside. Once you leave the secret path, this will permit you to go anywhere in the territory of the Heavenly Kingdom."

Bicheng wept as she listened to Shun'er and asked, "Sister Shun'er, after I leave, what will you and Sister Shanxiang do?"

Shun'er did not reply. She pushed Bicheng into the secret path and rushed to close up the face of the painting. By then, Shun'er had decided to die.

Three days later, the executioner announced, "In the case of the outrageous events in the Embroidery Hall, it is the death penalty for Yang Bicheng and whipping for the other servants. The execution is to be carried out tonight by *diantiandeng*."

When the executioner arrived at the Embroidery Hall, Shanxiang was already there and the prisoner had been wrapped with linens. The executioner wanted to check the identity of the prisoner, but Shanxiang shouted, "It was the Eastern King who ordered me to supervise the execution. If you don't trust me, you don't even trust the Eastern King!" The executioner retreated in fear.

The *diantiandeng* was carried out using the cinnamon tree in front of the Eastern King's palace. The prisoner, saturated with oil, was suspended by her feet and the torch was applied at that point, in accordance with customary practice. The fire burned slowly through the night. Shanxiang stood by the window with no expression showing on her face, which was illuminated by the fire.

In her mind's eye she could see, through the pall of smoke from the gruesome fire, that Bicheng was already in a remote village, safely settling down for the night. When Bicheng opened the bag, she would find to her astonishment the beautiful lamp. The codes for assembly of the lamp were written on the cotton wrappings. Shanxiang had received this lamp at a birthday dinner some years before Bicheng arrived at the palace. It had been presented by an old man. Inside the lamp box was a poem that Shanxiang had never told anyone about. It read:

> *The wind destroys the eastern garden's willow,*
> *Shattered red flowers fly away,*
> *Best to not mention oranges and plums,*
> *In late autumn the forests will be empty.*

Note: The willow refers to Yang Xiuqing, the Eastern King; red flowers refers to Hong Xiuquan, the Heavenly King; oranges and plums refer to the two commanders, Chen and Li; and forests refer to the decline of Hong's capital, Jinling (today's Nanjing city).

The poem appears to be a prediction of the fire. After that, Shanxiang suddenly disappeared. Her absence was so complete—there was no evidence that she had ever existed—that people wondered if she had ever appeared before.

Another person suddenly disappeared—Si Chen, the favorite commander of the Eastern King. It was rumored that he had gone to Xitan Mountain to become a monk, assuming the name Fa Yan.

9

I think Shun'er was the true hero of this story. We may conjecture that when she returned to the Eastern King's residence all was in chaos. The scene and the sounds have echoed down to us through an entire century, and are all too familiar to us even now: the shouts, the pounding feet, the screams and sobs, the women's furtive efforts at concealment, and the employment of whatever means were available to escape notice, like folded paper hidden in a drawer, or melting clouds, or birds flying away, or a drop of water evaporating.

Only one woman was exceptional. That night, Shun'er walked to the Eastern King's residence without looking back. She walked to her own death.

Shanxiang and Shun'er, we must presume, had an argument, and for the first time the brave young servant disobeyed, choosing death because she knew in her heart that this was the only way to assure that Bicheng would have a good chance to escape. Not pretty, never having experienced romantic love, having come from a village at a very young and impressionable age out of belief in what she thought was a noble cause, and after a brief period of happiness before she became disillusioned with the Heavenly King and all the other depraved despots and their corrupt minions, she had shown her willingness to die, if necessary, for what she had believed to be a great cause; now she had willingly died because no other act of which she was capable would be proportionate to the great sins of her masters and her own one mistake, which was to believe in them.

It came about in this way. Although she was not a close friend to Bicheng, she was an admirer, and treasured the small sample of embroidery Bicheng had given her, on which was depicted a pair of mandarin ducks, the symbol of marriage. She extracted the embroidery—a pair of insoles—from the bottom of her trunk and placed them in her shoes. Then she wrapped her neck in a length of pure white satin and employed it as a noose to hang herself.

When Shanxiang found the body she cried bitterly. She knew the young woman had chosen a method of death that would be bloodless so that her body could be used as a substitute for Bicheng. With the help of two reliable girls, she then wrapped the body from head to toe in pure white satin in preparation for the ritualized execution. Now all the girls knelt before the body to pray.

And now a choir came down from heaven. The wind supplied music, and in the wind, the sisters felt rather than saw a naked eye fixed firmly inside the lair of the moon, an eye that was clear, tranquil, and full of longing.

10

What is the difference between past and present? In many ways, the present is simply a new version of ancient history. Only one new technology represents a profound change: cloning. But no matter how superior the new technologies are, nothing can replace human feeling. A poet once wrote:

> Debasement is the password of the base,
> Nobility the epitaph of the noble.

The difficulty for human beings is to resist the lure of living. Even this poet is gone, his epitaph left behind. Between the password and epitaph, is there another way of life? For the young, to lose purity is to lose beauty. For the aged, beauty means something in between male and female. A person can wear a false hat all his life, but maybe once he may have to show his password—or identity.

If not, humans will turn into ants and worms, cloned products of the electronic age.

11

And now we return to the beginning of the story. Let us recall that isolated place and the mythical lake. In her childhood, Yushe often saw a huge freshwater mussel lurking in its shallow waters, its opening sealed by a black feather. Occasionally the shell opens, revealing that it is empty inside. Five years ago Yu left that place. Now we see her returning. It is twilight and the trees surrounding the lake have grown taller and more beautiful. They wave in the breeze and create symphonic music. In the fragrant dusk, Yu sees scattered red oranges among the darker greens of the forest. Here must be an ancient graveyard where a concubine was buried. Today grass has grown over the resting place of the deserted concubine.

But when Yu lay down at the edge of the lake as she did during childhood, she could no longer see the mussel. Now tattooed, she sat weeping by the lake. One by one, her tears crashed down. The tattoo on her body, according to Master Fa Yan, was the most beautiful he had ever created, and her blood had redeemed her sins. She had returned to Jinwu's home with rekindled confidence, but found a letter left on the table, a letter written by Jinwu.

Jinwu was once her future, her most beautiful inner fantasy. To redeem her sin she had endured excruciating pain. She thought Jinwu would like her tattoo, would praise her, and thus the past would be buried. With that hope, she had clenched her teeth and endured the pain. But now that Jinwu had left, all Yu's pain suddenly returned. She felt like her body and soul were shattered. Her whole being had been reduced to tears that solidified as they fell, making loud sounds when reaching the ground.

As in her childhood, Yu put her head into the lake, her hair spreading out like a floating jellyfish. Only this time there were no calls from her mother or her grandma.

CHAPTER 5 | YOUTH

1

Yushe was banished by the world to a more remote and barren place after she found out Jinwu had left.

Perhaps it was a self-imposed exile.

She had no sooner arrived there than she fell ill. But her new home was located in a place so ferociously cold that you could not comfortably remain in bed to recover from an illness. At night people huddled together in their beds for warmth. Occasionally an icicle would fall from the ceiling, crashing into the sleepers, but they were too cold and tired to pay attention. Yu was different. Night after night she remained awake, as if waiting for something to strike. Her coughing and vomiting reverberated in the wee hours when everyone else was asleep. When this happened, a girl whose bed was a long way from hers would appear beside her with a handful of pills.

Yu could see a pair of lustrous eyes by her bed in the dark and she knew the girl would look stunning in the daylight. Her name was Xiaotao, and she seemed especially fond of Yu. Her skin was so translucent that if you looked closely you could see her veins. She had high cheekbones and a well-formed chin. But it was those eyes that most attracted Yu. They appeared to sparkle and glow as if stars had fallen in them, an effect that was somehow enhanced by eyelashes so long that they cast tiny shadows under bright lights. To Yu, she seemed like a doll from a foreign country.

Xiaotao was attracted to Yu because in the short time since her arrival Yu had been mysteriously quiet; she must have wanted to escape everything, but had failed. One often wonders why those who are noisy are not heard, while those who have been reduced to shadows can establish a huge presence. Xiaotao thought Yu would be pretty if she put on a few pounds.

One day Yu fainted after working long hours in icy water. Her job was to gather hemp stalks along the riverbank. Her body was blue and lifeless as Xiaotao carried her to a tractor for transport to a local hospital. She did not regain consciousness for a day and a half; and as Xiaotao watched over Yu, the others told her to prepare for a funeral. When Yu finally revived at twilight, a major snowstorm had just commenced, coating the dirty hospital walls in a bright white.

The first thing she said was, "Is it snowing?" "Heavily, but how did you know?" asked Xiaotao, grabbing the frail girl's hands as she did so, afraid she might pass out again.

"Everything is so white. It's so bright that it makes me uncomfortable," said Yu.

Xiaotao was puzzled.

"I am hungry, I want meat."

"What else?"

"Dumplings, anchovies marinated in lots of oil, pineapple, hawthorn berries . . . but I know that none of these things are available here."

Xiaotao smiled, showing a pair of deep dimples. And before Yu could say anything, she bounced out of the room like a big rubber ball.

2

At nightfall, the door to my ward opened and a fresh breath of icy cold air washed in, along with a few flakes of snow falling from Xiaotao's hair and coat. The light switch clicked loudly, and the room was flooded with light. I saw a large bag of goodies, with Xiaotao behind it.

It was like the proverbial bag carried by Ali Baba: the goodies just kept emerging. I was amazed to see the magnificent cans. At a time when everything was deadly monotonous, the cans were indeed magnificent. There was the enormous white pig, seeming to smile from its home on the label of the luncheon meat. It stimulated my taste buds just to see it! I recalled a Chinese New Year celebration when my father saved two pieces of luncheon meat just for me. I put them in the middle of a big white steamed bun and relished the intense flavor one small bite at a time. Now the mere sight of that silly pig, plus the anchovy, pineapple, and hawthorn berry cans, were tantalizing.

With a pleasant smile Xiaotao said, "Only the dumplings are missing. But I brought you this." She pulled out a big package of spongy muffins that were not available anywhere else. Covered with layers of pureed yoke of duck egg and sprinkled with roasted sesame seeds, they were wonderfully crisp and fragrant.

The two of us had a fantastic banquet in the small room of the hospital, with the wind howling and snow swirling outside. We were for a time oblivious to everything, but the world had not forgotten us. Suddenly, the skies broke open to give us a big smile. A great gust of wind blew the window open and snowflakes suddenly danced into the room, breathing a life of their own. They blended together in a fusion of dim and bright light, wild yet harmonious, like the variegated hues of a spring garden or the stained glass of a rococo cathedral when the sun suddenly bursts forth. Such splendid moments are always illusionary.

Xiaotao seemed to me an angel sent from heaven to effect my rescue. Such a lovely girl, I thought, must have a lot of suitors.

"Do you have a boyfriend?" I asked.

Blinking her eyes and draining the last drop of pineapple juice into her mouth, she replied, "Of course. He's on the other side of the lotus pond, raising deer. Do you want some deer antler? When spring comes I'll ask him to cut some for you. How about you? You must have a boyfriend."

My head nodded in affirmation, as if controlled by a ghost.

"My boyfriend is tall and handsome, and he can ride a horse," she said. "What's yours like?"

I could feel the color coming to my cheeks as I replied. "Umm, yes, he's very handsome, too, much better looking than I am, and full of energy. An old abbot at a temple thinks very highly of him."

"Oh no, you must tell him not to get too close to monks. If he becomes one himself, he cannot get married."

I felt my heart sinking in my chest. Why would I describe my imaginary boyfriend using Yuanguang as the pattern? So handsome, but he is already a monk! I had revealed something to myself, a painful experience. It was a pain as fresh in my memory as the feeling of having my first menstrual period, as fresh as my memory of that day when two plum blossoms were tattooed on my breasts. That was a day when my heart and soul were so focused on another person that I was able to shield myself from the painful reality of my first experience of sexual intercourse and the attraction of a handsome young man.

I seem to myself to be always one step behind reality, then too soon giving up entirely. Throughout my life, I have given up time after time. Many years later I learned the real identity of Yuanguang. On that day, when he finally showed me his ID, he suddenly disappeared. Then more years elapsed, and we had another chance meeting, but by then that handsome young man had already disappeared forever.

That day when I so easily fabricated a boyfriend was the first time I had some fun telling lies. It gave me an unprecedented happiness that stayed with me quite a long time. Having reappeared, his face—so long neglected in memory—was now so much clearer, as if viewed through a magnifying glass. I understood his dilemma and recalled the details vividly. His eyes betrayed his kindness. He was moved to tears by my suffering, and though I was a stranger who used him as a mere tool in a tattooing procedure, he did all that he could to ease my pain; how could I have been so cruel? How could I have accepted such an intimate moment with a strange man?

Now, once again, the wind had its way with us, sending snowflakes flying about as the window was flung open. Here was a scene at once beautiful and dreadful that somehow eased my pain.

3

Xiaotao once said to me, "I envy pregnant women. When I was little, I wrote a poem of one line that went like this: 'Pregnancy is the most beautiful moment in life.' My mom was shocked and slapped me!"

"Did she often hit you?" asked Yu immediately.

Xiaotao shook her head. "She couldn't bear the thought of hurting me. We lost my dad when I was small and I think that was why she pampered me."

Yu sighed. "So, ultimately, you have had your mother to protect you."

Xiaotao opened her eyes wide. "Your mom didn't?"

Yu couldn't think how to respond, but Xiaotao was oblivious to her reaction and continued, "My mom is the best mom in the whole world! Even in those years when food was scarce, especially in cities, I still got whatever I wanted. Although I'm just a village girl, it was like what is written in books: living where grain is abundant, nobody starves."

Looking at Xiaotao's tender face, Yu was lost for words. She couldn't imagine how a village girl could have everything she wanted.

Soon there was an answer. One day after work the two girls made a trip to town and went straight to the only shop. Wrapped in a loose-fitting cotton coat, Xiaotao flitted about. Stopping for a moment where Yu stood, she whispered, "I will show you." Yu watched in fascination as Xiaotao waltzed into an aisle where canned foods were shelved. Her eyes, too, were waltzing from can to can, scanning the labels and everything else around them, until finally she fixed her gaze on a landscape painting that hung on a wall. While Xiaotao seemed absorbed in the details of the painting, cans of food seemed to be flying off the shelves like bits of metal attracted to a magnet.

Yu gasped, but Xiaotao remained calm. Later, when the girls were sitting in a corner of a small restaurant, she extracted the food cans, one by one, from pockets in her coat. She seemed as carried away as if she had been playing glorious music on a grand piano. This was her work of art.

Yes, real performance art, Yu thought.

4

Earlier we told the story of Meihua. She was one of Ruomu's servant girls who had been forced to marry a male servant, Old Zhang. After that she vanished from the Qin residence, but not from the earth as we might have imagined. Meihua was a smart and beautiful woman. All such women possess great vitality. They can be crushed by fate, but they can also revive and be reborn. In this sense they are like some plants—hardy and capable of regenerating themselves, even though they seem fragile.

After her marriage to Old Zhang, Meihua followed him to his home village. He was the eldest son in his family. Arriving from her journey, she was tired but still looked like a flower. An air-dried flower is sometimes more fragrant than a fresh one. One granduncle sighed when he saw Meihua, deciding that her face revealed that she had been cursed, a curse that would lead to her husband's sudden death. He even thought that the curse was so strong that it would extend to all men in her life, but he kept his thoughts to himself.

Soon after, the fate predicted by the family elder came to pass. There were bandits in the area, and late one night Meihua woke up to find a face at the window. It seemed an ashy green color in the gray moonlight, a face that looked like a rubber mask. Meihua cried out in terror, waking the whole family. Before she could dress herself, the bandits were inside, by the bed. Later, people recalled that she hardly put up any resistance, that she had probably passed out or was paralyzed with fear.

Meanwhile, Old Zhang lay dead in his own blood. There were five slashes on his throat, like a print of five crescent moons. The granduncle tried to stop the bleeding with an herbal concoction, but to no avail.

5

Meihua found herself in a bandit's hideout where she was given the position of honor at the table. A man named An Qiang was in charge. He was young, handsome, fair-skinned, and could have passed for a scholar, not much stronger in build than Tiancheng, and not at all the ruffian she expected. He liked to carry with him a book titled *Dialogue of Qingping Mountain*, and his movements were lithe and graceful. Meihua even thought he must have been, somewhat like herself, kidnapped and locked up here in the mountains. He must be a young master from a good family who had fallen on hard times.

Unlike Tiancheng's bashfulness or Old Zhang's eager lustiness, An Qiang betrayed little emotion upon seeing Meihua. He quietly asked one of the servants to take Meihua to a bathroom to change and then return for dinner.

The bathroom was huge with a built-in stone tub. Now someone brought a large leaf and instructed her to use it like soap. Meihua looked at it in disbelief, but as she rubbed it softly it became spongy, like the inside of a young squash. A trickle of fresh green bubbles formed in her hands, and she felt somehow refreshed. But after a while, she felt a slight nausea and vomited. Her stomach was not, however, really upset; the condition passed quickly and she felt strangely renewed, as though she had been detoxified. When she walked out of the bathroom she felt like a newborn baby.

Then Meihua was given a bowl of chicken soup that was boiled with milk vetch root, not a bit oily, with a few bits of green scallion floating on the surface. Having worked for a rich family, Meihua saw that this place possessed something like the settled, quietly sophisticated ways of a home long used to wealth and comfort. These people did not appear to be bandits who had become rich overnight and were now living extravagantly. At dinner, she was given a jacket embroidered with red feathers and silver buttons. Meihua stole a look at the two women seated at the table with her; they were acting neither like servants nor like mistresses. They remained silent, not even raising their heads. Both wore informal dresses, one in bright green, the other in deep yellow, with no decorative jewelry other than large silver bracelets such as those worn by foreign ladies. Meihua had seen them on the snuff bottles collected by the old master of the Qin household.

After the meal, the maid brought a nightgown, telling Meihua it was Mr. An's instructions. All the maids called An Qiang "Mr. An." They didn't call him old master or young master, or the usual names used among bandits. Meihua thought this was very strange.

The garment handed to Meihua was not an ordinary nightgown; rather, it seemed to be the kind of thing Western women wore as a wedding gown—knitted with layers of snowy flowers, topped with shining pearls. As she looked in a large mirror, she could hardly recognize herself, feeling disconnected from her own image. No longer was she an adolescent girl with bright eyes and smooth skin. She was amazed by her own beauty, but felt she was no longer the same person. Standing there a long time, Meihua got used to her new image. Or you could say that the woman in the mirror was finally acknowledged by Meihua.

Meihua was more bewildered as she walked down the stone corridor and into An Qiang's bedroom. He looked at her calmly, then opened a coded lock on a small jewelry case and withdrew a pearl necklace. He ceremoniously placed it around her neck, looking this way and that, and seemed pleased with what he saw. Then he said, "Good night."

6

When I couldn't sleep at night I kept thinking of the story Xiaotao told me. Her mother was called Meihua. I vaguely recalled my mother and grandma mentioning a servant girl by that name; she had been both the prettiest and most capable of the servants they had. When Mother was cross with me she would sometimes say that even a stubborn servant girl they once had—a very capable woman—eventually had to be married off. As the sayings go, a married woman is used water, only to be dumped out; when married to a chicken she stays with the chicken, when married to a dog she stays with the dog. Such expressions always seemed to make me profoundly sad.

From those early days on, I always divided women into two categories: one, prototypical mothers; the other, prototypical daughters. Even in this cold, remote place I did not escape maternal control. Mother types were everywhere. One of them, whose name was Chen Ling, was now sleeping nearby.

Chen Ling was only a few years older than me, but she was relentlessly controlling. When her deeply slanted eyes moved sideways, a crease would form on her forehead, giving her a cunning look. She was a born leader and easily kept all of us, thirty girls, firmly in line. No one could escape those sidewise looks.

When we were in the fields, we each had to work in our own row, which added together stretched out more than ten miles long. One day I had diarrhea and every so often had to run to the side of the field. When I returned I was behind the others, who were busy planting, each in their own row. Chen Ling shouted from the head of one row, "You must each plant one row by the end of the day. Cry about it if you want to, I don't give a damn!"

Chen Ling's voice was threatening. I was doing my best despite feeling weak and exhausted by illness. I was so far behind when lunch was brought up on an ox wagon that I was too far from it to get my share of the meal. All I could see ahead was black earth, nothing but black earth, seemingly stretching up into the sky.

By the time I finally reached the end of my row it was pitch-dark and I saw people sitting in a circle. Chen Ling was criticizing me: "Yu is a little mistress from a family that is part of the exploiting class." Her pitched voice filled up the dark sky and echoed in my ears for a long time.

7

Only after many nights did An Qiang and Meihua share a bed. On that occasion, while caressing the string of pearls gracing Meihua's neck, he said: "Did you know that this is called a teardrop necklace? It's a truly priceless piece of jewelry. Emperor Xuanzong of the Tang Dynasty at one time had a consort called Mei who was his favorite. But with the arrival of Yang Yuhuan—who was to become the emperor's ultimate favorite princess consort Yang Guifei—Mei lost her favored position. With the intention of consoling her, Xuanzong had a string of pearls sent to Mei, but she refused them and sent them back to the emperor along with this poem:

> My willow-leaf eyebrows long lacking in care,
> My red silken finery stained with makeup and tears;
> My old home devoid of the joy of toiletries and dress,
> Oh, there's no way that pearls can ease this distress.

"Later a famous ballad was named after this rejected offering: 'A String of Pearls.' I have heard that Xuanzong's gift was just such pearls. What a coincidence that your name also includes the word Mei."

Hearing this, Meihua smiled. "Comparing me with Consort Mei makes me feel embarrassed. Besides, it's not a good omen."

"It's just a story. Don't take it seriously," said An Qiang with a smile.

Meihua didn't say another word. Again she thought, as she had so often since coming to this strange place, how amazingly poised, how debonair was this bandit king.

Meihua soon learned how these pearls found their way to this hideout. She now began to understand An Qiang. It happened on a dark, blustery night. Since her capture, it was the first time An Qiang took Meihua anywhere. They rode for three hours in a horse-drawn carriage, finally stopping at a street corner in the town. Even in the pitch-dark, Meihua knew they had stopped near a jewelry shop—it was the best-known shop in the area, and it belonged to the family of her old mistress, Xuanming.

Meihua's job was to serve as a lookout, disguised as the young mistress of a wealthy family. The shop was protected by a cast-iron railing with gilded pillars and a double lock. Meihua looked on as An Qiang, taking his time, used his cigarette lighter to melt the solder that had been used by a repairman to hold together two parts of the fence; this was something An Qiang had planned long ago. An Qiang's action astonished and stimulated Meihua. Neither Tiancheng nor Old Zhang had stirred such feelings in her.

In the days to come, Meihua watched many times as An Qiang cleverly opened locks, doors, gates, and coded safes to add to his rich store of jewelry and other valuables. He remembered the history of every item he possessed; when he talked about them it was as though he was talking about his family treasury. This reminded Meihua of her old mistress, Xuanming. She, too, had stories about each item she owned, but while her stories were abstract, his were dynamic, with more than a hint of danger; and she could reach out and touch each item as he spoke of it. Things that can be touched become more attractive.

Life went on in this fashion for about two years. Then one winter night, with no wind or snow, just deadly cold, as she again served as lookout, she blew her warm breath on her freezing hands, stamped her feet, and wished the job was over. And then a new thought intruded: Why stand here and freeze to death? Why not go and taste the thrill of stealing jewelry? But the thought departed as soon as it came. What a curse! How can I even think of such a thing? She blamed herself for having such a thought, as though the fleeting notion was already known to Buddha. Just then she heard gunfire.

At first she thought it was a firecracker; perhaps a nearby family was celebrating some major event. But then came a series of such noises, and there was no mistaking what it was. It all happened so fast, before she even had a chance to fear. In the moonlight she saw An Qiang, this time walking very quickly, his back bent low. Behind him came Kuizi, his bodyguard, carrying a heavy sack; obviously they had got the stuff. Now they began running toward Meihua, leaving the gunfire far behind. Meihua climbed into the carriage, looking on as the two men came running, now moving as fast as they could. Their escape seemed assured, but then she saw an old-fashioned jeep coming at them at top speed, so fast the jeep rammed both men, running over one and sending the other flying through the air like a paper kite, but landing with a muffled, cracking sound, a horrid sound that Meihua would always remember.

This was the first time Meihua had ever seen fresh blood. It looked black in the moonlight, sticky like a barrel of bitumen spilled on the road. So much blood over the dry, frozen ground, it filled the cracks as though providing nourishment to a tortured earth.

8

Xiaotao received a telegram from home as the third wheat harvest was beginning. She showed it to Yu: "Mother gravely ill. Hurry home." Xiaotao's eyes filled with tears. "I couldn't get leave! The boss said it's harvest time, no leave can be granted."

"What to do, then?" asked Yu.

"What to do? Run," said Xiaotao.

Yu was silent.

The two girls remembered the motivation speech by Chen Ling two days before: "It's a busy season. No one can ask for leave. Anyone who leaves without permission will be punished as a deserter. Those who know deserters' plans but fail to report them will be criticized in writing. Those who help the deserters will also be punished."

Xiaotao insisted that she would leave. It was more than thirteen miles to the nearest railway station. The two girls discussed it in detail and decided to get up at three in the morning before anyone else was awake. This would give them enough time to walk the distance if they were unlucky and couldn't hitch a ride. Xiaotao fell soundly asleep soon after they reached the decision, but Yu remained awake. In this season there were no more icicles dropping from the ceiling, but there were countless bugs, including swarms of mosquitoes. Occasionally a bug would fall into a sleeper's open mouth.

Long past midnight Yu drifted into a troubled sleep and had a bad dream: She and Xiaotao were carrying their luggage and arrived at the railway station. She was too tired to move her legs and called out to a woman standing on the platform, "Momma, Momma!" Yu didn't know why she had suddenly reverted to the familiar form, and it made her sad. Then the woman turned around, showing her face for the first time, a pale face without features that so frightened Yu that she woke up. Xiaotao was still soundly asleep. Yu began sobbing at the thought of nesting in her mother's arms, being loved just like other girls. Yu imagined how Xiaotao's mother would shower her daughter with love when she arrived.

When she saw on the clock that it was 3:00 a.m., Yu woke up her friend. They didn't wash, slipping quietly out of the room, each carrying a small bag. There would be no problems getting out of the village, although it was dark and the road was tough going. The two girls stumbled along with difficulty. There were no vehicles for them to catch a ride. The only thing they heard was wolves howling in the distance.

9

In the days after 1947, Meihua stayed beside An Qiang, whose ankle had been smashed by the jeep. He had done his best to avoid the vehicle, but it had nearly severed his leg at the ankle. White bones showed, and blood spurted with each beat of his heart. Meihua held his foot on her lap, wrapped tightly in pieces of their clothing. Kuizi's body lay still, his eyes open and lifeless, blood oozing from his ears. He was beyond help.

Although permanently crippled, An Qiang didn't seem to have suffered much emotional damage. He continued to mastermind new exploits, each one cleverly calculated. One day, as they woke from a nap, An Qiang suddenly asked Meihua, "You have been with me for some time; let's see how much you've learned."

Then he laid out three identical jewelry boxes on the table, labeled "diamond," "ruby," and "opal," saying to her, "But the contents don't match the label. Here's the problem: how many boxes do you need to open to determine where all the jewels are? Is this too hard? If so, we can start with an easier one."

Meihua was used to this kind of game. Without hesitation, she said, "Opening one box is enough."

"Why?" An Qiang was surprised and raised his eyebrows.

Meihua smiled and opened the box labeled "diamond," to find it contained the opal. "You just said the labels do not match the contents; since the diamond is not here, it must be in the box labeled 'ruby,' because if the diamond is in the box labeled 'opal,' then the ruby has to be in the box labeled 'ruby.' But that is not what your question is. Therefore, the answer is: the box labeled 'diamond' contains the opal, the box labeled 'ruby' contains the diamond, and the box labeled 'opal' contains the ruby. Correct? Let's open them all and see."

An Qiang took Meihua's hands, smiling. It was the first time Meihua saw him so relaxed and happy. "Not necessary," he replied. "Your answer must be right. Meihua, you are as bright as ice and snow. Your sky is unlimited."

What An Qiang said contained the seed of a profound implication. When women lose love, they always become more daring, spurred by a desire to do something extraordinary; what can be as thrilling as falling in love? Intelligent and beautiful Meihua is destined to have a life filled with excitement. Or must Meihua make a choice to have such a life?

Since that time, in the area around Xitan Mountain, there has been a legend about a female bandit referred to as Aunty Mei. The story has been passed around for more than forty years, along with a tale about Master Fa Yan. These are the legacies of Xitan Mountain.

An Qiang lived until 1953, fifteen days after his daughter, Xiaotao, was born. He died without pain. The birth of his daughter brought ample joy. Calm, adaptable, and very smart, he lived a life free of worries despite his hazardous occupation. Meihua gradually learned that he did not really care much about the jewelry and other treasures; he loved the process more than the results. For him it was something like a child playing a game, pouring all his energies into an effort to win, or at least complete the puzzle. When he was done, he pushed the puzzle away and picked up another game. In every game, he invested all his energy.

He seemed to know right from the beginning that Meihua did not love him, but he didn't worry about it. Instead, he soon accepted the reality, just as he accepted the cruel reality of becoming permanently disabled. He carried himself as though he was from a well-to-do family, but never gave any hints of his previous life. To Meihua, he remained a riddle. Long after his death, she grew to love him.

10

Yu initially wanted to go with Xiaotao, but after pooling their money they only had enough to buy one ticket. With what was left, 6.20 yuan, they could buy a good meal. While waiting for the train, they went to a small restaurant near the station and ordered salty boiled peanuts, braised pork, deep-fried prawns, and boiled eggplant and potato. They wolfed down one dish after another, causing the owner to stare at them in astonishment. Maybe these two delicate young girls could swallow a whole deer without exerting too much effort. He couldn't know how much they had missed real food. On an average day he could make only twenty or thirty yuan; few people would spend more than one or two yuan for a meal. No one ever spent more than six yuan. Delighted with their presence, he tried to strike up a conversation. "You two girls are not local, are you?"

With greasy lips, Xiaotao lifted her eyes, saying, "Right. We are from far away. We are sent-down youth."

The owner blinked his eyes with sympathy, and then sat down on an empty bench. "You don't say. The sent-down youth from big cities really suffer in our small place! Nothing to do here, nothing available, and the locals are wild. Did you know this used to be a labor camp for prisoners?"

Mimicking the local accent, Xiaotao went on, "How could we not know? We will put up with any discomfort to build and protect the frontier. This is called knowing the tigers on a mountain. We go to the mountains with good intentions. Surely you know this."

"Yes, yes. Of course. Where are you girls going?"

"Home," said Xiaotao, alarmed at the question.

"Going home? No kidding? The train to Bei'an left an hour ago. Isn't that the only way to get to the city?"

The girls raised their heads, suddenly alarmed. Xiaotao asked, "Isn't there a direct train?"

"Oh, no, my little granny! That was ages ago. Take a good look at the ticket. Where would you board the train? This station hasn't been in use for a long time. Only occasionally does a freight train stop briefly. The higher authorities decided on this to deal with people like you, the sent-down youth, because so many fled by train. Now there is only one long-distance bus from here to Bei'an Township. You come back tomorrow!"

Xiaotao was close to tears. "Big uncle, please find a way for us!"

The owner took the ticket, scanning it front and back. He said there was a freight train carrying grain to Bei'an. But no free ride! At least two or three cans of luncheon meat for the train operator.

Xiaotao stamped her feet. "Had we known that, we wouldn't have splurged on this meal!"

As the time passed, Yu seemed oblivious to what was going on. She poured some hot water into the empty bowl and began to drink it slowly. Finally, in a break in the conversation, she spoke up. "I could work for you for a day, would that be enough to buy three cans of meat?"

Later, Xiaotao got on the grain freight while Yu spent the whole day washing dishes, cleaning the floor, and disposing of garbage. By the end of the day she stopped for a break . . . and then began throwing up. All that delicious food was gone.

When Yu returned to the village it was already past ten at night. The air was fresh and stars were visible. As she drew closer, she heard a roaring tide of noise, as though from a broken record player. Finally she saw that the yard was filled with moving heads. She was bewildered. The eyes of the crowd were upon her; it was like walking between two mirrors. Then she heard a voice seemingly from the sky, a voice that roared like thunder.

"Look, she came back! She dared to return! Bring her up onstage, let everyone see her!" Yu recognized the voice of Chen Ling.

"Confess! Confess!" Chen Ling was excited by the opportunity to humiliate a miscreant. "How did you get together with An Xiaotao and give her cover, help her escape? You failed to report her and conspired with her. Don't you know this is a double crime?"

A chorus of whispering voices intertwined. These rolling waves of sound suddenly frightened Yu. It was like the whispers she used to hear in her childhood. When she heard this whisper, she knew that disaster was about to strike.

Yu was pushed by many hands up onto a stage. Suddenly she felt close to the sky, as if at any moment she could hear voices from above. The sky was so huge, the stars bright, beautiful, cold, and indifferent, as the bloody games were played out on the ground. But the ground could not tolerate their indifference. The ground suddenly burned.

A fire had suddenly broken out in the compound. Many years later it was recorded in the history of the sent-down youth. The cause of the fire remains unknown. It started from a stack of beanstalks and then quickly spread to the stores of grain. The crowd charged at the fire, trying to put it out, but without tools. It was a fantastic display of bravado; each person was trying to outdo the other. That was an exceptional era. Everyone possessed exceptional vitality. It was a time of triumphs and disasters, infused with exhilaration and sorrow. Many seem to have forgotten that fire could eat them alive; they were so filled with fervor and thought their time to be heroes had finally come.

Yu was never again seen after the fire. No one could tell one burned body from another. Thirty-one tombstones were prepared, according to the camp's records, but Yu was excluded because Chen Ling insisted that she was not a member of the working class. She could not become a member of a revolutionary team, dead or alive. But the local villagers saw an amazing thing that night. They saw a girl clad in red from top to bottom riding on a star, riding, riding, until she vanished.

But Yu did not die. Or at least we can say she was reborn after death. She possessed the ability to be reborn. Simply put, she did not vanish. Our story is about her death and rebirth. A cat has nine lives, and Yu experienced nine deaths. Precisely, she died eight times. The ninth death was described at the beginning of our story when her mother requested a lobotomy for her. This last time was her real death. So she was still alive prior to the end of our story.

As we expected, Yu returned to the city where Jinwu lived. One day she happened to pass the snack bar at a famous department store. Looking through the windows, which reached to the floor, she saw Xiaotao sitting inside. Although none of her clothes were the same, Yu recognized her immediately. Next to her was a man and they were eating butter-fried cake, a famous snack at this store, and bean porridge. A little spoon was traveling in and out of Xiaotao's red-glossed mouth. She was wearing a fashionable blouse with embroidery on the collar. Occasionally she glanced at her companion, a look both sour and spicy; the man returned her glance approvingly. This was the early 1970s; it was a luxury to eat butter-fried cake and bean porridge in that famous department store.

Standing outside the window, Yu looked at Xiaotao's face and eyes, a countenance so familiar, so beautiful. Yu didn't go in. She just stood there for a while and then slowly walked away. Xiaotao never sent Yu a letter after they had parted. Only later did Yu learn the true reason she had left: Xiaotao's mother had found a job for her in the city. The telegram was a put-on. Her mother, Meihua, was not sick, and she was living well.

CHAPTER 6 | EMPTY CORNER

1

The city seemed empty when Jinwu was no longer living there. I never thought I would return here. Wandering about the dusty house, I tried in vain to find or remember something—anything. I had had several previous lives but could not remember any of them, and that's a good thing.

Silk pajamas lay on the bed. Their rich blue color suddenly brought me back to the azure lake of my childhood home. I recalled the time when I jumped into its clear waters. Once in the water, I saw the huge mussel and from its black interior, as it slowly opened, a female arm reached out, gently pulling me in. Warm yet transparent, the arm embraced me. After the initial darkness had passed I slowly opened my eyes and found myself sitting in an enclosed boat, sailing alone in the boundless water. But not quite alone: a man was operating the boat with his back to me. There were many cabins. I wandered from cabin to cabin until I came to the largest, where there was a huge bed, a wedding bed, with the covers turned down. On the bed sat a female mummy facing a mirror. It had been dead a long time, and there were many pieces of jewelry scattered about, together with bits and pieces of rusted metal. The whole scene was covered in spiderwebs. Outside there was gunfire, and bullets rained down upon the boat.

Recalling the lake brought waves of pain. The dream had ripped open the curtain enclosing my memory, a curtain that had remained closed for many years, but I didn't have the strength to face the past. After changing into the blue pajamas I lay down on the bed, where I seemed to be floating on the surface of the blue lake, watching the sun and the moon and the day and the night chasing one another before my eyes. I forgot time, but time kept on going. For seven days I lay on the bed until, on the morning of the seventh day, someone knocked on the door. As it opened someone quietly walked in and I felt a warm current of air approaching. It's Jinwu—it must be her! Like a spirit, the thought penetrated the darkness in my heart. I opened my eyes. It was not Jinwu, but a man, frail and old. It was my father, Lu Chen.

Sitting up, I now realized how weak I had become. My father was sitting beside me and tears welled up in his eyes as he slowly caressed my hair. I felt choked with emotion and avoided his eyes. Such strong feelings were foreign to me and I struggled for self-control. Now my father's hand seemed to burn my scalp, disturbing a deeply buried desire. I really wanted to push away his hand.

"It healed much better . . ." Father's tears were now streaming. "Come home. Mother and Grandma miss you."

I shook my head but said nothing; if I opened my mouth, the hot thing that was blocking my throat would gush out.

"Your eldest sister got married and came home with your brother-in-law. They all want to see you. Everyone is home except you. They also sent a photo for you."

His hands shaking, Father took out the photo and gave it to me. It was a typical wedding picture of that time. My sister was sitting with a strange man, their heads and shoulders touching, both in military uniforms. A message on the back was addressed to me: "For younger sister Yu from sister Lu Ling and brother-in-law Wang Zhong." His face was as plain as his name. So, older sister is now married. That means that marriage is not too far off for the rest of us sisters. A black undercurrent seemed to be moving beneath the surface of the photo, closing in on me from afar.

"Yu, you haven't addressed me."

With difficulty, tears streaming, I replied with one word: "Pa . . ." But I felt a burden lifting, and my tears were tears of relief.

2

Ling grew up under the direct care of our grandmother, who treated her like a pearl of great value, to be held only in the palm. Because Ruomu did not want to breast-feed, Xuanming found a wet nurse, Xiangqin. She was the daughter of Mrs. Peng, an old family servant. Xuanming thought the old connections would assure that the young woman would be reliable and honest. But an honest Mrs. Peng did not guarantee an honest daughter.

She was in all ways a typical village girl, and not unattractive, but what Xuanming liked most were those large, pendulous breasts. No need to squeeze, as just a light touch brought forth bountiful milk. Xuanming emptied out the largest room in the house for Xiangqin and Ling; in no time the tiny baby became chubby and Xuanming beamed with joy. She made rich soups for Xiangqin, who gradually became chubby as well.

By this time Ruomu had given birth to Xiao, and Shu'er was brought back to look after her. Ruomu started to call Shu'er Sister Tian, because she was no longer a young maid. Later, Sister Tian—who remained unmarried—became Aunty Tian, Ling's name for her. Loyal maids were not easy to find. Shu'er put up a makeshift bed in the hallway and took Xiao into her own bed so that Ruomu could sleep through the night. After changing the baby's diaper and feeding her, Shu'er would walk the floor singing *Sparrow and Child*, from a 1930s opera. Aunty Tian remembered it clearly:

> *Little Sparrow, little sparrow,*
> *Where has your mommy gone?*
> *Mommy flew away to fetch food,*
> *Mommy has not returned,*
> *My tummy is empty.*

You are my good friend,
I am your little friend.
At home, at home,
I have plenty of green peas,
I have plenty of worms.

If you want to eat,
If you want to drink,
Just follow me,
Just follow me.

My little sparrow,
My good friend,
Let's fly away, fly away, let's go!

Xiangqin was cut from a different pattern—she would never get up at night to look after the baby. To do so, she reasoned, would affect her milk production. Xuanming had to do that herself, so that her granddaughter would be disturbed as little as possible. She was constantly on duty: standing on her tiny feet, she changed diapers at night and cooked during the day, darting this way and that, the two diamond-shaped green jades on her shoes glittering like beams of light. The meals were elaborate: boiled meat paste for her granddaughter, soup for Ruomu and Xiangqin. And such soups! Crucian carp with turnips for Xiangqin to ensure healthy milk production. Lotus soup with preserved duck or black-boned chicken soup with milk vetch roots for Ruomu to revitalize her energy flow and blood circulation. Xuanming did all this with great joy.

Xiangqin's life was thus much simplified—eat, feed baby, eat again, and then one more thing, something unnoticed even by Xuanming: men. But as time went by, this could not remain hidden from Ling.

Although born after a difficult labor, her head damaged by forceps, Ling nevertheless showed signs of great intelligence from an early age. She was curious about the world and about herself. Using a mirror, she often examined herself carefully during a bath, every part of her body. She missed nothing. In her dreams a delicate and beautiful woman with fair skin would often appear, whose lips were painted scarlet red and who wore a beige silk dress—her mother. From her childhood experience she believed that women could live a carefree life only through middle age; thereafter, life became drudgery. This belief was reinforced when she spied on Xiangqin, who never dreamed that a five-year-old girl would climb to the top of the tall dresser while her wet nurse was bathing, and from there peep through a high window at her private moments.

Xiangqin's naked body was already familiar, but Ling found it even more amazing when examined surreptitiously. When Xiangqin reached back to unbutton her bra, Ling would feel a surge of excitement, anticipating the appearance of those two enormous breasts with their rosy areolas and tumid nipples. The sight made Ling dizzy. She wondered whether all women were like this, or if Xiangqin was something special.

One night, peering through the steam from her precarious perch, Ling saw another person—a man! His face was hidden by Xiangqin's long hair, but, like dried tree branches, his hands reached around from behind her naked torso to clasp her breasts, forcefully squeezing them, bringing color to surfaces normally creamy white. Ling watched as the hands clutched and squeezed rhythmically and the great orbs became redder and Xiangqin's body writhed, her face registering her agony. Her breasts were about to burst, like huge, soft fruit; scarlet juice squeezed through the man's sinewy fingers was about to splash bloody pulp in every direction. The shock of this imagined outcome deprived Ling of all control of her senses. She screamed and fell backward onto her bed, and as she was falling she had a clear view of the man's face: a strange face, reminiscent of the scariest of villains in films.

Ling's scream was drowned out by the rush of water in the shower. After a moment of numbness, she jumped to her feet and locked her door, then quickly dressed in a cheongsam that had been worn by Ruomu when she was young. It was made of soft satin and wool, trimmed with silver thread at the hem, the dark green material covered with large pink blossoms, each of them outlined in silver. Stuffing two scrunched-up hankies into the top after the fashion of the times, she suddenly saw herself in the mirror as the mature woman of her dreams. If we take the time to see and to think about it, we shall make a startling discovery: that in young girls' fantasies there is often a beautiful woman, imagined or real, who is the primordial image of her own mother and the point of origin of all her desires. Although this may be difficult for us to accept, girls' earliest desires are often aroused by members of their own sex.

Some years later, Ling's childhood sexuality took another leap forward. This came soon after Xiangqin's own child was born, a long time after she had left Lu's family. Ling was fourteen and spending a school break with her former wet nurse. During a hot summer day, Ling was roused from a nap by Xiangqin's painful moans. She found the woman lying in bed naked and faceup; the newborn infant skinny like a little mouse was nestled next to her and Xiangqin was massaging her breasts, apparently in agony. Her eyes still closed, she beckoned to Ling to be a good girl and come over and help Aunty by squeezing a little, she was in so much pain. Ling bent over excitedly and cupped her sweaty hands on the woman's breasts, those huge alluring organs, so familiar but no longer available. When she touched the nipples, squeezing hard as she did so, somewhere deep in her own body there was a tremulous response. At the sudden crushing pressure, Xiangqin opened her eyes wide in pain, and at that moment the two pairs of eyes locked momentarily. But Xiangqin soon withdrew her gaze, appalled because suddenly she had seen evil and cruelty in the girl's eyes.

Under the sudden pressure, Xiangqin's nipples became miniature jets, shooting out thin streams of thick and sticky yellow milk, which eventually turned thin and clear. Only then did Xiangqin feel less pain. Later, when Xiangqin's husband returned home, she told him that thanks to the girl's help, her mastitis had been relieved. As she said this, she was startled by the appearance of Ling's eyes, now strangely cruel and luminous in the dim light, their innocence gone, momentarily revealing the wanton gaze of an adult.

Ling was absolutely good in school, active as a leader in the Young Pioneers, taking great pleasure in issuing orders under the Young Pioneers flag. Only at night did indecent desires take a strong hold on her imagination, sometimes leading to intense anxiety and vague yearnings, even a kind of itchiness crawling in the cracks of her bones. This persisted until she was married, and from her wedding night on, for about six months, she was free of such feelings; after that they returned, staying with her until she discovered and bedded down with a new lover. This became the pattern of her life, her mood swings rising and falling with the highs and lows of her sexual adventures. Only after she reached middle age and her fifty-year-old husband of the time was promoted did this problem finally disappear.

Following the episode at Xiangqin's bedside, Ling's sexual desires became highly specific. She was crazy about the smell of Xiangqin's body, aroused by her sweat and her soured milk, and the remembered look on the woman's face as she had cupped her hands on those magnificently engorged breasts— a look of pain and infatuation, a look that fed her conquering desire. Ling surprised herself with the strength of her own desire, which was a mixture of lust, greed, and the will to conquer.

Xiangqin was always good to Ling, all the more so after the intimate scene in her bedroom. She made clothes for Ling and gave her a beautiful, intricately carved bamboo hairpin shaped like a butterfly. Years later, Ling learned that the hairpin had originally been a gift from Grandma Xuanming to Xiangqin's mother, Mrs. Peng.

3

Years later Yu heard her second sister, Xiao, saying to Yadan, their neighbor, that if she could accurately transcribe the details of Ling's life, she could win the Nobel Prize for Literature. Yadan is a writer. You will read about her stories soon.

Ling was indeed a strange woman full of weird ideas from the time she was little. Quick-witted, she was always able to safely navigate through troubled waters. Lu Chen often sighed, saying that "if only Ling could use her brain for the right things." Of the three daughters, Ling was the sole successor to everything there was about their mother, Ruomu, except for Ruomu's delicacy and aristocratic mannerisms.

Like all the girls in her family, Ling had large and beautiful eyes, with well-developed but, regrettably, slightly crooked eyebrows. Observant schoolmates noticed a peculiar resemblance between the shape of Ling's eyebrows and the hands of a clock, the hour hand seemingly pointing to eight o'clock, the minute hand to four—the twenty-minute position, and thus the nickname Eight-twenty was coined. In resentment, as a teenager she used tweezers to modify their shape. Now her eyebrows were truly unique, rather like quails with their tails cut off. Because her teeth were bad, she developed the habit of smiling with her mouth closed. Small framed, throughout her life she often heard the comment "Ah, you don't look your age, you seem so young!" To live up to the comment, she kept a ponytail till age forty and wore doll-like clothes till age fifty. Xiao often felt embarrassed for her sister, especially when she stubbornly insisted on wearing strange color combinations. When the two older girls quarreled, Yu would side with Xiao, who would never tease her. Ling, in contrast, took great delight in contriving elaborate and unkind surprises for her youngest sister. With hair pulled across her face and tongue sticking out, Ling would often suddenly jump out at the girl from behind a door. Xiao would meanwhile sit quietly on a stool, cracking peanuts and offering them to Yu one by one.

The Lu girls spent much of their time playing together. Each girl had a wicker basket where she kept small treasures: Western pictures, glass marbles, colorful rocks, dried insects with pretty wings; and buttons, mirrors, combs, and the like. Sometimes they would remove everything from their baskets and display them on the floor, a game they called "treasure presenting." Sometimes Ruomu would allow them to try on her clothing. She also showed them how, using soft stones, to draw pictures on the concrete floor. One day this led to a big family row. Ling, a pretty good artist, had created a salacious picture—a naked woman, her figure arched seductively, with some body parts shown in exaggerated form and in excessive detail. It was inspired by an illustration in a book, *One Thousand and One Nights*, which their father had bought for them. In a story called "The Tale of the Second Baghdad Woman," there was a picture of a woman whose clothes had been ripped off by her husband, who then beat her savagely. Merely lurid in printed form, the image as rendered by Ling went beyond the limits of familial decency.

Yu remembered that day when all hell broke loose. Father slapped Ling, Grandma smacked Father, little Yu charged at Grandma. Ruomu yelled from afar with a hankie covering her nose: "What kind of family are we? So violent! People are laughing!" Lu Chen panted, "Do you have no shame?" Xuanming, pushing forward on her tiny feet, said, "Lu Chen, let's make it clear. Who lost whose face? When my daughter married you, you didn't even have a decent set of clothes. I had to buy everything for you! No matter how wrong Ling was, she is still your Lu family's seed! It was left to me to bring up all your children. When it comes to teaching them, as long as I am still alive, you've got no chance!"

Xuanming's angry shouts could be heard all over Jiaotong University. Now a row of little heads had lined up at the window. Under their collective gaze Lu Chen lost all stomach for continuing the fight. His face turned ashen, and as Yu followed him to his room, she was afraid that he might just suddenly die.

4

When Yu first saw her brother-in-law, Wang Zhong, she knew that Ling's marriage must have been the result of her impulsive behavior. That, together with her fascination with illicit sexual activity, including practices bordering on sadism, had been her trademark since she was a little girl. Her father's slap after the discovery of the lascivious rock art had done nothing to curb her appetite for the strange thrill of deviant behavior—it merely resulted in her being even more secretive. Yu saw her sister drawing obscene pictures on scraps of paper; she especially liked to draw naked women, bound and helpless, with gaping wounds in their abdomens, their faces revealing pain and ecstasy simultaneously.

Anyone Ling was infatuated with was, in Yu's opinion, perverted. In elementary school she fell in love with her physical education teacher—the first male to become the object of her desire. The man wore his hair slicked back, revealing crude features, a man of low culture. Bowing to his will, one day when they were alone she willingly removed one article of clothing after another, finally standing naked before him. His big hands squeezed Ling's little body as if he were rubbing a skinny fish. Tumescent and breathing heavily, he stopped himself before reaching climax. He still had some sense about him, knowing the political consequences would weigh much heavier on him than on this young student.

Later, Ling fell for the Communist Party secretary of a rural commune during a summer labor trip; then again with a male actor in a Shanghai opera troupe. By now her exploits had come to her parents' attention, inducing anger, shame, and resentment. Each new man in her life seemed worse than the one before. Ruomu would curse while cleaning her ears—"Bitch!"—as if not to her own daughter but to a servant girl who had committed a mistake. Ruomu was not one to attack directly; she would always beat around the bush and in effect conceded the parenting role to Xuanming and Lu Chen. In this way she was a talented tactician; once having planted a negative comment, she retreated from the scene of action, preserving the option of playing the loving conciliator after observing the battle from a distance. Again and again Xuanming and Lu Chen regretted being used in this way; again and again they fell into her trap.

When Yu returned home after an absence of ten years, she was surprised to find that everything had become smaller, including her mother and grandma. Ling and Xiao had both become prettier, especially Ling. She was wearing a fashionable jacket of the time made of shining dark green linen, which accentuated the whiteness of her face. Her eyes, with the eyebrows still positioned at eight-twenty, shone with delight. She was the first to come forward and embrace her younger sister warmly; and as she did so, she pointed to the tall young man next to her, saying, "Call him big brother!"

Seeing the man from the photograph for the first time, Yu did as she was told. He was dressed in a uniform faded from repeated washings, also a fashion of the time.

Holding Yu's hand, Ling said earnestly, "Your brother's military uniform is genuine. He is a real soldier. He is the company commander sent to my former school during the big political storm to support the leftists. He is from three generations of poor peasants, a family background far better than ours!" As Ling was explaining all this to Yu, Lu Chen curled his lips in scorn, and Xuanming did the same. For once the two found themselves in agreement.

Until this point, Yu had been giving her undivided attention to Ling and her new husband; now she turned to her mother, finding that she had changed little: face much the same, no wrinkles, skin very white. But something in her expression was frightening, and Yu was startled. Summoning all her strength, she called, "Momma." But the word was strangely devoid of meaning and sounded hollow.

Ruomu's response was unintelligible and her flaming anger was not subdued just because the years had gone by. At the sight of her youngest daughter, she recalled a son that had once been hers, whose life had been snuffed out by this weird, skinny girl standing before her. Her life was rewritten forever.

Lu Chen rushed to break the ice. "That day you disappeared, your mother and I got terribly worried. No one thought you could have gone so far away, several hundred miles at least. You were only six or seven years old. How did you find the place?"

Yu looked at her father but did not reply. She could not remember how she found Jinwu. To her, what happened then seemed two lifetimes ago.

Lu Chen asked, "Where is Jinwu? Why have I never seen her? The tuition and living expenses; we owe her so much. We were very grateful. She was just one of my students; we can't let her spend so much money."

Ruomu chose this moment to fire her first salvo. Turning to Ling, her tone cold rather than passionate, she said, "No wonder your father has had nothing to say to us. He has saved all his words for his favorite person!"

Yu was already finding it hard to put on a happy face; now the past was like a knife to her, the wound too deep. She had never been able to disguise her vulnerability. Never a likable girl, always at a critical moment like this her defenses crumbled; she became even more awkward.

Ruomu looked at Yu again and said with a dramatic tone: "It's good you came back. If that cheap woman had not left, you would not have returned, right? Have pity on us, who for all these years have been worrying ourselves almost to death. You are so cruel. How could you do that? For three generations my family has been Buddhists and vegetarians. What did I do in a previous life to deserve a thing like you?"

And now another broadside, but it was nothing more than a moan. To Yu it was like a sharp, familiar sword piercing her nerves—nerves that had been numb for so long but were now again exposed. She knew that Father would now jump in with both feet, and the squabble would escalate. Yu leaned against the rickety old table and she felt one side of her face, the side facing her parents, begin to screw up; she was ready to flee.

Her father simply sighed heavily. He was getting on in years. The wrinkles on both sides of his mouth had deepened. They were bitter lines, reflecting years of repressed anger and outrage. His eyes were now habitually misty, as if tears were always just below the surface, ready to erupt. Yu heard his tone as much as his words, tones reflecting an effort to placate the family and smooth over this latest crisis.

"Forget the past. The child has just come back . . ."

At this point her father's words were overwhelmed by her mother's hysterical cries. And now Ruomu brought out her biggest weapon of all—self-flagellation. In a savage fury she began beating her hands against her own face, screaming as she did so: "I shall die! I really shall die! How can I ever forget she is your favorite daughter! What am I but a housewife with no means of support? I am old. Not like your daughter, who is at the age of flower and jade, so desirable."

And now Lu Chen was shaking. "How can you say such things? How can a mother be so hateful? Isn't Yu also your daughter?"

Ruomu raised her white bony hands. "All of you take a look. See how your father treats me! Lu Chen, I hit my face and now it is swollen! What more do you want from me? Shall I kneel and kowtow to your third princess?"

Yu grabbed her purse and ran to the door. But so did Ruomu, who at age fifty was still spry, ran and reached the door first. Prostrating herself, she began beating her head on the hard concrete. "My third princess, you cannot leave! If you do, I cannot get my share of food from your father!"

Yu saw her father collapsing into a broken chair. She felt ripped apart, torn asunder, reduced to a quivering mass and only barely able to move. And then it seemed that all were moving in her direction, all yelling at once, a huge noise pressing down on her so heavily that she couldn't breathe. All that noise became an amplified whisper and she suddenly recalled the scene ten years before, and this memory completed the destruction of her defenses.

She fought off the pushing, grasping hands and bolted for the street. No more azure lake. This was a city, dirty and derelict. But this was after all the city she wanted to come back to from that barren, remote place.

5

Yu was rescued by Yadan, the girl next door who was a few years older than Yu. Plump but not without charm, Yadan seemed to have retained her baby fat. Every day when she returned home from her job at a grain refinery she would sit at her desk, writing energetically. No one was allowed to see what she produced.

Yadan found Yu holed up like a frightened puppy, squatting inside a concrete drainage pipe. She took hold of one of Yu's legs and pulled vigorously. The girl was filthy with slime and mud. She had become an untouchable.

Exhausted, Yu no longer had the power to resist. All was dark in the Lu household, but a light remained in Aunty Tian's room. The woman was well over fifty years of age but still capable of quick, vigorous action; she sighed as she emerged from the house to take charge. Her demeanor was habitually solemn, which could hint of sophistication; but on closer inspection, it revealed only her bitterness. There was a mole at one corner of her mouth, which would move when she smiled. But Aunty Tian rarely smiled.

Matter-of-factly, she placed a large basin of water at Yu's feet. "Third daughter, wash up. Your mother has just lain down. Don't upset her again."

Yu seemed not to hear. She sat on the floor, arms around her knees, motionless. Aunty Tian sighed again. "Why do you behave this way? A girl should listen, read her books, do some needlework, keep clean, be a little bit sweet and likable. So what if Mom and Dad scolded you a little, you should just make a face and let it go. Why do you have to be so thick-headed and make your parents angry? Someday you will be a mother yourself, you'll find out that it's not easy to carry a baby inside for nine months . . ."

Yu said nothing. She was thinking, why bother bringing me into the world if there is no love? Then she raised her eyes and asked a question that made Aunty Tian think hard, then and later: "Tell me, was I born by my mother?"

Aunty Tian trembled visibly as she looked intently at those burning eyes. This girl is so obdurate, so passionate! No wonder her mother and grandmother disliked her so much! Pondering this, she said, "Third daughter, you really hurt your mother by saying something like that. Open your eyes: among the three girls, who looks the most like her mother? When she was pregnant with you, your mother liked to eat a kind of fish that was very delicious, but later she learned it had toxins that could poison her baby. This was terribly frightening. When your mom began delivery, I went with her because the old mistress was ill. Even though it was her third delivery, she was still afraid. She held my wrist so tightly that I had bruises. Of all three girls, you were the only one breast-fed by your mom, and she continued until you were three years old. You never ate meals without help until you were five. Talk about being spoiled, you were spoiled rotten! All the best, as though you were a boy! And then she finally had a boy after praying to all the gods, but then you . . . Ah, what can I say? All right, come and wash up. You are filthy!"

Yu suddenly pulled back her hands from Aunty Tian and held her knees, without a word.

That night, Aunty Tian didn't go to sleep until four in the morning. She and the young woman had continued their standoff and on that night Aunty Tian for the first time said some things she shouldn't have.

"No men would want to marry a girl like you! Even if one did, he would soon dump you!" This was so beyond Aunty Tian's usual discretion, she must have been really angry.

Yu turned around and silently stared, finally saying, "What about you? You are so kind, but still no one wanted you. Why?"

She raised her hand as if to strike the girl, but restrained herself. On trembling legs she made her way back to her room, saying angrily, "All the poison from the fish your mom ate was left in you. From now on I won't say a word, even if your mom and dad beat you to death."

Yu remained motionless. Under the dim light a cold smile crept onto her face. Such a sneer on a young girl's face was frightening.

Sitting in the corner of emptiness, Yu glanced about, looking at furniture that had been familiar to her since her girlhood, now worn and threadbare and somehow not fixed in place, its life span nearly exhausted. She suddenly felt that she, the house, the furniture, and the family itself were all transitory; all could collapse at any moment. Grandma's familiar snoring could now be heard. Nothing had changed, but everything had aged.

But from Ling's room came an unfamiliar sound, a strange moan. Yu could not imagine how her eldest sister could bring herself to be locked in the embrace of a total stranger.

In the early dawn, Yu felt something sticky within and below her groin—blood, sticky like pitch, and it was terrifying. She wanted to call for help, and regretted that Aunty Tian had been chased away by her.

Once again, she heard her sister moaning, strangely louder this time.

In the morning the doctor was called; he gave Yu several prescriptions, saying she was suffering from an internal disorder. Many years later Jinwu told her the medicine she was lacking was love.

6

Ling's bright face turned a faded gray in one month. Wang Zhong had used up his leave and had to return to his work unit. But Xuanming was beaming with joy. After his discharge he went to a job in the distant northwest, choosing to go there because Ling, as part of the first group of sent-down youth, was selected to work in a factory located in that region. For love Wang Zhong would sacrifice anything. Xiao joined them there, working at the same factory. All of this was according to Ling's preference; anything she wanted, she could usually get.

When Ling started to vomit, an old woman arrived from a distant place.

The old woman was tall, with some pockmarks on her face and a thick accent from the central plains of Shaanxi. She was Wang Zhong's mother. Three women can put on a show, now we have three old women, three old exceptional women at that. Mama Wang Zhong was diligent and took over most of Aunty Tian's work, including preparation of meals. Her style of cooking was different, not so refined. This reminded Ruomu of the time when she was a young lady and they had employed a cook who used to work for the imperial family. Portly and able to prepare many different styles of food, the man had a perfect Mandarin accent. He knew the old Peking delicacies. For instance, braised chicken wings in brown sauce from Spring Flower Restaurant; stewed bird's nest in light sauce from Mt. Tai Harvest Restaurant; soft fried duck gizzards from Hundred Scenes Restaurant; braised shark fin from Buddha's House; lotus pastry from Lotus House; pancakes fried with chicken oil from Rich Men's Pavilion; mushroom dumplings from Eardrop Shop—from appetizers to entrees to desserts, rare delicacies from the oceans to the mountains.

After going through the war, Ruomu had become more adaptive, so now she had no complaint at Mama Wang Zhong's giant stuffed buns. It wasn't so bad to be served ordinary food, just as long as she didn't have to lift a finger.

But Xuanming was not so generous. She could not help herself; she was a perfectionist, and everything had to be flawless. When she saw the giant stuffed buns—one of them taking up the whole plate—she curled her lips in disapproval. That expression was like a dull and rusty razor on Lu Chen's sensitive chin, but to the implacable Mama Wang it was unremarkable.

Like Xuanming, Mama Wang had her feet bound when she was a girl, but the result was far less delicate. Stout and large-boned, her pounding footsteps would herald her arrival from afar. Whenever Xuanming heard the stomping sound, her lips would curl and she would announce, "The heavyweight is coming."

Mama Wang Zhong was oblivious to refinement of any and every kind. When chatting with Xuanming, she asked, "How many have you laid?"

At first Xuanming had no idea what was being asked; later she complained to Ling, "Why on earth do you have to bring someone like this to our home?

Since when do we call giving birth to children 'laying a kid'? We are not animals! Oh, what a curse! What did you do to deserve an in-law like that?"

Ling's reaction to this complaint was heartbreaking. "Mama Wang is a daughter of a working family, three generations of her family are poor peasants. You cannot compete with that." Ling would always address Mama Wang as "Ma," right in front of Ruomu, which left her mother confused. Once when the family was assembled for supper and Xuanming had made a delicious turtle dish, Ling picked up a choice piece and said, "Ma, for you."

Ruomu handed over her plate without thinking. But Ling, with her beautiful eyes hung beneath her eight-twenty eyebrows, cruelly overlooked her own mother. "I am not calling you, I called my ma."

The long-suffering Lu Chen, not waiting for Ling to finish, put his bowl on the table with a loud clatter and got up and went to his room.

For the first time in her life Xuanming was cross with her favorite granddaughter, bellowing, "You don't think she is your mother? Who do you think gave birth to you?"

Whenever Ling knew she was losing ground, she used tears as her first line of defense. Now, with her mouth open and displaying a multitude of rotting teeth, she started to cry, hoping this would gain a pardon from Grandma. But not this time. Xuanming pounded on the table and continued to bellow, until finally Mama Wang Zhong waved a fan and said in a flat tone, "Old Granny, don't get so worked up on a hot day. She's a kid, what does she know?"

Xuanming did not respond; her stormy temper was like a man's early ejaculation. Once discharged, it went flat quickly.

But Ruomu had more stomach for the fight. Having remained calm when the others were in a rage, she had time to continue picking through the tasty dish; when she had found and eaten all the best pieces, she threw her chopsticks on the table. With bloodshot eyes, she dabbed her nose with a hankie and then declaimed, "I have a lousy fate! I went through painful labor for three days and nights, my father paid for a Belgian doctor who injured her head with his forceps, which worried me for years. But thanks be to God she could read *Little Women* at age six. Not until everyone agreed she was smart could I stop worrying. I always knew raising a daughter is doing someone else a favor, but how could I know that someone else would come to the door to capture her heart! Thank heavens, I am at my own house and eating my own husband's food!" She was working herself into a rage. Then she saw Yu in the mirror; Yu seemed to have a sneer on her face, and that was the trigger for dramatic action. Pushing the table away, she threw a spoon at Yu's face with all her force, too fast for Yu to duck. It cut her forehead as it flew by. Ruomu's voice went up an octave as she was launching her attack. "Damn you! What are you laughing at? Are you happy when your own mother gets bullied?"

Ruomu was back to her favorite game: scaring a monkey by killing a chicken. Mama Wang Zhong was still an in-law, no matter how annoying; Ling was well into her pregnancy, so Yu was the perfect target.

But Yu hadn't grasped these nuances. She was only seventeen years old, her emotional wounds from all that had gone before were still raw, and her mother's nasty emotional game had found its mark. Completely losing control, she threw herself across the room in defense of her dignity. Several hands reached out to stop her, stern voices scolded her at high and low pitches, and after she was stopped she was forced to endure the usual bromides of filial piety: "No matter, what, she is your mother . . . she can hit and curse and you can only listen . . . you must never lay a hand on your own mother."

When this had run its course, Yu finally said what had been bottled up. "You shouldn't have given birth to me if you don't love me!"

"Heavens, this girl will murder someone someday!" Ruomu opened her tear-filled eyes wide; she was stunned, along with two other stunned old women. By that time, Ling had returned to her room, not wanting to get burned by the fire she had started. But all three of the older mothers were united in their expressions of outrage. It was Mama Wang Zhong who led the charge. Picking up Xuanming's cane, she swung it violently, hitting Yu across the lower back; without a sound, the girl fell to the floor.

From his room, Lu Chen was heard moaning, "Fight, fight, fight! Fight till I die!"

And from Ling's room, loud sobs—if she didn't begin crying, her father might redirect his anger at her. Xuanming and Mama Wang Zhong called to her, pleading for calm, don't hurt your baby, and began making soup for the expectant mother; the two pairs of tiny feet, clearly of different status, moved about busily.

Meanwhile, Ruomu sat alone by the window, cleaning her ears with the gold ear spoon. In a tone of high drama, she addressed Aunty Tian: "Take the third daughter to a doctor. Maybe she is hurt; maybe she needs some medicine. She doesn't accept me as mother and she is hot-blooded, but I still care for her." To herself, she was thinking hateful thoughts about Mama Wang Zhong. "It's my family's business, who asked her to get involved. Even pigs and dogs want to become our in-laws."

7

The day wore on, becoming exceptionally hot. By noon, two daughters from the Lu family were admitted to the hospital at the same time.

Ling went to the women's ward, accompanied by Xuanming and Mama Wang Zhong. When her husband entered her room, Ling cried out, "Look what you've done! I have to bear it all! Look at me, so ugly." The two old women joined her crying, thinking about their days as young mothers. The doctor arrived, did his examination, and found that her cervix had dilated to eight inches. Soon she was wheeled into the delivery room.

Outside the delivery room, three people were waiting anxiously. A life is about to be born. It has thousands of ways to grow; it can be as simple as a tiny seed growing in the dark. That day a huge rainstorm followed the brutal heat. Outside was a scene of exquisite beauty. Shafts of sunlight intensified the colors in a garden surrounding a pond where lotus leaves had caught some raindrops. Birds took flight, soaring high into the sky, leaving one or two white feathers falling.

But inside the delivery room there were terrifying cries when a life was forging through. Ling's voice was penetrating, louder than anyone's. All three anxious people were beside themselves. But the screaming went on, growing somewhat fainter late in the afternoon as the expectant mother's voice began to fail. The head nurse appeared, saying the delivery was very difficult, they had tried every-thing, now they were ready to initiate a cesarean; would the father please sign the form? Sweaty, his hand trembling, Wang Zhong signed the paper just as a gur-ney was pushed out of the delivery room. All was covered by a white sheet; only Ling's soaked hair showed above it. Wang Zhong burst into tears at the sight, as did Xuanming. Between sobs she cried out, "Quick, where is the chocolate you brought? Hurry and give her a piece, she needs the energy."

But it was Mama Wang Zhong who remained calm and knew exactly what to do. Running alongside the gurney, she pulled up the sheet from the bottom, then in full voice shouted, "Stop! Stop this minute! I see the baby's head! Forget the knives, we can just pull the kid out right here!"

Many years later, Wang Zhong would still be proud of his mother's sound-ing judgment at the critical moment, said to his wife, "If not for my mother you would have gone under the knife. Ungrateful whore!" Of course, this is to be described later; to say any more now would be out of place. How un-predictable is this life we lead.

That day, the nurse held the bruised infant upside down, patting lightly, but there was no answering cry. The nurse said it was a girl, and then placed her in an incubator. The doctor noted on the medical record, "Fetus had sei-zure inside the uterus. Five minutes before breathing started."

Ruomu was sitting by the window, cleaning her ears, as the call came through. She called Aunty Tian: "Tell them I have a name. One word, Yun." With eyes cast down, Aunty Tian asked, "Do you have a special meaning for this name?" Ruomu responded impatiently. "What is there to say? It just crossed my mind, that's all." Then she murmured, "Just a girl. What is there to say? But you just reminded me. This is the first daughter of our Lu family's third generation. She must use our family name, Lu. Later, you go to talk to that old woman. If she is willing, the child can use the given name Yun'er and stay here, so they won't have to take her to that shameful mountain place. But if she is not willing, we are not forcing anything. Tell her whole family to take the baby and leave. Don't stay around here, wandering about, annoying me." Aunty Tian nodded and asked in a hurry, "Then what about daughter Ling?" Ruomu stared at her. "Why are you so confused? Are you getting old and losing your memory? Hasn't she already announced that she belongs to the Wang family? It's up to them now."

Aunty Tian paused and grew thoughtful. How strange, so many years after the liberation, her young mistress has changed completely. While in front of other people, polite and respectful to people, even humble; but not at all when the two of them are alone together. Closing her eyes, she could summon the memory: a room white as snow, the young mistress playing on a swing under the trellis in the garden, accompanied by Meihua. The two of them were so beautiful. They seemed to give off light to their surroundings. Later the young mistress chose her, Shu'er, and for this she remained grateful the rest of her life.

By the night, the whole family had gathered peacefully, acutely aware of the momentous events of the day, as if they had gone through a life-and-death situation. Aunty Tian carried the newborn little princess, walking around to show everyone. Lu Chen returned home late and gloomy. He peered at the tiny face of his granddaughter and sat at the table and stuffed in a mouthful of rice, then sat back as he chewed silently. He was not feeling well, and said so.

Aunty Tian rushed to find a hot water bottle. "Mr. Lu never complains about anything, now he says his stomach aches. He must be really hurting; maybe he should see a doctor."

Ruomu had finished supper and bathed; now looking rested and complacent, she moved forward to show concern for her husband. Lu Chen stared at her.

"Where is daughter?"

"Over there lying in bed. The labor lasted all day, she needs rest. Even though it cannot compare with what I went through in delivering her."

"I mean Yu," replied Lu Chen.

Then Ruomu changed her tone. "Really! Where is third daughter? Her big sister gave birth and she didn't even show her face."

Aunty Tian said hurriedly, "You forgot. Third daughter has back pain and Yadan took her to a hospital."

Lu Chen dropped his hot water bottle and stood up. Just then the door opened, and in walked Yadan. She was breathing heavily.

"Uncle Lu, let Yu stay in my house tonight. I came to tell you so you won't be worried."

But it was Ruomu who responded. "How can we trouble you so much? You should bring her back. What exactly is wrong with her?"

Yadan kept her eyes fixed on Lu Chen. "She had a herniated spinal disk. The doctor said it was caused by external injury. She should stay in bed at least a month. I see you are all quite excited here and no one can really look after her. Let her stay with me. My parents are away and she can keep me company."

Lu Chen was about to say something but was cut off by Ruomu. "That is a lot of trouble for you." Then, turning to Xuanming, "Yadan is such a good child. Since she was a little girl she has always been considerate. She can even get along with someone as strange as our Yu." And back to Yadan, "It can't be an external cause. She had muscle spasms in her lower back when she came home. You take good care of her. She is very odd, you have to be tolerant."

Only then did Lu Chen have a chance to speak again. "Yadan, you have to go to work every day. Better to let her return here. Aunty Tian can look after her."

Yadan's gaze had remained fixed on Lu Chen, as though he was the only person whose opinion mattered. "Yu said she didn't want to return here," she said. "She would rather stay with me. As for my work, I can leave a key with you so that Aunty Tian can come and go as needed." Handing the key to Lu Chen, she headed for the door.

"Walk slowly, it's dark out there," said Ruomu, poking her head out the door as the girl left. "Don't twist your ankle."

Lu Chen stared at the metal key in his hand. His face was a mask, but there was something churning painfully in that space within his chest where, for so many years, so many injuries had remained untreated and uncured.

CHAPTER 7 | A PLAY

1

One autumn day many years ago, when the falling leaves were getting swirled up in the passing breezes, a woman walked into the Lu family's front yard and knocked gently on the door. Xuanming was in the kitchen cooking, Ruomu was in her room getting dressed, Lu Chen had gone to tutor his Soviet students, and Ling and Xiao had gone to school. Only Yu heard the knock. She peered through the window and saw the woman, well dressed in a light green jacket of soft wool with a beautiful silk scarf hung around her neck. She was coiffed in the latest style—long, permed hair flowing down to her shoulders. She even had a light touch of makeup. In those colorless years, she was an instant beauty in Yu's eyes. Yu was transfixed and stared a moment before opening the door. Around the house the honeysuckle bushes were bare; only the roses near the windows were still struggling to offer the last of their pale redness to offset the drab grays and light browns of the season.

Soon Yu saw the flaw in her nearly perfect beauty as the woman walked in, followed by a skinny girl who was even thinner than Ling. Addressing

140

Yu, the woman smiled and said she must be the daughter of Sister Ruomu, whom she strongly resembled. Yu flushed immediately; she did not like to hear that she looked like her mother. She announced loudly, "Some guests have arrived."

Xuanming and Ruomu emerged from their rooms at the same time; instantly their faces soured. Bowing first to Xuanming, then to Ruomu, the woman said, "Mom, Sister Ruomu, I have brought the child for a visit."

Xuanming turned on her heel and went back to the kitchen. Ruomu put on her usual contrived smile, and told Yu to call the woman Aunt Mengjing, then left to make some tea. The woman ignored the cold reception. She smiled softly and asked Yu not to call her aunt, but *jiu ma*, uncle's wife. Although her voice was soft, it was somehow weighty, like thunder heard from a distance. Yu saw her mother's hands tremble as she poured the tea, spilling a few drops.

"Mom, Sister Ruomu," said the woman, "Tiancheng and I became a couple even though we never took the time to get married. I don't care about the formalities. This child is Tiancheng's flesh and blood. And I know Mom is most kind . . ."

That day went on like this: Xuanming brought out lunch—braised fish, vegetable-stuffed steamed buns, and Chinese cabbage soup. The Lu family's meals at that time, although much better than those of their neighbors, could not compare with their repasts in the days of old. After putting the food on the table, Xuanming said bluntly, "Eat and leave. There is no room for you here." The little girl ate six buns, one after the other, leaving only two that were broken in the basket for Ling and Xiao when they returned from school.

Mengjing seemed not to have heard; she just gazed at the buns. Yu heard Ruomu murmuring through closed teeth, "Thick-skinned!" Mengjing ignored this, and without pause spooned up the soup and devoured the remaining buns. Then she put a piece of fish on her daughter's plate. Xuanming watched Mengjing eating with disdain and couldn't help glancing at the little girl. Sensitively, the girl put down her chopsticks, and with her head bowed and her brow furrowed, she looked around. In a hoarse voice, she suddenly called out, "Granny," which surprised everyone at the table.

Mengjing immediately corrected her. "You should call her *jia po*," which was the word for "grandma" used in Xuanming's hometown. Xuanming was visibly pleased, and said with a smile that "Granny" was just fine; that any way little children addressed her was just fine. Xuanming's words, kind and warm, lit up the little girl's dirty face.

Just arriving at the table, Ling saw that Xuanming was warming to the visitors. She pushed the girl away, then sat down on the chair, saying, "This is my chair, don't you dare take my chair." Ling was slight but strong, and the girl went down hard, knocking her head against the stove as she fell, producing a thin trickle of blood across her forehead. Slowly the blood was oozing out, dark purple in color, like the old roses outside the window, faded by the autumn winds.

Yu was shocked and instantly went to help the girl; but she got up on her own, still holding an unfinished piece of bun in one hand. It was covered in ashes, but the girl swallowed it in one gulp for fear someone might snatch it away. She seemed oblivious to the blood. Only now did Mengjing put down her soup bowl and bring warm water to give the child a wash. Xuanming patted the girl's head and handed her the half-eaten bun from her own hand.

Thus, the two visitors got to stay.

At that time, Lu Chen's position at Jiaotong University brought with it for his family a row of single-story houses that had been built by Soviet experts in the early 1950s. They were square and clumsy, ugly yet sturdy, reminding people of the square sugar boxes made by their big Soviet brothers.

The next morning, while Yu was still tucked under her quilt, she smelled something delicious. At the same time, she heard her mother complaining. "Shameless! She even used peanut oil to fry the pancake!" At that time peanut oil was rationed: one hundred grams per person per month. For cooking, Xuanming used only vegetable seed oil bought at a higher price.

Yu noticed that Xuanming was not in the kitchen; instead, she was slowly combing Ling's hair, using castor oil to give it shine. Then she created two long braids tied with bright ribbons. Grandma did this every day for Ling and Xiao, using different-colored ribbons for different-color effects: bright red, orange, or dark green. Every day as she did this she would sigh, "What beautiful hair! So shiny and smooth!"

That day, as Grandma was doing their hair, Mengjing brought golden fried pancakes to the table. "Mom, you eat," she said, "all of you eat." Xuan-ming blinked her eyes and told the others to eat first. Ruomu and Lu Chen did the same. Only Ling jumped to it, like a cat, grabbing a pancake with her bare hand and stuffing it in her mouth just as the girl, with a bandage on her head, was reaching with her chopsticks. Later on there was a price to pay for her gluttony; having overeaten, Ling became ill. But Mengjing seemed to have a hole in her stomach, and her daughter, too, did not let her mother down. Mengjing and her daughter continued eating heartily. The Lu family's rationed food saved from the previous months was soon depleted by the two houseguests, like dispersed clouds driven away by a gust of wind.

Mother and daughter got to stay and stayed for three years, while a famine raged through the country. At the end of the three-year famine Lu Chen was banished to a remote frontier, and Mengjing got herself married to the newly appointed president of the university.

That little girl was, of course, Yadan. Later she said she would always remember that it was Yu who helped her up when she fell down.

2

Xuanming was the first one to discover the tattoo on Yushe's back.

Yu felt wild with joy after she moved in with Yadan. When Yadan went to work, Yu would stay home alone. Then one day when brilliant sunshine slanted in through the curtains, like a magic brushstroke, lighting up the walls with sprinkles of filtered sunshine, it made the entire room as fresh and delightful as a cup brimming over with crystal-clear water. Traveling clouds in the skies shot their drifting shadows into the room, changing its hues constantly. Just as it had been in her childhood, whenever such a moment presented itself, Yu felt that something special was about to happen.

And it did. It was the whisper that Yu had not heard for a long time. It came back to her, whispering softly. It was her guardian angel. Her guardian angel had not deserted her. She was overwhelmed with joy.

The voice was still calm and peaceful: "What you longed for is about to arrive."

"What is it? A person, an event?" Yu asked hurriedly. No answer.

She immediately began to think about what she longed for, and she always knew she had been longing for something, living in her inner world, feeling the outer world distant and strange. This was the source of her strange behavior and it made her absentminded and awkward and caused those near her, including her own family, to laugh at her and mistrust her. Their scorn was palpable, and she began to believe they were right—she was useless. Her existence was meaningless. Having once believed in herself, she was now embarrassed and filled with self-pity.

Now that whisper was a decree from God. Once again she saw the first light of day. She saw herself become a new person, dressed in a white shirt and blue skirt, walking happily on a tree-lined boulevard. She was walking closer and closer, but she couldn't see her own face. She felt that face could be anyone's face. She forgot what she looked like. Now she saw a close-up of a film. When she walked very close, she suddenly saw her own naked body with the two plum blossoms on her breasts that had turned blue. She cried out and woke up. It was a dream. Grandma was sitting next to her, reminding her of those times when she was very young and ill and Grandma had been kind to her.

Xuanming had lifted her shirt and was examining her back closely. She was not pleased by what she saw. "You got tattooed?"

Yu didn't respond.

"Do you know what it looks like?"

Yu shook her head. She really didn't know. Once she had tried to get a good look, using two mirrors. She thought it was beautiful, but could see only part of it.

"It's a serpent, a feathered serpent."

Without knowing it, Yu trembled and her face went pale.

"The tattoo is beautiful. Why did you do it?"

"For . . . redemption."

"Who did it?"

"Master Fa Yan."

"What!"

"Master Fa Yan at Xitan Mountain. You told me about him."

"But Master Fa Yan died sixty years ago . . ." Xuanming's whole body was trembling, her wrinkles moving uncontrollably about her face. She didn't know whether to laugh or cry.

Yu stared at her grandmother, feeling numb. She searched her memory, trying to reconstruct the events of that snowy winter day. Never for a moment had she forgotten her sin. On the day when she learned that Michael from America had taken Jinwu away from her, she received a decree from God, conveying to her an important message, telling her about Jinque Temple on Xitan Mountain. She wanted redemption and hoped that through suffering—the pain of tattooing—she would win Jinwu back. But Jinwu was gone—nowhere to be found. Yu jumped into the lake near her childhood log cabin, but as in the past, she didn't die. She survived not knowing who had saved her life.

Her memory of all these details was clear enough now, but she decided not to try to explain it all to Grandma. Just like when she was a little girl, she didn't feel like talking. All grown-ups were foolish. To them, to understand something was simply too much trouble.

But Yu's reference to Fa Yan was truly disturbing to Xuanming, who believed that the girl had actually had dealings with a ghost. So she burned some ambergris joss sticks and silently chanted *Incantation for the Past*. When Xuanming was praying for Fa Yan's soul, the past reappeared clearly before her eyes.

3

Naturally Xuanming thought of the last words of Aunt Yuxin. Seven days after receiving the lamp, Aunt Yuxin died. Xuanming soon found where Xitan Mountain was located, and was pondering how to deliver the lamp there. But then an event occurred that put her plans on hold forever.

The event was the source of the story of "Empress Dowager Cixi cuddling Xuanming in her arms in the twenty-fifth year of Guangxu's reign." Soon after Yuxin's death, a favorite consort of the imperial family paid a visit to Xuanming's family. There she happened to see Yuxin's unusually fine embroideries. The consort was amazed; she had never before seen anything nearly so well done. She took a sample with her to show to the empress. Old Cixi liked it, so she immediately summoned Xuanming's mother, Lady Yang, to the palace, and to show her fondness she asked that Lady Yang bring along her youngest daughter.

Lady Yang trembled at the thought of visiting the empress. A distant relative, Yang Rui, had been involved in the Hundred Days' Reform in 1898 and was arrested. Lady Yang's family, however, was not investigated. Whether it was an oversight or an intentional pardon, the family was off the hook. In the past, the family relied on their powerful connections with consort Zhenfei and her sister consort Jinfei to enter the palace. After the Hundred Days' Reform, consort Zhenfei was imprisoned by old Cixi, and there had been no word of her after that. Lady Yang had been in the palace for a long time, and she was aware of old Cixi's tricks. It was particularly worrisome to her that old Cixi wanted to see her youngest daughter, Xuanming. Her husband was not at home, thus leaving Lady Yang at a loss.

The consort was amused at Lady Yang's fears. "The old empress is in good spirits today, don't ruin her mood! Just choose one or two of the best embroideries and bring them along. You have nothing to fear." Lady Yang gathered up all the embroideries in her possession and off she went, together with Xuanming and the consort.

Xuanming remembered that day clearly. She had of course dressed in her best clothes. She saw an old woman dressed in golden satin sitting upright on her throne, a dragon chair. Her dress was embroidered with large peonies and her crown was lavishly decorated with jewels, a jade phoenix, and fresh flowers. She wore a dazzling robe over her dress made of 3,500 perfectly matched large pearls, with each one attached to a bit of jade, and all strung together in a fishnet pattern. Xuanming thought to herself what a shame that encased in such beautiful jewelry was an old, dried-up woman.

Xuanming recalled that her mother was speechless when she saw the old woman. She kneeled down three times and kowtowed nine times, chanting something Xuanming couldn't understand. Upon completing the obeisance, she ordered her daughter to do the same. But then, very unusually, the old lady suddenly extended her hands to the girl and took Xuanming in her long-sleeved arms. "She needn't perform a formal curtsy," she said. "How old is she? She is very clever with words. Why not leave her with me at the palace? She would be good company." Lady Yang kowtowed once more. "Old Buddha is much too kind, the girl is spoiled, lacks training, and is sometimes naughty. She may disturb you."

Old Cixi threw back her head and laughed heartily. "I am just having a little fun. I know she's the apple of your eye, I wouldn't think of taking her from you!"

She was punctuating each clause of each sentence with her hands, sometimes pointing directly at Lady Yang's bosom with the golden caps on each of her long fingernails. Xuanming was amazed to see the old woman, addressed by people as Old Buddha, behaving so intimately. She was quite human! Not a bit frightening, as rumor had it. But Xuanming's mother remained terrified, unable even for a moment to relax her face or let down her guard. Eager to change the subject, she rushed to open the bag of embroideries, saying, "Look, these were all made by a relative of mine. The needlework is not bad. If Your Highness likes any of them, please keep them and treat them as small rewards."

The empress began looking at them carefully, her rheumy eyes opened wide. Xuanming noticed that her mother was still trembling visibly. The scene brought forth a fleeting insight: what an incredible feeling to be a woman who is above all and who holds everyone in awe. How pathetic to be a person like her mother who has to behave according to the colors of other people's faces, and thus be controlled by them. Xuanming resolved that in her adult life she would rise above all this.

Then that old voice came again: "Am I so ignorant? Or are my eyes not focusing?" Calling to the head eunuch and his sister, who were standing in the corner by the curtain, she said, "Little Li and Big Girl, come and have a look! I had no idea that such fine work was possible! We must burn all the other things of this kind presented to the court as gifts!"

Li Lianying and Big Girl Li came forward and kneeled. "Old Buddha, your ladyship's eyes are not fooling you," said Li. "This needlework is unique. We who are your humble slaves are so lucky to get to see such treasures!"

Big Girl Li was also sighing with astonishment. The empress raised her eyes and smiled, saying, "Arise! All of these are exceptional. If I kept them all, I could be accused of misusing my power. You have no idea how the rumors fly around here. I would like your daughter to choose a couple of things from the palace so that we can have a more or less equal exchange of gifts."

Lady Yang could not suppress her unctuousness. Once more she prostrated herself, pushing her head down on the polished floor as though mashing a clove of garlic with her forehead. "Your Highness, please! This humble slave is embarrassed! I worried that you wouldn't like them. Don't mention these pieces. My family members owe their lives to you! We can't be happier if you should like some." Cixi nodded her head. "You are thoughtful. Still, we should have an exchange." Xuanming suddenly spoke up in her clear, girlish voice: "Your Highness, I request a reward."

Lady Yang immediately gestured to the girl to be quiet, but the empress stopped her. "Let the child speak. Such a little girl, a child's words are harmless!"

The reward Xuanming requested stunned both heaven and earth. She asked to meet with her aunt, consort Zhenfei, and have her picture taken with her.

4

Yu had become obsessed with the idea of seeing the tattoo on her back. The only way to do this, she thought, would be with a photograph, but it must be a reliable person. For some reason, she was reluctant to ask Yadan, but Grandma was quite old, her hands might shake too much and the photo would be out of focus.

But Yu could see the two plum blossoms on her breasts, just above the nipples. They always reminded her of that young monk, Yuanguang. Time had made his young face more handsome. That night she dreamed of a window opening quietly in a soundless night. A huge shadow illuminated by moonlight moved across the adjoining wall. And then she saw an enormous bird slowly flying toward her through the window. Strangely, the apparition was not scary, perhaps because the bird was calm and its eyes peaceful. But her eye contact was suddenly interrupted as the bird lay down beside her bed, and then, after glancing away for a moment, she could see that what had entered her room and was displayed by her bed was not a bird at all, but a *kasaya*, a Buddhist monk's patchwork outer vestment.

This was a familiar garment, not only its color but also its smell. When she suddenly woke up the vestment was gone but its odor lingered, an odor that somehow impelled her to do something out of the ordinary. She delved into Yadan's writing. She picked up one sheaf of paper titled *Q&A Behind Bars*.

She strolls along a tree-lined path in the evening breeze, the last rays of the setting sun casting a lonely shadow. She is about twenty years of age. Fate has doomed her to be lonely. In appearance, she is quite unlike the girls in this city, those fashionable, contented, sentimental girls. Her eyes are deep and clear and she projects a gaze that commands attention: at once curious, authentic, and purposeful. She is a knowledge-seeker, and that alone sets her apart from others of her generation. Three years of chaotic existence have not diminished her vision.

What does she want to do?

She wants to seek truth.

Several years ago when she was still a schoolgirl she began her quest for eternal verities, reading everything that might shed light. She came across quotations on "truth" by historical figures, quotations such as: "The life of one person is valuable, but the truth of an entire generation is more valuable. If death ensures truth will prevail, such death is worthwhile." Deeply buried in her heart, this has become her motto. Yes. To die in defense of truth; how glorious that is! She is full of romantic fantasies about pouring out her "pure heart" for her country.

Then three years ago on that unforgettable morning, fate threw her out of a pink almond candy wrapper, and she began to taste the true life.

The best years of one's life were gone, gone in such a way that it felt like a nightmare. Harsh labor destroyed her health and ruined her beauty; her first blossom of wisdom and emotion was crushed. But she did not give in.

Her quest for knowledge continued. Finally she concluded that truth in this society is wedded to power, and that leaders have been endowed with the godlike power to determine that their latest utterance is the essence of truth. A horse is called a deer one day but the next day it becomes a horse once more. They can never give a convincing explanation, but demand others to unconditionally "follow closely." In the herd of obedient followers, one cannot avoid being singled out as a scapegoat to be slaughtered. Truth is brutally ravaged and castrated. She weeps, demands her true identity be returned to her. But in this society smart people don't play jokes with their own life. Truth becomes cheap, meaningless, and as tasteless as a marriage without love.

Life is at a crossroads.

One road is smooth, garlanded with olive branches, red-carpeted, and leads to fame, money, social status, favoritism, convenience, and a happy, cozy family. In short, one can have all personal gains. Another road is a winding, bumpy path, overgrown with bushes; with tigers, lions, and wolves peering out of the dark, hiding somewhere along the way. This road leads to a dangerous life, endless physical pain, mental torture, unknown blacklists, shameless smearing, imprisonment, and disaster for families and descendants. On this road, no comfort, no personal happiness is in sight.

But years later, ten years or a thousand years later, history—the honorable judge—will give people a well-deserved judgment. There are always two ways to live a life: one is short, the other eternal, with sun and moon.

Which way to go? It's time to choose.

"The road is vast and long, I shall seek high and low," she murmured— Qu Yuan's poem—in the gray twilight on her stroll.

Suddenly, she heard a wave of singing blended with the breeze.

"Feeling the pain of no freedom
You lost glorious life.
In our hard struggles,
You bravely sacrificed your head . . ."

It was a male voice, depressed, low, and riddled with emotion. In the midst of the light breeze, the song was very touching.

What is this? At this time and place, singing such a song? Is this an illusion? She stopped to listen attentively.

"Bravely, you sacrifice your head bravely . . ."

The sound became lower, as if the singer was intoxicated with his own song. She never heard such a sad and touching voice. She stood, felt her hot blood trembling with weakness. She hadn't felt such emotion for a long time.

"Glorious Sacrifice." She certainly knew the name of the song. It was a famous song during the Soviets' fight against the fascists. Now she was driven by a strong curiosity, oblivious of the descending darkness and cool evening air seeping into her burning flesh. She wanted to know who in this deserted shooting range sang "the forbidden song" without fear.

Jumping over wild bushes and a watery ditch, she arrived at a gloomy house. It was dilapidated and dirty, but quiet and dark. Since this shooting range was shut down, almost no one had come here, not to mention a girl, to be in the dark alone. To come to this place, she must have been brave.

The song suddenly stopped. Deadly silence was all around; tall, black trees waved like strange beasts in the cool air, sending out a soft swooshing sound. In the mysterious gray gloomy shade, there seemed to be a pyramid of eyes and a sense of frightening fear surrounding her.

She held her breath and looked inside through the iron fence. Under the pale moonlight, behind the bars, there stood a tall young figure. She was scared and suddenly remembered the rumor of an important criminal prisoner locked up here.

5

"Yadan, I want to see the world outside this room."

"The outside world is horrible. It's better you don't see it."

"But it's equally horrible inside the room if you stay inside all day long."

"Comparing with the outside world, it's safer here."

"I don't want safety."

"What do you want, then?"

"I . . . I want to seek, I want to discover . . ."

"You will know you will find nothing, discover nothing."

"But I have looked. What I wanted to find may not be visible, may not be things that have shapes."

"But once you walk out of this room, you may never be able to come back in."

"Why?"

"Not everyone has such luck: able to come and go freely. The door to this room is a threshold to you."

"Then what kind of person can realize that kind of good fortune, can come in or go out anytime he or she pleases?"

"Someone who has practiced religious discipline."

"Someone like you?"

"No—I am totally unsuitable."

"Then I can undergo such religious discipline."

"Then you will have to think the matter through carefully. Not everyone can successfully undergo such discipline. The Monkey King, Sun Wukong, is the only being who has successfully used the pills from Laozi's immortality oven to achieve Nirvana."

"Do you mean to say that if I don't successfully emerge from such discipline, I'll end up as a heap of dust?"

"Yes. Wouldn't you regret that?"

"No, I would not."

6

In Yu's eyes, Yadan's image has changed. She was no more than an average-looking girl, thin above the waist, a bit thick below, like an old-fashioned plaited willow water pitcher, such as those used by the peasants in north China, with an unremarkable face. But now the girl who wrote *Q&A Behind Bars* has become an enigma.

It was Yadan who brought Yu to the outside world. It happened on an evening in springtime when so many things start at this time of year. Both girls breathed in the spring in the air. Yadan removed her blouse, put it close to her nose, and inhaled. "It smells of spring; can you detect this?" asked Yadan.

Then, with Yadan holding Yu's hand, they walked into the darkness. Yu's lower back had healed. Yadan felt that the person she was holding by the hand was weightless, floating unsteadily like a spirit at the will of the wind. Only her eyes had substance, flashing this way and that, glittering and reflective in the dark.

They walked together into a *hutong*, an alleyway in the western part of the city. Well along the alleyway, they came to a courtyard, and facing the courtyard a room with illuminated windows, where Yu could see many people, some standing, some sitting. Yu was a little frightened and stayed just behind Yadan, looking closely at each of the strange faces in the room. Suddenly there appeared a familiar and very handsome face. He should have been bald, but now his black hair had grown in neatly. She was startled, and her heart began to race. What had appeared before her was a soul from her previous life, yet visible in stark clarity. She was unprepared for this moment. She was reminded of the unresolved whisper: what you longed for is about to arrive. Was this the man she had been longing for?

It was Yuanguang.

7

"I know you. You are Yuanguang," she said.

"I am not called Yuanguang. I am Zhulong," he replied, slightly startled.

Smiling inwardly, Yu thought, what's the difference? Call him Yuanguang, or call him Zhulong, it's still him; it cannot be anyone else. He is the monk from Jinque Temple on Xitan Mountain, the man who merged her body with his and then engraved two little plum blossoms just above her nipples, which had now turned blue. She thought to herself, now I have found the person who can take a photograph of my tattoo.

Then Yu was amazed to see Yadan, the average-looking Yadan, suddenly open up like a flower, alluring as the chrysanthemum or some richly colored broadleaf plant. She was also blazing, so hot one could feel her heat from afar.

She and Zhulong stood in the center of the room and began a dialogue that Yu could not understand:

Yadan (excited, voice trembling): "Tell me, who are you? Why are you here?"

Zhulong: "I am a man who has been condemned to death. They put me here to be away from the world."

Yadan (even more agitated, eyes ablaze): "Why . . . why were you sentenced to death?"

Zhulong: "Don't ask. You are too young to be told."

Yadan (insistently, in tears): "No, I want to know. And I am not so young. I understand everything."

Zhulong: "Lower your voice. There are guards nearby."

Yadan looked around; Yu instinctively also turned and looked. Outside there were only the black shadows of trees waving in the wind.

Zhulong: "I thought my life's journey would end here without anyone knowing. It didn't occur to me that God would arrange an opportunity for me to express myself one last time. You must be frightened to see me like this. This is because young people are accustomed to seeing beautiful things and hearing positive propaganda. You are unwilling to hear, see, or believe in what is evil, ugly, and dark."

Yadan: "No! I am not that kind of person!"

Zhulong: "All right, I shall tell you my story . . ."

Then Yu heard a bearded man next to her shouting, "Stop! This part is finished. Now start again from 'Give me a supporting point.' Once again, start!"

Then Yu saw Yadan and Zhulong trading positions. Yadan's face was so red it looked like she was bleeding.

Zhulong: "Remember, Archimedes said, 'Give me a place to stand and I will move the world.' I believe that in political life, freedom of speech is just such a base point for leverage. Although it is not everything, it is the most visible, essential, and fundamental of freedoms, the one freedom upon which all others depend. Those who oppose this concept are afraid that free speech will undermine the foundation of the established order; they actually believe that wrongful thoughts are more powerful than righteous thoughts."

Yu found these ideas hard to understand; she was also puzzled by the transformation in which Yuanguang had become Zhulong, yet retained elements of his previous existence: his face, hands, and even his smell and bored expression.

Zhulong: "I'll stop here, I've said too much . . . It's going to rain, hurry home." (As if to prove his prediction, from the background came the rumble of timpani and the clash of cymbals. Yadan was frightened and fell into his arms.) "Hurry! Go!"

Yadan: "How long will you be kept here?"

Zhulong: "Not long. It will be finished by four this morning."

Yadan (suddenly in a panic, panting rapidly): "What!"

Zhulong: "You . . . what?"

Yadan: "I'm thinking . . . we should die together! At least once in our lives we should be true to ourselves, true to our identity! Now is the time!"

At this moment the timpani and cymbals grew very loud and the beat much faster. In the background a chorus began chanting, but not in unison.

First male:
> *The stench of blood and death is everywhere,*
> *Blows are struck but find no target.*

First female:
> *The night rages on and on,*
> *The storm takes full control.*
> *But the wind can wail no more.*

Second male:
> *The moon, so very, very old,*
> *So, too, may I be ancient.*

Second female:
> *You are a graceful wound,*
> *Your heart floats in the moonlight of midautumn,*

> *Not a shred of red cloud.*

Then suddenly, Yu heard a clear voice:

> *Debasement is the password of the base,*
> *Nobility the epitaph of the noble.*

The lights go out, the curtain descends. It is a very heavy curtain, impenetrable to light and sound, a barrier that separates the play from Yu.

8

Many years later in America, I saw a play called *Black Widow* that was staged in a famous theater. There I also saw a sculpture made of pure silver, adjacent to which stood a huge mussel made of metal. It was actually a metal framework and black feathers were glued to it in the shape of a mussel. Inside the opened mussel a naked woman revealed herself; slowly the mussel opened and closed, its motion imperceptible but for a slight tremble.

When it opened again, the woman was visible again. So secretive and so quiet, she concealed herself under her second protective skin—the black feather, which became her prison. It was a kind of solitude, but more a self-protection.

The naked woman presented herself as a virgin, and maybe she was. A virgin can look like a loose woman and a loose woman can very well be a virgin. Perhaps a virgin should look like one and a loose woman should not try to look like something else. But two negatives, one added to the other, may sometimes yield a positive.

How did that huge mussel that belonged to my childhood find its way to America? Many a play had I seen in my life, but only two of them left a deep impression: *Q&A Behind Bars*, and *Black Widow*.

9

Since she was very little, Yadan had dreamed of becoming a knight; yes, a female knight. When she was only eight or nine she could recite poems written by the nineteenth-century woman rebel Qiu Jin.

It's our own fault our country is in turmoil,
That I must wander homeless everywhere,
My blood boiling, afraid to look around me,
My gut as cold as frostbitten spring blossoms.
I'd spend everything for a fine sword,
And boldly swap my finery for wine;
My boiling blood raging in fury,
Threatening to become an encompassing blue wave.

That vivid phrase, "boiling blood," appears frequently in Qiu Jin's poems, and Yadan found that it resonated with her own feelings. Later, it was the "boiling blood" that ruined her.

When she was fourteen, while playing rough games with some boys, a sudden gush of boiling blood poured out. Surprised and embarrassed, she stood against a wall, hands behind her back, announcing, "I am not playing anymore."

Not so easily do boys give up their games, and they pulled and pushed her along. As she slowly sank to the ground, she began to cry, but even then they persisted, dragging and bullying, and this went on until it was nearly dark. Only then did she peel herself away from the wall, knowing that "boiling blood" had soaked through her clothing.

From then on, Yadan lived alone with her secret, dealing privately with a condition for which her mother had not prepared her. Nor were there any books on the subject back then. At times when the blood was due to come and had not appeared, or the days when it was supposed to stop but did not, she experienced terrible anxiety as well as pain.

She could not keep "pure thoughts when alone," as Confucius had advised. When she was alone she felt an irresistible desire to explore and caress her quietly changing body. One night when the moon was full she removed her clothes and opened the curtain, letting a bright shaft of light illuminate her rapidly growing breasts—like porcelain, she thought, yet pliant. Massaging both breasts, she felt a surge of current, like electricity, and an all-consuming excitement gripped her body in its deepest recesses, but centered just there! And as she touched that spot the electric current surged again and again, and a sudden flame of excitement drove away all other sensation until she began writhing, twisting, trembling from head to toe. It was fully ten minutes before she regained her equilibrium, and then wished she had never indulged in the game. In fact, so strong was the shame that she resolved never again to indulge in such a wicked act. But so strong was the urge that she could not resist its attraction. When her next period came and the desires returned, she repeated the massage, with the same result.

It was only years later that Yadan learned that this phenomenon had a name—female orgasm. It was a feeling of pleasure and satisfaction like no other; yet many women, she learned, would never experience it. Two people are not required, no need to search to the end of the land for the other half created by God; no need to follow the procedures created by civilized society. The whole thing is so simple! It can be one person's joy and pain, one person's enjoyment and sacrifice—entirely one's own. Many years later Yadan realized the deep love given to her by God; yet many people do not find the key to the secret door in their entire journey through life. But God granted her the ability to decipher it at a very young age.

Unfortunately, enjoyment comes with a cost. Several years later Yadan found that she seemed to be aging more quickly than other women; could this be the result of her secret activity? Could this affect her facial skin and cause her breasts to grow loose and flat? She believed that it did, but she could not control her desire. She thought that the only way to manage the problem was to find a man to love her, someone who could provide love, not just sex. Someone she would love, too. Love and sex are two different things. Sex born from love is different from pure sex. The man who could love her would undoubtedly rescue her.

But for many years, the man who could love and be loved never showed up. She thought she looked much older than her years. And then, at age twenty-five, she met Zhulong, the man she had been waiting for.

10

The people in the play, including Yushe and Yadan, made a trip to a suburban town more than a hundred kilometers outside the city. They were all riding beat-up bicycles, singing and laughing as they pedaled along the roads. They were young and healthy, and their hormones—even though in those days they had never heard of such a substance—increased their vitality.

Along the way they came to a huge lake. Groves of trees clustered about its banks. Around much of the lake ran a broken wall, with vines climbing up the sides and through the cracks. Where plump green leaves touched the water there were fish hiding below. Above the water robins hid in the shade of the trees; all was peaceful and quiet. Yu saw Yadan changing into her swimsuit, which left her looking like a magnolia, her body full, white, and beautiful. Her firm and full breasts showed plainly through the fabric and were visible in all their contours. She was now swimming right behind Zhulong and the two of them moved off into the distance. Yu slipped into the water.

Although she couldn't swim, Yu found the water relaxing; it seemed much like wading in that lake that was filled with her childhood stories. Now the water was above her shoulders, like a cool, silky satin lightly touching her body; she felt buoyant, able to move gracefully and easily in any direction. Moving her arms, she felt she was flying through the sky, then stopping to rest on the clouds, which had somehow turned from white to blue, rising and falling. Through the water washing around and over her she could see that the sun was gradually sinking, and that it seemed to be doing so in the same rhythm as the rise and fall of the water.

She swirled her toes around the sandy bottom, flexed her legs up and down, and again experienced the silky satin of the water as it caressed every surface of her body; it was an unprecedented moment of tranquil beauty. Warmth was circulating through the interior of her body and her blood was being purified; her organs were being washed, and so, too, the acupuncture meridians, those channels flowing with vital energy. In the quietness, she heard hundreds and thousands of voices, as though coming from a symphony orchestra; she was hearing the fugue of the universal soul.

The music and Yu seemed to have known each other before this moment. Therefore, she forgot time, forgot her own existence, and was unaware that twilight had come to the lake. But now a man was standing at the edge, looking at her through water so clear that even by starlight the bottom was visible. The man saw a pure white shadow, silent as the moon. When a star fell next to her, the man could see her entire body, with all its blood vessels and organs, translucent as a jellyfish.

But none of this startled the man. What arrested his gaze was the tattoo on her bare back, a work of rare perfection, and the two plum blossoms on her naked breasts. His memory was stimulated by the plum blossoms; he recalled that in a dream long ago he once met a girl. He was enchanted by the girl's soft demeanor, coupled with her sure and certain sense of herself, and by her expressive eyes. She seemed unable to live in this world, this girl who made him weep in his dreams. How could she have been thrust into this rough and brutal world?

The man stood silently, that man named Yuanguang or Zhulong, withdrawn from the world, lost in thought.

11

Late in the evening, the girl called Yushe emerged from the lake, her thick hair weighted down with water, which streamed across her back and down her thighs. Her waist was so small it seemed like the neck of a vase. Her breasts were small, perfectly formed cones and her lower body emerged in a long, soft curve. As she walked, two curved lines seemed to glitter and sparkle as starlight caught the beads of water. About twenty feet short of Zhulong she stopped.

Although the girl was totally naked and totally visible, Zhulong was not touched by desire; this watery ghost could not arouse human passion. If moonlight could last for a year and thus open a water lily, this would be the result: fragile, proud, untouchable. The plum blossoms on her breasts, bathed in moonlight, radiated wisdom, like the words of the Buddha:

Her eyes are the beacons of a transcendent love,
Her arms as beautiful as golden pomegranates,
Her lips plead silently in the coral light;
Finally she departs through that door,
Once entering the river she has cleansed her soul,
And shines again like a white stone in the rain.
Without a backward glance,
She swims to emptiness, to her death.

Only fish in the ocean experience complete freedom,
From their silence we create vanity,
The success of this era brings us to a dead end.
Wisdom is not random though trees may well be so,
Those who are surprised are not emperors,
But dinosaurs.

"What is your name?"

"I am Yu."

"Why Yu? Feathers detached from wings don't fly, only drift with the breeze, because the wind controls the hand of fate."

"And you? Why are you called Zhulong?"

"Zhulong is Zhurong, the ancient fire god. My mission is to bring fire to the dark."

"Yu, have we really met in some other time?"

"Yes, I've seen you before."

"Time and place? Do you remember?"

"Certainly. Jinque Temple, Xitan Mountain . . . after a big snowstorm."

"Master Fa Yan. You must remember him."

"Then the tattoo on my body, surely you remember that?!"

Almost in anger, Yu turned and showed her back to Zhulong.

The man called Zhulong looked closely in the moonlight. A feathered serpent was coiled around her vertebrae. He felt a sudden pain but said nothing. He did not want to say anything.

Looking at his expression, Yu felt her heart breaking piece by piece. She and this man had been so close, so intimate, his contours so merged with hers that their bodies became one. His expression, his smell, the sweat on his face had mingled with hers. It was he who drew from her those drops of virgin blood; the two of them together could generate steam amid the crystalline snow. But now snow had given way to moonlight, and what was cold remained so. She must recognize this reality: that he does not recognize her.

"I would like to ask you to take a picture for me."

"Why?"

"I just want to see the tattoo."

"All right. Your tattoo is very beautiful."

And right at this moment Yadan appeared from the shadows. A few words destroyed the amber island.

"Yu, get dressed quickly! Do you want the security patrol to arrest you?"

Yadan emerged fully from the shadows; like an angry hunter she charged at the fence that was confining the prey.

| THE SQUARE

1

Ruomu was twenty-six when she entered university. Rumor had it that money was offered to the school by her well-connected father. Decades later, Ruomu insisted that she had earned her entrance by passing the examinations. Shu'er, her personal maid, defended her mistress, saying such criticisms were merely the result of envy. Shu'er, unmarried all her life, was always completely loyal to her mistress. In the family, she was called Sister Tian after the age of thirty and Aunty Tian after forty.

Perhaps Ruomu did pass the entrance examinations, because that whole summer, after Meihua had been forced to marry the male servant Old Zhang, Ruomu shut herself in her white-as-a-snow-cave boudoir, not even going as far as the grape trellis outside her room. The only ones who could enter her room were her mother and Shu'er. For many weeks, Shu'er burned ambergris incense after cleaning Ruomu's room to mask its bad odor. She didn't know that it was Ruomu's own body odor caused by drainage from an infected cyst in her armpit that Ruomu had scratched until it broke open. Every day Ruomu used a powder given to her by her father's Belgian doctor-friend as a deodorant.

On the first day of school, Xuanming followed her daughter into the classroom. As Ruomu settled into a front-row seat, her mother planted herself in the back row, and taking out her embroidery, she began to work on it casually while listening to the lecture. Students, who had heard about what happened to Tiancheng, turned around in astonishment, thinking she must be suffering from one of her mental episodes. Ma Jing, the professor, was known as a no-nonsense man at Jiaotong University. Seeing the wife of the bureau director in his class, he approached her. Despite trying hard to contain his anger, he blurted out, "Old lady, please go home!"

Her needle was moving deftly, and without raising her eyes, Xuanming simply said, "Why? Am I bothering you?"

"No, old lady, but this classroom is not open to everyone!" Professor Ma regretted these words as soon as they slipped from his tongue. The director's wife had a stormy temper; she could be a formidable enemy.

For once, Xuanming restrained herself. She gave an impish grin, saying, "Mr. Ma, I had only private tutoring. I've never been in a classroom before and now I find it quite interesting." She asked the esteemed professor to be generous with her and even offered to pay tuition.

Ma Jing was speechless. From that day forward, Class Two of the Department of Management at Jiaotong University had an extra body—an old lady, a sit-in student. She always kept herself spotlessly clean, even during the times when she was suffering from a mental breakdown. When she was ill, someone wrote to Heshou. Although he didn't write or visit, he sent money, enough to pay for her treatment and to provide better food for Xuanming and her daughter. They had been living on a diet of bean sprouts, the only thing available. For the first time in a long while, she sensed the importance of having a man in her life, but she was not about to yield to him just because of this. She saved the shining white silver dollars and used the money to open a small store, selling groceries and an odd assortment of other items, including embroidered pillowcases and the cheongsams that she and her daughter no longer wore. The business prospered.

When she was young, Xuanming acquired a taste for clothing in modest earth tones that gave her a look that was classic but never extravagant. In the summer she often wore a black satin cheongsam or a white linen blouse and pants. But her daughter could be moderately flamboyant—sometimes wearing a feathery satin cheongsam in a golden pear color, with raised embroidery, depicting a peacock tail trimmed with dark green and silvery white threads. Another of the daughter's satiny cheongsams was pale red, with a heart-shaped crystal pin on the collar. Sometimes Xuanming dressed her daughter in a beige silk blouse with matching pants, together with a dark silky shawl embossed with floral designs. But variety and good taste in Ruomu's clothing didn't seem to help her daughter's personal cause. Of the four female students in the class of thirty students, Ruomu was the only one without a boyfriend.

The other women were Guan Xiangyi, Mengjing, and Shao Fenni. Guan Xiangyi, wealthy and worldly, was older and engaged to a Professor Wang at the university before enrolling in classes. An average student, she was chubby but pretty, sweet, and articulate. Nothing could bother her and any dress was becoming on her. She soon became Xuanming's favorite houseguest; anything that might be troubling Xuanming would soon disappear in this girl's vivacious presence. Xuanming fell into the habit of cooking delicious dishes that pleased Xiangyi in exchange for the girl's great stories. Ruomu was unmoved by these stories, but all the other students were pleasantly envious of Xiangyi's seat at Xuanming's table.

Mengjing was the prettiest of the four girls. She was the only daughter of a clock repairman, a widower who doted on his daughter and encouraged her to attend university in order to enjoy a better life. She had been indulged in childhood and was a bit narrow-minded. Sometimes she would become upset over small things. Others would ignore this, but Ruomu would offer a caustic rejoinder, smiling sweetly so that Mengjing could not justifiably explode in anger. Besides, Mengjing had been deeply in love with Ruomu's younger brother, Tiancheng, which gave her another reason not to tangle with Ruomu. But her petulance and irritability were plain for all to see, whereas Ruomu was calculating and multilayered, each layer providing a protective coating to the one below and thus insulating her inner core from harm.

To Ruomu, Shao Fenni seemed the most difficult of the three. She was also the smartest and most accomplished—always on top of her schoolwork and a skilled pianist. She was able to penetrate below the surface of things and to know what you were thinking or about to say. She had pretty eyes, a delicate nose, a beautiful mouth, and an inviolable aristocratic air; but she couldn't be described as pretty. Her face had a yellowish hue that made her seem perpetually ill. During class she would take out a handkerchief and softly cough into it. Fenni reminded Ruomu of Lin Daiyu, the leading—and tragic—female character in the classic Chinese novel *Dream of the Red Chamber.*

And so Fenni was the focus of male students' attention in Ma Jing's management class. Xiangyi was articulate, well organized, and secure in her status as fiancée of Professor Wang. As a result, she was deeply respected by everyone. Mengjing, young and pretty, was generally tolerated despite her occasional bouts of irascibility. But Ruomu, poor Ruomu, seemed to lose out on all counts, which instilled in her a great sense of loss. Sometimes Ruomu wanted to take the initiative in socializing with male students, but confidence, the one thing she needed in this endeavor, was just not quite there for her. Perhaps all of this was the bad residue from her "first moldy love."

But that was not the case with Xuanming, a strong character throughout her life, who would never beat a fast retreat without putting up a fight. Her constant presence in the lives of these students changed the equation. For four years, she sat at the same desk, her tiny and beautiful feet tucked under her, seemingly focused on both her embroidery and the class, but nothing and nobody escaped her sharp and observing eyes. Those eyes of hers were hidden deeply, like a periscope under the sea. Her spotlessly clean sitting room became the informal salon for the class, where on holidays and during festivals she entertained other people from the university, as well as her daughter's immediate colleagues. Cooking, to her, was never a big deal; she could make first-rate Hunan dishes, needing Shu'er only to help with details. That's why, though almost thirty years old, Ruomu couldn't even make herself a simple bowl of noodle soup.

By that time Jiaotong University had been relocated to Qiao Jia'ao in remote Guizhou Province, to move farther away from the war against Japan in the north of China. Xuanming somehow for four years made extraordinary dishes for all these people on a small, coal-burning stove. Students helped her prepare the fuel. During the period of near-famine, when bean sprouts were virtually the only ingredient available in quantity, Xuanming found ways to combine them with spices and small bits of other foods to produce savory dishes that were prized by everyone fortunate enough to be invited to her home.

One day, Xuanming cooked a whole duck, simmering it for the entire day and then combining it with red wolfberries, green cilantro, black mushrooms, and yellow angelica root to make a soup, with droplets of oil floating on top. The duck meat was so tender that a chopstick could be used to break it apart. The guests were Xiangyi and her future husband, Professor Wang Jiewen, who was the head of the body of students and faculty—known as the Hunan Fellowship Association, who were all natives of Hunan Province.

As they were enjoying the succulent meal, Xiangyi said, "Aunty, I have made an inquiry on the subject you asked about."

"And what did you find out," the older woman asked, while placing a hand warmer, a small hot water bottle, in Xiangyi's hands.

"Lu Chen has a girlfriend. Guess who? It's Shao Fenni!"

"Shao Fenni? That sickly ghost!" Xuanming was intrigued by this news, but was not surprised. Shao Fenni had the best academic record among the female students in the class, she was attractive and intelligent, and Xuanming feared that Ruomu could not compete for the romantic interest of such an outstanding young man as Lu Chen. But Fenni was not well; she could be heard coughing in every class, and Xuanming would sometimes put down her embroidery, so disturbing was this evidence of frail health. Lu Chen seemed not to notice, and as the intellectual leader among the students, he was naturally inclined to favor the most outstanding of the female students. But to Xuanming, the incipient "love" among the young people seemed no more than games among children, subject to the ebb and flow of immature emotion.

Professor Wang burped from deep in his abdomen, a sure sign of having eaten a little more than necessary; and then he deftly reached with his chopsticks for one more irresistible morsel and became deeply absorbed with the beginnings of its pleasurable journey through his system.

"This Sunday the Hunan Fellowship Association will have its big party, right?" inquired Xuanming. "Let's make that an occasion to get Lu Chen and my daughter together!"

Xuanming's words were to have a decisive effect on the future of her family.

Lu Chen was unanimously regarded as the most outstanding student in the entire Jiaotong University. This much became known to Xuanming within a week of her joining her daughter's class as a "sit-in" student. Soon she made inquiries about his family and his past, and then observed him carefully for three full years.

To make Xuanming happy was not an easy thing.

2

The weather was cooling down, as if the heavens were aware of Xuanming's scheming, and Fenni's illness became worse. One day, she went to see a doctor without telling Lu Chen, where she encountered Xiangyi. Xiangyi looked at her with loving concern, saying, "You look more and more like the sickly Xi Shi, our ancient model of the beautiful woman. Why didn't Lu Chen accompany you?"

Fenni covered her mouth with her handkerchief and coughed twice. "I can't ask him to come," she said. "In truth, I wanted to avoid him. My illness is not a thing of a day or two. Why bother him with my problem? Besides, he is so busy with rehearsing for the show."

"You are truly selfless." Xiangyi smiled as she said this. "Most women would cling to their boyfriend, not caring about anything else."

Fenni was deeply impressed by this comment. Forcing a smile, she said, "Sister Xiangyi, we have been so close all this time, please tell me the truth: if this happened to you, what would you do?"

Xiangyi's face turned gentler. "I don't think about things in such complex ways. I'm inclined to simplify my problems and then act one way or another. If I were you, I would take a leave from school for a year, return to Hong

Kong to recover completely, then resume my studies. What's the rush? If Lu Chen cannot stand the test of being apart for a while, then perhaps his love is not as deep as it should be to spend your lives together. Do you agree?"

Fenni's tears welled up. "I think so."

Xiangyi took Fenni's hand and was surprised to find that it was very smooth, very cold and firm, almost metallic. By comparison, her own hands seemed more like flour dough—white, soft, and warm. Since entering the university, Xiangyi understood that she would spend her life working for the railway, that it would be her iron rice bowl, an utterly dependable source of sustenance. Ruomu's father, Qin Heshou, had worked for several decades in the railway system; his network of connections was like the railway lines extending throughout the entire country—rich and complicated. Xiangyi knew not a single student in this class could escape from this network. So she must get on the good side with Xuanming and Ruomu now.

Xiangyi nodded approvingly at Fenni's sensible decision. "I always knew you would do the right thing for yourself and others once you thought about it. Let's go to Aunt Xuanming's house and ask her to make something delicious for you."

Fenni raised her head, revealing tears that glittered. She wasn't a weak person, but illness could drain anyone's strength. "No, Sister Xiangyi. My illness is not welcomed at people's homes. Why bother Aunt Xuanming?"

But Fenni couldn't resist Xiangyi's persuasion. As soon as they walked into Ruomu's home, a fragrant draft of air caressed their nostrils. Xuanming was stir-frying the stuffing for moon cakes. The midautumn festival was just around the corner and she was making preparations. She was making twelve different kinds of moon cake, stuffed with many different ingredients: laurel blossoms, sugar, dried longans, red bean paste, lotus seed paste, ham, bacon, taro, date paste, five different nuts, shredded coconut, and salty duck egg yolks. She made the cakes in the shape of the twelve zodiac animals and placed them on a simple device for cooking, consisting of a flat sheet of metal raised above the little coal stove. The result would be moon cakes that tasted entirely different from those bought in the stores. Xuanming's stir-fried moon cake stuffing became the talk of Jiaotong University; the fragrance wafted all the way to the little store she maintained near their apartment, lingering for days. Anyone coming to the store would inhale it deeply and then say, "Mrs. Qin is making stir-fried moon cake stuffing. Midautumn festival will soon be here."

Fenni was not happy at the time of the festival. She worried about the changing season, especially about the weather that lay ahead. Since the end of summer she had suffered from a minor fever. Lately she had begun to see blood in her sputum, but didn't tell anyone. Her parents had asked her to return home during the festival, but she had been hesitating. Now all seemed clear.

Fenni chose a moon cake stuffed with salty duck egg yolk, and after one bite couldn't stop praising it. Xuanming quickly placed two more on her plate that were just off the hot stove and asked the girls to stay and eat. After several protests, Fenni agreed to eat just one more, which was stuffed with laurel blossom and sugar. She took one bite but couldn't finish.

"Not good?" asked Xuanming.

"Very good," said Fenni. "I'm afraid I cannot eat much because I'm not feeling well."

"I know about your weak health," said Xuanming, "so I used only vegetable oil, which is easier to digest. Ruomu can eat two pieces in one meal, and she's not as healthy as you are. Today, no matter what, you must eat this piece."

Fenni then had to finish the moon cake and sip some tea. "You are such a dear girl," said Xuanming.

"Where is Ruomu?" asked Xiangyi.

Xuanming gestured toward the bedroom. Xiangyi and Fenni both laughed as they walked into the room. Ruomu cut a comic figure, all elbows and hips, half on, half off the bed, leafing through a dog-eared copy of *Manon Lescaut*, a blank look on her face. Now the setting sun sent faint rays through the curtain, bringing some color to Ruomu's wax-pale face.

Xiangyi covered the book with her hand and smiled. "Hey, little bookworm, look who is here!"

Ruomu raised her eyes languidly. "Is it Fenni? Please sit down."

Actually, Ruomu was acting. She had followed every detail of their conversation with Xuanming, and only as they entered her room did she grab her copy of *Manon Lescaut* to use as a stage prop to cover her face. Her performance was convincing and now, masked by her look of woozy ennui, she was scanning Fenni for useful clues; in this game, Fenni was outmatched.

That day the performances staged by the mother and daughter reached a climax when the Belgian doctor arrived. It began when Ruomu casually remarked, "Ma, that Belgian doctor who treated you last time . . . is he still in China? Why not let Fenni give him a try?"

Dr. Hoffman specialized in neurology, internal and thoracic medicine, and even gynecology. With the exception of pediatrics and urology, he was competent to deal with just about anything. Ruomu's suggestion immediately met with Xiangyi's approval. And with no further prompting, Xuanming walked over to the old-fashioned telephone. Fenni looked nervous as the dial rotated through its staccato whirs and clicks. Fenni was wearing an old pale pink wool coat, her usually yellowish face now showing a bit of reflected redness from below. Her long, permed black hair was tucked inside the coat. Her appearance reminded people of a postponed if not faded glamour, like that of flowers that open and close quietly without reaching full blossom.

If Fenni had been more observant, she might have noticed that the Belgian doctor came a little too quickly. But Fenni was immersed in her own feelings of gratitude to these helpful friends. The Belgian doctor was courtly and respectful, and projected an air of professional skill that inspired confidence. Fenni felt entirely comfortable as he inspected her from head to toe, employing all the usual scientific instruments, taking a full three hours to probe all the usual orifices. As Xuanming brought hot taro soup and tea, the Belgian doctor assumed an air of utmost gravity as he announced that Fenni was suffering from tuberculosis, together with chronic bronchial asthma. He advised her to immediately stop attending classes to receive treatment; that if she did not follow his advice, the consequences could be serious.

Fenni's face turned from yellow to a pallid white. She took the bowl of taro soup from Xuanming, slowly stirring it with a porcelain spoon and a look of intense concentration, as the spoon slowly shattered into fragments . . .

Afraid to look up, Xuanming and Xiangyi kept their heads low as they ate. But Ruomu could no longer restrain herself and used the book as a cover while she watched Fenni's tortured face. She was afraid her twitching lips would betray her impulse to laugh.

After the guests had gone, Ruomu hid in her room and indulged in the first bout of completely hysterical laughter of her whole life. The sound was so piercing and sinister that it would have been truly frightening to anyone passing by. Meanwhile, Xuanming was standing on her tiny feet and pounding hard on her daughter's door, sounding a drumbeat that was strangely in tune with her daughter's shrieking, the two of them generating a cacophony such as had rarely been heard in Qiao Jia'ao.

3

Fenni left the mainland on a windy, moonless night. That night the entire university—teachers, students, and their families, and the various other professionals employed there—gathered in the auditorium to watch a Peking opera, *Shi Kong Zhan*, a complete three-part traditional opera set in the Three Kingdoms era (222–277 A.D.) of Chinese history, performed by students. Lu Chen played the lead role as the great strategist Zhuge Liang. As he walked on the stage, wearing a *bagua fu*, a long coat printed with the eight *yin-yang* trigrams, and waving a feather fan, he sang the classic lines, *"While I was viewing the mountain scenery from the city wall, I heard chaotic noises . . ."* As he sang, his eyes scanned the audience, looking for the familiar pink coat.

A few days prior to this, Fenni's parents had arrived from Hong Kong. At first Lu thought he should wait for them to propose a social get-together; then he realized that he was being a little too self-centered. But Fenni seemed to be hiding something from him. He worried about this but was silent, and rehearsals were taking much of his time. He thought that after the performance he would have a good conversation with her. He used the remaining pittance of scholarship money to travel more than thirty miles to Guiyang City's best pastry shop, where he bought a box of cookies for Fenni's parents. The cookie box was imprinted with three gilded characters: "Honorable Guest House." He thought this couldn't compete with what was available in Hong Kong, but at least it conveyed his good intentions.

The auditorium at the Qiao Jia'ao campus down in the south had been designed by some big-shot architect. The interior was lavishly decorated. Hanging from the huge dome were a crystal chandelier and a large banner—featuring the national railway logo and incorporating a red star in the design. Massive dark gray velvet curtains enclosed the stage. This was a luxurious facility, accommodating three thousand people for the presentation of a Peking opera, while a war was raging in the north of the country.

Lu Chen's costume was striking—a feather fan, black silk scarf, red and golden *bagua* symbols, all exquisitely designed and made. Lu Chen was not a trained artist, but enjoyment of Peking opera was a strong family tradition and he himself was a great opera buff. His father was particularly attached to the role of a dignified older male, the *lao sheng*, that had been developed by the famous actor Tan Xinpei. Naturally, this led to Lu Chen being heavily influenced by performances in the Tan style. He could not be compared to professionals, but he was amply qualified for a university production. On top of this, he was very popular in school, with the audience cheering him on during every musical interlude. Professors, rigid and stern-looking on other days, and female students, always models of decorum, now also shouted "Bravo!" with their hands halfway touching in a Buddhist gesture of reverence and their eyes squinted. It was a glorious event: stentorian shouts of approval mingling with the shrill reverberated from the marble surfaces of the great domed hall, and echoes of Lu Chen's vigorous voice seemed to linger for days on end.

> *When Sima's soldiers arrived,*
> *Skies were ablaze with their feathered flags.*
> *But our streets and strongholds were lost*
> *Because we had no strategies and skills,*
> *And our commanders were in discord . . .*

As he sang these lines, Lu Chen was trying to perk up his spirit, but deep within he felt despair. The pale pink wool coat that should have been part of this occasion was nowhere in sight. That old worn-out coat had become an eternal flower in his eyes, a heartbreakingly colorful flower whose beauty could lead to danger.

That was a night Lu Chen would never forget. The auditorium looked like a sacred temple, gaudy with lights but immensely dignified, as Lu Chen stood on the fresh grass and looked back at it. The locals had never before seen such a structure, and they talked about it excitedly as they returned from a street fair and gazed at its imposing facade. The sheer brightness of the lighting made them think something might happen. For people who lived in darkness, such light was long overdue.

That night some people saw a young woman dressed in a pale pink coat with a large-brimmed matching hat climbing into a horse-drawn carriage. The brim was not large enough to screen her melancholy expression as she sat between a couple that appeared to be her parents, who were well dressed and concerned about her comfort. The departure of this gloomy young woman dressed in that pale pink coat was quiet and slow, not so much a rolling on wheels as a floating away, from shining reality to dark vapors.

Lu Chen fell ill for some time. Whenever his eyes drifted to that *bagua fu* that he wore in his role as Zhuge Liang, he felt a stirring of nausea. The girl whom he deeply loved had left no message for him, except through Xiangyi, and it was cryptic: "Returning to Hong Kong. May not come back. Rest well. No need to make contact."

When Lu Chen began to recover, Xiangyi sent over a bowl of Xuanming's duck soup. Lu Chen found the old connection between stomach and spirit returning. When he asked for more, Xiangyi said with a grin, "Good. Let's go to Aunty Qin's home. You've lost weight, you need some good nutrition."

Lu Chen, after all, was a man with normal needs, not a monk or a saint. At a party at the Hunan Fellowship Association a few days later, Professor Wang Jiewen dragged him over to Ruomu, urging him to ask her to dance. As it happened, they didn't dance, but his interest was kindled. Lu Chen was a one-woman kind of guy. When courting Fenni, he paid no attention to other girls; now, after four years, and for the first time, he looked with romantic interest at another woman. Here was a pale, frail but supple figure, with eyes that were strangely lifeless. The white part of her eyes projected a glacial blueness. That, in fact, was her true color: cool blue. After the warmth of the pinkish hues that leaped out from Fenni's personality, this was a change, but after a bit of hesitation, Lu Chen accepted this new color scheme. Although his passion had not been rekindled, he found that the new object of his desires was clean, fresh, and acceptable.

The events that followed went very smoothly: Lu Chen was found frequently at Xuanming's table, tucking into duck soup and other dishes that were intensely flavorful; Xiangyi was happy to be matchmaker, Professor Wang to be host of the wedding. Mrs. Qin paid to have the ring made. The couple went to a photo studio to have photos taken. Eight banquet tables were arranged. It was not exactly what Mrs. Qin had in mind, but for wartime it was not bad at all. Lu Chen learned on his wedding night that the bride was a full five years his senior.

4

Lu Chen could no longer stand me. He frowned even at the sound of my footsteps. Since getting a duodenal ulcer he has been eating less and less. The doctor advised against oily or spicy food, but that's all we had. As the old saying goes, "Even a capable wife cannot cook without rice." Mother does the best she can with whatever we find at the market. Meat is rationed—we are permitted half a pound per person per month. Seafood is unavailable. To make our food more appealing, Mother adds oil and spices, but oil is also rationed. So she renders bits of pork fat and buys a little of the high-priced vegetable seed oil; this is the way we get by, and it's a disaster for any stomach.

As I grow older I am no longer content with sitting alone in a wicker chair and fumbling with the ear spoon. I need to walk around. I entered Yu's room the other day and despaired at what I found—a pigeon cage—that's what it's like. Stuff piled up, things I hate to even look at. Yu's strange treasures: spiders, centipedes, and bats with extended wings, all made with bits of wire that are now getting rusty. Her desk was covered with colored drawings and I began looking at them. One showed a reclining mummy dressed in a green copper cloak. A trickle of red blood oozed from the cloak. Two young girls who looked alike stood alongside, one at the head and the other at the foot, staring at the mummy.

Another picture showed what seemed to be the same two girls, but now grown up, their naked bodies elaborately festooned with beautiful Arabic jewelry. They appeared to be staring hypnotically at a large fish tank filled with water in which a deformed creature was transfixed by the women's gaze, as though under a spell. Adding to the chilling mystery, it had no body, only four limbs.

In the center of the third drawing there was a young girl facing forward. She had flaming red hair—a bizarre contrast to her sheer, cold face. Her entire body looked unrealistic, like dead white porcelain. Just in front of the girl there stood colorful wineglasses. Behind her was an open door, beautifully colored in gold and green. By the door was a mysterious woman with silvery skin. She had the appearance of someone just arriving for a birthday party, but was ignoring the girl. The girl's expression conveyed indifference to everyone and everything—even death, which somehow suffused the scene with a stillness that might have lasted a thousand years. The drawing expressed an unknown fear.

The next drawing was unfinished. A shepherd girl was shown dressed in an ancient Greek costume and seemed to be standing on clouds or in water. Surrounding the girl were sheep also on clouds or in water, and the sheep's hooves glimmered like the petals of cherry blossoms. The girl was cupping a shaft of ambiguous light in her hands. Above her was a pale sun, looking like its scarlet red had been sucked away. On top of the sun Yu had drawn a man without a head. The empty spot reserved for the head was cut out and had fallen into the hands of the girl. At the bottom of the picture a line read: "Apollo is dead."

Looking at Yu's drawings, I was astonished. They were scary, the work of someone who was demented. I thought to myself, "In the past I just thought she was a little strange, but she's really mentally ill." This was shocking. Treatment would be very expensive. Such were my thoughts for the next sixteen years, until the lobotomy was performed.

If the drawings had been the only evidence of Yu's weirdness, that would have been bad enough. But I couldn't resist the urge to look for more. Throughout my life I have had a strong inclination to snoop. Perhaps this can be traced back to the incident under the grape trellis forty years ago. Ah, that fragrant trellis—that was where I met my Waterloo. It opened for me a small part of the curtain of life, giving me an astounding glimpse of desire. But then the curtain was closed again. Desire concealed in colorful fabric: impenetrable, forever unknowable—that was what I had seen so briefly. To break through the wrapping would cost a lifetime of effort. I had made such an effort, but was unwilling to admit it. Whenever I hear people talk about their lives, their desires, I must cover my ears; on this subject, I am beyond hope.

For many years I have been tormented by hope alternating with despair. When feeling hopeless, I look around at others, and if they, too, are having such feelings I take comfort. Reading other people's letters and diaries gives me boundless joy. But Yu's diary was not interesting; it was filled with words I could not understand. Even words I understood seemed senseless—words such as truth, meaninglessness, jail cell, decay, absoluteness, black cotton, brass gong, nobility, indecency. Such words mean nothing to me, they are just more indicators that third daughter is mentally ill. As I leafed through more pages, some new lines jumped out at me:

> *Apollo is dead,*
> *Is Apollo dead?*
> *Let the dead die,*
> *Are the living souls*
> *already singing in the first morning light?*

I have studied classic poetry and prose, but these words were not poetic or in any way lyrical. They were signed by someone named Yuanguang. They gave me an uncomfortable feeling.

I had a good formal education, and in the old days I listened to broadcasts and read newspapers, although they were not important in my life. (Sometimes they made me fall asleep.) Today's young people cannot understand what it was like then; the government had an unusual method for communicating with everyone, all the time, through loudspeakers hung on walls everywhere—in shops, offices, homes, restaurants, public squares. Mostly it was just propaganda and, like the proverbial water torture, it never stopped. It produced some strange wonders; for example, it was very common for people who were mentally retarded or mute to go about chanting phrases such as "Long live" and "Boundless longevity." The media were an important tool for manipulating people's minds, especially in a society in which there was only one public voice for the whole nation, and almost no overarching beliefs or values apart from what was preached through the media. No matter how indifferent to the media I had been, I could tell that the message in these lines of poetry was wrong and would be regarded as reactionary. After all, I had not been out of touch with the world.

Such thoughts were stimulating. I wasn't cut out to be a housewife, and it was unfair that fate arranged for me to stay home. Now things were changing—Mama Wang Zhong was long gone, and my two elder daughters had left home. Yu had moved in with Yadan. Xuanming could think of nothing but her great-granddaughter, Yun'er. She didn't care to talk with me. The same was true of Aunty Tian. And Lu Chen was busy either writing self-criticism or reporting on others. He didn't even have time to see the doctor about the blood now showing up in his stools. Everyone had deserted me, no one cared about my thoughts or feelings, and this was unfair. So unfair.

That night I called Lu Chen to my bed. I tried to talk with him and became so emotional that I began crying. He just sighed, again and again. This scene had been repeated over and over in our nearly thirty years of marriage. Then I showed him the lines of poetry that I had found in Yu's room. He was stunned, and then shouted, "Bring Yu back! Bring her back home!"

As an echo to Lu Chen's roars, Yun'er started crying in the next room. It became louder. Mother and Aunty Tian rushed to the cradle at the same time. Aunty Tian lovingly picked up the tiny baby. As she fondly gazed at the infant, who lacked the beauty of her mother and grandmother, Aunty Tian began singing that song of years past:

> *Little Sparrow, little sparrow,*
> *Where has your mommy gone?*

5

Yun'er's mother, Ling, was hundreds of miles away, in a distant city in the northeast, sleeping with a man in a factory dormitory. That man was not Wang Zhong.

From when she was very small, Ling had enjoyed playing games, and her eagerness in this line far outstripped that of her mother. The man, whose name was Hu, turned out to be a teacher to both Ling and Xiao. He was short, hairy, and full of restless energy. He was divorced, and being a bachelor for the second time made it tough to pass the time. Among the few women he had eyed with interest, only Ling was easy prey. Best of all, her husband was working at a factory just far enough away.

Ling enjoyed rough sex and lots of it. After her wedding to Wang Zhong she soon lost interest in him—too conventional, no variety. But Hu was, for a time, all that she desired, at least in the bedroom. Both of them were insatiable and went to great lengths to inspire each other. One of her favorite games was to be tied to all four bedposts and then bend her strong and supple body into a beautiful arch, just like the woman in *One Thousand and One Nights*. Years later, when pornographic videotapes flooded into the area, Hu had the luck to see again that beautiful arch Ling had created for him.

Hu was amazingly good at finding the thin line between pain and ecstasy and then traveling that perilous boundary to prolong Ling's pleasure. He would lie on his stomach like a dog and employ his heavily coated tongue to explore every part of her lithe torso, sometimes gently, sometimes viciously. She would moan and scream and fling herself about in paroxysms of agony and pleasure, like a female cat rutting about with the neighborhood toms. They both enjoyed the constant search for variety and surprise.

Then one night, after hours of such carnal delight, Hu gave a great sigh. "Too bad," he said.

"What's too bad?" she responded, stretching her body to sit up, having forgotten that she was tied fast to the bed.

"Too bad you are so thin," he said, untying the ropes.

"You like chubby girls?" She was offended. "That's easy. My sister Xiao is quite fat. Go after her if you're so hot for more flesh!" She pulled the blanket up to cover her exposed breasts.

"Don't be childish. Why talk about other women? You are the best. I've always said you are the best."

Ling, who was also insatiable in her desire for compliments, swallowed everything Hu said, as she was always ready to believe the best about herself. Growing up, she had never felt much competition from her sisters when it came to the attention of men and boys. She disdained her younger sister Xiao. Everything about her was plain and her manner was clumsy. Xiao had nothing like her sister's coquettish eyes and seductive body. Such attributes come from birth; they cannot be taught. Like her grandmother said, "One mother can raise nine different kids." Ling's personality stemmed from invidious comparisons of Ling and Xiao offered by unthinking adults during the girls' childhood: she's so pretty . . . or clever, or cute—all with reference to Ling, as Xiao stood by, looking all the more awkward and slighted.

Now, perhaps to demonstrate her confidence in herself, she took the initiative to get Xiao involved. "Hu, my love, you should taste my sister's cooking. It's really very delicious."

As in all things, when preparing to cook, Xiao was very meticulous. She cleaned the rice thoroughly, got the right seasonings ready, and deftly added each item at the right time. On this occasion, she prepared twice-cooked pork, stir-fried string beans, and a local dish from northwest China called pork rolls. While Xiao was still preparing the soup, Ling and Hu had eaten most of the dishes Xiao had already served.

From childhood, Ling was so pampered by her grandmother that whenever there was good food Ling would always get a little extra put aside by Xuanming. No one complained except Ruomu. But Ruomu would only say it to Lu Chen and Lu Chen would get angry and condemn Ling for always "eating more and doing less!" Ruomu was a born politician, knowing how to balance problems and focus on main issues. The main problem in the Lu family was of course between Xuanming and Lu Chen. Their problem could be traced back to the 1940s when Lu Chen found out on his wedding night his bride was five years his senior. His immediate conclusion was that he had been deceived by someone, and that someone was none other than his clever mother-in-law. The old lady sat in the last row of his class looking as if she was paying attention only to her embroidery, but Lu Chen always felt a pair of eyes penetrating him from behind. As the years went by, Lu Chen and his mother-in-law disagreed about almost everything, including child rearing. Since Ling was Xuanming's favorite, she lost favor with Lu Chen. The opposite dynamic was at work with Yu and her father. Xiao was the classic middle child—not as much love, not much mistreatment either.

Xiao said nothing as she sat down to eat her soup. She was flushed and ate quietly. She was still quite pure, quite self-conscious in the presence of men. Her shyness stimulated Hu. He was experienced in seduction, and knew exactly what to do and say and how to conceal his motives. A few days later, when Xiao had gone to take a bath, she encountered him unexpectedly in a narrow space in the boiler room. He was calm and serious, and again she was flustered. She was wearing a loose-fitting T-shirt, no bra, not expecting to meet any men at this time and place. The free-swinging motion and detailed architecture of her breasts was revealed, and she knew it; instinctively she hunched her shoulders and turned away.

Hu looked slightly to one side and gave no outward sign of his excitement. He smiled reassuringly and said, "Thanks again for the great meal the other day." Then he pulled a Chairman Mao button from his pocket, one of those that shine in the dark and were still a novelty at the time. It emitted a greenish light in the dimly lit boiler room and Xiao was immediately interested. He took a step closer and, gathering a bit of cloth between his fingers, carefully pinned it on her shirt, taking care not to let the sharp point touch her skin but brushing against her left breast with the back of his hand—ever so lightly. Even this slight touch made her quiver and brought more color to her cheeks.

Within a month, everyone at the factory knew that Hu and Xiao had become lovers. In the evening, people often saw her sitting by the door of the workers' housing unit, busily knitting a pair of socks. One of the older women offered a pleasant greeting. "Take it easy, don't ruin your eyes. As they say, when night falls, chickens always return to their nests." Xiao just maintained her concentration, not wanting to profane something as serious as her newfound liaison by bantering about it with strangers.

Xiao could not have imagined that her affair had been orchestrated by her own sister. Ling was a pioneer in sexual liberation. Soon after reaching puberty she had resolved in her own mind questions that are subjects of endless debate among famous scholars—questions about the relative importance of love, sex, and family. She felt that these three things must be kept separate. All are important to women, and ideally none can be omitted. Love is a moving target—changing constantly, requiring constant renewal, and requiring of its participants that it be given and received without coercion. Sex is a thing of the moment. Presently, Hu was her sex. He could satisfy her cleverly, without restraint, and indulge all her secret fantasies.

As for marriage, no husband could be more ideal for Ling than Wang Zhong. He was loyal, considerate, romantic; and he followed her around like an obedient and well-trained dog. Best of all, at least for the present, he was not with her every day; even if he wanted, he could not control her. She wore her hair gathered in two clumps at her back, swinging from side to side, and she dressed in doll-like clothes. Old workers, when they saw the two girls together, would joke that "older sister looks young, younger sister looks old." Ling loved hearing jokes like this. So for the time being, with her beautiful eyebrows arched at twenty past eight, she enjoyed her career as a nubile female to the fullest possible extent.

Clever as she was, Ling had forgotten one important thing: life constantly changes. Personal attraction fades, and the end of a story cannot be foretold by reading the first paragraph or two.

Hu began to change. Subtly at first, then gathering momentum, his attraction for the two women gradually shifted in favor of Xiao. Ling would posture or smile in ways that had previously sent shock waves through his libido, but he began to ignore these signals. Meanwhile, Xiao quietly knitted sweaters and socks, ironed his clothes, and prepared perfect meals. More important, Xiao made no demands; to men like Hu, this was crucial. He gradually began to find excuses to avoid Ling, and that, unfortunately, stimulated her powerfully. Oblivious to a truth she could not easily believe, she would look for him with ravenous intent, even inventing small excuses for her be-havior: my younger sister is looking for Hu, have you seen him?

People at the factory looked on as the sisters' comedic duet played out. Finally, a female worker burdened with slight paralysis from polio gave Ling the ultimate answer: "Isn't your sister with Mr. Hu? The two of them sneaked into the woods after dinner. Didn't you notice?"

The scene in the woods has remained in Xiao's mind to this day. She saw her sister coming on her bicycle riding madly into the woods. Fire shot from Ling's eyes, enough to kill someone. As she arrived in a hidden coppice she threw her bicycle to one side and charged up to Hu. Hu was strangely calm, as if having anticipated this for a long time. Before Xiao came to grasp the gravity of the event, she saw her sister catch Hu fully across the nose and mouth with her open hand. A loud muffled sound followed, like a heavy object landing on a cotton sack, his blood spurting immediately, soaking his beard. An image of a red mist clouded the scene and obscured Xiao's vision. At that same moment a shrill torrent of invective pierced through the mist directly into Xiao's ears.

"You shameless, stinking hooligan! You ugly, hairy bastard! You don't de-serve either of the Lu sisters and you certainly can't have both of us! Xiao, if you are still my sister you will never again speak to this stinking hooligan!"

Ling was too impatient. Her emotions clouded her judgment. In this way she was like her grandma—when she blew her stack the explosion was enormous. Had she been more restrained, the results might have been totally different.

Xiao was dumbfounded but not in tears; she was shaken with a gush of nausea. Perhaps this gush of nausea is what people describe as the feeling of love. Then that alone is enough to break a human's heart. As the sun was going down, two blotches of "red cloud" had formed on her cheeks like fruit on a snowy day; Xiao looked so simple and homely. That pair of cloth shoes handmade by her grandma appeared still and quiet on her feet.

Her first love had been aborted before it had fully blossomed. She closed her eyes tightly, refusing to see herself without love. She knew that all her heart and soul had gone into this love, which was now gone, gone forever.

Following that, Ling lived amid the laughs and disdain. It had never oc-curred to her that despite her making such great efforts to launch this game, it would end in total disaster. Two months later Wang Zhong came to take Ling away after receiving an unsigned letter. No longer was he the adoring lapdog. "Ungrateful whore! Bitch!" After giving her a thorough beating, a taboo that, once broken, would be repeated, he realized he could never trust her again. The seeds of their divorce, which was to come ten years later, had been sown.

6

Ruomu felt uneasy as she knocked on Mengjing's door. She vividly remembered the day when Mengjing and Yadan dropped in on her for a brief visit some years ago, and then stayed for three years. Those were the years of natural disasters and famine. Ever since then, the Lu family had been in turmoil. Lu Chen had been banished to a remote place. Meanwhile, Mengjing had moved up in the world, marrying the president of Jiaotong University.

Ruomu had never bothered much with Mengjing when they were in college together. She was an attractive woman but the daughter of a clock repairman, a provincial by the standards of Ruomu's family. Always, in every phase of their lives, Ruomu had treated Mengjing as an object of scorn, but she never criticized her openly.

Mengjing was inclined to claim more of the family's affections than they were willing to give. She would describe her relationship to Tiancheng in idealized terms, emphasizing the depth of their love and their mutual respect, and insisting that Tiancheng's last days in this world were spent with her, and that Yadan was the result of their love. Perhaps the most disturbing thing of all was that she insisted on calling Xuanming "Mom." Ruomu, always on the alert for emotional weak spots, had learned to exploit this one. Whenever Xuanming was distressed about something, Ruomu would subtly introduce the subject of Mengjing's place in the family. Like a spark in a room filled with explosive fumes, this would ignite the old lady's pent-up fury, and she would give vent to her anger over Mengjing's presumptuousness and Tiancheng's premature death. No matter how cruelly Xuanming and Ruomu had treated Mengjing, Mengjing's marriage to the new president of the university represented her ultimate triumph.

Mengjing herself opened the door; each woman was surprised at the presence of the other. Always quick to adapt, Mengjing willed herself to smile, saying, "Sister Ruomu, please come in, you are an honored guest. I see you so seldom, please come and taste the excellent green tea I brought with me. It was a gift for my husband, our Old Yang."

Ruomu concealed her annoyance at the overly familiar "Old Yang." Mengjing constantly mentioned "our Old Yang" in her conversation, just like ever-so-handy Tiancheng was constantly brought up when she first arrived at Ruomu's house. But for all her disagreeable traits, Mengjing's vitality was admirable. She was constantly in motion, making things happen. When she walked, it was always with a quick motion, creating a little swirl of wind. To Ruomu, seemingly born to be mistress of a mansion and passive by nature, Mengjing's pace was dizzying. She was annoyed by Mengjing's youthful, energetic outlook, and by the fact that the two of them were aging so differently. After spending so much of her life in quiet repose watching other people work, Ruomu's steps were like those of a much older person, and she would grow tired after a short walk.

Ruomu kept her real feelings about Mengjing well hidden as she responded to the invitation to tea. "Ah, you are so kind. But I cannot drink tea. When our Old Lu was given some green tea I drank a small cup, but found it too stimulating. I couldn't sleep that night! The two cans of tea, this year's crop, are still at home; if you like, I'll give them to you."

Mengjing thought to herself this woman still had the air of the young mistress she was several decades ago and still liked to manipulate people. But Mengjing managed to smile and said, "Sister Ruomu must be here to see Yu. She went to work with Yadan as a temp. Didn't you know?"

Mengjing took malicious pleasure in watching Ruomu's face as she received this news. At first she turned pale, then color came to her cheeks as she snorted, "Damn that girl! Such a contrarian! As though we can't feed her, she has to go to a miserable factory to a temporary job! Shameless!"

"Shameless" was one of Ruomu's favorite words, and it reminded Mengjing of coming to this city alone with Yadan, and of all the insults of this kind they endured from Ruomu, most of them expressed behind their backs. Despite being classmates, and despite Mengjing's bonds with her brother, Ruomu had offered no affection, no respect, only calumny.

"Sister Ruomu, try to be open-minded. When children grow up, they must lead their own lives. You cannot control them. Look at our Yadan, she didn't even tell us about her boyfriend. Yu must be more than twenty by now. You can't always worry about everything they do."

However well intended, these words were a torch to Ruomu's pent-up anger. She had been holding a piece of paper in her hand, the one containing the lines of blasphemy she had found in Yu's musty room.

"You look at this," she screamed at Mengjing. "Talk about control, you should control your daughter! Yu is unsophisticated and naive and she cannot write such a thing. Look at this garbage!"

In a gush of ungovernable rage, Ruomu threw the paper at Mengjing and slammed the door loudly as she stalked out of the house. Through the closed door, but loud enough to be heard inside, she yelled, "Please tell Yu to come home when she returns!"

This scene, so unexpected and so inexplicable, left Mengjing shaking. It was several moments before she could open the paper and scan its contents. The inflammatory words, signed by Yuanguang, jumped into her eyes like flying knives. But it was at once clear to her that Yadan had no apparent connection to these words; the signature was Yuanguang's and the handwriting was Yu's. But who was this Yuanguang?

7

"I ask you, who is Yuanguang?"

"Never heard of him—why do you ask?"

"Come on, you little demon, tell me the truth! Sooner or later you will ruin your father and mother!"

"What exactly happened?"

"Who said anything happened? You think you have outgrown your mother. Let me tell you something—you are still immature. Could you even exist without your mother? Think back to the time when you and I were a lonely widow and her orphaned child. When we arrived here I had to ignore the hostility and unspoken insults. Was it easy for me? You think because you are now making a little money you have become somebody? Let me tell you—your mother is always above you. Do you think that eyes can rise above eyebrows?" Mengjing started to cry.

"Ma, what are you talking about? I haven't a clue . . ."

"No clue? Look at this; is this a clue?"

"Oh, Yuanguang. This was written by Zhulong, my boyfriend."

"Don't say that! Don't ever say that! Listen—from now on, if anyone asks, you must not mention this Zhu-whoever. If anyone asks, you must not mention him. Are you sure you're old enough to be dating? Let me tell you, being together with a man is a big deal! It may be years before you realize all the consequences."

"Momma! . . . Give me the paper!"

"No!"

"Momma, I tell you this: if you ever betray him to the authorities, don't ever, for the rest of my life, count on me to call you Ma!"

"What! You would turn your back on your own mother for a man? Shame on you! I know a married woman is just wastewater. But before you're even close to marriage, you're ready to discard your old mother; even your finger-nails are ready to grow in other directions! Whatever you call me, whether you like it not, your body came from mine! You can get a new boyfriend, but never a new mother!"

"Why do you say such mean things? I am leaving, and don't cry if I never come back!" Now it was Yadan's turn to cry.

Lu Chen: "I ask you, who is Yuanguang?"

Silence.

Lu Chen: "Tell me, this is your father asking, who is Yuanguang? Are you listening?"

More silence.

Ruomu: "Stubborn girl! Again she is being obstinate! Say something! You want to drive your dad crazy?"

Still more silence.

Lu Chen: "Yu, tell me, who is this Yuanguang?"

Yu: "A friend."

Ruomu: "A friend! Look, she's taking it so lightly! Since you were a small girl, you were always difficult. How could you copy stuff like this? You want to drive your parents into the ground! No wonder your grandma said that when a demon showed up the family would decline. You are the demon of our family!" And now it was Ruomu's turn to cry.

Lu Chen: "Okay, okay. Stop crying now. Yu, Dad's been worrying about you, concerned about your thoughts. You are so young, but you harbor negative thoughts. You are really worse than your two older sisters in this regard. This is a small mistake but it will lead to larger mistakes. Dad is not trying to scare you, or accuse you of being a terrible person. Among my students in their twenties, many have committed small mistakes. But you have to own up to them."

Ruomu: "It's a terrible thing when you give birth to a ghost. You do terrible things and we beg you not to drag us in! It's not easy for us, to have returned to the city from that shabby place. It's such bad karma to have a ghost born into the family!"

Yu: "What right do you have to read my diary?"

Ruomu: "Oh! What an obstreperous girl! So full of reasons for being so headstrong! I am your mother, your whole self came from me, how can I not have the right to read your diary?"

Yu: "Reading another person's diary without permission is a crime!"

Lu Chen: "Stop! You cannot speak to your mother this way!"

Yu: "You can be certain that I'll never drag you in. I am leaving and will never return."

The above two episodes occurred in two families simultaneously; two young women left their homes at about the same time, going to the same place: a vast, freezing, and boiling Square.

8

That April was both freezing and boiling. All history books have reserved a space for that April for its extraordinary consequences. During the entire month of April rain seemed to fall ceaselessly. At night, as raindrops splashed through the leaves of the maple trees surrounding the Square, the sound of trickling water grew louder and louder, a cry from the heavens for this rotten and crumbling world. Every raindrop was reminiscent of a diamond, the purity of diamond. On the night of freezing and boiling rain, Yu was engulfed by the sea of people. To her eyes the people in the vast Square became raindrops; their hearts were as clear as water. A tall, grayish white monument stood among the people, looming in and out of the rain, like a soul floating in the raindrops, the soul of the gathered crowd.

> *Let the dead die,*
> *Are the living souls*
> *already singing in the first morning light?*

Yu found surprising warmth in the cold April rain. Silently the rain was falling in the blowing wind like the tears of those who could no longer cry. That vast Square, soulful, clamorous, and disturbing, was now covered with garlands and wreaths. Never in her life had Yu seen so many flowers gathered in one place! And what a pity these were not real flowers.

Only in her childhood had Yu seen such a floral profusion—the vast sea of wild spring flowers that spread across open fields and woodland glades. There, in its tranquil majesty, was that azure lake of her childhood with its mystical fish, bleached to ghostly shades of white and pale blue, swimming in schools along the rocky shore. There, too, when she placed her hands in the water, its ethereal blueness seemed to penetrate to the marrow of her bones.

To Yu, the paper flowers in the Square, alive in the rain, were as beautiful as any field of wildflowers seen in childhood. The Square assumed a variety of forms: a vast sheet of white paper, a huge expanse of tortoise shells, an ancient bronze, or a tombstone. What was common to all of them was that they could contain words. People were writing. Words were inscribed everywhere, each and every Chinese character inlaid as though by a master artisan.

Yu was suddenly impelled to touch the inscriptions on the tombstone. To caress the thoughts of a thousand minds: this was her irresistible impulse, and with it came a moment of clarity, a life-changing instant of emotional maturity. She suddenly discovered the root of her suffering. Since childhood she had been longing for love—the love of her parents; later, the love of friends. Only love and friendship would be good medicine; nothing else could bring zest to her life. But in the course of such a long illness, clarity about its cause could bring only modest relief. Like a blade of grass that has withered in a long drought, one drop of dew might prolong her survival; but no one gave her a drop of dew. People were not kind. She was physically and spiritually drained. The pain was dulled but not ended with the recognition of its cause.

Yu had wandered to many places and began to think she might spend her entire life as a wanderer. She had searched for a home and not found it. Standing in the Square and looking across the seething ocean of passion on display there, she realized that everyone present on this momentous occasion was in quest of a home; everyone was, like herself, a wanderer. All had once loved, all had been cheated by love. A nation without love, faithless, would forever wander. Wander to the point of no return.

Now she heard a whisper coming from her heart, which transformed into a loud voice echoing in the Square:

> *Apollo is dead,*
> *Is Apollo dead?*
> *Let the dead die.*
> *Are the living souls.*
> *already singing in the first morning light?*

She saw that the person who uttered the loudest sounds was standing on the base of the tombstone. He was the man named Yuanguang or Zhulong. Next to him stood a woman. It was Yadan.

Yadan had not arranged to meet Zhulong here, but once in the Square, in the midst of the vast throng, she knew she would find him. She had many things to tell him, but the rain put out her burning fire as she suddenly realized that in this world there were problems bigger than her own. She couldn't stop her tears as she struggled to say, "I could not stay at home any longer." Zhulong took her hand and walked to the base of the tombstone. She held on tightly, fearing this hard-won happiness would suddenly slip away. In those days a simple hand-touching was still considered to be more than a casual signal of intimacy; it conveyed a tacit understanding of something much deeper. So when the two of them walked forward, Yadan's heart was filled with the music of a wedding ensemble.

No one noticed a tall, buxom woman taking pictures from one corner of the Square. A reflection from some unknown source turned the woman's otherwise beautiful face a gloomy shade of blue. The birth child of an international collaboration of revolution and love, she had just returned from a nearby city where she participated in the dress rehearsal of a musical play. The point of the production was to eulogize a great man of the times, and to sing the praises of workers and peasants. The woman's name was Jinwu; she could not understand the purpose of the musical, but to participate in it was a good cure for boredom.

She had other ways to occupy her time and stave off boredom. She was the kind of woman who knew how to enrich her life at any time; performance was merely one of the things she had found stimulating. She had the leading role in the musical *On the Grain Delivery Road*, which required dressing in the colorful costume of a woman of Dai ethnic heritage, a people from the mountains of Yunnan Province. In the audience, she knew, were hungry men who would stare at her ample chest, so revealingly displayed in a tight-fitting costume.

In those days, all musicals were formulaic—learn one dance and you knew them all. The songs were the same, or at least the lyrics were more or less the same; learn one and you could sing them all. In this advanced nation, even before the principle of cloned life was well known, the reproduction of material and artistic products was commonly understood. This was an intelligent nation, and these were the same people who through the centuries had conceived four great inventions: the magnetic compass, gunpowder, paper-making, and printing.

> *Walking eastward in the morning sun,*
> *Bathed warmly in its golden light,*
> *Dai girls carry baskets of grain,*
> *and the goodwill of our peasants.*
> *Oh, flowered skirts dancing in a breeze,*
> *Oh, laughter echoing from mountains and valleys.*
> *We bring bountiful grain for our country,*
> *and boundless happiness to fill our hearts . . .*

Thus, as though playing a game, Jinwu led the dancers earnestly, repeating the steps to the up-tempo music, something she could do in her sleep if that became necessary. In rehearsals she also took delight in correcting small mistakes in the orchestra, sounding out the correct notes in her clear alto, as though she, not the conductor, were their leader.

But here in the Square, she knew she was not witness to a playful musical; she knew that "grain delivery" meant tears, not joy, to peasants. She came to the Square wanting to record the unscripted scene with her camera, conscious that a momentous event was in progress, one that should be accurately portrayed for future generations. In her vascular system ran the serum and albumin of a brave people. She was the child of revolution and love, the earliest result of what would later be labeled and praised as "international collaboration." Among the crowd in the Square, she knew she would stand out, and so she did her best to conceal herself.

9

On that night, that historical night, an elegy was rising strongly to the heavens. Rain poured down violently and thunder muffled the sirens. But they were heard, and people fled in all directions. Mud flew off panicky feet and bullet-like raindrops thundered down. Yu was surprised at her own sense of calm; she wiped the rain from her eyes and licked the rain that trickled onto her lips, tasting blood and mud. She felt pulled by an unseen force as she dashed through the muddy puddles. Everyone had the same plan: to vanish from the Square instantly, like butterflies in a spring breeze. Something terrible was about to happen. Something terrible, something terrible—that whisper came back to her.

Now Yu slowed to a walk as she saw many people charging into the Square, sticks in hand, while a monotone voice repeated its orders from a loudspeaker. Just ahead, Yu saw a beautiful couple, Yadan and Zhulong; she had never realized how beautiful they were when moving in unison, struggling forward, tumbling yet unwavering, filled with the passion of their idealized vision of the future. Yu momentarily forgot the fleeting pain in her heart and watched them in silent appreciation of their beauty at that moment.

A police car whizzed past, nearly knocking her down. She saw the car stop briefly behind the couple. Such a brief stop, a flurry of motion, and then—they were gone! Disappearing before Yu had time to cry out.

Now Yu was screaming into the night rain: "Yadan . . . Zhulong . . ."

Yu heard a voice speaking in the darkness: "Evidence shows that Apollo is dead, and this means that the sun is dead." This was an utterly counterrevolutionary remark.

10

Three months later the city where I lived had temporarily vanished. The big city nearby was also shaken violently. I was not at all surprised, because this was as I had predicted. I knew that the boiling lava at the Square could not possibly be extinguished by a single rainstorm. The lava was running beneath the earth; I thought it would surely break through the earth's crust and explode. I came to the big city before the earthquake, remembering I still had a home here. Also, I was hoping that my young friend Yu—who stayed behind when I left—would be there. I had been missing her for a long time. The reason I left this place was to search for my mother but also because Yu had grown too dependent on me. I thought this would be best for her future.

After the death of my adoptive parents, all leads to the identity of my birth mother had been cut off. When Michael was leaving to return to his own country, I said good-bye to him at the airport. He promised to help with my search. If he got any news he would send it right away, through someone reliable. Still, I was anxious. Looking down the endless green corridor leading to the boarding and departure gates, I thought that someday I would pass this way as I left the country, never to return.

I strongly believe that my mother, Shen Mengtang, who was known for her energy and passion, is still alive. One night in May 1943, she and Wujin, a soldier, were strolling hand in hand along the banks of the Yan River. The moonlight and the scent of flowers seeped into their pores. When together, they forgot all else. Western-educated and filled with romantic notions about love and destiny, she had thrown herself into this young man's arms without reserve. He restrained himself. "Don't be like this," he said, "you must remember what happened to Liu Qian and Huang Kegong."

The tragic story of Liu Qian and Huang Kegong had served as a warning to all young men and women in the Yan'an area and inspired them to remain chaste; no one wanted to suffer Huang's fate. Wujin was no exception. Knowing that violations of human nature would be punished, Wujin had conflicting emotions that were causing him actual physical pain, sapping his strength and tormenting his mind. To serve at the front, throwing himself into the thick of battle: that, he thought, would be the way to ease his mind and resolve his conflicts. In moments of calm detachment he feared that such thinking was self-deception; still, at that time he was inclined to believe that all personal desires during wartime were a sign of weakness, a distraction from the task at hand. When the Japanese enemy has invaded, all worthy young men should throw themselves into the fight.

But this young woman argued that he was confused, that there was no conflict between love and one's duty to defend the nation.

My mother had told him many stories about revolution and love, for example the tale of Insarov, the Bulgarian rebel, and Elena, the Russian girl, in Turgenev's *On the Eve*. Both he and my mother had cried as she was telling the story. As they were both in tears, a strong flashlight pierced the darkness. Their expressions at this moment were pathetic—like tiny insects trapped in a spiderweb. Any hopes for escape were futile as the gigantic bug opened its mouth and prepared to swallow.

Wujin wrote many lines of self-criticism and managed to please the examiner in the third version. My mother, who was experienced as an underground Communist working in the KMT-controlled area before coming to Yan'an, escaped punishment by cleverly manipulating the two interrogators.

"Your mother fooled all of us, but we still liked her," my adoptive mother said. Such was the strength of her personal charm, and it made me proud to hear about it.

I found the house empty. My beautiful blue silk pajamas were still lying on the bed but my little friend was gone. Although sealed off, the entire room was covered with dust. The air pollution in this large city had reached epic proportions. I could sense it in my throat and nose. I used the pajamas to brush some dust off the bed and then lay down.

Had I been cruel? She was such a small, frail girl and she had come a long way to live with me, to take sanctuary from her hostile mother. She regarded me as her only trustworthy relative, but I left without saying good-bye. How did she deal with my sudden departure? Has anything bad happened to her?

I stared at the ceiling, glad for the rare opportunity to think without interruption. As I considered the matter, I stopped blaming myself for Yu's troubles; she had given me little choice. After she arrived on my doorstep I soon found that she was tougher than her appearance suggested. Her love for me was too possessive. She curtailed my freedom and was hostile and disrespectful to my friends. Just by looking at those tortured eyes, the unsuspecting Michael had been taken in; he could have been swallowed by her! This was intolerable. I am free and must remain so. Through freedom I endure; I can never focus my love on one thing in the world—not a beautifully painted landscape, not a needy, if emotionally appealing, human being.

Now, as I lay on this dusty bed in this musty room, I begin to think of that strange girl—odd and yet lovely, unbending and affectionate, who evokes both sympathy and annoyance. She was so out of place in this world. No matter what time and place, she was doomed to be out of harmony with the world's symphony, or at least that part of it that craved peace, friendship, and love of mankind.

11

After that destructive earthquake, the Russian-designed buildings constructed in the 1950s remained standing. The building occupied by Yu and Yadan suffered no damage; still, its occupants shook with fear. The entire community surrounding the university moved into makeshift tents to stay safe from aftershocks. Everyone except Yu.

Yu had been unable to sleep on the night of the mighty earthquake. At three in the morning she got up, noticing that the sky outside her window was a dark, savage red. Just as she began wondering why, the overhead light fixture began to sway, the very ground on which the house was built rumbled and roared, and the building lurched violently, as though it were being torn apart by some great, unseen hand.

On the evening following the disaster, as aftershocks continued, people wearing red armbands went from house to house rendering aid and encouraging people to vacate their homes to prevent further injuries from collapsing structures. In fact, people required no persuasion; their will to live was sufficient motivation. People desire to live even if they live in hell. Naturally I refer to those "normal people" in a general sense.

But in this matter as in so many others, Yu's eccentricity once again became manifest. An old woman from the neighborhood committee stayed until two in the morning, saying, "Young woman, come out now. We have promised not to leave one brother or sister behind. We have received a rating of excellent for three years; now you are the only one in the area who insists on staying inside. You cannot ruin our reputation!"

Finally, a piece of paper was tossed from the window. On it, Yu had written that she would take responsibility for herself and intended to remain inside. Finally, the old woman gave up and slowly trudged away. Before going far, she looked back and said, for all to hear, "The third daughter of the Lu family must be sick!" This became a neighborhood mantra, repeated by many in the vicinity of Jiaotong University. By the time of Yu's frontal lobotomy, in the 1990s, it had become accepted wisdom that she was mentally defective, so the surgery seemed unsurprising.

When the sky began to show glimmers of the new day, a few people sleeping in makeshift tents saw the third daughter of the Lu family leaving with a school bag on her back. She was a shadowy presence, drifting among the other phantasms of the predawn darkness, soon arriving at her family's tent. Ruomu pretended to be asleep but heard her whispering to her father.

"Dad, I'm leaving for a while, going to work."

She drifted away again before Lu Chen could respond. But Ruomu had already formed an opinion. "What a curse! More aftershocks are predicted, but she just goes wandering off! Why is she doing this? As though she has not given us enough to worry about already."

She might have said more, but was somehow inhibited by being outside her own home. Lu Chen closed his eyes, giving vent to a series of his characteristic sighs.

On the day that people began dismantling their tents, Ling and Xiao returned home for a visit from their remote factory jobs in the northwest. They had sent cables on the day of the disaster, which made the headlines in the nation's largest paper. The wording revealed to Lu Chen's perceptive eye that they were not in close contact with each other.

The sense of having survived disaster somehow brought people closer. So it was that the Lu family were, for the first two hours of their reunion, happy and at ease with one another. But then, as Xuanming placed food on the table, Xiao asked, "Where is Yu?" The room went silent.

"She's never home," said Ling. "Does she have a boyfriend?"

Ruomu took a bite of a chili pepper, then coughed slightly. "Her affairs are her business," she said. And then she turned to Xiao. "But I'm worried about you. You are old enough. You should start dating; otherwise, you'll become an old maid."

This remark brought color to the cheeks of both sisters. Xiao vomited a slurry of just-swallowed fish onto the table, then ran to the bathroom, where she vomited again and again, following this with loud crying.

Lu Chen threw down his chopsticks. "This family is a mess! All day long, the old crying, the young wailing. Are we getting warmed up for a funeral?"

Xuanming threw her chopsticks down even harder. Pointedly facing

Ruomu and ignoring Lu Chen, she said, "Listen to that! The old one is still sitting here and he is howling for a funeral! You ask him, whose funeral?"

Before Ruomu could reply, Lu Chen turned his wrath directly on his nemesis. "Mother, you have no cause to throw bricks at me! What happened to Xiao no one knows better than your favorite darling first granddaughter. You should ask her!"

It so happened that Lu Chen had earlier received a letter from Xiao relating in detail her older sister's disgusting behavior. In his response he had done his best to comfort her, saying this was not her fault, she should not be too sad, and that other opportunities would come her way, and so forth. But perpetual worry was his specialty and he had lost three nights of sleep over the emotional issue. He didn't even sigh loudly for fear of awakening Ruomu. As usual, he had chosen to keep his family scandals to himself. But also typically, he then erupted with suppressed anger when the topic was suddenly revealed.

Now Ling entered the fray, defending herself in her usual manner—with tears that were calculated to draw sympathy, and they did. It was then Xuanming's turn to burst into tears. Aunty Tian soon followed, creating a cacophony that ceased only when Xiao emerged from the bathroom, her finger pointed aggressively at Ling's nose, and began to declaim loudly a complete history of the sordid affair. It was then followed by more of the same from Ling. A crowd of eager spectators gathered at the windows to enjoy the row.

Seeing this, Xuanming reverted to her emotional specialty of last resort: forcefully slapping her own face, wailing bitterly between each slap.

"So shameful! All of you were born into a good family." Slap, slap. "If this were the old days each of you would be suitably married by now, heading your own household." Slap, slap. "Oh! What a scandal! This is such bad karma. Was I so evil in my last life that my son had to be taken away? If Tiancheng were still alive, would I come here to live under the roof of another man, like a mote in his eye or a splinter in his finger?" Slap, slap. On and on she went, alleging damage to her reputation and loss of face, reminding them that she was an important figure in the community.

That day, the only person to maintain a measure of quietness in the heat of this great battle was little four-year-old Yun'er. Already she understood how to derive victory from turmoil. With all of the family concentrating its energies elsewhere, she seized the moment to take possession of a tempting but forbidden object: Ruomu's box of buttons. Not only did she have great fun playing with them, but she also discovered a few large and pretty ones to confiscate for her own store of treasures. As a bonus, she also found an irresistible box of chocolates and quickly reduced its contents by half. Her appetite slackened over the next few mealtimes and her stools turned chocolate brown.

12

Yushe had concealed from her family the nature of her new employment. She had signed on to become a stevedore. Yadan told her about the opening but thought the work would be too heavy for someone so slight. But Yu was intrigued: Yadan was underestimating her strength, as she had once carried bags of wheat weighing eighty pounds; she was made for this kind of work! Yadan looked her up and down, her expression conveying disbelief. "I don't want to call an ambulance and see you confined to a hospital," she said.

So Yu went to work, paying no attention when people shook their heads at her slender build. There were a few women on the dock, but they were muscular and looked tough. Yu was about one-third their weight. The pay was figured on a piece rate, so no one could complain that she was not doing her share.

Her first commodity was bags of urea, some weighing fifty pounds. She bent her back, waiting, full of confidence, but when the first bag landed on her back she stumbled. She steadied herself and by a sheer act of will managed to carry the sack to the warehouse. Looks of disbelief followed her. She found the pain in her lower abdomen frightening.

She suddenly came to understand the true value of being young. Just a few short years ago, youth helped her ward off disasters. But now, although she had not changed much in her appearance, her internal organs were changing every day. All the yesterdays are gone and every today exists only one day. As an ancient Greek philosopher once said, a man can never enter the exact same river twice. The human body changes like a river, perhaps even faster than a river does.

Yu clenched her teeth and held on to the job. When she received her first month's pay, after deducting only eight yuan for food, she gave the remaining twenty-two yuan to Yadan. She did not want to owe anything to anybody. Yadan couldn't overcome her stubbornness, so she deposited the money, thinking that one day Yu would need it.

After the earthquake came another disaster, a huge rainstorm. A local grain warehouse began to flood and the stevedores were called out to wade through the rising water to remove sacks of grain to prevent spoilage. A black, oily substance oozed from a rubber warehouse across the road, contributing to the mess. The workers pulled on high rubber boots and quickly waded into the water to save as much of the precious grain as possible.

Each sack of grain weighed a hundred pounds. When Yu attempted to carry one, she could almost hear her bones cracking. Even the large, tough women could not bear it. Yu carried one sack, stumbling as she did so, but one of the strongest women shouted at her, "Don't even try! No one will reward you, no one will care! You'll pull your insides apart and never be able to bear a child!"

Yu's tears ran down her cheeks along with the rain. She paid no heed; since that rainy night in the Square she felt she had grown up. She was not the only one in the world who was suffering. She was worried about the beautiful couple who had been carried away in the police car. Since they disappeared into the police car on that rainy night, she had not traced any news of them. She admired them. How much she wished she could live and die with someone. But some people are born to be lonely in this world, born to be isolated from others. Yu unfortunately sank into that isolated swamp, unable to rise from it. How many times she prayed, hoping for the whisper to bring her a decree from God to rescue her. But there was only silence, deadly silence in her heart.

Now we can see that young woman, pale and frail, carrying a huge sack of grain on her back, like Jesus carrying his cross. We cannot tell what she was thinking. She looked as if she was listening. She was indeed listening. She was listening to the cracking sound coming from her bones, replacing the whisper she was hoping to hear. By the warehouse wall she sat down, seemingly no longer listening, and took out a rather dirty handkerchief and spat something into it. Should we have been standing a bit closer, we would have seen a small glob of fresh red blood. Surprisingly the young woman didn't show any fear. On the contrary, she looked much better after spitting out the blood.

Yadan was released on the third day. She looked terrible. "Zhulong was jailed at Banbuqiao prison," she told Yu. "Can we sue them for false arrest?"

"But where can we file the suit?" asked Yu.

"There must be someplace," replied Yadan. "We must go to the highest office holder who has direct authority."

As they were talking, Yadan looked closely at Yu. "What happened to you? You are as pale and limp as a cold noodle."

Yu didn't reply. After a moment she raised her head, saying, "Let's go and look for the highest leader."

13

Yu walked into the huge lobby but Yadan was stopped outside. This is like a scene from ancient history, Yu thought. In the Qin Dynasty of 221 B.C., Jin Ke, who went to assassinate the emperor, walked into the hall alone, but his assistant, Qin Wuyang, was stopped outside the door. Yu was filled with pride at the thought of facing the authorities alone.

But Yu's memory always turned reality to illusion. In her memory, on the top floor of the building was a large conference room with a long, red table in the center. On either side sat neatly dressed men, deep in discussion. Such sophisticates! They covered their faces with fancy handkerchiefs as they talked in low voices. They were like bees swarming around a hive, she thought, their voices rising and falling, quiet for a moment, then buzzing again. At first they didn't notice her.

She made no sound, but the men noticed her shadow projected across the polished surface of the long table. The sun, entering the window at a low angle, was at her back, which obscured her features. When they realized that a stranger had intruded they became alarmed. "What's she doing here? Guards! Seize her!"

But it was too late. Yu jumped nimbly onto the top of the table. Her small, delicate feet were prominently displayed. She walked calmly to the end, adjacent to a large, open window. There she dropped a note on the table on which she had written, "Zhulong is jailed at Banbuqiao prison. He is a good man. Please release him."

And then she did an extraordinary thing. Many years later, they would still be talking about it. Without pausing—she didn't want any of these creeps to touch her—she leaped through the open window!

Yu had interrupted an international conference of VIPs. All of the men—whether they had big or small noses, yellow or black hair—were frightened by this apparition. None could remember precisely what Yu looked like, and a huge uproar ensued. All the guards were interrogated, with the security chief swearing he had blocked two young women from entering the building. Could it have been a ghost?

The explanation given to the international visitors was that this was a servicewoman who suffered a severe mental disorder; much later this episode would be recalled as part of the justification for performing a frontal lobotomy. Meanwhile, the big noses and small noses, who had all been gathered at the table, expressed to one another their intense dismay that someone so beautiful—she must be beautiful, they thought, remembering only those delicate feet—could have come to such harm in their presence.

That day and long afterward, passersby would remember that they saw a young woman falling lightly in the afternoon breeze, like a leaf from a sycamore. It was a wondrous scene.

Yu didn't bleed when she hit the ground. In five minutes the ambulance came and gently removed what some people assumed was a dead body. At the hospital they found that she had broken bones, severe contusions, and internal injuries, the worst of which was a tear in her liver. They did surgery, repairing the internal injuries and splinting the fractures. After recovering, she walked from the hospital. Another chapter, a new era, had begun in the remarkable life of Yushe.

CHAPTER 9 | MOON ART EXHIBITION

1

Jinwu felt that a new era that truly belonged to her had arrived.

Jinwu was a performing artist. She had played the role of a spy, but she was not satisfied with being an actress. Whenever a new era arrives, many of the things that come with it can unnerve people. But Jinwu jumped right in without a moment of hesitation and began a new career as a nude model for artists. With this job's good income and flexible hours, suddenly money and freedom came her way, bringing the promise of more desirable things. Her life had taken a positive turn.

When, for the first time, the top art academy in the country began recruiting nude models, a major controversy erupted. But asceticism as a cultural norm had prevailed for at least ten years. Many felt that a genie had been released from a bottle, just as in the Arabian myth; and it could never be put back into the bottle again. A devilish spirit had been unleashed and roved across this ancient Oriental land, running into a residue of broken "isms," thus giving birth to or aborting a cluster of deformed fetuses.

Not all were deformed, though; there were favored children of the new era as well, and some of them were favorites at the art academy, the royal art palace of our country. Ten years of asceticism for them had been a wasted lifetime. They were overwhelmed at the sudden opportunity to paint from a live nude model, a rather common thing for art students in other countries.

The newly recruited models were gorgeous, especially when compared with those who had worked at it previously and were now well into middle age. The new ones were less inhibited, less burdened with guilt or shame. In that respect, Jinwu was typical: posing without clothes was just a job, no different morally from being a teacher or actor. Clear and healthy of heart, free of guilt, and narcissistic: that was Jinwu. Thank heavens, we have only one Jinwu.

When Jinwu stepped out from behind the screen that day, she was poised, self-confident, and lively. She was greeted by a collective gasp. Teachers and students, men and women—all were amazed by the iconic beautiful body that now stood before them. She was slender but large breasted, and her golden, curly hair, like some kind of special artificial fiber, suggested that she was not a pure Han Chinese.

Taibai, one of the oil painters, took special notice of the goddess now standing before him. He had been one of the first to grow long hair at the beginning of the new era. That, together with his worldly and solemn expression, gave him a priestly demeanor, reminding people of a medieval cathedral. Taibai began painting but was finding it difficult to keep his mind on his craft; his thoughts were drifting from his palette and brushes to the model. After two sessions he was behind. So, not surprisingly, he invited Jinwu to work extra hours for him, at night, in his room.

Taibai was married. His wife worked at a cultural association and had her own quarters. His roommate, Gulu, was a student leader who was usually out until midnight. Thus, Taibai had privacy and space. Taibai was talented, proud, and passionate about beauty. His one mission in life was to discover, capture, and possess the world's beauty. And then move on to new beauties. When he first saw Jinwu, his impulse was to capture and possess her!

It was late spring and there were hints of chilliness in the air. Jinwu wrapped her body after removing her clothing, glad that she had brought her own towel; her host's blankets and sheets were typical of a bachelor. A strange odor pervaded the room—a combination of cheap cologne, men's hair gel, musty clothing, and paint solvent. She opened all the windows.

"You are too warm? Really?" Taibai liked to use inverted sentence structures, giving a question-mark tonality to everything he said. He began to mix paints on his palette, showing his intention to employ lots of blue for her nude body.

"One does not notice the fragrance if one stays too long in a room filled with orchids. I suppose you cannot smell whatever is in your room." Jinwu liked to put people on the defensive in conversation. She unceremoniously removed the towel and arranged it so that her body needn't touch the bed as she struck a reclining pose.

"You are tough?" said Taibai with a knowing look as he sprayed a bit of cologne on the bed. "Better now?"

"I think you had better hurry up, my working time has already begun," she said.

Taibai missed the point of her remark, a mistake that would later prove costly. In the presence of this naked, alluring body, he lost his focus. His brush shook, strange blobs began to appear in the vivid blue. Oh well, he thought to himself, this is expressionism.

All three lights in the room were fixed on Jinwu. The light masked out the shabby scene in the room, accentuating the curves of her body, which helped the expressionist artist, but the light gave the scene a false sense of unreality; that semitransparent body with dimly visible veins became an object of art. While beauty remained, she didn't look real anymore.

He approached his subject, putting aside brush and palette. Following the bright light, his hand soon moved lower and lower, pausing momentarily at curves. Touching, he hoped, could shed some more light on his art. Right now he'd rather have a woman with some flaws lying on his bed, rather than a perfect, flawless piece of art. Her skin was warm, soft, and smooth, exquisitely smooth, like the best silk. Having confirmed one exciting sensory input with another, he plotted his next move.

"Are you going to do performance art?" the silky woman suddenly asked, in a voice as warmly smooth as satin.

Later, even Jinwu wasn't sure how the words "performance art" traveled through time and space and rolled off her tongue. Yu had used these words many years ago and they were now suddenly fashionable. They struck the artist forcefully. He raised his face and searched hers for clues. She was squinting slightly, her brow was arched, and her mouth was poised in a tentative pout; she was mocking him. She was in control and showing tolerance for his weakness. Her expression was the look of someone who had survived much and was observing a newcomer just stepping onto the world stage.

Under the pressure of this look, the artist began to tremble; and then his anger flared. Eager to prove his strength and potency, he forgot about posing as suave, if not exactly debonair. When he pressed his entire body on that piece of silk and satin, he suddenly felt a vacuum in his heart. Such a feeling was scary and debilitating. He barely moved, then deflated, sudden and complete, like a balloon pierced by a needle. Meanwhile, Jinwu's face remained close to his, full of mockery.

"You are now finished?" she asked, looking at her watch and mimicking his uptalk. "Okay? Altogether, one hour and forty minutes?"

"What are you saying?" he stammered.

"Models are not free. And at night the rate is doubled. You forgot?" Jinwu was putting her clothes back on as she said this and sprayed a bit of perfume. "And you should pay extra for the damage to my sense of smell." She giggled as she spoke. "As I said, the clock began running when I started posing."

The angry artist had no response. He emptied his wallet, his hand shaking. She accepted the money, smiling graciously.

"Actually, I just wanted to know," he said hesitantly. "You . . . you don't seem to be pure Han Chinese? You seem to have some Western blood?"

"You spent all this time to ask such a question? Ah, so expensive. I can only say, I don't know."

"All right." Taibai's anger was again rising, and his fist was clenching involuntarily. Fighting to regain composure, he tried to conceal his face in the shadows as she opened the door.

"By the way, next time you do performance art, it would be best if you spray a bit of this kind of perfume." She waved her own small bottle in front of his eyes.

Now he really lost control and slammed his fist against the door panel, opening a small cut on his knuckles.

"Whore."

"What did you say?"

"Whore."

Jinwu, smiling deceptively, stepped a little closer, saying one word at a time: "Listen, little man . . . you . . . are . . . a . . . fool!" And before he could dodge the blow, she had slapped him full across the face with the loose ends of the bills. Still in control, she didn't want to throw away the money to prove her purity. This was no Hollywood B movie. Money is important in a commercial society.

2

When Yushe was released from the hospital, Jinwu took her to the dusty house where they had lived together for several years. This was a time when everyone in her circle was preparing to enter college. Jinwu wanted Yu to do the same. There is much competition for good jobs, she explained, you'll need a college diploma, without it you will lose out. Yu asked what Jinwu would do; Jinwu just smiled, didn't respond.

Jinwu got everything ready for Yu: canvas, easel, brushes, and more than fifty tubes of paint, more than what she had seen at Taibai's apartment. She had one simple instruction: "Start painting! I know you can do better than those lousy men who have been gawking at my body!"

Yu had already painted seven pictures when someone knocked at her door. It was a stranger who introduced himself as Gulu, a friend of Taibai. He didn't care that she didn't know Taibai, he was there to see her paintings, which astounded him from his first glance at one of them.

The colors of Yu's painting were a horror: heavy reds, greens, blues, and purples; all became unearthly colors under her brush. The dark reds looked like solid blood; the deep blues and dark greens looked like the paint had been soaked in ocean water. In one painting, what appeared at first glance to be a flower, when examined more closely became a bird. In another, when Gulu discovered a bird's head embedded in a rose, he looked more closely and was rewarded with another insight—it was also a fish head, and what had been feathers became scales. Eyes were hidden in unusual places and monstrous beasts with evil intent lurked in the shadows, poised to leap out at the viewer . . . Gulu was amazed to see how easy it was for evil to hide in beauty. Some of the images conveyed ordinary subjects rendered in bizarre ways: an oddly shaped black woman, a bronze devil's mask, cloudlike birds, colorful spiders hidden in flowers, a golden apple lost in blue feathers . . . a gush of poisonous fluid filled the colorful air.

One of the finished paintings was truly astonishing to Gulu. It was quite a simple painting: a serpent coiled up on a large metallic structure shaped like a mussel with black feathers all over. Strangely enough, the feathers did not remind him of flying birds, they rather looked like a heavy curtain conceal-ing the serpent in a mysterious way. It was rendered in the highly detailed way that was popular in the photo realism school. Gulu found the image scary; he could not look at it for long. He was like a young boy seeing a grown woman's naked body for the first time, or seeing a crocodile for the first time; he was scared but wanted to look at it again. So he retreated to a safe place and glanced at it once, then glanced at it again. It was exciting; it was loathsome; it was irresistible. He then had the frightening sensation that the serpent had coiled around his torso. He sucked air and shuddered at its clammy, muscular embrace. A few drops of urine dribbled down his leg.

"What inspired you to paint this?" he asked.

Yu looked at him closely. He didn't look slow-witted. How, then, did he come to ask such a foolish question? She didn't respond.

He paced back and forth and stepped more closely to examine her paint-ings. As his courage seemed to return, he looked as if he were trying to insert his head between the paint and the canvas. At last he asked, "Do you know that in ancient history the serpent you painted represents the highest spirit of mankind?"

Yu threw down the brush. Was he joking? But there was no trace of irony or mockery in his expression. She thought of asking him to take a photograph of her back. But she didn't. She had once asked Yuanguang to take a picture of it. His reply was a commitment. For anyone else to do this would be to violate a sacred trust.

Yu never learned that, about a year later, a hugely successful but unofficial art exhibit featured her painting. It was placed in the most visible place in the first exhibition hall, with one slight change: the artists' names, Gulu and Taibai.

3

The news that Xiao got into a major university in the late 1970s was the first good news for the Lu family in a long time. She was no longer the timid girl with red clouds on her cheeks, knitting socks and sweaters for her boyfriend while waiting for him on the doorstep. Though still simple and plain, she had changed a lot. She was spirited. She was self-confident. As Xiao entered the Lu family home, Xuanming had to look closely before she recognized her own granddaughter.

The family gathered to welcome her. Lu Chen, a top student in his own time, smiled broadly; he had always wanted his daughters to attend university. "The children were delayed ten years," he would always say.

Ling was there, too. Xuanming wept as she held her hands. Her beloved eldest granddaughter hadn't been home for a long time; now her complexion was sallow, her expression wan. Her eyes were red, as though from frequent crying. Wang Zhong did not return with her. Although Xuanming did not admire him, he was after all the husband of her eldest granddaughter, and without him the family gathering was incomplete. Yun'er was there; she was turning into a pretty girl. Eventually she would, by consensus, become the prettiest girl in the family, even prettier than Ruomu in her prime. Her spirited good looks went straight to Xuanming's heart, perhaps because she was reminded of her own childhood. The memory of those days would stimulate the old lady to tell again of her own fairy-tale adventure, when she visited the empress dowager in the twenty-fifth year of Guangxu's reign.

In the dynamics of this family: among its nine members, including Wang Zhong, there were three pairs of enemies. Xuanming and Lu Chen were one pair, Ruomu and Yu another, Ling and Xiao the third. Just because she was now experiencing validation as the result of entering university, Xiao could not forgive Ling. On the contrary, she had achieved clarity about many things. Her eyes, once dull and uncomprehending, revealed a newly sharpened perception. For the discerning, they also revealed a secret: Xiao had a sweetheart.

He was a classmate and his name was Hua. Xiao knew he was the right man for her the first time she saw him; in fact, she thought predestination was at work. In a classroom exercise designed to relax the atmosphere on that first day of school, each student was asked to offer a brief performance, and then select someone else to be the next to do so. When Hua finished his singing, he arbitrarily asked that the next person be the eighth student to his right. Everyone turned to look for the eighth student. It was Xiao.

She stood straight, putting aside all timidity, and sang a childhood song, *On the Beautiful Field*. Hua had not expected to hear such an accomplished performance. He watched closely, and with just that one glance, he felt an unknown feeling float across his heart.

Objectively, Xiao was no beauty; but she stood out, not because she was flashy and shining. Rather, it was her simplicity. On that day simplicity became a special quality. Her rekindled liveliness was enhanced by her simple outfit—blue jeans and a light gray T-shirt. Simplicity and vitality: exactly the qualities that most appealed to Hua.

Their mutual attraction was soon apparent to both of them. They began spending time together. When she was with Hua, Xiao felt that her innocent girlhood had been restored. Life with Ling had deprived her of those feelings; although younger, Xiao had always assumed the role of older sister. Someone had to be responsible. Now she felt a sense of release.

Xiao had been a flower hidden in the dark, lonely and beautiful. Now the stars had risen, bringing the fresh and cool scent of flowers; her heart was now open to rich possibilities and warm feelings.

This university was in the distant north. In spring, lawns came to life and students began spending time in the open, inhaling fresh air and absorbing the sunshine into their bones. Xiao felt the presence of only one person; all of her senses had opened to him, and his to her.

One day, while she was alone in her room, he appeared on her doorstep and asked for a private conversation. Closing the door, he said, "We both know there is something special between us: you feel it and so do I. We are grown-ups and cannot be coy. But we must control our feelings because nothing can come of them."

That day Hua told Xiao that he was married.

Strangely, it was not hearing that Hua had a wife that sent ocean waves crashing through Xiao's inner spaces; having a spouse in this era is no longer an unconquerable barrier to the expression of love. It was hearing the word "control" that opened the floodgates, releasing her emotions. She wept on his shoulder, but her own cries could not move her, just like flowers could not hear their own sighing. It was in her tears that Xiao was drowning. Because these tears had been held back for so long, now, like a river, they crashed downward. He, too, was drowning in her tears. Rarely shedding tears, he felt as if he had become a bare tree, all its leaves stripped off.

Xiao went home. She needed someone to share her sorrow. At that time, the Lu house had just installed a telephone, so she phoned. "Where is Yu?" she asked.

4

Yushe was the last person to enter the classroom for the college examination. The middle-aged female teacher looked at her disapprovingly as she said, "I am going to ask a question designed to test your imagination. All of you know the story that begins 'Fragrance followed the horse's hooves on the way home from a flower garden.' And as you also know, the punch line is that 'bees and butterflies were flying around the hooves.' Now, I want to recite a poem and ask you to use your imagination in that same way and draw a picture representing your response to the poem. Draw anything you like." And then she recited the poem:

A willow tree on the east,
A willow tree on the west,
A willow tree on the south,
A willow tree on the north.

The students looked at one another, completely lost. This delighted the teacher, who continued:

Thin willow twigs
in hundreds and thousands
cannot hold back the departing person.

Now the students felt released from the suspense and misery, thinking they'd begun to understand what the teacher was looking for. But she continued:

Partridge was weeping,
Cuckoo was weeping,
Brother, don't leave,
Rather return, rather go,
Partridge was weeping.

How strange! This was neither prose nor poetry. Now the students looked even more puzzled than ever. And then they went to work, but it was in various directions: some drew a pair of cuckoos, some began by sketching the four willow trees, and some began by depicting a pair of lovers.

The teacher walked among the students, glancing at the variety of interpretations, but she spent most of her time examining Yu's work. She was drawing a naked woman whose arms were raised high, but in the form of tree branches. With a series of firm strokes and using fine lines, something like the floral patterns seen in wallpaper, she gave the figure no depth, working in only two dimensions. No shadows, no shading, just changes of color; these were ways of indicating a hidden message. Meridian acupuncture channels were displayed and visibly connected to the heart, but there was no blood in the blood vessels—no blood in the entire body. This was a picture with no emotions.

"What is this?"

"This is a maze."

"Why a maze?"

"A human being is a maze. Soul and body—both are part of the maze. A body is the wall of the maze and the soul is the little path connecting everything to the center. To enter is to live, to leave is to die."

"But you left the theme a thousand miles away."

"Not a bit. Your poem is about a woman, perhaps a prostitute. A woman who wants the man to stay, but she is doomed to failure. The willows and birds are part of her, her imagined ciphers for body and soul. I've outlined all her codes in this picture. Now you can go ahead and break the codes."

With that, Yu picked up her things and left, leaving the teacher and class dumbfounded. Only now did the teacher realize that this student had not obtained a permit to take this examination.

The other students gathered around Yu's picture. Shaking his head, one of them said, "If she's not mentally disordered, this girl must be a genius."

The teacher took the picture with her.

5

Yadan published her first short story in the early 1980s. This came about by chance. She had just entered the literature department of a major university. To her great surprise, on the first day she saw Zhulong, who had just been released from prison and had enrolled in the physics department.

At the center of the campus was a water fountain, a nice place for students to meet and fall in love by moonlight. The moonlight caressed the fine and sensitive emotions of the lovers. One evening, Yadan sat at a spot where the moonlight melded with the yellowish streetlight to give her hair and face a golden glow. Next to her sat Zhulong; he seemed absentminded or in a trance, his thoughts drifting to another world.

"Why don't you try to publish all your writings," he finally asked. "You have great potential."

"Do you really think so?"

"Of course!"

So Yadan wrote a few more stories, working mostly at night, but showed them to no one. She lacked confidence.

One day, a teacher named Yuan assigned his class a writing project. It was to write a story titled "Encounter." Yuan had previously been the editor of a large magazine, and he was a very exacting critic. Yadan wrote thousands of words, in and out of class. Responding to this assignment, she wrote a story about a young girl named Xiao Fan who met a former classmate named Shasha at a bus stop. Shasha was wearing so much makeup that Xiao Fan hardly recognized her. Xiao Fan passed the examinations and entered a university. Her mood was buoyant, which contrasted sharply with Shasha's, whose joblessness affected her attitude. Mainly through dialogue, the story described Xiao Fan's optimism and Shasha's despair. When the bus came they parted; Xiao Fan assumed this was their final meeting. Deep in Yadan's heart, she was Xiao Fan and Yu was Shasha. She had learned that Yu had not been admitted to the art academy, despite all of Jinwu's encouragement and material support. Yadan was very disappointed by this news. So much talent, but now Yu's future was definitely at risk.

Yadan hadn't seen Yu for many months. Jumping out of the window had been a heroic act. And then all those months in the hospital. She loved Yu passionately, as much as she loved Zhulong, and she had spent three months of her own time caring for her in the hospital. Now she copied a poem by Qiu Jin, intending to give it to Yu.

> It's our own fault our country is in turmoil,
> That I must wander homeless everywhere,
> My blood boiling, afraid to look around me,
> My gut as cold as frostbitten spring blossoms.

Yadan thought that this poem applied to Yu. When she was released from the hospital, all patched up like a rag doll, her recovery surprised everyone.

Many had expected she would never walk out of the hospital. Old women talked about it: "The third daughter of the Lu family—what a story! Her organs had been torn apart, but then they put them back together. Is she not a ghost?"

After her release, Yu stayed at Jinwu's house. Yadan went to visit, but Yu remained silent and listless most of the time. One day, Yadan made a delicious soup and brought it all the way from home in a thermos, splattering her dress. Pouring it for Yu, she said, "My mom brought a live turtle home from the market, then chopped off its head herself so that I could make the soup from fresh ingredients." Yu just frowned; was it the soup that displeased her or was she just not willing to have company? After a while, Yadan lost interest and seldom visited.

But Yu remained in her heart and often appeared as a character in Yadan's stories. She tried to achieve some objectivity about her, giving some of her qualities to different characters with different motives and ideals. Sometimes one character led to another. In this way, Yadan gradually improved her understanding of human nature. One day she bought a puzzle for Yu, a Rubik's Cube. Yu held it under the sunshine filtering in through the curtains and looked at the patterns on each side. That moment left a deep impression on Yadan: wasn't it true that every person is like a Rubik's Cube, presenting a different face with every twist of the cubes?

Yadan's story was used as a model composition by Yuan, her writing teacher. He passed it around among her classmates and asked if she had other stories. She gave him one that told of a young girl who loved her mother deeply, but tried in vain to gain her love. After beginning to earn money, the girl bought a buttercream cake from her first month's pay. The mother said it was not made of real butter and, not knowing how much the girl craved the cake—whether made with real butter or not—fed it to her cat. The girl grabbed the cake away from the cat, stuffing it into her own mouth, and in this way choked herself to death. Yuan showed this story to editors at the magazine where he used to work. They were all quite at a loss as to its meaning, finding it didn't fit into any of the usual categories—not a tear-jerker, not a provocative story, not about sent-down youth. They were so constricted in their thinking that no one wanted to take on the job of editing it, nor did anyone want to send it away, as the story was somehow touching.

Finally, it came to the attention of the chief editor, who slapped his thigh and said, "Good! What's wrong with it? It pokes at the problem of social classes. Even love is separated by class! The mother and daughter were one family, but the mother was obviously bourgeois and the daughter a worker, a proletarian. This is a symbolic way of writing, with great depth."

Buttercream Cake became Yadan's big career breakthrough. It was published as the lead story in an important magazine in a section reserved for new writers. It turned her into an overnight celebrity in the world of writers and editors, and she was even interviewed on TV and by newspaper reporters. She began to receive fan letters and was occasionally recognized on the street. All of this attention did wonders for her self-confidence, which carried over into other realms of her life. Thus, one day she felt that it was time for her to speak up, and she asked Zhulong to meet her at the water fountain.

That night, moonlight spread out on the water like broken pieces of silver. Yadan saw Zhulong walking quietly toward the fountain.

6

My obsession with jewelry began in the mid-1970s, before the Cultural Revolution had ended. Often I would visit a nearby pawnshop in search of valuable items at cheap prices. What a strange time in history. Fear pervaded everything. It was at the pawnshop that I met Xuanming.

It was midday in autumn under gray skies. As usual, I was lingering in front of the jewelry counter. An old woman came walking through the door on tiny feet. It was her feet that first caught my attention, along with the delicate black shoes she wore. The tips of the shoes pointed upward and they were decorated with diamond-shaped bits of green jade. Her shoes overshadowed all the antiques at this pawnshop named Benefit the People.

Concentrating so much on her feet, I almost missed seeing the jewelry box she carried in her hands. At one glance I could see it was made of golden rosewood, heavy looking, with an embossed copper cap on each corner depicting flowers. Her manner was dignified and proud. As she opened the little door in front, four beautifully made drawers came into view. She pulled out each one; people in the shop came closer to see what treasures would be revealed.

I was awestruck. Here was one of the last living representatives of that long-ago world of wealth, beauty, and privilege. She symbolized a class of people of which I knew little and longed to know more. Here was an opportunity and I would not let it pass.

In the first drawer was an exquisitely carved ivory seal. Yellowed with age, it depicted a boy playing a flute and a buffalo with a boyish face. It was inscribed with the name of a high-ranking official in the Qing Dynasty. The official was well-known for his brutal campaign to crush the Taiping army; could this old lady be his descendant?

The second drawer contained a bracelet made with silver and agates. Each stone was scarlet, like red berries found in a deep forest. Silver had been used to create a spidery web of contrasting color and texture around each berry. Jinwu noticed that several strands were broken but had been repaired. Cleverly done, but the repairs would detract from its value.

In the third drawer was a pair of pearl earrings. The pearls were in the shape of teardrops, milky white, and perfectly matched. The old lady said this was a rare treasure that had come down through her family; previously there had been a matching necklace, creating a jewelry set that was unique and immensely valuable. But a nephew named An, who was an ingrate, had taken possession of it and subsequently given it away.

As the old lady was giving her recitation a small group of customers had gathered around to listen and ask questions. She found this stimulating and her spirits perked up as she expounded the fine points of her treasures: "The teardrop pearls are rare because they grow only where the two shells join, resulting in one end being narrow and the other fully rounded. Finding two that are perfectly matched in color as well as shape, as these are, is extremely rare. In the old days, according to rumor, there was another pair like this that belonged to one of the several imperial families. They came into possession of a man named Zai Zhuan. When his family was driven out of the Forbidden City he became poor; but no matter how desperate he was for money, Zai would never sell them. They were not perfectly matched like these in our possession, but they were large and considered a rare treasure. Zai Zhuan would loan them to others but never sell them. So, all of you . . . can you imagine the value of this pair? They are a real treasure, and if I didn't really need the money I would never sell them."

I immediately asked, "Are you selling because of a wedding or a funeral?"

Annoyed by this question, the old woman said, "For my eldest grand-daughter's wedding."

The last drawer had a diamond ring set in platinum. Saying nothing, I guessed the diamond must be twenty carats. Lines of scarlet birds were carved on the platinum. Two Chinese characters, *gao* and *yao*, were engraved on each side of the setting. I found this very curious and said, "*Gao* is written with the character for sun on top of the character for tree. *Yao* is written with a sun beneath a tree. Is this significant? Any special meanings?"

"Yes," said the old woman. "According to the book *Within the Four Seas*, 'Beyond the south sea, between the black and green seas, there was a type of wood called Ruomu.' What is Ruomu? That's the golden branch of the sun's tree god. *Gao* means the sun on top of the tree. *Yao* means the setting sun by the base of the tree. This ring was made for my daughter Ruomu's wedding."

And now I knew this old woman was the grandmother of the three Lu girls. She was the mother-in-law of Lu Chen. I took her hand in mine and asked, "Is your eldest granddaughter named Ling?"

All of that happened a few years ago. Thinking about it now, it's still interesting. That day Jinwu followed the old woman to Lu's house. Jinwu used to be Lu Chen's student, majoring in railway economics. Then she was selected by a film studio to play a couple of roles and decided to make acting her profession. Jinwu and Lu Chen had no relationship but Ruomu hated the younger woman. She believed that Jinwu intended to seduce her husband. Sensing this, Jinwu deliberately became friendlier, even a little flirtatious, just to aggravate Ruomu.

Finally, Ruomu issued an ultimatum, "Jinwu must not enter our door!"

It was Lu Chen who signaled the end of this little game. "If you want me to live a few more years, do not come here again."

Jinwu looked at his thin and yellowish face with astonishment, wondering how a man of strong character and high intelligence could so easily be dominated by a woman. But she held her tongue out of sympathy for her teacher.

Jinwu helped the Lu family financially. All three daughters stayed with her at no cost while attending school—the two older children while Jinwu's adoptive parents were still alive. The couple had no children of their own and loved having them around the house. They left some money for Jinwu, which they claimed had come from her biological mother; but as the couple died suddenly, the woman had never been identified. So the connection to Jinwu's real mother was forever lost.

Jinwu remained true to her word to Lu Chen for a long time, not returning to his home in order to avoid upsetting his jealous wife. But after meeting Xuanming she changed her mind. It was a rare opportunity because only Xuanming was at home, and Jinwu wanted to see Xuanming's treasures and hear more of her stories. This was a woman with an interesting connection to the past.

Jinwu made afternoon tea for Xuanming and a dish of spicy beans, knowing she was originally from Hunan Province. Jinwu had been to the Lu house many times before, but had never met Xuanming. From Ling she learned that the old lady did most of the cooking; she must have been in the kitchen all the time. On this visit, by preparing some food to take with her she could keep Xuanming to herself and indulge her as she deserved. Xuanming brought out some rice wine to accompany the spicy beans and asked Jinwu to drink with her.

When she learned that it was Jinwu who had helped the girls while they attended school, the old lady squinted and said, "You are lovely. How old are you?"

"I am ten years older than your eldest granddaughter and eighteen years younger than your daughter; how old does that make me?"

"You are over thirty but don't look it."

Jinwu giggled. "I am an actress. There's another actress named Fang who is over forty and still plays a teenager." She took a big sip of the wine and liked it very much.

Xuanming said, "It's easy to make. I just made a large bottle of it; you can take it home with you."

So the two of them sat and drank and chatted like old friends. Finally, her head spinning a little from the wine, Jinwu said, "I saw the jewelry you brought into the shop. You must love those pieces very much. You wouldn't sell them unless you had to."

The old lady curled her lips in resignation. "That's right. Lu Chen has been useless. My husband used to run the railroad and supported a whole family, a large one. We lived well."

"But it was a very different time and can't be compared with living conditions today. Wasn't Lu Yu's mother a college graduate? Why is she not working?"

Xuanming sipped wine and chewed on beans. "Well, it was Ruomu's father's idea, he said it was a woman's duty to have children; she should stay home and cook. If not for me she couldn't have entered a university."

Jinwu rolled her eyes and said, "To tell you honestly, my mom left me some money. I like that diamond platinum ring. If you're willing, just give me a price and I'll pay you for a long-term loan. When you have a little more money you can have it back. That's better than letting it go to some stranger."

Pondering a moment, Xuanming said, "All right. I had the ring made when Ruomu got married. It cost me nine hundred Chinese silver dollars at that time. Now it must be worth at least three thousand yuan. But at a time such as this, don't mention the real price."

Jinwu took out a wad of money and counted. Three hundred yuan was on the table. "How about paying you a thousand three times?"

Xuanming nodded silently, wrapped the ring in a hankie, and gave it to Jinwu. Seeing the aged hand with its veins throbbing, Jinwu felt regret and said, "Whenever you want it back, just let me know. I'll bring it back immediately. I live at the last stop on the number nine bus line. The place is called Yang Qiao."

"I can see you are a straightforward person," Xuanming said with a smile.

Xuanming was wondering whether she should show Jinwu the lamp. That was a real treasure. Several times she was about to mention it, but in the end she decided not to. When Jinwu asked again if there was any other treasure, Xuanming firmly shook her head.

Some years later Jinwu saw the lamp in a large museum. She looked at it a long time and wondered why Xuanming had kept it hidden. Had the old lady shown her the lamp, she would have wanted to have it, even if it required selling her house. But now it was forever beyond her reach.

7

If her eldest granddaughter had not asked for jewelry, Xuanming would have forgotten all about the place called Yang Qiao. But by the 1980s Ling had thrown away all revolutionary feelings and was ready to enjoy material objects. It happened rather suddenly; one night it came to her that she had been entertaining foolish thoughts. What is real? For a woman, money is real. What is freedom? Freedom comes from money. And freedom is like opium: one lungful and you are addicted. Ling had swung from one extreme to the other and now truly believed that money provided the key to freedom.

Ling knew all about Grandma's treasure. In that large rosewood trunk and the small rosewood jewelry cabinet, there were countless treasures. So she began asking Grandma for jewelry. She knew she must make her wants known before her sisters began to think along the same lines. And Grandma never said no to her eldest granddaughter. Recently all three Lu children had begun working and sending money home; Ruomu's only expenses were three meals a day and a bundle of ambergris incense each month, so she had saved some money. Since Ling had fallen in love with jewelry, Xuanming decided it was time to go to Yang Qiao.

When she saw Xuanming, Jinwu couldn't help thinking how much the old woman had aged in the ten years she had known her. She couldn't imagine what she herself would look like at that age. Live while you can, drink until you get drunk, hurry up and get a life—this was especially true for women. At least that was what Jinwu believed.

When Xuanming arrived, Jinwu was busy with preparations for Yu's art exhibit. Frames were all over the bed and floor. Xuanming couldn't even find a place to sit.

Jinwu was in high spirits, but as usual Xuanming began by making complaints. In her previous life she must have been deeply indebted to the Lu family; she had served them for so long, yet the debt was still unpaid. Jinwu just laughed, saying this outlook should be applied to her; as for the grandmother, was it not sufficient to say she was acting from a sense of duty? Xuanming smiled.

Jinwu brought Xuanming to her bedroom, where they could both be seated comfortably. Then she brought out tea and cookies. Xuanming, who had become a servant to her own family after an early life as lady of the house to an important man, was deeply appreciative of such generous but informal hospitality. She sat on the bed with her legs crossed, thinking she really liked this young woman. Perhaps she could adopt her. But she was too young to be a daughter, too old to be a granddaughter.

"Do you have children?" she asked Jinwu.

"I don't even have a husband, where would I get a child?" Jinwu returned her smile.

Xuanming reacted spontaneously. "You should get married! It's no good to pass forty without a husband!" As she said this she was thinking of her own aunt Yuxin, who remained unmarried all her life. Perhaps it is true that beautiful women are ill-fated. But Jinwu's beauty was still at its peak and there were no indications of ill fate. This thought led to another: times had changed. Today many women age better than men.

Jinwu moved in and out like a swirling breeze. Smiling broadly, she said, "I'd have gone to the market if I knew you were coming. Maybe shrimp dumplings, I remember you like that. Tonight you must stay for dinner. Yu will be back. You must not have seen each other for a while."

Jinwu made a sweet dumpling soup. After serving a bowl to Xuanming, she left the room a moment and returned with the diamond ring. Xuanming had been reluctant to mention the subject and here was Jinwu, thoughtfully providing the ring of her own volition. The old lady was moved.

Jinwu sat next to Xuanming and blew on the hot soup to cool it. "Honestly, I wanted to wear it when I married. But that didn't happen, and it's a waste to let it sit here unused. I wanted to return it long ago, but I'm always busy and it's still here. I am so sorry you had to come all the way here. Now eat the soup while it's hot. I made the dumplings a little soft so they will be easy to chew."

Xuanming caressed Jinwu's hair. "Good child, you are so thoughtful. Look, I still have good teeth! At age eighty-nine I've only lost two! But about this ring: it's worth at least seven thousand yuan. Think it over."

"Of course, I know. But it's not mine and I cannot keep it. Back then we said this is on loan to me, you didn't sell it. I will not go back on my word."

Again Xuanming was moved. On the edge of tears, she said, "Good child! People like you will be protected by Buddha all your life. When we first met I knew we had some predestined connections. You know what life is like in the Lu family. I'm an old woman who has served them for so many years, but I have run out of energy and am terribly lonely even while living in the midst of my own family. I once had a son, but he died during the war. Had he lived, life would have been much better for me.

"Imagine! Living with a daughter, who has been spoiled by everyone since she was a small child and has never done any work herself. She expects me to account for every last penny! As I'm getting older, my mind is not working well. Often, if I return from the market short a few coins, Ruomu nags me about it for hours. And Lu Chen won't even speak to me. Although I have many faults, I am still an elder in the family; how can they show so little respect? I can't count on my granddaughters. I raised the eldest of them single-handedly. For what? All she wants from me is money and jewelry! I do pamper her, but I know what she is up to. Selfish as she is, she's still a dear child. How I wish I had a granddaughter like you. But I had too many sins and don't deserve such good fortune." This speech was uttered with much daubing of the handkerchief.

Unhesitatingly, Jinwu said, "Then love me as your granddaughter! Take me as the daughter of your lost son. I don't have any family and I don't even know who my mother was. From now on, I'll show my filial respect only to you. Okay?"

Xuanming was overwhelmed by this expression of love. "Good child, you are so smart! Old people need to hear such wonderful appreciation. It doesn't really matter whether you can show filial respect or not.

"You know what our girls are like. The eldest one has a bad temper, but of course I'm to blame for that. The second one is honest, but nothing can make her talk. The youngest one, Yu, was odd since she was little. She caused so much trouble for the family. Outsiders all thought her mother and I treated her badly. But who can get along with that child? She killed her own little brother! Could her mother ever forgive her?"

Jinwu reached out to cover Xuanming's mouth, protesting "Granny, don't ever say that. Yu was too little to understand. She was filled with sorrow. She went for a tattoo for this and endured so much pain. Can't you talk with her mother and convince her to let these old feelings go? After all, Yu is her daughter."

They chatted till after dinner. Yu did not return and since it was getting too late for the bus, Jinwu sent Xuanming home by taxi—bearing the ring, much lighter in the heart, and smiling to herself.

8

Xuanming did not sleep that night. She was thinking of Jinwu. What an amazing woman—so accomplished, frank and straightforward, warm, shrewd but gallant. She thought also of her own youth, and of what a curse that none of her granddaughters, not to mention her own daughter, not even her great-granddaughter, was as good a person.

Xuanming had been born in turbulent times at the end of the nineteenth century. Her family name was Shen. Her father was the richest businessman in the provinces of Hunan and Hubei, and owned many jewelry, satin, and silk shops. Later the family joined the Manchu court in Beijing, assuming official duties there. Xuanming's father was the eldest son, and he had several brothers. All of them were scholars. The whole family was eminent. But unexpectedly, her father's fortunes began to decline after the move to Beijing. First, it was Lady Yang's distant relative who got into trouble. Although this had no immediate consequences for their own family, Lady Yang became fearful and insecure.

Xuanming's father never kept any concubines. In those days this was a rarity. Because of her father's example, Xuanming strongly opposed her husband doing so. Lady Yang had given birth to all seventeen daughters of the Shen family, and she managed the household. She had doubted the wisdom of going to Beijing. Another source of anxiety was Yuxin. When she died and Yang Rui got into trouble, Lady Yang's worries seemed to overwhelm her and she became gravely ill. At the same time she had become preoccupied with finding a husband for her youngest daughter, Xuanming. She was fully aware that the girl was headstrong and naughty, but nevertheless hoped to arrange a match with a highly respectable family.

Xuanming's third uncle had a close friend, Qin Tianfang; he was well-known for his role in building the Beijing-Zhangjiakou Railway together with the famous Zhan Tianyou, who was known as the father of railways in China. After construction was completed, Qin became the regional chief for the railway. His son had recently returned from studying in Japan and asked Xuanming's third uncle to help him find a wife. It was these connections that led to Qin Heshou's becoming Xuanming's husband.

In China, as the twentieth century approached and European ideas were making their way into the Far East, and after the defeat of the Hundred Days' Reform, many people with breadth of vision began leaving the country to study abroad. When he was only about ten years old, Qin Tianfang's second son, Qin Heshou, was already capable of leading his Boy Scout troop in song:

> *Forward march, forward march!*
> *Little boys with little ponies,*
> *Filled with military spirit!*

In the grand drama of the twentieth century,
If you don't fight, how can you survive?
We love our country as we love our kin,
We love our troop, as we love ourselves.
May we live long lives,
May we live forever,
May our triumph be glorious!

When he first saw her, Qin Heshou was not impressed with Xuanming. He was forward-thinking and no longer wore his hair in a pigtail, yet here was a woman who reflected the old ways, with dainty feet, the very feature that Lady Yang wanted to show off. But as his eyes ranged up and down Xuanming's body, like a video camera, he found much to admire. She was enchanting! She was a well-mannered mistress from a respectable family. As the youngest among many siblings, she had been indulged and was used to having her own way, but she also had a capacity for work. Having developed an early aptitude for business and finance, she had helped her father with accounting and had been exposed to many people who were professionally and socially accomplished.

As for Xuanming, the task of sizing up this young man was simpler. At a time when most marriages were arranged by parents, including those of her older sisters, her family had made an exception and brought the two youngsters together. Qin Heshou arrived wearing creased trousers and a striped shirt, over which he wore a Western-style vest. His hair was neatly combed and pomaded, his face slightly oval, his eyes spirited, and the bridge of his nose straight. Xuanming was pleased at what she saw, and they spent a few moments exchanging remarks about their ambitions, what they had read, and so forth.

Thus, the marriage was arranged.

In 1911, the year of the Xinhai Revolution, which ended the Qing Dynasty, Xuanming married Qin Heshou, the second son of Qin Tianfang, head of the Beijing-Zhangjiakou Railway. The wedding was a grand affair and the gift list included the following items:

— six carved jade bowls with raised decorations in green on a white background

— ten pearl-studded fans in individual boxes

— one pair of folding screens decorated with ruby-studded golden pheasant frames and a wide array of scenes from Chinese opera and literature, complete with black-lacquered cases

— one pair of pearl-encrusted, lined jute bags finished perfectly with a ring of twenty-three northern pearls

— one double-sided, fine-toothed comb with handle, perfectly set with sapphires

— twenty floral wine cups carved from rhinoceros horn

— ten sets of jewelry boxes

The dowry list included the following items:

— two padded-cotton quilts embroidered with gold thread, each trimmed with pearls, emeralds, rose sapphires, and green and white royal seal jades

— one bronze mirror set with dozens of rare pearls

— one pearl and jade head ornament, inlaid with dozens of rare pearls

— one carefully embroidered wedding dress trimmed with gold thread and pearls

Before daylight on her wedding day, Xuanming's mother woke her from a sound sleep and brought breakfast. Two maids were assigned to help Xuanming with her hair. Lady Yang took out the rouge Yuxin made from flower petals and they spent two hours turning the bride into a heavenly beauty. Lady Yang personally set the tiara in place. It was decorated with pearls, jade, and other semiprecious stones. Attached to this was a veil, as prescribed for the bride of a prestigious family, on which Aunt Yuxin had embroidered images of phoenixes. Although her jewels were not as sumptuous as those seen on Manchu princesses in the Forbidden City, the embroidery was of the highest quality.

By noon, all the sisters- and brothers-in-law were gathered in the front hall. In a mood of festive gaiety they helped the bride into her sedan chair. But after it had been raised by four strong young footmen, she suddenly jumped to the ground, saying, "Ma, I will return in three days and prepare a batch of pastry." Lady Yang, who had been holding herself in check, suddenly burst into tears.

"My child, please don't worry about such things. When you are living with your in-laws you cannot always do as you please. If you want something, let me know and I'll send it over."

Master Shen frowned on this much indulgence. "Never heard of such a thing, sending food to a married daughter. You spoil her too much. She should do as the Romans do, live according to the customs of her in-laws."

Xuanming twisted her face into mock despair, saying, "Dad, don't you love me anymore?"

Master Shen held her hand and sighed, "Dad would like the Qin family to finish taming my coltish daughter."

Then the housekeeper urged her to return to the sedan chair, the trumpet fanfare was sounded, and the wedding procession began.

9

On my wedding night I arrived at the Qin house but did not sleep with my husband. That evening, two men—in their midtwenties, wearing leather hats—came to visit Qin Heshou, who took them to the study. They talked all night. Twice I sent them tea and heard them speaking of "the corruption of the Qing government . . . foreign powers slicing up China . . . people suffering . . . Sun Wen's three principles."

Out of curiosity, I asked, "What are foreign powers?"

My husband replied, "Foreign powers are a few big countries, imperialist countries."

"And who is Sun Wen, and what are his three principles?"

"Sun Wen is Dr. Sun Yat-sen, my teacher. We knew each other in Japan. His principles are 'nationalism, democracy, and people's welfare.'"

He hesitated a moment and then said softly, "Don't ask questions now. We have things we must discuss this evening. I'll tell you when I have more time."

In those days Heshou was good-natured and patient, and I tried to be the same. He was from a big family, the second eldest son, with a big brother, four younger brothers, and one younger sister. Because the elder sister-in-law was not in good health, all the household affairs for the whole family fell on me. Fortunately, I had experience doing this in my parents' home, but it was tiring. I had expected that life in his family would be quiet and I could use the time to read and learn to play music. But all six brothers' families lived under one roof and there was endless housework.

I had to plan and supervise preparation of meals; monitor the cleaning, gardening, and maintenance; and anticipate and prepare for seasonal holidays and birthdays. The work was constant and I was responsible for getting it done. Early in summer all the family's winter clothing had to be pulled out of cupboards and closets and aired out in the sun, including both Chinese and Western jackets and coats. The same for everything made of wool, satin, and leather; all had to be aired out, together with paintings, books, and calligraphic art. Every summer I had to organize the cooking and preservation of food for the winter: a dozen or more jars of marinated vegetables, pickled cabbages, soybean paste, chili bean sauce, and berry jelly. For holidays I made rice wine, marinated fish, bacon, and sausages. And then there were the desserts and treats, such as pine seed candies, winter melon and popcorn candies, cookies with orange stuffing, and dried dates. During the day I dealt with social affairs, and at night I managed the bookkeeping, needlework, and embroidery. Although the Qin residence had many servants, by the old rules everything had to be personally managed by the daughter-in-law. Failure with anything would bring complaints, even scorn. The eldest sister-in-law collapsed from the pressure of work; now she was suffering from a tubercular disease. Her face turned waxy yellow and sometimes she was delirious. I was young and healthy, but after a day's work I was sometimes too tired to speak at night. I tried my best to perform flawlessly and soon won the respect of all the brothers and their wives. Every time I returned to my own family's home, my mother would be concerned and point out that I had lost more weight. But this is a typical situation for women, she said; after being a daughter-in-law for thirty years, if you survive you'll then be a mother-in-law, and life should become easier.

Heshou was popular. Friends often visited and they would talk until late in the evening. This was a problem for me because after working all day, I was expected to be available as hostess; often when I was serving them tea I was too sleepy to keep my eyes open. The interest I had in marital intimacy early in my marriage soon evaporated. Occasionally I would complain. I had only a few years of private tutoring, I told my husband, and "I thought that after marrying you I could attend school for a few years; instead, I've become a servant for this big family."

Heshou would smile and say that things were going to improve, that if I could support his efforts for a couple of years, "we'll go to Japan and you can get a civilized education." This gave me hope, and when I was too tired to move, I would think about his promise. "Going to Japan" became a delicious treat that was deeply buried in my thoughts. But time went on, and on. The treat got stale, then moldy and rotten. Heshou made many promises. None of them came true.

In the autumn of the first year of our marriage there was a huge event, one that broke up our dull routines. It was the third year of Xuantong's reign. Puyi, the last emperor of China, was overthrown and Sun Wen, known to most Westerners as Sun Yat-sen, established the Republic of China. This brought my husband great joy. "Just wait," he would often say, "a better life is coming for all of China." His optimism was reflected in the mood of the street. Overnight, men rejected the old hairstyle and removed their pigtails. Women no longer bound their feet. Freedom and equality were in the air.

Years went by and the good changes promised for our family did not materialize. I worked as hard as ever. Seven years into the Republic, I gave birth to a girl and named her Ruomu. She was very pretty and I was proud, but Heshou had no interest in baby girls. Then, after a few more years, I gave birth to a son. This brought great happiness to my husband and he named the boy Tiancheng, meaning heavenly achievement. Heshou had meanwhile been promoted; now he was head of the Gansu-Shanghai Railway. We moved to a house of our own in Xi'an, a large and beautiful place with a courtyard. I hired four servant girls, two cooks, and three old women for part-time work. Life was simpler, but the kind of life I'd dreamed of did not come true.

Heshou had for some time been an occasional user of opium; now he used it daily and began having elaborate dinner parties for friends and showgirls. We began to fight about that, and in retaliation I took up activities of my own. Mahjong was something I enjoyed, and now I became obsessed with it. Since you play, I'll play, too, I thought to myself. Heshou no longer commanded my respect, and when I would complain or argue he would throw a tantrum, pound on the table, even smash tables and chairs. He had no patience with the children; even for the smallest bit of misbehavior he would make them kneel as punishment. I began to feel insecure and started putting money away. Gradually, beginning with funds that I had saved from my wedding, and with money saved by being frugal, I accumulated enough so that the children and I could survive if something happened.

10

Yushe's solo art exhibit, titled *Moon Art*, finally opened as scheduled.

Jinwu's efforts were crucial. Through persuasion and pulling strings, she got the local arts and cultural minister to come to the opening.

The minister gave a little speech: "In this time of reform and change we wish to encourage the practice and enjoyment of art . . ." Then he enumerated the four principles that should guide artists. He wanted them to support the efforts of their leaders to improve everyone's life and realize the aims of the revolution. He pointedly referred to the youth of the artist and concluded with the usual platitudes and pleasantries, then left the gallery in a hurry, head bent low, without a glance at the exhibit. The crowd came alive after he was out of sight and lingered over each painting, discussing the artist's intentions and technique.

There was much to discuss. Here, in one of the nation's most prestigious galleries, Lu Yu's eccentric visual universe was on display. It included paintings of donkeys' heads; a television set made to look like it was made of soft, edible materials and then hung on tree branches, and which was attracting flies; desiccated butterflies and parts of human bodies; a hand holding enlarged genitals; and the gigantic mouth of a dinosaur painted in photo-realist style. After seeing these works, a student of the art academy named Red Dawn rushed to the ladies' room and vomited. But she returned to see the rest of the exhibit. When leaving, she signed the guest book, commenting, "Amazingly decoded Freud! Oedipus awakening!"

In the main hall was a painting of a totally different style. It contrasted strongly with the darker visions displayed in the other rooms. On top of a bright blue wash the artist had painted enlarged snowflakes; each was treated differently from the others, yet all partook of the same vision: at once simple, tranquil, and mysterious. Adding to the enigmatic qualities of the work was an adjacent label which read simply *No Title*.

Reporters from a television station arrived with their cameras and lighting equipment and walked toward Jinwu, whose radiance and proprietary air made them think she might be the artist. She glanced around, not realizing until then that Yu was not in sight. With the lights glaring and the cameras recording, she explained that she was not the artist, only a friend; but she said the artist was very young. This remark whetted the appetite of the reporters; all were men, with men's appetites for youth and beauty. Also, this would give them an angle that might increase viewers' interest.

So when Jinwu found Yu sleeping under the table where the guest book was placed, all the TV people were disappointed. As Yu stood up and rubbed her sleepy eyes, the cameras that had been facing her were suddenly turned off and the lights went dark. The artist was indeed young, but she was also shabby and listless. Moreover, she had paint smeared on her face. How disrespectful! How foolish! In one thoughtless moment she had forfeited her opportunity to achieve what so many people crave above all else, even more than riches: fame! Or at least a few moments of that precious intangible.

Television people are above all professional assassins. No matter how much fame you have already achieved, if you break one of their unwritten rules you are in trouble. They will wipe you out, reduce you to ashes, turn

your good name to mud. Three bows and nine kowtows may not be sufficient to restore yourself in their good graces.

In the rarefied world of the TV reporter, there is no space for unconven-
tional behavior, no appreciation of the value to society of an outcast or mis-
anthrope. Yu had no idea how important the mass media would be for her.
She looked far away from this noisy exhibition hall, fallen in deep thoughts
in another world. We could see this young woman in the midst of the crowd
was all puzzled, her eyes were deep but drifting and her face stained with oil
paints. She looked so lonely standing in the crowd, like a single bare bush in
a tall forest. She felt embarrassed, not knowing what to do.

A newspaper reporter walked through the crowd.

"Excuse me, Miss Lu Yu. May I ask you a few questions? I personally
think that twentieth-century artists use their visual language to exhibit their
fears—of reality, mystery, the universe. They are seeking a haven from these
fears in this quiet space. I think your art is filled with fear and anxiety about
sex. The themes are castration, masturbation, intercourse, and impotence.
All of this may be a source of madness at the same time as it fosters unbridled desire. If I am correct, you are a typical Freudian, right?"

"What is a Freudian? I don't understand what you are saying."

"What?" the reporter almost shouted. "You don't know Freud?"

The reporter's reaction was not exaggerated. In the early 1980s, whether
you were brilliant or dull, aristocratic or plebeian, knowledgeable or ignorant, to know about Freud was the first step on the ladder of sophistication.
To be ignorant of Freud was to sign your own death sentence in the court
of intellectual crime. An artist who didn't know about Freud could not have
anything to say to readers of art criticism.

But this reporter had exceptional patience. "Okay, let's change the subject. May I ask, which artist influenced you the most? For example, Rubens,
van Gogh, Cézanne . . . ?"

"I don't know. I haven't paid much attention to other painters."

"My God! You don't know about Freud, you claim no influence from
Western masters. Then where did you get the fear in your art?"

"I . . . I don't know."

Jinwu had been standing next to Yu, doing her best to control her tongue; now, finally, she interjected, "Of course it came from her own feelings, from her own life experience."

The reporter squinted his eyes, thought for a moment, and then asked, "Which one among all your paintings in this hall is your favorite?"

Yu looked around like a child taken by grown-ups for the first time to a shopping mall, and then pointed to the painting that depicted snowflakes against a blue background.

"Why is it called *No Title*? If you were asked to give it a title, what would it be?"

"*A Childhood Snowstorm*." She had finally produced an answer. As she said this, she noticed a young man watching from afar. It was the man named Yuanguang or Zhulong. They had not seen each other for a long time. He had lost weight and seemed fatigued, as though from a long journey; he was still very handsome. He became visible just as the crowd began to disperse. They left in haste, just as they had gathered around her in haste.

He spoke quietly. "This afternoon I'll take part in a debate for my election. If you have time, please come." His look was serious but neutral, as though he was looking at one of her paintings.

As they were talking in the middle of the exhibition hall, people were noisily walking out, occasionally jostling the artist. She overheard phrases of their conversation as they passed by: ". . .what modernist painting? She never heard of Freud!" ". . . said she never heard of Freud. Must be lying!" Yu smiled softly and saw Zhulong frowning. He had heard it, too.

11

The election held at that famous school in the early 1980s became a feature of the country's landscape.

Yushe, now a worker, entered the school on a tatty bicycle. To attend the lecture she had arranged to work the night shift. A huge herd of bicycles had come together spontaneously and were now clustered in front of a huge office building. Inside, laughter and applause were, to Yu, the sound track of another world. Sudden applause brought her out of her trance. Then she heard a voice she knew well, although its timbre had deepened.

"To reach purity, one must be ignorant; to be correct, one must be fatuous; to be steadfast, one must be brainless. This formula shares no common ground with true Marxism!

"Right. There are always people who are too lazy to think for themselves, and who willingly hand over their right to choose their personal beliefs. In China, such people claim they believe in Mao Zedong. If they lived in the Soviet Union, they would claim they support Brezhnev. If in India, they would be devout Hindus. If they lived in Libya, they would be Muslim fanatics!"

A round of laughter followed this colloquy. The human wall jamming the entrance to the auditorium, now filled by two thousand people, was moving a little and Yu managed to squeeze into the area behind the last row of seats, where people were standing shoulder to shoulder. Now she could see that spectators were jammed into every conceivable space—on the stage, under the stage, in the aisles, on windowsills, even on top of the steam radiators. The scene was reminiscent of another lodged deep in Yu's memory—that night in the Square. Normally averse to crowds, Yu was not fearful of this one but she did wonder: would Zhulong survive yet another encounter with authorities? For this was the same brave young man who had stood on the base of the white tombstone, just as he was now standing on the podium, as though on an altar, totally exposed. He seemed destined to sacrifice himself for a cause. Danger had become his hobby. Yu worried: he had escaped once, but he cannot make good escapes every time.

"To punish thoughts is, in reality, to regard all citizens as suspects. If a comrade can be convicted of a crime because of his reactionary thoughts, then how can this be restricted to what is published? Why not put a listening device in a family's home? Why not open a personal letter? Confiscate and hold as evidence a private diary? Thoughts can be conveyed by the style of one's speech, or expressed by silence. Why not punish 'illegal cries,' 'implied smiles,' and 'reactionary wordlessness'? In fact, all of these travesties have actually occurred in the last ten years. They were logical extensions of the concept of punishing thoughts. Just imagine the implications of a doctrine that holds that thinking can be a crime; this is like the proverbial dragonfly. As long as we keep the dragonfly's body, no matter how many times we cut off its evil tail, it will grow back again!"

Yu looked around fearfully as though she had done something wrong. Those clubs, which in the Square had seemed hidden right there among the audience . . . could there be clubs here, flying out at any time to attack people, beat out their blood, smash their bones to pieces? Stop! Run! If you don't run now you will never escape.

"Allow me to ask," a student said earnestly, "shouldn't evil verbal attacks be limited, kept in check by authorities if necessary? Please note that I said attack, not just criticism!"

"Good, let me reply. What is an attack? In a legal sense, a false charge can be defined, a slander can be defined, only an attack cannot be defined! We all know in the past ten years how people used this label of criminality to send many honest people to death. The essence of the matter is this: how to tell the difference between an attack and a criticism."

This response was received enthusiastically. Then one of the students asked a dangerous question; instantly it was followed by cries from the podium, "Don't answer! No, no, don't answer!" Yu saw that Yadan was among those shouting for caution; her face was alarmed, as it had been the night when they played Q&A Behind Bars. But some other students shouted, "You must answer! Must answer!"

Zhulong just smiled calmly, and then reminded the student voters that he was in this race for a people's representative, not for a post as state chairman. This single joke got him out of a danger zone.

Through all the stimulating speeches more than a dozen video cameras were recording, and hundreds of still cameras were in use. Every facial expression was captured, every word as well, and the voices from the podium were blasting through loudspeakers. Question slips from the audience were piling up in front of Zhulong like a little hill and Yadan was helping him by dividing the questions into categories for response. Once again a stage, a play, and the leading roles acted by Zhulong and Yadan.

A loud voice from the audience: "May I ask, do you really understand what people want? The freedom to think and speak is very nice, but what they really want is a raise in salary, shorter working hours, better housing! You are making nice little speeches, but what we really need is someone who can actually do something, not just talk a lot! You never mentioned a word about the actual needs of students in this university, so why should we vote for you?"

Zhulong smiled again, this time showing signs of fatigue, but continued:

"The tone of your first question suggests you have already decided that I do not understand people. It is thus a statement rather than a true question. This kind of logic is not entirely unfamiliar to us. If I say I am one of the people, you will say that there are classes among people; if I say I, too, have been a worker, you will say there are workers who are in the vanguard and those who have regressed. In short, because you decided that I do not understand people, therefore I cannot represent them. Your premise is that you can apprehend the true needs of the people but I cannot—right?

"In your second question, once again really a statement, you say we need real action, not empty talk. Excellent! Let us see what a people's representative should actually do. Our workers must have skills, our doctors must know how to treat patients, judges must deliver fair decisions. So what about a people's representative? First, he must be a legal entity; second, he must be able to speak for all the people. So, the first duty of a representative is to do what? Talk! (Laughter and applause.) Of course, he or she must speak the truth and do so with dignity, have firm theoretical training, be able to get along with other people who have different views, and so on. For example, Lei Feng was a very good man, but if he were to be elected as a general commander, that would indicate we are not treating politics as a serious subject that can be scientifically analyzed, but as merely a stage for the achievement of fame and glory. (Applause.) Furthermore, when Mr. Ma Yinchu proposed population control at the National People's Congress in the early fifties, almost all the people's representatives opposed him. And the result? One man was wrongly criticized and three hundred million more people were born. Can you say that all those in opposition were bad people? On the contrary, they were good people! What concerns me is having the kind of people's representative congress that is composed of one hundred percent flawless people who know absolutely nothing about politics!"

The applause was deafening. The speaker had to shout out the next sentence:

"This—I believe, what I just said, should represent the highest interest of all Chinese youth and Chinese people, including all of our students!"

He can't escape. He can't escape. Like a whisper, this refrain echoed again and again in Yu's ear. Good heavens, that worrisome whisper! For years it had not appeared, and now it overwhelmed the cheers and acclaim that were directed at the speaker. It was like an explosion at the center of Yu's brain. She covered her ears with both hands as if to drown out the inner voice, the voice of a fear so great it was taking possession of her mind.

The audience had meanwhile become calm. Now the students were asking personal questions. "Who did you revere as a teenager?" or "Who do you think are the great men?"

"Sun Wukong and Jia Baoyu."

This was a strange reply. It aroused an unexpected reaction from the women in the audience. Sun Wukong was the Monkey King in the novel *Journey to the West*, and Jia Baoyu was the leading character in the Chinese classic novel *Dream of the Red Chamber*. One of the women walked forward and asked, "Why?"

"Sun Wukong, the Monkey King: resilient and brave. Jia Baoyu: affectionate and emotional. Put them together—would not such a person be perfect?"

More applause and laughs. The sound of Yadan's laughter was the loudest. Yu thought she should leave at that point.

But women students had more questions.

"What are your views on love? Do you love anyone?"

Zhulong had been responding smoothly, dispassionately, but this question clearly touched him. Under the bright lights his eyes softened, dreamy thoughts intruded; he was suddenly vulnerable. Yu saw that Yadan's mood instantly reflected his; she seemed on the verge of collapsing.

"Speaking candidly, I have been fond of a girl. It was she who saved my life with her own; to save me, she almost died. But I can never go near her. I don't know why. This is a great mystery to me. Perhaps it is also my real sorrow."

Yu watched Yadan's face turn from bright rosy sunshine to pale white paper. Then, beyond all those among them who were gaping and staring, she saw Zhulong's eyes, penetrating through space like a laser beam, coming straight to her. He had found hers in the sea of faces. Involuntarily, Yu turned away, afraid that she could not withstand such a penetrating gaze. She began walking toward the door, feeling other eyes, those of people on both sides, eyes that created holes, like bullets. And from her own eyes she felt tears gushing forth in profusion.

Oh, Zhulong, Zhulong! Say no more, that's all I need to hear. Now you must look back at Yadan. Without your love, Yadan will die.

Almost immediately another candidate jumped on the stage. He was excited and he spoke with animation: "We decided upon December eleventh as our election date. This is one day after the anniversary of a famous event: the election in 1848 of a notorious liar, Louis-Napoléon Bonaparte, who became both the first president and the last monarch in France. We cannot allow such a tragedy to be repeated in our socialist country today!"

Yu turned around at the door and saw Zhulong looking crushed and defeated, as though shot in the back. Run, Zhulong, run! The world offers thousands of ways to apply your energy; why do you have to choose the most dangerous path?

12

It was nighttime and Zhulong again walked into the *Moon Art* Exhibition Hall. Yushe was sitting there like a statue, her head bowed and her back bent. A misty shaft of moonlight drifted through the window, drenching the interior with its creamy residue. The banner for the show had fallen and was now spread on the floor, covered with an assortment of footprints. With just one step into the hall, Zhulong left behind the world of profaned dust and frustrated desire. Here was the serenity of an unearthly world, a world of tranquil beauty that engulfed his senses. And here was a girl who used her beauty not as a spear but as a shield. Slowly, surely, she led a proud young man through the mist of awakened desire and straight into an enveloping web of deepest love. He remembered a startling glimpse of a gray water ghost on another moonlit night at a distant lake—a glimpse that was forever etched in memory.

This man, the man called Yuanguang or Zhulong, had sealed himself off from extraneous temptations; he believed he was destined to pursue one mission and must not be distracted by the usual pleasures of the world. He would work tirelessly in pursuit of that mission. He could not devote his love to one person. And yet, there had been that one night by the water fountain when he had walked into a trap. Who says women are water? They are fire. A girl in love is a blazing fire; she rages through all fuel and nothing can stop her; she burns others and then burns herself. She burns all that surrounds her to the ground, and from the ashes she continues to spark and sizzle. Women are possessed of that kind of love that is catastrophic, unforgettable, overwhelming. That night by the water fountain, Yadan's caressing hand was boiling hot and her black eyes blazing as she opened his shirt button by button, and he was engulfed in a cauldron of desire. In an instant, all those beautiful abstractions conjured by Feuerbach, Socrates, Nietzsche, and Sartre were neutralized. He was a young man, after all. He couldn't resist. When he saw her virgin blood he understood he must be responsible for her.

For the first time Zhulong was in thrall to a girl. Not because he was deeply in love, not because she would be his ideal wife, not because she was his intimate friend. His obligation was of a different kind than usually leads a man to commitment, yet he could see no way to discharge that obligation short of marriage.

But in the depths of the night when he was alone with his own thoughts, he had only one girl in mind. That girl had jumped from a building, had broken and torn and crushed her tender body, had spread her blood across the filthy pavement in order to save him. That girl who had an exquisite tattoo on her back. That mysterious girl. He could not enter her body, nor could he invade her mind. Everything about her was saying—No!

There in the misty moonlight of the exhibit hall as the couple sat shoulder to shoulder, the girl raised her eyes; but her gaze was not inspired by physical desire, nor was his in response. Instead, they were possessed by something inchoate, something akin to religious inspiration. Their souls were sparkling through their eyes. Zhulong's manly beauty and Yu's female tenderness were intertwined like a coiled serpent. Scattered stars seen through the window seemed to have turned into some symbolic and mysterious signs. Yu seemed to be saying, "I am a reincarnation of a dream. My love is real, but will always be metaphorical."

Zhulong understood, saying, "Yu, remember what I said at our last meeting? That a detached feather is not soaring but drifting."

"Because its fate is held in the hands of the wind," said Yu.

"You remember clearly."

"I remember all your words clearly."

"Including my statement at the debate?"

"Yes."

"But that was only a political statement."

"I was outside the door, but still heard you. You asked, 'Who gave us yellow skin and black hair? Our generation is bound to either sink or fly with our country.'"

"But deep down I don't really think so. Human kindness has limits but human evil is boundless. The past ten years have allowed the genie out of the bottle; the devil has slipped out and can never be put back in the bottle. The country will rise, economic material will be gained, and we will catch up with advanced countries; but what about the realms of the spiritual and metaphysical? Will they ever be restored? This is a quandary that is more frightening than being poor."

"If that really concerns you, why not bring it up? Why not tell the truth?"

"Yu, consider this parable: A child asks his mother, 'Why are we still eating cabbage? Yesterday's song said our tomorrow will be sweeter than honey.' Mother replies, 'Silly goose, there is a tomorrow after tomorrow. The tomorrow in the song is far away from us.' If the mother said, 'Tomorrow is never coming,' what would the child do?"

"You use tomorrow to lie to people. But more people care about today."

"Naturally, everyone is most concerned about the time in which they live. How much does it mean to an ordinary person to discuss prospects for human life after hundreds or thousands of years? Modern men have no ideals, no sacred nation, no precious citizenship; they are drifting feathers. 'A detached feather is not soaring, but drifting.' I did not use 'tomorrow' to lie to people. Many people need a tomorrow they can believe in. When a teacher asks you to solve a problem, would you like to do it?"

"Of course."

"You like to solve a problem because you know there is a method for doing so. If you face a problem that you believe is irresolvable, one that would take your whole lifetime and the lifetimes of your descendants, would you still be willing to attempt a solution?"

Yu had no answer. Her mind was churning, her gaze frozen like ice. Their streams of thought had diverged, like a river seeking multiple channels. She had known from the time he walked in what he wanted to say.

Music was softly floating on the night air, coming down from heaven, floating through a door, separating their souls from their bodies.

"Is there a church nearby?"

"Yes, just across the road."

"No wonder it is so clear . . . ah, today is Christmas Eve."

> *What a friend we have in Jesus,*
> *All our sins and griefs to bear!*
> *What a privilege to carry*
> *Everything to God in prayer!*
> *O what peace we often forfeit,*
> *O what needless pain we bear,*
> *All because we do not carry*
> *Everything to God in prayer.*
>
> *Have we trials and temptations?*
> *Is there trouble anywhere?*

We should never be discouraged;
Take it to the Lord in prayer.
Can we find a friend so faithful
Who will all our sorrows share?
Jesus knows our every weakness;
Take it to the Lord in prayer.

They both found this music, these words, inexpressibly beautiful. Zhulong said, "Church, music, choirs . . . this was unthinkable five years ago. But now it's right here with us. Who can predict the future of China? The futurists said they can predict the future of the United States, Africa, and Europe; only China is beyond prediction. Can you imagine ten years later what China will look like?"

Yu put her finger to her lips, motioning Zhulong not to talk. The music was floating over her, it suffused her being. Her beloved sat beside her, very close, as they listened to what had been sent down from heaven. He, whom she loved, loved her; what happiness! What she had longed for for so many years was now happening, right now, before her eyes, within her ears. She was feeling the presence of God, her own God, who had guided her for so many years. He was next to her, right now, in the deep darkness, and he was smiling at her. She was so excited that she was about to cry out, "What you have longed for is about to come true!" Yes. Only now did she realize what she had longed for. It's about to come true. She held her breath, still and motionless, fearing if she moved that that huge happiness would be scared away.

"Yu, I have something to tell you."

"What is it?"

"I am going to be married. To Yadan."

"Congratulations. Congratulations to both of you."

"But what I wanted to tell you is not about this."

"Then what is it?"

"You must know . . . I have always loved you." Zhulong was finding that, for once, the words were not coming easily. "I love you and I want you to know it. But I also know that we are not suitable for marriage. We cannot enter each other's worlds. But I will keep you in my heart forever. I am selfish. If I marry you, you will no longer belong to me. But now I can keep you in my heart and you will belong to me forever."

Zhulong softly caressed Yu's long hair, tears gleaming in his eyes. "Now let me tell you a story. When I was young, I had a dream. You were present in my dream. I did a tattoo of two plum blossoms on your breasts. You were my first woman and I was your first man. But in my dream, you ignored me and left me alone. I was very sad. Later, when I woke up from the dream, I could feel the pain in my chest . . . that was only a dream, so when you asked me several times, I did not admit . . ."

"Why do you—like so many other people—separate reality from dreams? Here is a secret: reality is a dream. Because the soul, like our body, must work and must rest as well; when the soul works, it is reality. When the soul rests, it is a dream. Think carefully: is it not true? And when my soul works, it's the time when your soul rests. To me, that is reality. To you, it is a dream. Correct?"

"You are unique. I have never known anyone like you. I am a materialist and do not believe in spirituality, the soul, heaven. But I cannot oppose you, because my reasons are insubstantial. Do you believe you have the power to be reincarnated? I really want to know."

"I don't know. If I really had such power I'd rather give it to you. Zhulong, run away! Run while you still have time!"

"Run away? Why? If a shabby barricade blocks our path, we should walk around it. It may remain standing after we die. But if I strike it with my head, it falls and I die. Yu, I understand, I've prepared for it all."

"But some things are much more cruel than death."

"I know."

"If one day you look at yourself in the mirror, you may feel that the person in the mirror is no longer you. You cannot recognize yourself and forget what you looked like before . . . if that happened, what would you do?"

"But it won't happen." Zhulong slowly stood up. "It won't happen."

A priest's voice could be heard from the church. "God loves everyone, including those who are nonbelievers. God saves the drunken, the criminals, and those who hurt him. Even those who nailed him to the cross! Jesus used his life to bring rebirth to others, and to bring forgiveness and joy. Truly spiritual love, pure love, true love cannot end, because God is love! God is eternal!"

> *Are we weak and heavy laden,*
> *Cumbered with a load of care?*
> *Precious Savior, still our refuge:*
> *Take it to the Lord in prayer.*
> *Do thy friends despise, forsake thee?*
> *Take it to the Lord in prayer!*
> *In his arms he'll take and shield thee;*
> *Thou wilt find a solace there.*

We can see the young man walking slowly out the door. We cannot see his expression. We can see the girl sitting there, raising her head after a long while. Her face is stained with tears, her expression is poignant. She suddenly remembers one thing, but it's too late, and the memory brings regret. "I forgot to ask him to take a picture of my back." Now she may never see her tattoo.

CHAPTER 10

FOREST OF TOMBSTONES

1

Many years later I came across real forests of tomb-stones in Europe. Cemeteries in Europe are as beauti-ful as their churches, yet each and every one of them is an entity unto itself. In Vienna, they are exquisite. Each piece of sculpture is a work of art. The gates are com-monly wide open, and scattered throughout you can see all kinds of sacri-ficial offerings, wreaths, holy lamps, flower vases, suits of armor, quivers, silver masks, and the like. Statues of guardian angels stand tall, along with the statues of great musicians like Bach, Brahms, Beethoven, and Mozart, which are very lifelike, ready to play for us or deep in thought. Among all these departed great masters, perhaps the most stunning incarnation is that of Mozart. Below a cerulean Viennese sky, this golden god on his marble pedestal evokes trills and chords, contrapuntal complexities and voluptuous fervor, entire sections engraved in our memories. Fallen petals lie scattered by the wind, and they add to the feeling of tranquility.

But that tombstone forest was not the one I kept in my heart.

In another cemetery, this one located in southern Serbia, I discovered much older graves, some dating from medieval times. Here were tombstones cracked and weather-worn, some tilted and fallen, adorned only by geometric figures and some uncommon names; here no remembered melodies, no sonorous overtones, only the clash and clang of ancient battlegrounds, and they added to my sense of reality and sorrow.

But this also was not the tombstone forest I kept in my heart.

2

Zhulong did not marry Yadan. Years later those who knew both of them said should the two have married, each would have been a different person and the course of their fate would have altered.

What changed Zhulong's fate was a simple evening meal.

He intended to eat at the school cafeteria, but it was closed. By chance, that was the day he had received his monthly stipend. At that time, there were a number of students who received a salary while attending school. So with his pay in his pocket, he walked into a small restaurant near campus and ordered pan-fried dumplings, stewed cabbage, and a small bottle of sorghum whiskey. While he was waiting for his food, a girl sitting at another table caught his eye. Her rare complexion and bright eyes, like a brilliant color on a gray palette, were fresh and untainted, the likes of which Zhulong had not seen for a long time while living in a big city. And that wasn't all. In front of the girl was a table loaded with food: braised jumbo shrimp, salt-and-pepper shredded pork, stir-fried chicken, steamed frog legs. These were the most expensive items on the menu and not the usual fare for the frugal customers like Zhulong who patronized this place. The young woman faced this hearty spread, with the refined table manners cultivated only in a good family, sampling the dishes elegantly, like a princess—with no hint of hurrying.

Zhulong was intrigued.

Now we behold this young woman through Zhulong's observant eyes. She had black hair, a delicate pink complexion, lustrous dark eyes that looked as if a pair of stars had fallen inside them, eyelashes so long that in bright light they cast tiny shadows, and high cheekbones and a well-formed chin that made her look like a beautiful foreign doll. We seem to have met this girl before. She has not changed much since then. Her hair perhaps a bit shorter, she is An Xiaotao, and we heard her story in Chapter 5.

We of course remember that she is the daughter of An Qiang and the servant girl Meihua. But we would never have guessed that An Qiang was the son of Xuanzhen, the fourth sister of Xuanming, and that his father was one of the four famous *yamen* police chiefs in old Beijing. As a boy, An Qiang seemed to have taken much from his father's heritage: He was fond of guns and swords and was skilled in martial arts. He was vigorous but refined, agile and high-spirited. Much to everyone's surprise, on his wedding night, at the age of twenty-two, An Qiang disappeared. His mother, who was greatly disappointed, blamed herself. She later told Xuanming, her youngest sister, "Never force marriage upon your sons and daughters. An Qiang must have been so unhappy with his arranged marriage that he simply walked away from it. Just like that. Had I known he was unhappy, I would never have arranged it!" Just the mention of this subject would bring Xuanzhen to tears.

By now we know that Xuanming learned nothing from her sister's experience; she herself turned out to be a calculating and controlling mother. Her tough, unyielding manipulations engendered frail and devious behavior in both her son and her daughter. Then she schemed and worked to bring Ruomu and Lu Chen together, which was good for no one, especially not for herself.

As for Meihua, that pretty and clever servant girl, that withered young woman's eventual capture by and marriage to An Qiang was perhaps the best thing that ever happened to her. In the ensuing years of life with An Qiang, Meihua's own life underwent a transformation and rebirth. It was that brand-new Meihua, no longer naive and affectionate, but matured and experienced and full of spirit, who created Xiaotao. From the moment she was born and as far back as Xiaotao could remember, her mother was always coming and going like a lonely knight. And every time, her mother would without fail come back with her prize. Her mother occupied a supreme place in Xiaotao's heart and remained a mystery from the time as a child she heard the legendary story of "Aunty Mei on Xitan Mountain." Meihua was not a woman of many words; she never preached to her daughter about rules of behavior. Having had an indulged upbringing, the girl became a free and unbridled youth, yet was able to look out for herself quite well. Xiaotao clearly was blessed with her father's free spirit and sense of chivalry and her mother's wisdom and spiritual serenity. The concept of playing by the rules never entered her mind. When her mother died, she made her way to Beijing. Once there, like a fish in water, life became for her an unstoppable free-for-all. And she was not about to be intimidated by the corrupt and sophisticated urban dwellers. After getting away with her games a couple of times, Xiaotao became more daring.

When the young student walked into the restaurant and ordered pan-fried dumplings and stewed cabbage, Xiaotao immediately noticed him. His eyes were like swords, sharp and clear, and his gaze commanded instant attention. From his whole being there came a force of personality and strength of character that were well beyond the ordinary. Xiaotao had been in the city for two years and seen much, but this young man's charisma was instantly attractive. Since she never restrained her impulses, she immediately invited him to join her. He refused, with a smile. Entirely appropriate, she thought, and as she was thinking of how to make another approach, he lowered his eyes and went on with his eating.

Seeing the young man about to complete his meal, Xiaotao called for her bill, and when it was presented, she suddenly screamed, "See what was in the soup! Look, everyone, a toothpick! How could you let this happen? Luckily I noticed it; my life would be in danger if I swallowed it. Call your manager!"

All eyes were on Xiaotao. Zhulong watched in astonishment as she continued with her scam: evidence presented, the foundation laid, a threat implied; then a brief bout of "reasoning" with the manager. The poor man was overwhelmed by the sheer force of her attack and quickly offered that the meal would be free if only she would not pursue her complaint. "We do not want to lose our license," he said, thus losing the game. Xiaotao's fiery charges gave way to delight, and she threw a playful, satisfied, and altogether seductive look at Zhulong as she sauntered through the door.

An old man sitting nearby was clenching his teeth as this scene unfolded. "That's what we call a rice worm! A time bomb! What a shame. Such a pretty girl. So many surprises these days."

"I knew what was going on," said the manager, "but without evidence that she herself dropped that toothpick in the soup, I just had to let it go."

Zhulong paid his bill and left. Around the corner, he caught up with Xiaotao. "I just knew you would follow me," she said with a warm smile.

"I wanted to know about the toothpick," said Zhulong.

His seriousness and tone of voice made Xiaotao giggle. "That's so funny. I want to know where you work. I can't believe that the world could produce such a lovely man as you!"

Zhulong flushed. He never lacked for confidence with girls and felt superior to them. But now from nowhere had come a girl who treated him like an equal. It was so sudden, so surprising. And stimulating.

"Don't you think it's awfully cheap to do something like that?"

She giggled again. "Good God, what's cheap about that? You must be a big-time scholar. I am nothing but a country girl, never finished middle school. But I just had a banquet at no cost and you, a big-time intellectual, ate cabbage and had to pay for it. So who is the winner here?"

Despite his fury, Zhulong was intrigued. He wanted to study this girl.

Within three weeks they had moved in together. Another three weeks went by in which Zhulong graduated and was assigned a job at an institute on the outskirts of the city. Soon they were married, which stunned all his friends. Among the three girls who loved him, he had chosen Xiaotao. He felt guilty about Yadan and Yu, but what were the choices? When loved by three women, a man is bound to make two of them unhappy; he hoped that in time they would forget him.

It never occurred to Zhulong that he did not understand women. He was regarded by friends as a highly adept professional revolutionary, quite capable of understanding and explaining the intricacies of economics, politics, philosophy, and much else. Yet he had no understanding at all of the woman he had chosen as the subject of his "study." The one who was thoroughly studied was none other than himself.

3

Yushe was unable to attend Zhulong's wedding. She had checked into a hospital again. When she heard the news about Zhulong's marriage it upset her so much that wounds from her fall ripped open and had to be repaired surgically. She was unable to cry hysterically like Yadan, nor could she vent her woes by ceaseless talking like Xiao. Having no such outlets, she could only take out her frustrations and sorrow on her own body.

It was dinnertime when she checked into the hospital. Dr. Danzhu was the physician in charge of the surgical ward and he immediately interrupted his dinner to give her a thorough examination. Jinwu brought Yu her favorite food: eight-treasure rice porridge, pickled vegetables, and anchovies.

Impassive by nature, Dr. Danzhu said nothing when he observed the two plum blossoms on Yu's breasts, but he was surprised. This was the early 1980s and tattoos and other bodily adornments were still uncommon. To Dr. Danzhu, all bodies, male or female, were the same without clothes. But the plum blossoms were unique, and his eyes lingered on her breasts. Of the hundreds of women he had examined, this young lady's breasts were without doubt the most beautiful he had seen: petite, gracefully formed, elegant. The plum blossoms, just above the nipples, added an exotic flare. He wondered where Yu came from; what was her story? Yu's languid expression gave him no clue.

Dr. Danzhu came from a long line of physicians, and his father, a high-ranking official in the Health Ministry, had been with the Red Army on the Long March in the 1930s. His son, however, had no interest in revolutionary matters. He was pragmatic, devoted to science and his medical practice. He was a kindly man, but like most physicians he avoided personal involvement with patients. His wife was also employed in medicine, as a laboratory technician. Everything about his life had been routinized. When it was time for him to marry, his mother introduced him to an eligible lab technician. She seemed to him no different from other women—no better, no worse. His response to courtship was similar. Why waste so much time? His fiancée was also keen to proceed, so they tied the knot within a month of their first meeting. Once the business of marriage was out of the way, he quickly plunged back into the business of medicine. He earned a reputation as an exceptionally skillful surgeon and was soon elevated to the rank of chief surgeon, the youngest doctor of such rank at the hospital. Before his mutually interesting encounter with Yu, Dr. Danzhu felt that his life was quite fulfilling—nothing missing, nothing regrettable.

Thinking about such matters, we often neglect the real meaning of the term "mutual encounter." In human affairs, mutual encounters are not all that common! Some people only have such an encounter with another person—meaning getting to know each other at a deeper level—once in a lifetime, and that one-time encounter is unforgettable. Others live together throughout their adult lives without penetrating to that deeper level even once. Danzhu and his wife had been married for five years, never once arguing about anything. They were a model couple in the eyes of their friends and relatives, but Danzhu was fully aware that theirs had never actually been such a mutually enlightening encounter. In his mind those couples who argued indicated that something they both cared about had deeply engaged them. To Danzhu, arguing was one possible form of such an encounter.

As usual, Danzhu made his rounds before leaving the hospital at the end of his shift. He noticed the food on Yu's night table had not been touched.

"Why didn't you eat?" he asked softly.

Yu was in a daydream-like trance. She was startled by his question and shook her head.

"You must eat; otherwise, you will not make it through tomorrow's surgery," the doctor said sternly.

Yu said she couldn't lift her arm to reach the food. So Danzhu sat down and began to feed her the rice porridge with a spoon. She was embarrassed by such attention, but said nothing. Now she saw his face. His pupils were not black but a hazy, bluish gray. He was tall and heavily built, handsome but phlegmatic; no hint of emotion flickered across his face as he spoke. Was there just a hint of sarcasm in his voice? Yu felt sad as she tried to see herself through his eyes: to him, she thought, she was of little more significance than a small animal.

Yu, a psychologically sensitive child, had been a late bloomer in physical development. At the time of her first meeting with Dr. Danzhu, she had
just arrived at the full bloom of puberty. Mentally depressed and physically
run-down, she nevertheless felt an unfamiliar and rousing vigor coursing
through her body. A yearning for love had been a part of her makeup for
many years, and now it included a hunger for adult expression of such feelings. Even a tiny spark would ignite a blazing fire in her heart. Right now,
this doctor seated by her side, a man she had never before met, through the
simple act of feeding her, one spoonful at a time, had aroused her to a point
where her feelings were almost painful.

Jinwu had said she was Yu's cousin when checking her into the hospital.
Danzhu certainly recognized the older woman as a movie star who had recently turned to working as a model for artists; newspapers and magazines
carried stories about her and color photos. Even overseas media had begun
to take notice. But her classically beautiful face held no interest for him; he
even felt a slight natural hostility because she signified glamour as popularly
defined. This was much like his aversion to his father's generation of old
revolutionaries; he would show his distaste through comments like "They
were a bunch of red-flag wavers who went against another bunch of red-flag
wavers."

Jinwu said to him, "I am very busy. I hope you'll take the trouble to look
after my young cousin."

Dr. Danzhu nodded in affirmation, but resented her casual manner and
condescending tone. Now, with the day winding down and visiting family
having gone home, most patients had gone out for a stroll, and doctors were
making preparations to leave for the day. The ward began to quiet down and
Dr. Danzhu had a moment to sort through his thoughts. Looking at this
young woman who was lost in her own thoughts, who seemed not to belong
to any of the usual classifications of young women, he was suddenly smitten
with a profound and long-forgotten emotion. He wanted to talk with her.

"None of your family is coming tomorrow?"

"Jinwu will come."

"She has a performance tomorrow. She told me as she was leaving."

"The rest of my family doesn't know I'm in the hospital, and I don't want them to know."

"But we need a signature for your operation."

"I will sign it myself."

"Okay. Tomorrow morning I'll ask the nurses to prepare your skin."

"What do you mean—prepare my skin?"

"With all those scars from all the operations you've had, you still don't know what skin prep means?"

"All of the others were done while I was unconscious. I either fainted just before or had been given a general anesthetic."

Danzhu was surprised to hear this and felt sorry for his young patient. He said softly, "All that happens is that the nurse will shave off any body hair. Not painful, but it will go more easily if you're not nervous about it."

After spoon-feeding her the rest of the rice porridge, Danzhu was on his way out, but then heard Yu's feeble voice calling him. Turning back, he saw a strange expression on her face. "What's the matter?" he asked.

"Nothing, really; I'm just a bit scared . . ."

He went to her side and turned on the light near her bed; the rest of the ward was now dark. In the dim light her face was pale. Her expression was sad and vulnerable. He sat down again, not daring to leave.

"I just had a dream, but it seemed so real. I dreamed that I became very light and rose up to the ceiling. I was frightened and said, 'Please let me down, let me down.' Then I awoke in fear, even sweating a little. But then, just as I was thinking it was only a dream, I began to rise up again. Just like that, it happened three times. To be weightless was really scary. What was the dream trying to tell me? Doctor, can you interpret dreams?"

Danzhu laughed. He rarely laughed. "How come I have never had a dream in my entire life?"

This was dreamy Yu and dreamless Danzhu's encounter. Fate arranged it. Although citizens of the same country who spoke the same language, they belonged to two different worlds. These worlds were far apart and their chances of meeting slim. But an encounter that happens against such long odds is bound to produce stories.

The next day, Yu saw his eyes above the surgical mask. This was the first time she had entered an operating room fully awake. The room seemed enormously large and its white sterility gave her a chilly feeling. For a long time she had been afraid of whiteness. The huge snowstorm in her childhood and the winter plums in the snow in her teenage years had given her the same feeling, a chill that emanated from the marrow in her bones. Now she was lying on the operating table and trembling so hard that she could see the sheet covering her quiver. Then she heard Dr. Danzhu say simply, "Begin."

That word, "begin," reminded her of the play *Q&A Behind Bars*, from several years earlier. The play's bearded director had said to Zhulong and Yadan, "Begin." It took place in a large room, containing many people, and they were putting on a show. There were many people present; but now Yu was all alone, facing the daunting, soulless, empty white stage. She could hear the scissors and felt weak and afraid. Her tears welled up and began spilling down her cheeks. Gradually, against her best efforts, she began sobbing uncontrollably.

"What's the matter?" the doctor asked.

She saw beads of perspiration on his forehead. She tried her best to stop, but the tears kept coming.

"Why are you losing control?" he asked. "You've had plenty of anesthetic for such a minor operation. It cannot possibly be painful."

"A grown-up crying like this," scolded the head nurse. "If you interfere with the doctor and the operation is not successful, you will be held responsible!"

But that little speech made things worse, and now she was hysterical. The doctor paused.

"What's the matter?" The doctor's voice was, in marked contrast to the nurse's, soothing. A drop of his sweat fell in Yu's mouth. It felt icy cold, not like the heat of Zhulong's sweat. But she liked the smell of his sweat; unlike that of most men, it smelled like pure and fresh olive oil.

The patient's and doctor's eyes met, and in that instant Danzhu understood her tears. He spoke as softly as he could. "Relax, be calm, it's almost done. Almost. Your friend is waiting outside the door. What shall I say about your red eyes? You have endured much bigger operations, why cry about this small one? There, there, I'll give your skin extra care later, okay?"

The head nurse looked at Dr. Danzhu in surprise. In the six years they had worked together, he had never before tried to communicate so directly with a patient. In fact, he rarely said much to anyone. Every day, he saw blood, often death, and very often endured the emotions of patients and their families. Always he had seemed stoic, even stolid. So what was his connection to this girl? Perhaps they were related? Holding back her frustration, the head nurse did her best to comfort Yu until she fell into a deep sleep.

Yu woke up at midnight to find no friends around her. She was the only patient in a small single room in a different ward, with a man sitting on her bed with his back to her.

"You awake?" Danzhu had turned around, observing her steadily.

She could tell he was extremely tired. She curled up her body and then sat up. A thick bandage was wrapped around her upper torso. He slipped a shirt over her bare skin, although she was not concerned about being naked. Clear-eyed and alert, she watched him.

"Why do you cry so much?" he asked. He spoke in flat tones, but she could see a glimpse of warmth in his face. That little sign of emotion brought tears to her eyes.

"I look very ugly when I cry, don't I?"

He didn't answer.

"But I don't want you to find me blubbering . . . I . . . just want . . ."

"You must learn to wear a mask. Your life would be easier."

She looked at him in surprise.

"Really. You must wear a mask. I don't say you should be deceptive. It's a way of protecting yourself from interference from others. To live in this society you must not reveal too much of yourself."

She was puzzled, but listened carefully.

"These are matters of common sense that you should learn from your family. I am sorry, I don't mean to be too personal."

"Then, when can one remove the mask?"

"Only in the presence of those you trust."

She lowered her eyes, her expression thoughtful. "How about now? Is it okay now to take off my mask?"

Dr. Danzhu slowly and gently placed one arm around Yushe and held her close to his chest. She was soft and compliant, like a hibernating serpent.

4

Yadan had become very unattractive. Years later when friends saw photographs taken when she was young they would say, "Oh, you were so beautiful when you were young."

Her change in appearance was due mainly to a lack of sleep for a month. With dark circles under them, her eyes now resembled those of a panda. She lost sleep because she had discovered she was pregnant. It happened when she lost her virginity that night by the water fountain. She was one of those women who are so fertile that one touch of a man can start a new life. If not for the one-child-per-couple policy, she could have become a heroic mother in the best sense of the word.

In the early stages her pregnancy was not easy. Adding to her fatigue, Yadan couldn't keep her food down.

"Who is the father? Who?" Her face turning pale, Mengjing demanded a reply, but none was forthcoming. "It must be that Yuanguang!" Women's intuition is surprisingly accurate.

Hearing Yuanguang's name induced a small smile but still no reply, as Yadan bit her tongue. But that small smile infuriated Mengjing; she showed her love for her daughter with a mighty slap across her face. Yadan fell to the floor from the force of the blow. Mengjing had entered menopause, which reduced her tolerance for unwanted news. She began slapping her own face, crying but controlling her screams, then pulling her hair and throwing herself against the wall; around midnight she ran out of steam and fell asleep in the arms of her gentle, older husband.

Early the next morning she went to the market and stood in line to buy a turtle. Later she emerged from the kitchen with bloodstains on her hands and a malevolent look in her eye, scaring her daughter. But then her look changed, reflecting a small note of triumph, the result of hearing about the ill fortune of her neighbors, the Lu family. "The news next door is not too good, either. Yu is in the hospital again, and Ruomu and Lu Chen are quarreling."

Bad luck in the Lu family had always given Mengjing a boost, but Yu's hospitalization was disastrous for Yadan because she couldn't visit her. Yadan was unwilling to reveal her condition, even to her best friends. "Pregnant," this stigmatizing label, which in her life thus far had been such a distant concept, had suddenly been attached to her. She had just graduated from university and had been assigned to work at a government office, so she had no choice but to lie.

Four months later, lying about her condition was no longer possible. The entire Jiaotong University knew that Mengjing's daughter was pregnant, though not married. When Xuanming stood in line to buy groceries, she heard people talking about it:

"Look at Mengjing's daughter. Her body has changed shape but they don't know who the father is. She's driving her mother crazy!"

"Girls are a big worry when they arrive at a certain age. Your family is so lucky to have only sons."

"Look! She is out in public! Just look at those udders!"

"She had big breasts to begin with. But they are all meat. She won't have milk enough to feed the child! . . ."

Yadan walked up and stood by Xuanming and called her granny. Xuanming said she would buy whatever Yadan needed. Yadan thrust a ten-yuan bill into Xuanming's hand and said she wanted some chopped lean pork. As she walked away, she overheard the old women yapping.

"Her hips are quite big—looks like a girl!"

"Ah, the hips are much smaller than the belly. Must be a son!"

Arriving at home, Yadan collapsed on her bed and buried her head in her pillow, giving vent to her feelings in long, choking sobs. She had been reduced to nothing. A colleague she liked came to visit her and informed her that the authorities had been intending to elevate her to the position of a secretary to a minister, but that this proposal had fallen through. Thereafter, Yadan sought refuge at home, refusing all sustenance. Her face became a sickly yellow. Mengjing, after inquiring at several places, found a gynecolo-gist willing to induce labor. She was five months gone, so outright abortion was out of the question. From the beginning, Yadan had opposed abortion and in one of the worst scenes with her mother had held a small knife to her own wrist, saying, "I must keep this child!" After giving this ultimatum, she passed out.

Seeing Yadan at the point of a life-threatening breakdown, Mengjing went into life-saving mode. Forget about saving face, that possibility was be-hind them; now she put her energy into preparation of tempting foods and drinks; but, still, Yadan was eating virtually nothing.

Her fifth-month ultrasound exam showed that Yadan was carrying a baby boy. At last some red color returned to Mengjing's pale face. When they got home she learned that someone named Zhulong had come to visit Yadan. "What an odd name," her stepfather had said. But Mengjing noticed that Yadan trembled upon hearing it, her eyes lighting up but soon fading like a dying meteorite. For months, Yadan's face had displayed resignation at best. Now it went through a series of contorted expressions, ending up in screams and sobs. At last, Mengjing thought, we know who the father is—that son of a bitch originally called Zhulong, who deserved to suffer a thousand cuts.

Yadan locked herself in her room, once again overcome with grief. From outside the door her mother begged her to control herself, that she might harm the baby. But how could she digest what her mother was saying, when her thoughts were with Zhulong entirely? At this moment she loved him more than ever, but she had made up her mind not to see him, because she was truly ugly now. She might die giving birth to his child and then he could visit her in death, knowing she had sacrificed herself to give life to his child. His heart would be broken, just as hers had been all these months.

Imagining Zhulong's future sorrows brought her some relief, and at din-ner she ate a bowl of the lily-bulb congee her mother had specially made for her, then asked for a refill. From that day forward her appetite was restored. Day after day she feasted on Mengjing's tasty meals and added layers of fat. Six meals a day, then chocolates and other sweets after dinner with her legs raised high as she watched television. Plus a midnight snack.

One week prior to delivery, just as Yadan was gulping down an afternoon snack, she looked through a window and saw a man walking toward the house. Slender body, long legs, broad shoulders swinging slightly from side to side as he walked: she knew that body before seeing the face and treasured its strength and virility. A gush of happiness rushed to her throat but then choked her as it conflicted with her pent-up sorrow, bringing her once more to the brink of emotional meltdown. She leaned on the windowsill and watched him with hungry eyes. He was, as usual, in a hurry, looking ahead. At just that moment the new life stirring within gave a hard kick and then another; was this a sign of recognition of his father?

Mengjing was sitting on a sofa knitting a sweater. She sprang to her feet and reached for Yadan's elbow. "Is it him?" Not waiting for Yadan's reply, she rushed to the door. But Yadan blocked her way.

"Mom, tell him I'm not home."

"Why? How strange! Aren't you thinking about him every day? I want to ask this SOB if he knows he is about to become a father!"

Now Yadan had become deadly serious. "Say just one word and we'll no longer be mother and daughter!"

This was reminiscent of a scene seven years earlier, when the subject was a man named Yuanguang. On that occasion her daughter had given the same ultimatum. Good heavens, this was the same man. Perhaps he had changed his name. Once again, proof of women's intuition. Whoever he is, she knew she hated this man who had mercilessly deprived her of a healthy, happy daughter. What a good child she had been. Now ruined, poor child. Why was she so hot-blooded? What had gotten into her?

Mengjing was rarely emotional. But now she wept every night under her blankets. Such a price, she thought. All those years ago it was Tiancheng who had taken possession of her body, her heart, and her soul. But he was a good man, honest and gentle. This guy Zhulong, or Yuanguang, or whatever, was a total jerk!

Yadan's composure had returned. She knew that in the end her mother would retreat. Her stomach was frighteningly huge and projected upward. Without exaggerating, a glass of orange juice could stand on top. Now this belly was a dividing line between mother and daughter, and the mother could not cross.

From the story of Mengjing and Yadan, we may conclude that experience in dealing with the ordinary vicissitudes of life is unique for each individual. It cannot be reliably passed along from one person to another or from one generation to the next. Sadly, experience is like a one-way border: once it has been crossed, there is no going back. Such a paradox! If only experience could be cumulative, life would be simpler, with much less sorrow. Mengjing could easily tell Yadan that love, if not returned, is bootless. If it flows only in one direction, an increase of love will change nothing. In that situation, the person who receives love may be touched and make small efforts to be responsive, but that is not love and will lead to grief on both sides; if the efforts are large, the grief will be greater. The alchemy of love is beyond rational analysis, and, for all we know, the capacity for one person to love another may be foreordained by the mysteries of life in the womb.

As was to be expected, it was Mengjing who yielded. She opened the door and, in a flat tone of voice, said, "Sorry, Yadan is not home. She is very busy these days. You don't need to return."

Yadan, out of sight, was listening, and she felt all over again a constriction in her throat.

Yadan began having contractions, perhaps as a result of excitement and emotional turmoil. In the room reserved for women in labor, there were four other pregnant women, all moaning in pain as doctors checked their progress. One doctor was not very sympathetic. He even yelled at a woman who was seated near Yadan: "Lower your voice! Look over there," he said, pointing at Yadan, "her contractions are much stronger and she has not asked for pain medication."

But how would the doctor ever know that Yadan's pain was more severe than mere physical contractions? She thought she was really going to die and never again see Zhulong.

By the time she was on the delivery table she felt she was no better than an animal. Doctors and nurses skillfully stripped off her gown and covered her with a sterile yellow sheet. And she lay there totally naked, unresisting, while all her pubic hair was shaved off, and she was pushed this way and that by anonymous hands, entirely subject to the will of others. Her feet were placed in stirrups, spread widely to give everyone complete access to parts of her body even she herself had never seen. She heard one doctor shouting "Push!" and "Push harder! You're open and ready to deliver."

So she began pushing with all her might; but it was no use—her contractions subsided and it was time for the doctors to change shifts and take their meals. Yadan was left where she was, legs open wide, with people walking back and forth looking audaciously at her nether parts, some of them poking a rubber-gloved hand here or there casually, almost absentmindedly. She burned with shame. She was still quite young, had experienced sex only once, but now she had been turned into a slab of meat, a birth machine. She had no mental preparation for the role she was now playing. In fact, she still felt like the girl she was only the day before. Only now did she experience the cruel reality—in the eyes of others, in the eyes of doctors—of being merely a woman delivering a child. Only now did her at-oneness with village mommas and mares and bitches and cows become fully apparent. These thoughts stayed with her subconsciously and stubbornly, and every time they rose to the surface she felt an odd constriction in her chest and throat.

Yadan spent much of the next three days and nights on the delivery table. The physician in charge was an authority in the field of obstetrics and she was in the midst of a heated debate with another authority on the topic of natural versus cesarean birth. Yadan's doctor insisted on the natural method and repeatedly urged Yadan to tough it out, bite the bullet, cooperate. Suction, incisions, forceps—any and all techniques could be used, indeed were used, all to avoid surgical intervention. But nothing worked for Yadan. By the end of the third day, the doctor in charge began to wonder if Yadan's case might be the exception that proved the rule. However, seeing Yadan's sunken cheeks, she decided to try once more to turn the baby, which until that moment had not worked. She hastily pushed her rubber-gloved hand all the way up the birth canal, at the same time pressing with great force on the outside of Yadan's abdomen, and turned the fetus so that its head was pointing downward.

This sudden and unexpected realignment of her own interior anatomy precipitated a hoarse scream from Yadan, who had been clenching her teeth for days. Mengjing was dozing in the hallway. When she heard the scream, she rushed into the delivery room, shouting, "Murder! You've killed my daughter!"

Relatives of other patients rushed to the door. The assistant and head nurses tried to block the crowd. In the chaos, the words "It's out!" were heard, but there was no crying from the baby.

Mengjing almost fainted. "My grandson! Now he's dead, too!"

The grandson was not dead. He was fat and vigorous and loud, just a little out of breath for the first few moments.

The following day, as Yadan was wakening, a nurse wheeled a baby into her room and put him at her breast, commenting that he was strong and tough. Yadan examined his features, thinking he looked just like Zhulong. Nose, eyes, lips, cheeks, tiny hands—all were perfect. She smiled and said, "How do you do?" Motherhood hormones were taking over.

5

In these days of turmoil for Yadan, Xiao's worries were exactly the opposite. If we say that Yadan was fertile earth, Xiao would be a saline-alkaline desert. Yadan's suffering would be Xiao's happiness beyond words. Xiao would be willing to go through hell on her way to having a child.

But in her entire life she did not conceive.

Today's Xiao was approaching fifty years of age and living in a midsize city in Europe. It was a beautiful city, dotted with gardens, pigeons, bronze statues, and churches of Gothic, Rococo, Baroque, and Byzantine styles. She had earned two college degrees but found them of no practical value there. She opened a small company doing printing—business cards, stationery, advertising mailers, and so on. Life was not great but at least it was quiet and secure. For a long time she lived with a Czech writer; in reading Milan Kundera's novels she had discovered an affinity with the Czechs. The one she lived with looked about sixty years old, with wrinkles deeply etched on his face. His appetite was excellent, especially for Chinese food. He could sit in a Chinese restaurant in the center of the city and consume a whole plate of braised pork. But no matter how much he consumed, his bony shoulders were always visible under his big, loose raincoat, giving him the look of a comic character in a cartoon film. It was that oversize raincoat that was his signature costume. He wore it whenever he and Xiao ventured out to the city's central square to watch the clock strike twelve noon. When the gigantic clock put its two hands together on the number twelve, a door would spring open, twelve oddball characters would slide out one by one, and then a skinny old man would raise a wooden hammer and pound on the clock bell with great force. Often at this moment, the square would be filled with people waiting for the big event, their faces turned up to the sky, all looking in one direction, at this show—unique among the world's spectacles. At that moment, the writer would put his arms around his Chinese lover and together they would watch the action as if they were seeing it for the first time. In the windy season, his big raincoat would fly up and cover Xiao completely. When this happened, Xiao would feel a sense of desolation—the bleak feeling of being a foreigner in a strange land.

Xiao's love affair with Hua had ended in the mid-1980s. It turned her into a self-centered little girl. Once, late at night, Xiao asked her roommate to fetch Hua and demand that he accompany her to the "English corner." This was diagonally across from Xiao's dormitory and was where students went to practice conversational English. Her school was known for producing top-rate students of English. On that long path Xiao and Hua would stroll and talk; under cover of night, they could even show a bit of affection for each other. Xiao preferred taking her own path to love, but to get Hua onto that path was not always easy. On that particular night, Hua would not go with her, claiming it was too late and not proper. This struck her as a feeble excuse, and she began to cry, feeling slighted. Hua did his best to console her, but it was no use. It suddenly occurred to her that Hua was controlling all aspects of their love affair—whether the pace be speedy or slow, the mood high or low, the feelings deep or shallow. He was an impregnable fort. When he did not want to open the gate, even if she had a thousand strong and able horses and men ready to help, she could not lay siege to his indomitable will. He held firmly in his hands the power to initiate love. Never before had she felt so vulnerable, so foolish, so unhappy. Thus, Xiao and Hua began that old story of Anna and Vronsky in Leo Tolstoy's *Anna Karenina*.

By then, the tragic ending of their affair came fully into Xiao's view.

But Xiao refused to take no for an answer. Xiao was losing her mind; Xiao perked herself up, bought expensive clothes and imported makeup; Xiao changed her voice from being revolutionary in tone to a soft and sweet charm; Xiao practiced a girlish smile before a mirror; Xiao posed in various sitting positions in class; Xiao couldn't sleep or eat; Xiao began to forget things and made numerous errors; Xiao was too nervous to laugh anymore; Xiao painted her lips a scarlet red that was totally unsuitable to her age and complexion.

But all her efforts were as useless as a river running east. Her efforts had an effect that was opposite to what she hoped for.

Xiao turned into the young widow Xianglin, a character in Lu Xun's story *The New-Year Sacrifice*. Like Mrs. Xianglin, Xiao talked on and on about her lost love to her sole audience, who was Yu. On weekends, when the family gathered in front of the TV, Xiao would sneak into Yu's room, close the door lightly and lay down next to Yu, then pat the bed gently. Yu's head would immediately rise to a listening position, patient as always. Listening to her sister chatting endlessly was like going to hell, but who else would go to hell other than Yu. She's my sister, said Yu to herself.

Xiao's lovebird flew away, unstoppable. She felt strongly that this was destined to be the only true love of her life. She had invested heavily in making her relationship with Hua work to the satisfaction of both parties. Now she was fatigued. Pouring out her heart was the only thing left for her, her only channel to let things out. This pouring-out could release months or even years of what had sunk to the bottom of her heart.

"Pouring out" one's heart is a happy image to some people, especially for certain women. It can be a beautiful thing: cleansing one's soul, brightening one's eyes, broadening perspective. But to do this one must have a listener. Without that, it is like oral sex—impossible to perform in front of an imagined person. The problem arises for the listener. The listener must possess great endurance and have a big heart. He must also have strong will, the will to draw the line and say "Stop!" when his interlocutor strays into foolish territory. If not, he would be like a secondhand smoker—inhaling unwanted poison, the poison and dirt exhaled by the other person.

When the person pouring out his or her heart happens to be a writer, then it is not just trouble. It is a disaster. He or she would throw all his or her filthy language and naughty thoughts to the reader. A story might go like this: the writer or his or her character talks interminably about getting up in the morning, then might go to the store to buy a pair of shoes. They may fit well at the store but be tight when he or she gets back home. Should or should not the shoes be exchanged for a better fit? After pondering, the writer might change into thin socks and try the shoes again. While changing socks, he or she might notice a corn on his or her foot. To pare away the corn, the writer could yak on and on about finding scissors, then a knife, then maybe a nail clipper.

Encountering such drivel, the reader must have strength of character and say "Stop!" when the outpouring starts.

Thank God, Yadan was not such a writer.

By the late spring and early summer of 1985, Xiao and Yadan met new boyfriends on the computer, in a matchmaker's love column.

One city became the leader of an entire generation of the new trend; it was the first to have a computer matchmaker. Young people of "over marriage age" made their way to computers, inputting their information and awaiting the output. Inputting and outputting, just like China's import and export businesses, was all started and popularized back then and during the following years spread throughout the entire country. From name, age, sex, and hometown to height and weight with or without clothes, a person's complete hardware and software, like a code, was inputted into the computer to become information for another person to consider in making a choice. So beautiful, fast, and modern. China's modernization and entrance into cyberspace began with the computer matchmaker.

Computers made everyone equal. Yadan's name at that time was well-known in literary circles, but in the computer, it was no different from whimsical names like dumbbunny or bubbleboy. All names were digested, compared, and sorted a thousand different ways in that vast binary structure. Devout young men and women who had passed the normal marriage age stood in line silently praying that good luck would fall from the sky. Xiao wrote in her wish list that her love must be from an intellectual family, a man of decency and integrity, a college graduate with many hobbies, over five feet six inches tall, in good health, and under forty years of age. In the space about herself, she wrote that she was a college graduate from a highly educated family; good-looking, warm, and soft; five feet three inches tall; an avid reader; and a good cook.

Yadan only put in one line in her wish list: hope that the man would be good to children. Yadan's self-description was also very simple: thirty-three years of age, healthy, five feet two inches tall, from a professional family, and a lover of literature.

Xiao and Yadan solved their marriage problems at about the same time and according to their own wish lists. Xiao found a man five feet six inches tall, from an intellectual family, and the same age as herself. More important, he had many hobbies, so many that Xiao could not keep up with him. His outstanding hobby was photography. Xiao's husband, Ning, could make a dewdrop come to life on a lotus leaf. Through the power of his lens, each drop looked like a pearl, glittering with subtle hints of gold and silver. Xiao was filled with delight. She loved her Ning like loving a child, protecting him under her wings, feeding him and warming up a cozy house from morning till night. Xiao felt fulfilled. Ning returned her love abundantly and trusted her completely. He delivered all his earnings, down to the penny, and let her manage the finances; he was always gentle and dutiful in the presence of friends. He also took many beautiful photographs of Xiao, which made her very happy. Average-looking Xiao became a stunning beauty in his pictures. On his advice, she let her hair grow long, holding it together with a large clip. For one shot, Ning personally looked after her makeup and turned Xiao into a melancholy beauty. Then he dressed her in an old-style Western jacket and tight-fitting pants and had her pose on a terrace against a railing with a sandalwood fan in her hand. This photograph went on the cover of a 1986 calendar. Ning's darkroom techniques added a washed-out effect to make Xiao look like a young mistress from a foreign mansion of 1930s Shanghai. Nostalgia was embraced by the many, both young and elderly, who took pleasure in savoring the styles and images of old times in the capital city. Suddenly, the metropolis saw middle-aged women dressed in old-style Western jackets that covered whatever they wore underneath. When visiting friends, they never left home without a sandalwood fan. The fragrance of perfume or powder would quietly fill the air when the fan was waved back and forth.

Yadan's computer matchmaker brought her a different experience. Her husband, Ah Quan, was a short man but to her great joy he loved her son, who was of course fathered by Zhulong. Although his house was on the outskirts of the city, she accepted his proposal. Her whole heart was given to her son. She stubbornly clung to the thought that she had Zhulong's blood and that one day she and Zhulong would reunite. Like a happy ending in a corny film, Zhulong by that time would be as sentimental and romantic as she was. Whenever she thought about this, she would be self-congratulatory. Raising the boy without his natural father's help was surely a noble undertaking. She even began to feel sorry for Ah Quan and felt that this arrangement was unfair to him; therefore, she was determined that she would by all means make it up to him.

She discovered soon after the marriage that no one but herself needed compensatory care. Ah Quan was impotent and had been that way from birth. Something not easy to cure.

6

As we tell the stories of the women in this family, we must not forget Yun'er. While we were attending to other characters, she grew into a blossoming sixteen-year-old. Earlier we mentioned that she was a very beautiful girl. At age twelve or thirteen, her beauty surpassed that of her mother, aunts, and grandmother; she even came close to outmatching her great-grandmother Xuanming. But now, Yun'er is far more beautiful than the young Xuanming

ever was. Hers is a rare sort of beauty, like a fine red wine, with a superior
quality you can taste, but which is hard to describe. And from nearby, its rich
fragrance is intoxicating.

The grown women in the family were preoccupied with their own problems and were habitually worried, depressed, or rushed, so they missed this
young girl's growing up. In their eyes, she seemed to have matured in one
night and now was taller than they. So they could no longer go about their
lives without noticing her. And she was, in a word, stunning. Even Ruomu,
who never paid attention to children, now looked on in silent amazement
while Yun'er combed her hair, wondering whether this child had stepped
down from a picture.

Seeing her grandmother staring, Yun'er called to her, "Granny . . ." very
sweetly. But suspicious as always, Ruomu would not be fooled by that sweet
voice. She continued to stare until she at last discovered that Yun'er was secretly using a dark red lip gloss. Ruomu asked, "Why are you using makeup
at such a young age? Are you not afraid of ruining your skin?"

Yun'er smiled sweetly. "Don't worry, Granny. Only a little bit of lip gloss.
Nothing on the rest of my face."

Ruomu looked at her again, saying, "It's not safe out there. When you go
out, be careful. A girl should not be too attractive."

Yun'er just grinned and hurried on her way.

Yun'er changed into a silk dress made from her mother's shawl, red with
gray orchids, making a nice contrast with her snow-white skin. She looked at
herself in the mirror, a fruitless search for imperfection, then left the house.

From a very young age, Yun'er did not live with her mother, so she was
accustomed to independence. She was also very intelligent, but not in the
same way as her aunts. The older generation of the Lu family knew how
smart she was but none of them guessed that she wouldn't get into a high
school. At age sixteen, she became a waitress at a big hotel and had already
collected two months' salary before her family found out.

The hotel was located in the busiest section of the city, close to the famous
Square. Yun'er could see the monument from the front desk. To her that
soaring marble monument was just a sightseeing destination, not any kind

of historic symbol. The feeling for it held by her aunts' generation—the feeling that this was a sacred place where transformative events took place—was dead for Yun'er. She had no god, no rules, no philosophy, only herself. Yun'er knew clearly that she could use her own wisdom to change any rules. And she had no fear in doing so, only the joy of success and sorrow for failure. She spent sixteen years witnessing the laughs and cries of the older generation. Not worth it! If she were in their shoes, all would be much simpler. Yu was of course the person who puzzled her most. "My youngest aunt is too serious!" She had once made that half-serious comment to Ruomu. In her eyes, all of Yu's bitterness and eccentricity was unthinkable. What Yu held most important and valuable was nearly worthless in Yun'er's eyes. In only two months working at this hotel, Yun'er had already built up many connections. Every night after work, Yun'er had all kinds of men who drove all kinds of cars coming to pick her up, vying to take her to all kinds of exciting places. Her life was full. She was too happy enjoying life to feel tired. For her, men were nothing but props. Or stagehands. On life's stage, they made the curtains go up and down.

One of the men in love with her was a Japanese businessman named Yamaguchi. He came almost every day. He was a rich sales representative for a famous line of Japanese cosmetics. He was generous, giving her big sacks of money. On Valentine's Day in 1989, for example, he drove up in a Lexus, holding a large bunch of roses. In those days, giving fresh flowers as gifts was not yet popular. One rose, perhaps; but he brought several dozen, of many colors. The managers as well as other young women were profoundly impressed.

Yamaguchi was cool. At age thirty-six, he had dark eyebrows and a close-shaved chin. He liked to nudge Yun'er's soft forehead gently with his chin, as if appreciating a flower or a piece of jade.

He had made elaborate arrangements for Valentine's Day. First they went to the James Café restaurant, where they ordered Napoleon beefsteak with black pepper, goose liver salad, jumbo shrimps with fresh clam sauce, Texas barbecue baby pig, a Mexican barbecue platter, Venice vegetable soup, and James Café house desserts. It was Yun'er's first time at a classy Western-style restaurant. Under the dimmed lights of the crystal chandelier, well-trained waiters dressed in tails, looking very handsome, provided impeccable service. Yun'er decided that the delight she was experiencing was not just that everything was so perfectly provided for them; it was the intangible joy of status.

From working at a big hotel Yun'er knew what status was. Many rich and some famous people came through this city, but few had status. This was the truth of a society that was in transition from one stage of development to another. Yun'er was determined to acquire both money and status, and she was starting right now while she was young. She disdained the conventional dullness of life in the homes of her mother and aunts; that would not be her path. She wanted to create new territory. Born to be beautiful was such a happy thing. When she was still very small, Yun'er had realized the value of her beauty. She already knew how to use it to best advantage. She would never give that up. Never.

After a meal that was far too large and could only be nibbled at, they went to the Coffee Garden. Yun'er was thrilled to see the diamond jewelry Yamaguchi presented to her. It was a Swarogem diamond necklace and earrings. He said this brand name was very hot right now in Japan. Yun'er enjoyed looking at Yamaguchi drinking Madeira while talking. His manner was suave, and he sang along softly to the melody played by the pianist. Yun'er was surprised to see how knowledgeable he was about women.

"Later we will go to a disco dance hall. You must redo your makeup. What you have is not bad, at least there's not too much of it, but I can help you improve it. For instance, under the lights it's better to use an orange-colored foundation, dark green eyeliner, black eyelash pencil, and bright red lipstick with golden gloss. Since you have short hair, you should use a little hairspray. Your current makeup is a little too light, right?" Yamaguchi ordered a glass of red wine for Yun'er and said with a smile, "Don't worry. Later I will take you to my company office. We have young ladies who are in charge of image creation. I'm sure that tonight you'll have the best time of your life."

Yun'er sipped the red wine and said unhurriedly, "Why are you so good to me?"

"Do you have to ask? Why are we meeting on Valentine's Day? Naturally, because we're in love."

Yun'er noticed the way he said "love." He made it very clear. Between sips of the smooth red wine, Yun'er clearly heard the word and savored its sound. But she asked herself, was it really love? Do I really love this Japanese man? Yun'er was puzzled. She lowered her head; her eyes were sparkling with all the fire and vitality that a beautiful girl just blossoming into womanhood can project. Yamaguchi was getting serious now. His mood had become earnest and he began reciting the famous words of famous people; a truly dazzling display of romantic erudition, she thought.

"Shakespeare said love was bittersweet; Aesop said those who were conquered by love were shameless; Solomon said love was stronger than death; Plato said love was a serious form of mental disorder; Cicero said blue represents reality, yellow is envy, green is decline, red is shamelessness, white is purity, black is death, and when mixed together, they form the color of love. Miss Yun'er, do you know that your beloved country has a poem that goes like this:

" 'Beside a vast, quiet lake, under an icy sky,
Black hair thinning, she kisses her youth good-bye;
Facing the moon alone, she longs for lasting love,
She envies only warm lovers, not cold spirits above.'

"Would you like to know what kind of man I am? I am precisely the man who envies 'warm lovers, not cold spirits above.' Ha-ha-ha!"

Laughing along with him, Yun'er queried, "Mr. Yamaguchi, it seems you have studied in China?"

"No. I studied Chinese in Japan for two years. Do you know why my Chinese pronunciation is so good?"

"Why?"

"Because I am very intelligent! Ha-ha-ha."

The laughter brightened his mood. Yun'er was also becoming more and more cheerful. She went with him to his office, but no young ladies were there to reshape her image. Yamaguchi didn't seem surprised; he just smiled and took her to his private office. "Oh, how did I forget that other people had to have a Valentine's Day, too?"

His tone of voice and graceful gestures were enchanting. For young girls such as Yun'er, there must be someone to worship subconsciously. In those times in that place there was no god, no faith, so the only one available to worship was this middle-aged man with money and status. He was twenty years her senior. That age difference brought with it a natural tendency for deference; she did not dare treat him the way she treated boys in her own age group. Besides, he was Japanese and had status.

Yamaguchi's eyes were softening. "Let's sit down. Make yourself comfortable, and let me show you how to fix yourself up. First, you need some makeup that's appropriate for disco dancing. You need a golden brown touch on the upper eyelid and silvery purple powder to touch up the corners of your eyes and eyebrows. For the lips, a cold color, like icy purple. Gold or silver for the nails . . ." He had taken out a complete makeup kit and applied its contents to her perfect face. The change was instantaneous.

"The secret is what you do between the eyebrows and the lips. If a woman just has one face. How boring. You know that a Hollywood star can change her face a hundred times. The famous Hollywood makeup artist Kevyn Aucoin was a great master of facial transformations. He turned Liza Minnelli into Marilyn Monroe, Winona Ryder into Elizabeth Taylor . . . that's what's called makeup!"

Yamaguchi was touching Yun'er's arm, his eyes filled with a dreamy expression. "You must remember, a woman is not just a face, there is also a body, which is more important. You, for example: you have beautiful legs, why cover them up with a long dress? You should wear a miniskirt and light green stockings. And your torso—do you know what I mean by torso? It's the sexiest part of a woman, including the chest, back, hips, and thighs—all so beautiful. Oh, your chest is a little weak."

Yun'er now saw his face getting red, his hands moving faster, and his breathing becoming heavier and heavier. Yun'er's heart was beating fast, and she wanted him to stop. Normally she would just play a little bit with men to use them, keep them interested, never thinking to do something serious. She was afraid. No matter how smart or experienced, she was only sixteen. In the company of Yamaguchi, after a little wine, her usual defenses were gone. The smell of a middle-aged man, a little musky, a hint of cologne, engulfed her. It also aroused her, but she wasn't sure what that feeling meant.

"You should use a form bra to increase the height of your breasts . . ."

He knew so much about women! His hands stopped on her breasts. His fingers were fumbling with her buttons. Suddenly, a curious and compelling desire firmly suppressed her fear. She wanted to give it a try. Imagining herself in a leading female role in a Western film, she felt natural and relaxed.

7

I don't know how it happened but I felt the whole thing was so simple. I must say it was the simplest thing in the world. I don't know why all my aunts struggled all their lives for happiness with men. I just thought this thing was so good for women, and women were the biggest beneficiaries.

I didn't feel much pain. Just a little blood. Not that much joy, either. The real joy was the next day when Yamaguchi took me shopping at SciTech Plaza. That was my favorite thing—shopping! To find something I liked from the dazzling fashion racks was so stimulating. Much more so than rolling around in bed. I soon picked out a bundle of clothes: a silvery gray blouse, a South Korean–made embroidered silk jacket, an apple-green light woolen fall jacket, a bright red long dress made of lamb's wool, and a light red heavy silk long dress . . . anything I wanted to buy, there was someone there to pay for it. To shop till you drop was unbeatable!

In the end, I put on a white silver silk and satin jacket, matched with a black miniskirt, and a whole set of silvery jewelry and silver-colored shoes, then brushed on some silver and purple makeup powder supplied by Yamaguchi. Standing before a mirror, I couldn't recognize myself.

I attracted many eyes. Yamaguchi was elated. He took me to the largest entertainment and recreation center in the city, called Ya Bao. I could tell that Yamaguchi was a regular there, as all the service girls knew him. He called the manager over and handed him a big wad of cash, requesting the swimming pool just for us, demanding that the manager tell other customers to leave. The manager forced a smile, protesting that this would be difficult to arrange. After lengthy negotiations, the manager said he would clear the smaller springwater pool for us. Yamaguchi bought me a bikini, smiling as he handed me the one he chose.

"Take this for now. Next summer I'll buy you a new one from Paris."

I can't swim very well. So Yamaguchi started to teach me. We were the only ones in the pool, and, as I hoped, he began to touch me underwater. The water was beautifully dark green, reflecting the tiles below. The poolside rest area was painted white and dark green, with broadleaf trees growing nearby, like a small section of a tropical island.

I asked him, "Do swimming pools look like this in foreign countries?"

He paused in his exploration of my body and smiled. "I will take you to see what a swimming pool looks like in a foreign country."

"Really?"

"No big deal. If you like, we can go this year."

Coming out of the pool, we took a shower and went to a room he rented just for ourselves, where food had already been set out. Japanese sushi. I didn't like it much. Yamaguchi said this was not authentic and someday he would take me to Japan to taste real sushi. He asked me if I liked to sing.

"Not wild," I replied.

"You don't seem to have a dominating interest. What do you like most?"

I thought about it and grinned. "It has to be fashionable clothes and cosmetics."

He pretended to be fainting and sucking in his breath, then said, "So long as you don't ask me to buy Mount Fuji!"

I couldn't stop giggling. He was so funny.

He sang very well, starting with a song called *Far Away*. He used to sing at karaoke bars in Japan. He told me karaoke was invented there because Japanese men were too tired and needed to sing to relax. Many white-collar Japanese men worked too hard during the day, so they went to bars after work to sing karaoke and drink whiskey. The mistress of the place would make stir-fried noodles, sometimes throwing in a dish of pistachio nuts. Some would go there for their birthdays. The mistress would then send in a cake and ask the small band to play *Happy Birthday*. When he talked about this, his eyes seemed to drift somewhere, as if recalling or avoiding something.

Under his continued urging, I picked a song titled *Dream Chaser*. The words went like this:

> *Let me have one look,*
> *Don't let me sleep with an empty pillow.*
> *No regrets for youth,*
> *A lover is forever.*

He nodded encouragement, saying my country had a poem with two lines like this:

> *Live life to the full while living,*
> *Don't drink alone with the moon.*

That was about what the song meant. Saying this, he put his arms around me and kissed me, and then we did what we did yesterday. Then he sang praises to me all over again, saying that I was the most beautiful woman he had ever seen.

"So, are there no beautiful women in Japan?" I asked.

He replied that pure Japanese women could not be considered beautiful. It must be some problem in the origin of the race. They all seem to have turniplike legs. No ankles. But mixed-race women in Japan are very beautiful. So I said, your mother must be a mixed-race woman. He stared at me with widened eyes. I tried to explain by saying that a woman with turniplike legs couldn't give birth to someone who had beautiful legs like yours. Now the veins on his neck were bulging. He suddenly looked very hostile, like he was going to slap me. I had no idea why he was so upset. I tried to make him calm down with light banter. Later, as I spent more time with him, I discovered that it was okay for him to make a joke, but I could not initiate one.

These kinds of guys are so boring. If it weren't for his money, I would have stopped hanging out with him long ago.

Later, he did take me to Japan. By then he'd told me he had a wife and a grown child. I was not surprised, as there were always stories like his reported in the newspaper. But I got to go to Japan thanks to him, so we each got what we wanted from each other.

8

In this city in the late 1980s, there was an explosive increase in the number of parties people were throwing and going to.

Jinwu's birthday party included almost everyone she knew in the capital city. Even Yu, who had not been seen for a long time, showed up. She was still shy and silent and sat alone in a corner, watching only feet and shoes through her half-closed eyes. Jinwu was in the big room where many feet and shoes moved about busily. Someone with a pigeon-toed stance and who wore a pair of T-shaped shoes was moving toward Yu after passing through many feet and shoes. That pair of shoes was out of fashion and unbearably ugly.

"Yu, how are you?"

Yadan stood in front of her. But this was only a shadow of the real Yadan. She had changed so much that Yu did not want to look at her. She was now fat and old looking, no longer the pretty but baby-fat-chubby girl Yu remembered from earlier times. She was overweight, thick through the middle. Her eyelids were so loose that they sagged over her eyes, giving them a triangular shape. Her skin was now coarse and lacking in color. But from her eyes you could see that she was obviously excited to be at the reunion.

Yadan held Yu's hand tightly and said repeatedly, "You are the same, no change! But look at me—I look so old, don't I?"

Yadan said the same thing to others. But everyone tried to comfort her: "No, no, not much."

But Yu was different, as always. She said, "You look so different, I almost didn't recognize you."

This brought a sad expression to Yadan's face. Tears were welling up, tears she had been hiding. "Oh, Yu, you are so good. Only you will tell me the truth."

Yu's response was also emotional. But to change the subject, Yadan handed her a stack of photos that were all of her and her son. Yu hadn't seen the son, Yangyang. Yu looked at a picture of Yadan breast-feeding her baby, one large, bare lobe revealed. Yu's heart choked with pain. Her mind had flashed back to the memory of that little girl who fell on the floor near the stove, holding an unfinished bun, so many years ago.

Yu took Yadan into Jinwu's bedroom, where no one would interrupt them. Now it was like old times, talking about things that only they knew. As they were catching up on each other's doings, Yu felt that Yadan was still the same girl, though she looked older; and she had not abandoned her thinking and writing. She told Yu about preparations for her next novel, to be titled *The Story of Xiao Feng*. It was going to be about a young woman who goes to the big city, working as a babysitter for a couple who are members of the white-collar class. Though Xiao Feng's life as a babysitter will bring difficulties and hard work, the story will nonetheless have a good ending. Yadan talked about this excitedly while Yu listened quietly.

Finally, Yu said, "Your heart is still so young."

Yadan thought about that and said, "The worst thing for a woman is that the body ages but the heart remains young."

Yu said, "That's wrong. The worst thing is while the body remains young, the heart gets old."

Yadan looked at Yu steadily, rolling her statement around in her mind. "Yu, do you have a boyfriend?"

"Maybe."

"What does that mean? You won't even tell me?"

"Not a secret. A man . . . a surgeon. We are together."

"Do you love him?"

"I don't know. I can't figure out what love is." Yu looked up quietly. "But we are together. It feels quite good."

"Then get married."

"We can never get married. He has a wife and he can't get a divorce."

Yadan grabbed Yu's hand. "Leave him! Listen to me! Even if he were an emperor, you cannot want him. He has a wife and family. And you have nothing. He can move forward or retreat, but you have no way out."

"Yes, I often feel that way. It's not equal. Is there equality anywhere in the world?" From this thoughtful question, she went on to claim that this world has no equality, and definitely no equal love. Those who write ideal equal-love stories must be those who were deserted by the world, or sexually impotent, or widows or widowers.

They heard a commotion outside, a familiar voice greeting the crowd. Upon hearing it, Yu seemed about to fly away to a distant but familiar scene. It was a snowstorm, there were plum blossoms, and a glaze of blood drop-lets on the thin spine of a young girl; and there was a young monk named Yuanguang, with drops of sweat on his shaved head and tears in his eyes. On that winter day, tears, sweat, and blood were mixed together. An impression remained in the snow, with its scattered plum blossoms, that could not be erased by history or re-created with the passage of time.

The voice startled Yu and Yadan at the same time. To Yu's surprise, Yadan—who looked so drearily resigned to her fate a moment before—suddenly came to life, as if she had received some kind of injection. Her expression reminded Yu of *Q&A Behind Bars*. In that play, Yadan was like a flower blossom; now she stared at Zhulong as he walked into the room. Her eyes shone like stars. Zhulong was captivated by those eyes.

At first glance, he had not changed much. But Yu knew him well; in her eyes, his change was profound, much more so than Yadan's. He used to have clear, transparent eyes, but now they were dull. He hid his feelings well, but now she could detect a hint of pain in his expression.

Pain that Zhulong could not hide must have been heartbreaking.

The reunion was not as dramatic as anticipated. Yadan's glorified moment was fleeting. Everyone politely nodded their heads. That was it! Just a greet-ing; no one pretended to be surprised or overly warm. That would be too ar-tificial. Zhulong sat down and began talking; clearly this was his way to hide his feelings. As he spoke he gradually lost track of reality. His eyes lit up as he spoke about the current issues on everyone's mind. Zhulong, this brilliant student leader from the past, commented on the current student movement from the cognitive frame of someone who had experienced it all. He said the country is undergoing a difficult time. Intellectuals should rise above their own dissatisfactions. "I don't think the current student movement will play an active role in solving our country's problems."

Yu had no idea that what he was saying would become a national issue a few months later, when he would be attacked from all sides.

He said, "In difficult times, intellectuals should keep a cool head, separate the salon discussions from actual political events and policies, separate academic ideas from reality. When we talked about avant-garde issues, we tended to be overheated, saying whatever came to mind. That led to two problems: first, the concepts were not mature and the terminology was inaccurate; and the definitions were not clarified or confirmed. Second, when ideas were put on the table for discussion, scholars were not really responsible for their thoughts. It was simply a forming process, a way to let an idea take shape. Before such thoughts are ripe, we should avoid using them to influence others. What we must do right now is minimize the confrontations, try to avoid disasters."

Others were now tuned in to the discussion, and Zhulong's words were soon buried under opposing voices:

"Zhulong, I'd be amazed if you dared to say these things on a university campus right now."

"I heard your debates during the election campaign. I didn't think that in only a few short years your edges would all be ground down."

"I heard your name often in those days. Today is the first time I've met you. They said you were a principled revolutionary who would 'use his head' to knock down a wall. What about now? No walls? Softer head?"

A deep female voice rose above those of his critics. Jinwu, brightly dressed, was descending a stairway that led to the upper floor; and she was, as usual, sparkling. She always enjoyed making a dramatic entry. She had wanted to meet Zhulong, see this man who was chased by so many outstanding young women. What she found was just an ordinary young man, conventionally dressed, nothing special about him. Jinwu couldn't understand why proud Yu would lose her mind over him and why Yadan, who dreamed of perfection, would allow her life to be turned upside down for such an unimpressive character.

Jinwu's puzzlement is only too typical in life. We often like one type of person and dismiss other types. But the one we drive away is often preferred by others. What is truly rare is a person who is admired by all, whether men or women, young or old. That is when we should be alert. In a period that lacks a legitimate idol, a person liked by all is very likely a liar or a yes-man.

Zhulong smiled. With that expression he looked like Yuanguang. Modesty combined with purity. In an instant his smile had disappeared. His eyes had met Yu's.

"If there are moths in the house, we can clean it; there's no need to burn it down. Revolution is not a good method," said Zhulong.

Jinwu had arranged for the party to move on to a nearby restaurant for the meal. Now everyone was walking out her door. Yu saw Zhulong standing in the dark, motionless. Yadan was slowly walking toward him. Yu saw Yadan's face and remembered again the play *Q&A Behind Bars*. Perhaps Yadan had the wrong impression: all this was a play, a suspenseful play without an ending. Yadan did not cry but her expression was heartbreaking. She had discovered that she still loved him, that this would never change. There was nothing anyone could do about it.

Yu heard Yadan ask him quietly, "Why did you come alone? Where is she? I always wanted to meet her." Zhulong's reply was indistinct. Yadan said, "I don't want to talk right now. But someday I will."

Yu felt a sudden gush of warm fluid in her nose that made her dizzy. She got up and walked to the door, deciding she would not continue with the others to the restaurant.

Yu heard light footsteps following her. She knew that step and heard Zhulong calling her.

"Lu Yu, why didn't you talk to me?" His voice was low, and he sounded hurt.

Yu stopped but didn't turn her head.

"I have a lot to say to you. Where are you living now? I'll come to see you!"

Yu still didn't turn and still said nothing. The voice behind her fell silent. But she knew he was just a step behind, a head taller than she, with his hands in his pockets, watching the elegant neck of the woman just in front of him.

"Zhulong, if you want me to speak, okay, but I still have the same thing to say. Run! It will be too late if you don't run now." She left quickly after saying this, without even turning her head.

It was growing dark. Yu walked out into a deepening darkness that was like a huge empty stage—there were no pedestrians, no vehicles, no buildings, nothing of human manufacture. She walked into this darkness, deeper and deeper. She had no regrets but there was a huge sorrow in her heart. Then a voice, seemingly from a different world, sounded in her ear. "Run! You must run! Otherwise you'll never escape." Yu looked around, but there was no one there. And then she realized—it was her whisper! Her spiritual message since childhood, and it was long overdue.

The last rays of twilight disappeared from the horizon.

9

When I saw Zhulong, I was reminded of the old adage "Everyone looks good in someone's eyes." And I thought the adage was true as it applied to him.

That someone who looked good in my eyes was far away in America. He left his school many years ago to return to his own country. It was ideology that separated us. After many years had gone by, he sent me a letter. He wanted me to know that he remembered me and had not forgotten my wish. He had discovered a clue about my mother in a small city called Alan on the West Coast.

I tried to picture that city. Houses stood along snowy streets, like something in a fairy tale. Flowers that are not seen in my country blossomed in the snow. The flowers were in several primary colors, all bright. The air was clear, chilly, and sweet. Since there was no wind, it was not like the bitingly cold winter in northern China. In this small city, in the winter, one could still wear a pair of red wooden sandals to go walking in the snow. Later, when I went to America, it became clear that what I imagined was correct.

Michael said that in that small town, people said there was an old Chinese lady who rarely left home after her husband had died. Only her neighbors saw her when she occasionally went to a pizza shop across the street to buy milk and fat-free pudding. They said that during World War II her husband was known as David Smith.

I got my visa to go to the United States without any trouble. I was the last one to be interviewed that morning. I was called to window number three. People said the old woman at window number three was very tough to deal with. But she was polite to me. After a few routine questions, she smiled and said, "It looks like you have no reason to return to China."

I knew this was a trap. I replied, "I certainly will return. China is everything to me. Here I was a movie star for twenty years, but in America I'll be a nobody."

The old woman smiled broadly. Foreigners are very simple, after all. They are likely to trust whatever you say.

I began immediately to prepare to go abroad. Before leaving I definitely had to find Yu; I couldn't leave without seeing her. I had found her a job in a small factory where they made sweaters by hand. Better than working as a stevedore. But where had she gone? Perhaps somewhere with Zhulong. Every time she saw him, she went a little nuts.

10

For Ruomu, the biggest thing to happen in the late 1980s was the centennial of Jiaotong University. Many alumni, including those in Taiwan and Hong Kong, were expected to attend the celebration. The news about Shao Fenni's coming excited Ruomu. Fenni's husband, Wu Tianxing, was also their classmate. As a student, Wu, short in stature and quiet, was inconspicuous. But with his gentle nature and persistent pursuit he surprised everyone by marrying Fenni, the flower of the class.

Ruomu read the letter from Fenni over and over again and read it aloud to Xuanming and Lu Chen. Xuanming was at this time ninety-nine years old, but her mind was still clear. Fenni's letter seemed like a message from another, distant lifetime. The old woman recalled the times in Qiao Jia'ao when she made moon cakes and plotted all the tactics for her daughter's marriage, a marriage that turned out to be unhappy.

Fenni and her husband arrived on June second, the day after International Children's Day. All three of the elderly members of the Lu family were waiting. When the doorbell rang, Ruomu greeted Fenni warmly. Forty years had passed; the beautiful young woman of the past had aged gracefully. She was dressed in a blue satin dress with a beige vest, and her hair was gray and fluffy. An elegant pair of glasses added to that once beautiful face and she still talked with the same soft accent. When she called Xuanming "aunt," everyone was emotionally touched, even Lu Chen.

Fenni brought many gifts with her as if to pay back what she owed to Xuanming. Sitting down to tea, Fenni said to Xuanming, "Aunt, in over forty years, I have never forgotten your moon cakes. If not for you and Sister Ruomu, I may not have lived past the age of thirty. Now we are all in our seventies. And imagine, you are almost a hundred years old. You are still so healthy. That just shows you have done something good."

On hearing this, Ruomu thought about the time when they called the Belgian doctor for Fenni as a scheme to get Fenni away from Lu Chen. But who would have thought that turn of events had saved Fenni's life? And Ruomu got Lu Chen to marry her and the fights between the two of them never ended for forty years; what an unhappy marriage. What a payback. Just thinking about all this upset her. She immediately changed the subject.

"No news about Sister Xiangyi?" asked Ruomu.

Fenni was overcome with sorrow, so her husband said, "Sister Xiangyi suffered from diabetes and died two years ago." Old Xuanming took this hard. "Oh, Xiangyi," she said, "that child. She was my favorite. I thought I might see her again, but she left before me." Lu Chen changed the subject. "Mengjing is well and lives next door. She is a grandma now. Her grandson is lovely. We asked her to come over for dinner." Fenni was delighted to hear this. "She was the youngest in our class, now she, too, is a grandmother. That shows how old we are now." So they began to talk about children. Upon learning that Fenni's three generations were all well, including two grandsons and five granddaughters, Ruomu took out the family album and showed it to

Fenni. "This is Lu Xiao, a graduate student now. This is Lu Yu, who is still a temporary worker somewhere; she is the most worrisome in the family. And this is my granddaughter, daughter of Ling, now in high school."

At this moment, Yun'er came home, dazzlingly dressed, lighting up the whole room. Seeing Fenni and her husband, Yun'er greeted them sweetly by calling them grandpa and grandma. This made Fenni happy, and she took Yun'er's hand, saying, "This child is so beautiful. She is prettier than all my grandchildren. Where are you going to school?"

"The high school affiliated with the Foreign Language Institute. It's nearby. Is Grandma from Hong Kong? Is that an interesting place?"

Fenni gave her a bag of gifts and said whether Hong Kong is good or not, Yun'er would find out when she visited, and she could stay with her for as long as she wanted. Yun'er was happy and walked away with her presents.

Things got livelier at dinnertime. Xiao and her husband, Ning, came, followed by Mengjing and her husband. Mengjing and Fenni held hands, cried, and laughed. Fenni asked, "Where are your daughter and grandson?"

"They said they would come. I don't know where they are now. I have no idea. This daughter of mine worries me all the time!"

Xiao was the chef and Lu Chen and Ning assisted her. First she made eight cold appetizers: goose web salad with mustard, boiled green peas, peanuts, cold cucumber, steamed chicken, tofu with scallions, sliced pork with minced garlic, and sliced spiced beef.

Fenni said, "They are all very good, as good as the dishes Aunt Xuanming made back then. I always remember the duck soup and told Tianxing many times that I hoped I would someday taste it again."

Ruomu said, "We knew you would crave duck soup. Lu Chen made it for you but we don't know if it will be the same as my mother's."

Ling came in when the hot dishes were brought to the table. She looked fatigued and ugly, which frightened everyone. Her pretense of being happy made people feel even worse. Tianxing looked at Ling and said, "This must be that child who was pulled out with forceps." Xuanming said, "That was so long ago, it's all right to talk about it now. That time her mother spent three days and nights in labor and still couldn't deliver her. It was life-threatening.

I went with Grandfather to a temple. I banged my head kowtowing two hundred times, making my forehead bleed. But eventually my prayers worked. That Belgian doctor who had gone back to his own country had suddenly decided to come back. He personally delivered the baby, using forceps to pull her out. Sometimes miracles happen."

Ruomu glanced at her mother, saying, "This was your reward? The child was born because of your two hundred kowtows?"

Xuanming was very deaf now; not hearing Ruomu, she continued. "But my prayers were only partially answered. Guanyin, the Goddess of Mercy, was angry with me and took away my little grandson. That poor child, he was not even one year old."

Ruomu threw down her chopsticks and went to her room. Lu Chen gave Fenni an anguished look and said, "You see, my family has been like this for several decades. The same old thing. Who can take it anymore?"

There was not much that Fenni could say. She searched for something comforting. "Every family has its own problems."

The two of them exchanged looks, then both looked away glumly. The past was coming back to both of them at the same time. Seeing Fenni's gray hair, Lu Chen wondered about the twists and turns that come in the life of a family. When he was young, he had thought that if he could not marry Fenni, he would become a monk and never marry. That was so naive. In reality, no matter who you marry, life goes on. He found this thought depressing.

Fenni almost didn't recognize Lu Chen when she first saw him. She thought they would not have recognized each other if passing on a street. The young and dashing Lu Chen! Now such an old and skinny man. He was too thin, as though suffering from an illness. He had trouble smiling, and when he did so, it was a bitter, heartbreaking smile. Fenni couldn't imagine what life had been like for him all these years, but she guessed that a proud and self-confident man such as he could not have a good life in a family such as this. Society and his family must have pressed him from opposite sides; perhaps that was why he was so thin.

Mengjing pulled Fenni to one side and told her in a low voice, "You don't know what happened to Sister Ruomu. She had a son when she was forty years old but the son died an abnormal death."

"How?"

"Choked to death!"

"What! Who did it?"

"Sister Ruomu's youngest daughter, Yu. That girl was strange when she was little. Now she is still not married and doesn't have a regular occupation. All day long she would take my foolish daughter with her, doing God knows what. We knew they would cause trouble someday!"

Fenni was shocked and said, "God, how could she have killed her own little brother?"

"It's true. The old lady told me this herself. Sister Ruomu almost died! The mother and daughter still don't speak to each other!"

Fenni and Tianxing coaxed Ruomu out of her room. She was crying and said, "You see, this is my family. Anyone may say anything without any concern for others. She is already ninety-nine, yet still so tough with her tongue. Sooner or later she will curse us all to death, then she will die."

Fenni thought this was too much. Luckily, Xuanming couldn't hear it. So Fenni and Tianxing got up and began saying good night. But just then, Yu arrived.

She had not been home recently. But she had received a letter from her father saying that on June second she must visit, as Aunt Shao and Uncle Wu would be coming from Hong Kong for the centenary. They had been friends for more than forty years, and she must come and pay her respects. Yu had heard the stories about Shao Fenni and was full of curiosity about this old lover of her father's. As usual, she was casually dressed, in fact rather sloppy. An old lady with gray hair was not what she expected. It was hard to imagine that that face was once beautiful. A woman without love loses her beauty, Yu thought. But in this world, how many people have met their true love?

Fenni was a straightforward person, without pretense. After hearing about the youngest daughter's supposed crime, she couldn't feel relaxed in her presence. Her tension was apparent to Yu, who immediately intuited the cause—they had been talking about her. The family had told this woman from Hong Kong what had happened a long time ago. Whenever such a situation arose, it made Yu feel self-destructive. Hide your face! Hide your face!

Yu's initial warmth in Fenni's presence was no longer possible; now she felt defensive, almost hostile, and turned her attention to Xiao. As for Fenni, her initial shock at hearing the story of the baby brother had turned to surprise upon meeting the eccentric Yu, who at first seemed so gentle. Then, as she thought about it, Fenni's mood shifted to disbelief. It must be a mistake. No one could believe that this girl could have been capable of such a heinous act. But as she continued to observe the young woman, she perceived a hard edge emerging. Was it congenital, unbridled viciousness coming to the surface?

Fenni suggested another subject. Feigning cheerfulness, she observed, "What a remarkable family! Three girls, all so pretty. Second son-in-law also outstanding! Where is first son-in-law?"

Then everyone thought of Ling, who had not spoken till now, being too busy eating. Her sunken, yellowish cheeks moved up and down as she chewed; the elasticity of her skin was a thing of the past.

"Really, why did Wang Zhong not come? Is he busy?" Ruomu felt something wrong in the air and she was trying to rectify the situation.

Ling was no longer quick with words. Dumbfounded, she stared at Fenni, finally blurting out, "We are divorced."

"What did you say?" Now it was her father who was dumbfounded.

"We are divorced!" The words were not merely loud and emphatic; they came out like an abusive curse, and she broke into sobs.

This ended the conversation. Everyone froze, not quite believing what they had just heard. The silence was broken by Yun'er's scream: "Look at Great-grandma!"

Great-grandma had slumped to one side of her chair. Drool was seeping from one wrinkled corner of her mouth.

11

In late spring and early summer, it was Yangyang who saved my life.

Later mother still talked about it, saying he was our family's lucky star. This much is certain: without him, I would have been long gone.

It was Children's Day, June first, of that fateful year—1989. The kindergarten teacher asked parents to pick up their kids early; the political storm was already in full force. After picking up Yangyang, I was stuck with him at home except for one night when I went to visit Fenni at Yu's house. To my surprise, the event unfolding at the Square now was much different from the one on that freezing and boiling April night some ten years earlier.

That April will endure in our memory. Looking back, it was a time of sorrow, expressed in the innocent tears shed at the Square; it was also a time when clarity and purity of purpose came easily. Now all that had been replaced by a complicated mix of personal and political objectives.

When hypocrisy is rife, people begin wearing masks. But when a mask is worn too long it may turn into the flesh and become a permanent feature. To win public support, people must devote themselves completely to a bigger cause than those that grow out of their own ambitions. Our situation may be compared to living in a large garden where only one crop is grown and all other plants must be rooted out.

This leads to the foundation of a collective idea of Nirvana that was no single individual's dream.

Sadly, I would now have to swallow my last bit of pride. I would have to give up ownership of my own body. Having given my first love to someone I deeply loved and thus produced a child, but without forming a union of husband and wife, I now owed it to my mother to find another mate, almost anyone, even someone I did not love, just to wash away the embarrassment of the single-mother status imposed on my mother and myself. It was seemingly all for the creation of a "safe nest," but it did not change the nature of the bargain, a business of prostitution even though it was carried out with one man in accordance with all legal requirements. Ironically, I had entered into a business deal in order to gain respectability.

I will never forget when, on the day of my marriage to Ah Quan, I walked into the small courtyard on the outskirts of the capital city. The air was filled with the odor of rotting plants. A small garden was crowded with squash still on the vine that had been left unpicked and eaten by insects, which had turned into worms. Some of the worms had hardened like date pits. Two long vines were sagging with aged squash hanging down into the dirt, with skins that had turned dark brown. The entire trellis was covered in dust and spiderwebs, with dried-up grayish squash seeds nestled inside. The whole thing was literally hanging by threads. I carefully walked behind my Ah Quan, avoiding the hanging vines studded with insects; he poked a worm, which immediately revealed a yellowish fluid. When I wiped my hand on a tree, a black cloud of flies swarmed about my palm.

The interior of the house was equally disgusting. Rusting metal furniture was scattered about the filthy floor; only the marital bed was new, painted an optimistic bright red and green. At that moment my mother-in-law rushed out. She had beady eyes set in dark circles and a surprisingly large nose and mouth. A large cyst bulged out next to her nose, but her worst feature came on display when she smiled: buck teeth. She was flat-chested, abnormally so. Without thinking, I drew in my own breasts. My father-in-law was tall and strong and ruddy-faced. He punctuated his sentences with an automatic clearing of the throat, often followed by spitting. There was another woman in the room who looked to be more than ninety. My mother-in-law told me to call her Great-granny.

The room was hung with heavy curtains and the light was dim. A musty, sour cabbage odor pervaded the hovel. Great-granny sat on her bed, spooning up soup from a greasy pot. Toothless, she was smacking her lips over a piece of pork shoulder, competing with several flies for every last morsel. With every bite the metallic purple of her gums came into view, changing to a darker color as she chewed. Oily soup seeped from one corner of her mouth and dribbled into a puddle at her feet, where more flies partook of the feast. Those flies were too fat to ever fly up again. As though sound effects were needed to complete this loathsome scene, a series of farts erupted as the great-granny worked her way into the delicious pork shoulder.

Nauseated, I swatted at the flies, but Great-granny pushed me away, leaving greasy handprints on my beautiful block-printed sweater. "Did they hurt you? Why kill them?"

As I was taking in this scene, I noticed that my mother-in-law and Great-granny had a strong resemblance. The bone structure around their eyes was triangular, as were their faces as a whole, and their teeth, or what was left of them in the mother, were small and protruded hideously. They also dressed alike. Mother-in-law wore a large, loose-fitting black sweater and her mother was dressed in a big, loose cotton jacket, also black; why would they wear such drab clothing on a day that was supposed to be happy?

That night, Ah Quan and I did not sleep until very late. Early in the morning, when the sky was still dark, I heard a knocking sound, like that of a woodpecker. Groggy, neither asleep nor awake, I covered my ears. But the sound became louder, like a drum, and I realized at last that someone was pounding on the bedroom door.

"Ah Quan, open the door!" It was Mother-in-law!

Ah Quan and I began pulling on clothes, but he opened the door before I had quite finished dressing; in front of the open door, my hands fumbling clumsily with buttons, I was confronted by Mother-in-law, whose knifelike gaze sliced right across my chest.

"What time is it now?" she said. "Great-granny is waiting for your wife to make breakfast!" Her face was waxy, her eyelids sagging. She was full of a deep hatred. Father-in-law had lost his smiles but not his habit of constant spitting. The great-granny sat at the table with a long face, knocking on the bowl impatiently. No one looked at me, but I felt their eyes. I felt their hateful gaze, under which I must get dressed quickly, and at the same time I felt completely naked. I thought of those worms hardened like pits hung on the decayed vines in the yard. I panicked.

"It is our family's custom that on the second day following the wedding the bride becomes the daughter-in-law and can no longer behave like a guest!" After I had served them breakfast, the three elders sat around the table, one side of which was against a wall. Mother-in-law took out two red envelopes and gave them to us followed by her little speech. "This is for good luck. From today on, we are one family. Consider it a deposit; next year we want a grandson!"

At that time, the elders had no idea I already had a child.

Ah Quan had done his best to cover up the matter, but after a time he gave them the news, in two parts: First, he told them that he could not father a child, a fact confirmed by a medical checkup. This was a huge shock to the tribal elders. Ah Quan had been the only son in three generations. Seeing the shock treatment on the elders worked, Ah Quan told them about handsome and smart Yangyang. Only then did the elders realize that their only son had married a secondhand wife. Though he was not one of their own by blood, it was better to have a grandson by this means than none at all. The elders had no choice but to accept the realities as presented.

After receiving five telephone calls from my mother, I decided to go home for a visit. Two days later, after a light breakfast, I dressed Yangyang in nice clothes and off we went on my bicycle. When I got to the main road, I felt something was wrong. The streets were eerily quiet. By the city's freeway, I saw a bus that had crashed and burned lying wheels-up by the side of the road, oily smoke still emanating from the ruptured carcass. Yangyang pointed with his tiny hand. "Mom, what's wrong with the big bus?" I didn't answer. The horror of the scene was overwhelming.

12

That day the sky was gray, the air was still, and everywhere the mood seemed fear-ridden.

As Yadan pushed her bicycle into the Jiaotong University compound, a former neighbor dashed up to her, scolding as she advanced, "Do you know what's going on? You dared to bring out your child!" Yadan didn't grasp the implication of the question but was frightened by the tone of alarm. Something was wrong. Very wrong. She immediately thought of Zhulong. God! Where is Zhulong now?

It was no longer the Square of that April, no longer that freezing but boiling rain when she had walked up to the holy altar with wedding music in her heart. Nothing was real now. Nothing was clear. All had passed. All had been lost. Nothing could return to its original state. As painful as it could be, Yadan felt all had been lost, forever gone.

Fenni was surprised that beautiful Mengjing had given birth to such an ugly daughter. She was even more surprised at her distressing expression.

Fenni and Tianxing had scheduled their return to Hong Kong on June sixth. But all transportation was halted. The express bus to the airport was not available. Yadan borrowed a three-wheeled flat-decked tricycle cart, and by taking turns with Xiao, she pedaled the energy-consuming contraption carrying Fenni, her husband, and their luggage to the airport. Xiao was stunned by the scenes along the way, the remains of a street battle; but Yadan was preoccupied with thoughts of Zhulong, of Yu, and of their presence on the Square that long-ago April. That era was a hot-blooded era; the events in the Square of that era were created by hot-blooded people who had thought they were all reborn, leaving an old embryo behind and entering a brand-new era. They thought they could board their Noah's Ark to resist the unwanted flood, but in the end they were defeated by their own fate.

Before entering customs inspection, Fenni held hands with both Xiao and Yadan, saying, "This was not a good time for me to come to the capital. We brought trouble to you and to your parents. This was our first reunion after forty years, little did we know . . ."

Yadan expressed her own sorrow in return. "Aunt Shao, we are all sorry. Our family had been doing well. This event was unexpected."

In a loving gesture, Fenni caressed Yadan's hair. She found that this ugly girl when caught in a moment of emotional expression was charged with high spirits, which let Fenni see that once this girl had been attractive and beautiful. The old lady spoke of returning for another visit someday, but both women knew that the chances were remote. And then Fenni and Tianxing gradually faded into the throngs beyond the gate.

Yadan thought of going to look for Zhulong to see if she could send him to Aunt Shao; Hong Kong might be a safe haven. But how to find him? This was a man who wandered everywhere at will. Neither fears of death nor the ordinary constraints of married life would hold him back. Thinking of his marriage was a source of comfort to Yadan. He never talked about it and was always alone at social events—the lonely knight.

Yadan and Xiao encountered another familiar figure at the airport. It was Jinwu, smiling and poised as usual, now dressed in her favorite red blouse.

"Are you seeing someone off?" asked Xiao.

"No, I am the one to be sent off," she replied. "Why would you come to say good-bye to Fenni but not me?"

"What? You are leaving?"

"So? Why can't I go abroad?"

"How did you arrange it? To which country?"

"To the United States, visiting relatives. It was arranged by an old friend."

"You just go like this without telling anyone?"

"Do I have to go with bells and whistles?"

"I mean, you didn't say farewell to anyone?"

"I am now saying farewell to you. My flight is tonight. I knew you would be here to see off your family friends, so I came early to meet you."

Xiao and Yadan looked at each other, and Yadan asked the question in both their minds. "Did you say good-bye to Yu?"

Jinwu frowned and with some feeling said, "She did not return the whole week. I called her factory, and they said no one knew where she was. Tell her when you see her that I will get in touch from abroad."

Jinwu disappeared, just as she had thirteen years ago. This time she did not escape from a small place to a large city; this time she escaped from a city on one side of the world to another on the other side.

That night the Lu family gathered around Xuanming's bed. The doctor confirmed that she had suffered a stroke. She was ninety-nine years old, no need to rush her to the hospital. The family should prepare for a funeral. When the clock sounded at midnight, Xuanming suddenly opened her eyes and said clearly, "Let me tell you all, the sounds you heard last night—the whole night—were not firecrackers. They were gunshots."

Everyone was stunned at hearing this. Then Xuanming asked for her special birthday costume, made of blue satin stitched with silvery thread, symbolizing longevity.

"Let her dress up as she pleases," Ruomu said. "It may lift her spirits." So they sat her up and helped her into the clothes she wanted, and were surprised at her remaining vitality as she gestured for her wicker chair. Everyone agreed this was a good sign, she may live to a hundred. The old lady gave Ling a ring of keys and asked her to fetch the precious lamp so that she could put it together one more time. And that's what she did, working piece by piece for two hours, threading each and every flower petal according to the codes. Under the dim light her hands gradually turned pale and she grew weak; eventually they seemed as white and thin as paper.

Her last words were "Give this to Yadan's son, Yangyang. He may be the real flesh and blood of Tiancheng." Her voice was weak and choked with phlegm, and they cradled her ancient head as she gradually slumped over. She was dead.

The Lu women began crying. The old lady had guarded her treasures all her life, not distributing them among her children, and now she was asking them to pass along her most valuable possession to an outsider. Ruomu and Ling at once agreed they did not hear clearly what Xuanming had said. Only Xiao confirmed that Grandma gave the lamp to Yangyang. Lu Chen sighed heavily. Ruomu said, "How could Xiao be so foolish? Grandma disliked Mengjing all her life; she couldn't possibly have wanted to do this. Xiao must be mistaken." So Xiao said no more, and she started to help Ruomu clean the body and begin making all the arrangements.

Yun'er woke up during the night and saw Xuanming's body laid out on the bed. She cried and felt remorse that she had done something that would have horrified her great-granny: she had a Japanese boyfriend, and the old lady would not forgive her for that.

13

When Xuanming died, Yushe was with Zhulong at the Jinque Temple on Xitan Mountain. As she was lighting incense sticks, one by one, the ninth one suddenly died. Yu said something had happened at home. "My grandma died."

Zhulong looked at her in disbelief and asked if her intuitions were ever wrong. Yu thought about it and said, "No."

They had taken a night train to escape from the big city and travel to Xitan Mountain. Zhulong looked surprised when they arrived. Indeed, he agreed, he remembered a dream many years ago. In the dream he was a monk named Yuanguang. On a snowy winter morning when red plum blossoms could be seen in the white snow, he assisted a Master Fa Yan, who was doing a tattoo on a young girl. This Xitan Mountain looked just like the one in his dream, but with no snow or plum blossoms. The Jinque Temple of his dream was now old and dilapidated. But this was the place he visited in his dream, and he was a monk named Yuanguang. This was all so unbelievable.

Yu was elated. Yes, this was it! Jinque Temple was still there. She took his hand as they entered the temple. All the monks in attendance were surprised, saying, "Master Yuanguang! You came back!"

Yu's memories were confirmed by the abbot. He said Master Fa Yan had died in the fall of 1969 at the age of 139. The last thing he did in his life was to create a tattoo on a young girl's back. Fa Yan said it was the best he had ever done. Then he went inside the hall and never came out again.

After his death, his assistant, Yuanguang, also left the temple. The old abbot looked at Zhulong and said, "This man looks very much like Yuanguang."

Yu quickly said, "Please accept him as Yuanguang. He wants to become a monk. Please shave his head."

For the first time in their long friendship, Zhulong was angry at Yu. He asked the abbot to let them stay here first and then he would decide.

They chose the room in which Master Fa Yan had died. What a change of scene! Only yesterday they were in the midst of the roaring Square. Today, as if today were separated by a whole lifetime, they were here. Zhulong had made arrangements to help his friends and left the burning city at midnight. Once on the road, he allowed Yu to lead the way. He thought the temple in her mind could not possibly exist.

But not only did they find Jinque Temple on Xitan Mountain, they also found the very place where Master Fa Yan's spirit had left the earth. Zhulong looked around the dusty room, idly searching for traces of the old man. The abbot said he had died in the Sleeping Buddha, or recumbent, position. Zhulong knew full well that he himself was not truly Yuanguang, but he was full of admiration for Fa Yan. He was only Zhulong, the fire god of ancient myths. Deep in the night he sometimes thought in the way he imagined a fire god would: he would burn himself to ashes, lighting the road ahead. But now his boiling blood was gradually cooling down in this cool room, and his thoughts turned to escaped comrades and to his own future. Everyone was in hiding; but, in time, someone must stand and take responsibility for the momentous events just concluded in the Square. The consequences of evasion would be unthinkable.

Yu knelt in front of Master Fa Yan's deathbed and again burned some incense and said a silent prayer for Zhulong: "Master, protect him. Whether or not he was your assistant, he is a good man. Protect him from the consequences of this disaster."

As she said this, a sudden gust of wind blew out the incense. She was stunned and, as she arose, said, "We must leave here. It's not safe."

Zhulong refused to budge. Tomorrow would not be too late.

Yu had no choice, so she sat down next to Zhulong. He held her in his arms, his eyes and smile reflecting an inner peace. He said, "I remember that dream now. I went into the side hall and a ray of twilight beamed down. I saw a thin girl but not very clearly in the dim light; she seemed obscured, as though by melting snow and ice. That girl was you."

She thanked him for revealing his memories.

He continued, "I remember that girl did not cry even once during the tattooing. Her endurance was remarkable, and I thought of testing its limits with a sharp needle; to test her body to see if it was or was not real."

Yu said Master Fa Yan used cotton to remove her blood and said, "Young girl, I know you are in pain. Your skin is too tense and I cannot continue. There is only one way to bring relaxation. This young man can help you, and then we can achieve the most beautiful tattoo in the world."

Zhulong said, "I knew I could not resist Fa Yan. I had no choice."

Yu said, "From the very beginning I knew you were not just anybody. So I accepted you."

"Later I took over the tools from the master and wanted to try doing a small tattoo of my own, but didn't know how and where. You turned and pointed at your breasts. And you said, 'Come, leave a souvenir.' It was dark, but under the moonlight I concentrated for thirty minutes and made two plum blossoms, one on each breast."

Yu was moved by all of this, saying, "You really do remember. Everything. At the end, when you were done, you collapsed and said, 'I can never be as good as the master.'"

Zhulong said, "Fa Yan did say, and now I remember this, that this was the best tattoo he had ever made in his whole life. And he went on to say it was 'the wonder and treasure of the world. I shall never do it again. Young girl, leave. Go far away and never let me see you again.'"

Now Zhulong and Yu embraced in the dark silence, and this dusty room was filled with their passion. Now there was no more blood, no more sadness, all was clear and unhurried. What remained was the purity of their passion, together with a renewed belief in the beauty of truth. Human feelings rose to no higher level than this.

Zhulong softly caressed Yu's skin, smooth like porcelain and cool, and the two tiny plum blossoms had grown darker over the years. This magic girl had become a woman; could she continue to practice magic in the dull world of settled workers? He employed his hands to revive her stiffened body. He touched the two tiny plum blossoms and she shivered—a strong reaction that aroused his desire. The dark blue blossoms turned to dark red, as his hand brought a rush of blood beneath her tender skin. Yu waved her long, dark hair across his face and chest, bringing a rush of exhilarated pleasure that reached down to the roots of his spine; never had he felt so real, so thrilled to the core. Yu was responsive to his every motion; and her own body, now thoroughly relaxed but thoroughly aroused, undulated and vibrated, like a fish exerting itself through an onrushing stream. Her own existence had entered a new stage of reality. Frozen for so many years, her body was now at last fully ready for merger with that of the man for whom she yearned constantly.

But it was not to be. He stopped, the veins on his forehead throbbing to the rhythm of his heart. He pulled his knees to his head and buried his face, saying, "Yu, forgive me. I can't."

Yu arose from a dream state. "What, what did you say?"

Zhulong said no more. But that night he was like a caged beast, moaning so loudly that he was heard by the monks.

Yu fell asleep. She woke in bright daylight. Rubbing her eyes, she got up and realized that Zhulong was gone. She found a slip of paper on which he had written, "Yu, I left. No matter what, someone must stand up and take responsibility for events in the Square. Don't look for me. We will meet again."

Yu saw her hands turning white. Her pulse was throbbing. She looked about the room for evidence that her memories of the night were true. She found something that had slipped from his pocket—a small bottle with pills and a slip of paper. This was a note from another woman. "Zhulong, I am so sorry. It's all my fault, passing my disease on to you. Take this medicine, get well soon. Wife: Xiaotao. May 20."

Yu read the paper three times, each time experiencing its message like a knife cutting her heart. To suppress her pain she curled up her body and pulled her hair. Her eyes were burning and she had no more tears.

Yu was running against the wind, under the burning sun on Xitan Mountain. It was under the wind and sun that she saw that vast forest of tombstones. They seemed to have appeared overnight. The forest of tombstones was spread over every part of the mountain, in the color of gray clouds. Yu noticed there were no inscriptions on the tombstones. No names.

The wordless tombstones had spread across the landscape as far as the eye could see!

Many years later, when Yu recalled this scene, it would give her a jolting sensation.

This was the forest of tombstones Yu kept in her heart.

CHAPTER 11

CROSSOVER

1

蛇 Five years later Yushe had a dream. In it all the stars in the sky were woven into a single, seamless net. In the pitch-black sky, a small boat shaped out of human bones rocked in the deep sea. Sitting in the boat was a person dressed as a servant, holding a skull.

Yu later modeled a painting on the dream. Michael from America said that the painting should be named *The Crossover*.

Grandma Xuanming had once said that the term "crossover" had a special meaning in Buddhism.

Yu pondered the meaning of the term. What intrigued her was that its religious meaning was the same in both Eastern and Western traditions.

Later she altered the painting, adding Zhulong's face to the skull and making the image of the servant look like herself.

2

I flew from the East to the West. It felt like the wings of the airplane were seemingly attached to my own body. Yes, now I was a big, lumbering bird flying over that famous ocean, leaving a huge, crescent-shaped trail across the deep purple sky filled with perpetual white clouds.

I could feel your body's warmth in the breeze. I knew I was getting closer and closer to you.

Washington, D.C., in April resembled a nineteeth-century British water-color painting, floating in a grayish fog, tinted with a faint aristocratic air, with pale pink cherry blossoms dangling harmoniously against the backdrop of gray. Only God's hand could mix the colors to produce such a dreamy illusion. This led me into another dream, not the kind that drifts along but a genuine, deep dream filled with thousands of unhealed wounds. It featured a withered beauty, like an old but once beautiful lady whose face had been wrecked over time, with only the slightest hint of her spirit remaining. An elusive charm might glimmer from her face but only if the right cosmetics were applied; her beauty now came only at great expense and effort. And now a world once exhausted and dying was rising up again. Traces of those times in different forms and shapes were found after the catastrophe, buried deep under the earth.

I couldn't restrain myself from falling on my knees to place a kiss on one such trace. The kiss was gentle, for I feared that fresh blood might suddenly spurt out like the juice from a fresh piece of fruit. Once before, that trace had opened up like a brilliant flower, filling in the dark skies.

You said, "Union Station, tomorrow morning at seven o'clock."

I held the phone not knowing what to say. I had not heard your actual voice for five long years, but its echo had lingered in my heart ever since our last meeting. In the forest of tombstones, that echo had lost direction, transformed into millions of sound tracks traveling like light beams through abandoned gardens, those gardens of thorns. The traveling sound of your echo sliced through broad palm leaves, turning their edges into the sharp teeth of a lumberman's saw. That was how the echo of your voice stayed in my heart, like those sharp teeth. I was deeply wounded.

I knew I would not cry when I saw you.

My tears had dried beforehand. They would come back only after I had seen you. But I would have no tears during our meeting.

I would not weep, not lose my words, and not use any body language. I would not even stare at you, not remain silent, and not get lost in my own thoughts. I knew you would do just the same.

This is not because we are no longer young.

On that night five years ago, you left on your own, walking silently into the darkness to the cross that opened up and swallowed you. You were crucified by the darkness of the night. You lost so much blood, more than the blood shed by Jesus Christ. But you were not Jesus, nor could you become him. This is not an era capable of producing another Jesus. On that dark night no one laid an eye on you; no one was there to bury your body. All of them seemed to have vanished instantly. No one dared to reveal their despicable acts in the face of your nobility. They attempted, to no avail, to explain that your actions came out of your own selfish and contemptible desires. Then they elevated you up to the heavens, building you up as a glorious hero with the most beautiful, gaudy, but worthless compliments, telling you all along to remain up there and never return. But you did return—the most terrible thing that you ever could have done.

3

At Union Station, the largest railway station in Washington, D.C., Yu recognized Zhulong with some difficulty among the crowd of non-Chinese. His big frame was intact but inside he had been completely broken. She quietly scanned his shattered face, trying hard not to betray her own emotions. He was wearing a loose, baggy jacket—perfect to cover up his fat belly. This fat man, bloated by a diet of fast food, with a gloomy face and slightly balding head, was a mere shadow of the handsome, spirited young man of five years earlier. He told her that he was now living with his wife, An Xiaotao, in nearby Baltimore. He said he was grateful to Xiaotao, for without her he would never have reemerged from the deep darkness.

Yu immediately noticed stains on his shirt collar.

There was nothing she wanted to say, nothing at all. A little mermaid swam off in the ocean after saving a prince. When the prince came to, he saw a beautiful princess next to him. Naturally he thought it was this princess who had saved his life. The little mermaid's tongue had been cut out. She could not say anything and nothing could be said. This is such a beautiful metaphor and warning, serving as a model for all misunderstandings and tragedies for a thousand years. No other story can be more suitable to explain such tragedies.

Some people are simply destined to have their tongues cut out.

He ordered tea. As in all Chinese restaurants in America, the waitress also brought fortune cookies. Staring at the cookies in complete silence, neither of the two uttered a word, nor did they bother to open them.

No. She did not want to see him in America. She'd rather he were dead than living like this. So she avoided his face; she kept her eyes on the fortune cookies and listened to his voice in silence, hoping to resurrect the past in his voice. At this railway station café in a foreign country, she was trying to recover the voice that had been lost for so many years—a voice that had appeared just at the moment when some music from a church filled the air:

Have we trials and temptations?
Is there trouble anywhere?
We should never be discouraged;
Take it to the Lord in prayer.
Can we find a friend so faithful
Who will all our sorrows share?
Jesus knows our every weakness;
Take it to the Lord in prayer.

Are we weak and heavy laden,
Cumbered with a load of care?
Precious Savior, still our refuge;
Take it to the Lord in prayer.
Do thy friends despise, forsake thee?
Take it to the Lord in prayer!
In his arms he'll take and shield thee;
Thou wilt find a solace there.

But now, years later, that night was long gone. In the empty and quiet hall of the railway station, the grayish blue moonlight engulfed the couple. Zhulong said, "Yu, remember what I said then? A feather that has broken away from its wing is not flying but drifting."

No one, it seems, can escape the fate of drifting.

"Run, Zhulong, run. There is still time," Yu had warned him back then.

"Run away? Why? If a shabby barricade blocks our path, we should walk around it. It will probably remain standing long after we die. But if I strike it with my head, it will collapse and I will die. Yu, I understand, I've prepared for it all." Back then, when he had uttered those words, Zhulong was young and spirited, full of energy.

"But some things are much crueler than death."

"I know."

"If one day you look at yourself in the mirror, you may gaze upon someone who is no longer you. You will not recognize yourself and completely forget how you once looked . . . if that happens, what will you do?"

"But it won't happen," Zhulong commented back then as he slowly stood up. "It won't happen."

Now, Yu realized, it was precisely those words that had hit Zhulong and hit him hard.

At that very moment back then, a preacher's voice was heard from the church. "God loves everyone, including nonbelievers. God saves the drunken, the criminal, and those who hurt him. Even those who nailed his son to the cross! Jesus used his life to bring rebirth to others, and to bring forgiveness and joy. Truly spiritual love, pure love, true love cannot end, because God is love! God is eternal!"

Love? Forever? Yu could only laugh. The church music of that night, the reflections from the glass windows, the fragrance of the apple blossoms in the air: all of these things were props to dress up the show. The leading male and female characters had entered the drama and performed as in real life. They had progressed beyond the time of *Q&A Behind Bars*. But after Yu saw the play *Black Widow*, she came to see the snake oil in the *Q&A Behind Bars*. *Black Widow* had reminded her of that freshwater mussel in her childhood—

such is life. But *Q&A Behind Bars* had indicated her life could be different. Yet any type of life contrary to nature would be punished, no matter how noble a person's faith. Noble deeds and forbidden actions are equally at odds with human nature.

As with Yu, Zhulong's thoughts turned to that night near the church. The young woman sitting in front of him, he thought, was actually part of a fairy tale, nothing but an illusion, an illusion that surfaced in his good young days. He had left himself and his illusions back in his homeland. That was the cost he should pay when leaving his home country. He was not sentimental when he thought of that night and the church, as he knew he had been destroyed, destroyed by an unbeatable power. When he was young, he often wondered why some historical figures ended up betraying their causes. Now he understood them, a lesson he had learned at the cost of his own life. That profound understanding applied here: not until you "cross over" is the essential experience gained. But once the crossover is complete, you can never return to the original place. Here lay the origin of most tragedies in the world. But now recalling and reliving the past was of little interest. He wanted to avoid anything that had to do with the past, including his illusions. That was his fragile defense line; once that line was broken, he would never again find reason to live.

He went with her to the Smithsonian Institution, where she asked him to take her picture standing next to a strange-looking sculpture made out of wire and some recycled materials. The wire was all rusty but somehow that natural rust formed a strange picture. She walked to the front of the structure and opened her arms wide so her shawl looked like the wings of a witch. She thought of the term "performance art," which led her to think of Jinwu, who lived in a city nearby, hopelessly searching for her long-lost mother.

By the time they had climbed the stairs to the third floor of the museum, Zhulong broke out in a sweat.

"So how do you make a living?" Yu inquired.

"Delivering food. I won't accept charity."

"How do you manage to deliver food when you're in such poor physical condition?"

"Well, it's not that bad. I eat two meals a day and I buy two bags of frozen dumplings at a small shop owned by a Chinese. They're quite delicious."

"Who is taking care of you?" Yu asked as she eyed the stains on his shirt collar.

"Why do I need anyone to take care of me? I'm not a patient."

"But you are sick. I know you have been very sick. You were locked up for three years in a jail cell only four square meters in size. There was a latrine, nothing but an open pit with a smell that in the summertime was unbearable. Maggots were everywhere and eventually you developed a rash, scratching your skin so much you exposed your own bones. You nearly died in that jail . . . but later you managed to slip out a message, demanding better treatment; otherwise, you would have ended up defending your dignity by death . . ."

He clenched his teeth. "All that was in the past."

But Yu was not about to drop the topic. "Also, you were sick even before you were tossed in jail. I saw a bottle of medicine at Jinque Temple . . ."

At that point, he suddenly roared, "I said all that was in the past!"

She opened her eyes wide, staring at him, and immediately was drained of every ounce of energy. Once again she felt the horror in the simplicity and precision of the Chinese language. One word, "past," was all you needed to erase everything. This led her to think of the word "cruelty," but it was pale and powerless in comparison to the word "past." Eyes can change from clear to dull; skin can turn from bright to gray; inner strength can fade from strong to weak; the mind can change from sharp to slow—all those changes form a terrible process. A beautiful creature can be broken without even leaving a sound in the universe. Once it's broken, it becomes a thing of the past. Thus, a broken body along with a broken soul is a thing of the past, left behind in another world.

And it was during this past time that she had gone to see Dr. Danzhu with great fear and sorrow, begging the doctor's father to issue proof that Zhulong's illness was so serious that it required assistance from outside the jail. After searching far and wide, she also had found him the best lawyer to help save him. She had no money, but for him she would cut her own soul and flesh to pieces.

"There is another thing that you have not settled." She looked at him calmly.

"What?"

"You have a son who is ten years old now."

His lips started to turn pale: "You mean . . . Yadan?"

Yu had an unyielding bitterness in her heart. She wanted him to feel the pain, to suffer. She laughed a bit. "Do you think you were fair to Yadan? Mr. big hero?"

He wasn't crushed. His eyes drifted to a faraway place. "Have you read *Man and the Forest God*? The forest god said, 'When our wisdom was born, it was time your wisdom ended.' Man replied: 'The time for fairy tales has passed, though a time without fairy tales has no charm.' In reality, modern men desire to escape from freedom as much as they long for it. In the past, I longed for freedom. But now, I only want to . . . escape it . . . Yadan is a great woman." He paused. Then, looking rather relaxed, he asked, "How is my son?"

Yu smiled again. Zhulong seemed to find her smile beautiful for the first time. Yu looked even more relaxed than he. She said, "Shall we open the fortune cookies now?"

They cracked opened their cookies at the same time. Zhulong's fortune read: "You will rub shoulders with your lifetime love." Slowly he rolled the small piece of paper into a ball. Yu read hers: "What you long for is about to arrive."

"What you long for is about to arrive." Yu raised her eyes in surprise. All the museum exhibits surrounding her looked the same. This was the largest museum in America. God's favorite people, with their blond hair and green eyes, walked around with happy and somewhat foolish smiles on their faces. But that whisper which belonged to another world was written in that cookie! How? Yu suddenly felt there was something in the dark chasing her, watching her, and guiding her. That something was telling her that what she longed for was not Jinwu, not Master Fa Yan, not Yuanguang or even Zhulong. That something was guiding her gradually onto a small path leading into a maze where the final answer was hidden deep inside.

What was it that she longed for? An overpowering suspense entrapped her. She was both longing for and afraid of the final revelation.

At midnight the last train for Baltimore finally pulled into the station. Lovers were hugging and kissing on the platform. Zhulong and Yu avoided looking at each other while spewing out irrelevant words. When the last bell rang, Zhulong quickly extended his hand before boarding the train. In a flash, when he turned around, Yu could see the tears streaming down his face.

Yu was such a hopeless pretender. She stood there for as long as she could, with not another soul on the empty platform and rain falling from a boundless sky. Whenever a wing flashes across the sky, there must always be a trace of a wound. Every wound, as beautiful as it may appear, must have a heartbreaking story of its own. But Yu's own bloody story could not make her cry out loud. She just stood there alone on the empty platform, letting her tears fall along with the incessant rain, as she wished her whole being could melt away in tears. She folded two tiny boats out of paper and put them in a puddle, watching them swirl and turn.

One month later Zhulong died of a brain hemorrhage. The circumstances of his sudden death were very simple. On his way to deliver a takeout order of food, he suddenly fell down, hitting his head, and was gone just like that. Living in a foreign country, he was regarded as an indigent and immediately taken to a public hospital. No name, no one knew who he was. Judging from his clothes, they knew he lived in one of the poorer sections of the city. As for An Xiaotao, she was in a different city. So by the time she heard the news, Zhulong had already been buried in the local commoners' graveyard. No tombstone. No one knew he was once a young man full of vision and ambition, a legendary student leader in a great country, and that he could have brought about the victory of a grand and glorious cause. The manager of the cemetery only remembered him as being a heavy man with a bald head, either Chinese or Japanese. With no relatives and his religious affiliation unknown, he was quickly buried, without even the simplest of ceremonies.

4

We mentioned earlier that Jinwu was ageless, existing in a perpetual present.

It is said that Jinwu had had innumerable men in her life. Her current beau was named Peng. They had met at a world-famous casino in America, a place filled with constantly moving images in the colors of the rainbow, and where at night the air carried a distinct metallic smell. As soon as she entered the casino, Jinwu laid her eyes on a slot machine with its twirling images of fresh fruit. A line of purplish red grapes seemed to indicate success, so when they came up she sat down and put in a quarter, but this time different types of fruit appeared as the machine swallowed her quarter. Four more times and the results were the same, but on her sixth try, instead of pushing the "go" button she pulled the handle. Presto! The light on the top of the slot machine suddenly blinked as the same four images of fruit lined up neatly. At that moment, the young casino woman whose job was to provide slot players with change for the machines pushed her cart in Jinwu's direction as the eyes of all the surrounding players looked at her in wonder. Jinwu knew she had won big-time.

It was at that moment of excitement and exhilaration that Jinwu caught sight of Peng, who was walking straight toward her. One brief glance and they knew they wanted each other. For Peng, Jinwu was the right woman at the right time, and for Jinwu, no other man could be better than this one.

That night they rented a room at a large hotel, in front of which were glittering images of skeletons and women, along with a cross. Women seemed always to be somehow connected with death, which was common in both Eastern and Western cultures. Jinwu and Peng didn't have sex that night, but, like two old friends caught up in a platonic relationship, they sat at a certain distance from each other, chatting and drinking coffee as Peng told Jinwu a story.

Like Jinwu, Peng also came from mainland China, where he had once been the owner of a large company with more than ten subsidiaries. But after becoming involved in a major financial scandal, Peng had been forced to leave China. Alone in a foreign country, Peng felt lost, as the halcyon days when he was surrounded by adoring and flattering people were no more. Gone was the satisfied feeling of issuing orders from on high, as he now had to contend with his limited knowledge of English, which for a former big boss like him was absolutely fatal. He was trapped. Witnessing Jinwu able to converse with the young casino worker in fluent English, Peng immediately decided to approach her.

Peng's story was not an uncommon one in China. He had worked as a partner and sometime middleman with an entrepreneur named Chi Dang in the real estate business. But the real man behind the scenes was a certain Mr. Li, a midlevel government official with considerable political and bureaucratic clout. Over the course of several years, Peng and Mr. Li had engaged in a number of private business transactions, with Peng providing bribes of more than a hundred thousand U.S. dollars. But like a bloodthirsty wolf waiting for his next kill, Mr. Li was insatiable, always impatient for the next infusion of cash.

Peng's troubles began when the entrepreneur, Chi Dang, was eager to buy a building. Through an associate named Zheng, Chi had met Peng at a karaoke bar, a place where Chinese businessmen met to engage in negotiations against a background of blaring music and flowing alcohol. Prior to his first meeting with Chi, Peng had acquired new information on the building's potential sale. Chi immediately jumped at the opportunity and acquired the rights to purchase the property in three years' time for nine million yuan. At that time, Peng thought the time provided by the contract was long enough to close the deal. But three years had passed and still no deal.

Peng's ability to consummate the deal all depended on the approval of Mr. Li. The real value of the building, Peng knew, was seven million yuan, which would leave Peng with two million. After providing Zheng, who had made the introductions, with a commission of three hundred thousand yuan, Peng could pocket the rest, while Mr. Li was paid the seven million in three separate installments, with Mr. Li providing the necessary paperwork that accompanied the sale of state assets to private owners. Everything was going smoothly; that is, until Peng discovered that before he had been granted legal ownership rights to execute the resale of the property to Chi Dang, Mr.

Li had fled abroad with the money and his family to America, leaving Peng at the mercy of Chi Dang. Now Peng was mired in a bog of trepidation, as he knew Chi Dang would come after him.

As a young man Peng had read the Chinese classic of military and political strategy, *The Art of War,* by Sun Tzu, and understood the concept of strategic retreat. His only choice was to flee China, and taking advantage of a multiple-entry visa he had managed to acquire earlier, Peng avoided disaster by coming to America.

5

At four in the morning, Jinwu and Peng emerged from the hotel into the sleepless city, with its nights filled with endless colors and sounds. With nowhere special to go, the two lingered in front of the hotel next to a water fountain that featured a statue of a mythical sea monkey with a horse's head and a fish tail, painted gold with a tint of red. Peng took many photos for Jinwu, who described her career as a movie actress in China, where she once played the role of a spy and also was cast as a character from one of China's ethnic minorities. Now, in America, her dream to be a movie star had been rekindled, with hopes of becoming an Asian star who would dazzle Hollywood. From the way she posed for his photos, Peng could sense Jinwu's manner and skills as a potential superstar. The only things lacking were an appropriate opportunity and the money.

Jinwu really got to know Peng one evening when they stopped in at a local topless dance club. As few of the patrons were Asian, both of them felt somewhat uncomfortable. Sitting alone in front of one of the dancers who pranced about bouncing her huge breasts in his face, Peng appeared distinctively unimpressed. Despite her bottomless bag of tricks, the dancer failed to get a rise out of Peng, who promptly got up, tossed a ten-dollar bill her way, and then motioned to Jinwu to leave. Here was a handsome and dashing man, Jinwu suddenly felt, who could be a true partner in life.

Jinwu brought Peng to her home in a small town about two hours' drive from the city of gambling and topless bars. It was a run-down place that stood in stark contrast to the glitter of the gamblers' lair. Jinwu's apartment was old, located in a nondescript, plain building, but it also had nice wood floors and walls that immediately attracted Peng, along with the interior decor that displayed the quality taste of its owner. Peng sat down on the carpet near the fireplace, while Jinwu took out a set of Chinese stemware and offered him a warm drink. This made Peng feel like he, too, was starring in a film about two people meeting for the first time. Jinwu added to the cinematic aura by putting on a record of violin music. Peng's sole desire at that point was to slow everything down so he could fully enjoy the moment of starring in a film, but then someone walked "onstage" at the wrong moment, ruining Peng's mood.

6

Peng was the first to see that pair of eyes glittering in the darkness. It made him tremble.

Jinwu introduced the two with a smile: "This is Yu, my young cousin. This is Peng, my new friend." Yu, a young woman with a soft and yellowish face, emerged from out of the darkness wearing a large, loose-fitting shirt with long sleeves hanging below her hands in the traditional Chinese fashion. Her body, soft as if it had no bones, moved freely inside the loose shirt. She also wore no makeup, and when she smiled her eyes exuded a deep-seated fear.

Later, Peng commented to Jinwu that Yu was the embodiment of the old saying about women's bones being made out of water.

7

Jinwu had gone to America in search of her mother.

Her first stop was, of course, Michael's place, where she was warmly received. But Michael had to tell her that the possible lead on her mother's location in the city had been lost. Three times Michael had shown up at the old lady's house, until one day the old lady mysteriously disappeared, making Michael even more suspicious. Now a sales rep for a large company,

Michael had received his early education in China. Despite his busy sched-
ule, he drove Jinwu all over the West Coast, going to each and every place
and talking to all sorts of people who might provide a clue to the mother's
whereabouts, all to no avail.

After six months, Jinwu decided to set out on her own to try her luck in
America, even though Michael had asked her to stay on at his place. Through
Michael she had met a movie director and landed a few minor roles, one
playing a Vietnamese refugee and another as an underworld character in a
film about Chinatown. Her mixed blood worked to her advantage, making
it a bit easier for her than the average Chinese who first moved to America,
but she was far from satisfied. Having once starred in a major role in China
as a spy, she was not about to be content playing subservient female roles in
America. After two small parts, she withdrew all her money from the bank
and headed for the gambling city.

Yu stayed with them. Since Peng had managed to escape China with a
good amount of cash, the three could go on living together without worry
for the next year and a half. Peng treated Yu carefully, not so much as a result
of talking with her himself, but because the story of Yu related to him by
Jinwu filled him with an unidentifiable fear.

"From a very young age," Jinwu explained, "Yu had engaged in witchcraft
and at the age of only six murdered her own little brother. She even tried to
kill herself, and not just once."

Coming from Jinwu, these words had a dramatic impact on Peng. Peng
already found Jinwu to be quite remarkable, smarter than anyone he had
ever known. Before he had even finished a sentence, Jinwu had figured out
what he was about to say. Despite having no formal financial training, when
told of Peng's financial disaster in China, she immediately grasped the situation and wrote a series of cables and faxes to China to rectify the matter.
Everything involving the case was put in writing, without any trace of it having come from her hand. Throughout his many years in China's business
world, Peng had met his share of women and divided them into two groups:
those he could take to his bed and those he could not take to his bed. As his
business prospered, the number of women pursuing him grew by leaps and

bounds, and whenever he entered a dance hall they came at him in droves. Those who managed to land a date with him felt a deep sense of pride. But Peng's desires in life were simple; he would not let any romantic emotions interfere with his business dealings, which for him were a constantly changing battleground. The thought of losing out on a money-making opportunity simply to be with a pretty face was unthinkable, literally making him ill. Besides, in his view the prettier the face, the less intelligent the brain.

But Jinwu now challenged all this. She was like bright sunshine, with flashing eyes that challenged his usual smug way of thinking. In her presence, he was immediately transformed from the tough, single-minded businessman into a little boy who had been seduced by a ghostly power. In fact, he would later learn that an ancient meaning of her name, Jinwu, was, in fact, "sun," a meaning shared with Yu She—feathered serpent—something he found even more frightening. Sandwiched between two suns, Peng felt not only the heat and glory but also a distinct suppression of his longtime hunger and anxiety. For the first time in his life, he had succumbed to the pressure of losing out to the superior intelligence of two women, suddenly finding himself in third place. Bedazzled by the intelligence of these two women, the man found his view of females was forever changed.

One Sunday, Peng wanted to splurge and drove Jinwu and Yu to a large nearby shopping mall; he told them to buy whatever tickled their fancy and not to worry about the price. For Jinwu, Peng's generosity appeared boastful, but without hesitation she took up his offer, picking out a fashionable dress suit with broad shoulders and slim waistline, made of musk deer leather in an olive green shade. This she matched with a Native American–style turquoise necklace and a broad-brimmed green sun hat. The items were expensive and elegant, with a total price tag of fourteen hundred dollars. In a flash, Peng took out his credit card and then turned to Yu: "What about you? Picked out anything?"

Wearing a long dress made of old linen, Yu settled on a bottle of medicine with a skull and crossbones on its label. Although he could not read the English on the label, Peng realized it was some kind of poisonous medicine.

8

Jinwu told Peng that from a very young age Yu had suffered from severe bouts of insomnia that became impervious to any conventional medical treatment. She had also attempted suicide on three separate occasions, but her body had evidently developed an ability to neutralize any intake of poison. Gradually, she had come to rely on drugs that contained poison to get some sleep. There was nothing more to it, Jinwu insisted, and so Peng should not be alarmed.

That night, Peng also had trouble falling asleep and had to resort to taking five Valium pills before he could drop off. Jinwu mocked him for this weakness, pointing out that he would end up in the same situation as Yu, needing a nightly dose of drugs. Jinwu quickly fell asleep, filling the night air with a slow and soft snore tinted with a light scent of Chanel perfume.

At dawn, Peng heard a rustling sound emanating from Yu's room. In the fresh, quiet mornings in such a small town, Peng's hearing was especially sensitive. He simply could not resist the urge to get up after hearing the door open and close. Looking off into the distance, he spotted the figure of a young woman limping away.

Located outside this small town was a forest with a mystical and ghostly quality exactly like the one portrayed in the famous painting by the French artist Jean-Baptiste-Camille Corot. Especially at twilight, the black treetops appeared like so many paper cuts pasted against a purplish blue sky. One could easily imagine a swarm of gold-colored forest nymphs dancing among the trees.

Peng followed the young woman named Yu into the forest. He watched her repeatedly bending over to pick up something, in all likelihood fresh mushrooms, as they often sprout after a rain. Peng wanted to go back but quickly realized that he had gone so far into the dark forest, where only shards of sunlight penetrated through the thick canopy of tall trees and bushes, that he would never find his way out. His only choice was to keep following Yu, which became increasingly difficult as the blazing sun began to penetrate the forest cover like a precious sword. Dazzled by the bright light, he was only able to catch a periodic glimpse of the woman. Her gray clothes, black hair, her hands, indeed her entire body seemed to have been suddenly fragmented by something. Her body now appeared somewhat unreal, like the reflection of the moon in a pool of water. The sunlight had become increasingly intense and now penetrated everywhere, so much so that the figure of the young woman had seemingly become a part of the light.

Peng was now exhausted and felt a sharp pain cutting through his left side. He could feel it coming—the kidney stone that had bedeviled him for many years, even after serious doses of herbal medicine, had under the stress of the moment returned with a vengeance. The stone could cause him excruciating pain, and ever since traveling to America, he had debated whether to buy health insurance and have it taken care of. Money was not the problem, though his preference was to avoid spending it on insurance. Should the kidney stone become a problem, seeing a doctor without insurance would cost him a ton of money. As he once again was pondering the cost of treating the stone, his eyes were suddenly dazzled by the appearance of an oddly shaped ancient tree that stood like a giant man, its branches curling upward and bending down like giant arms. The big lumps covering the tree trunk looked like the faces of newly born babies. Heavens, they did look like baby faces! Summoning up his courage, he reached out to touch one of the branches when suddenly it swayed around like a snake, scooping him up and wrapping itself around him so tightly that he could hardly breathe. Then, the tree branch suddenly loosened its grip and tossed him into the air. He whirled and fell heavily to the ground, totally losing consciousness.

When years later he related this story to me, I didn't believe it, as the description was too similar to a horror movie I had once seen. But later I checked out the movie and, lo and behold, the film had been made after Peng's experience. It was truly horrible.

9

Peng woke up to a rich and drowsy medicinal fragrance and immediately could hear Jinwu's magnetic voice: "Hey, you all right?"

Peng turned around to see that grayish pale figure, the mushroom picker, stirring a pot of herbal medicine with a long spoon. Yu had learned about Chinese herbal medicine, Jinwu explained, so every morning she went out to pick herbs. Jinwu was indebted to Yu's herbal medicine for her own smooth and shining skin, something that Peng had noticed right away. She also rarely fell ill and noted that she was much healthier than others in her own age group. "Try some of Yu's medicine," Jinwu suggested to Peng. Though he remained skeptical of all these wondrous claims, Peng agreed but wondered out loud why Yu didn't take some of her own medicine, since she looked like she needed it more than anyone else. But Jinwu said Yu had taken too much medicine in her life and now only poisons had a real impact on her. After taking a bit of the medicinal brew, Peng immediately felt great pain and be- fore he could cry out, urine and a bit of blood spewed forth from his body. Minutes later he was relaxed and felt dramatically better, realizing that Yu's concoction had caused the troublesome kidney stone to be purged.

That night Peng for the first time ever smiled at Yu and promised he would provide financial support if she decided to open a clinic. "That's not a small thing," commented Jinwu, for to open a clinic in America, one needed a medical school diploma along with legal immigration status and a business license. A friend of Jinwu's had earned a medical degree in another coun- try but could not obtain a license to practice medicine in America. Peng's attitude was simple: where there's a will there's a way. Once, in his middle school years, he had carved out of a turnip a replica of an official seal used in legal documents and managed to get official approval for a number of dif- ferent projects, including his own company. Back in the early halcyon days of China's economic reforms, starting up a company was a piece of cake, so easy that a company could be officially registered without a bit of real capital. Downing a few drinks that evening, he explained to Jinwu and Yu how he managed to get the company off the ground to the point where it eventually boomed. Jinwu listened carefully and grinned at Yu, who was staring at Peng as if she were listening to a fairy tale.

Peng was in a good mood. He had gotten rid of his old troublesome kid- ney stone and proposed to his two female companions that they take a trip to

Europe. It was there, during that trip, that Yu walked through the cemeteries and looked at the tombstones.

When they were in Vienna, with music playing in the background, Jinwu put on the nightgown Peng had bought for her, revealing to him her beautiful chest and amorous legs. Jinwu had a perfect body except for her two gigantic breasts, which were blown up like two balloons, with light blue veins running through them and dark rings around their luscious nipples, and which swayed as she moved toward Peng. Now he would learn everything about her past and everything about his present moment: never, not once, could a living man, he believed, resist what was dangling before his eyes.

They had a good go at each other well into the night. When long after midnight Peng got up to go to the bathroom, he saw a light in Yu's room, where she was fumbling around with an old computer whose black screen appeared, like some deep, dark void, reflecting Yu's blank face.

10

Some time ago, I had found an old computer at the hotel in this old city of Europe. It was my first time to face a computer. Not knowing which button to press, I pressed one, and suddenly the entire screen was covered with strings of the same Chinese word—*zi*. Repeated over and over again in different forms, the character filled up the entire screen, something I found really frightening. This character was itself quite scary. For a long time, I did not know its meaning, as it was the first response from the computer to my attempt at a dialogue with this machine. I was frightened by this first reply and did everything I could, frantically hitting the keys in hopes of wiping the character off the screen, all to no avail. The character in its multitude of forms just stared right back at me, without budging.

I began to sit in front of the computer, staring at it every night under the greenish lamplight that turned my own face a green color. Whenever Jinwu got up in the middle of the night and in disbelief saw me in front of the computer, she could never in her wildest dreams imagine the little secret I shared with the computer, a secret I would never reveal to a soul, not even on my deathbed.

This secret was started by simple chance. One night I woke up from a deep sleep and found myself still sitting in front of the computer, its screen appearing frighteningly large. It was a huge door of a dim red color. Behind the door was an empty void. As I leaned forward, I was sucked in by a powerful force.

I passed through the door at lightning speed, moving so fast that my body floated about weightless, which made me feel dizzy. Gradually and unconsciously I opened my arms, and like a bird I began to fly in the sky—a feather detached from a wing does not fly but only drifts. But I was flying, not drifting. It was flying that I myself could not control.

Suddenly I stopped as I arrived in a world that was completely still. There was a forest, the forest familiar from my childhood. It exuded a mysterious and ghostly feel. Especially at twilight, the black treetops appeared like so many paper cuts pasted against a purplish blue sky. One could easily imagine a swarm of gold-colored forest nymphs dancing among the trees.

I felt as if I had returned to my childhood. I was picking mushrooms that had sprouted up after a rain, but their color was unusually bright, giving them a frightening appearance. In the deep forest, a man walked toward me. His name was Peng.

Why was Peng here at this time? Was he following me? The blazing sunshine was now penetrating the trees and glaring in my eyes. When he walked close, I saw horror in his face: his lips were bloodred, his hair gray, and his eyes green. He was floating as if he, too, was weightless. He also began to pick mushrooms, but as soon as he touched one, it began to ooze blood. Heavens, what I saw was not mushrooms but little babies. Peng was breaking their necks! He threw them, one by one, beneath an odd-looking old tree nearby. That old tree stood like a giant; its branches were swaying around like giant arms. The lumps on the tree trunk looked like the faces of little babies. Heavens, they did look like baby faces! I saw him reach out his hand to touch a tree branch. It scooped him up like a snake, wrapping itself around him so tightly that he could hardly breathe. Then the tree loosened its grip and tossed him into the air. I was stunned. After a long while, I thought about the road back home, but I couldn't find it. A lake blocked my way, the lake in my childhood. I lay down by the lake. There should have been a mussel, a black mussel. But I couldn't see the mussel either. There was only an image sneering at me: bloodred lips, gray hair, green eyes, floating about as if all gravity had vanished, like a figure in a cartoon—that image was me.

I woke up crying. The hands on the clock revealed it was three in the morning. I was sitting in front of the computer.

11

Jinwu rushed out of her room when she heard Yu's scream. Yu sat leaning on the desk in front of the computer, having just awakened from a deep dream. Jinwu stared at Yu and suddenly knew that Yu had a secret, a secret that Yu would not tell even her.

Jinwu walked over to the computer and randomly touched a key. When two lines of English words jumped up onto the screen, she frowned and remained silent. Yu asked what the words meant, but all Jinwu would say was that she did not understand.

Morning arrived, and as Yu was coming out of the bathroom, Peng asked her if she knew what the English words on the computer meant, and then told her: "Your father is ill with cancer and your mother has asked you to return home."

At that point, Jinwu interrupted Peng and told Yu that she should not return to China, as she would never be allowed to leave the country again. "Think it over," she advised Yu, "it could be a trap." Yu did not say a word, and returning to her room, she started to pack. She looked at Jinwu and said, "Even if it is a trap, I must go back."

The night Yu left, Jinwu moved to the couch in the living room, clearly putting a cold distance between herself and Peng. Always the clever woman, Jinwu made Peng understand that she had lost all interest in him. Her sneering look and cold shoulders made his physical desire for her disappear in an instant. He felt sorry and was filled with shame.

Jinwu said she wanted to leave here, too, and continue the search for her own mother.

12

That blue lake was the last stop for Yushe before she left America for home.

It was a windy day; strong gusts rocked all the boats anchored in the lake.

When Yu laid her eyes on one craft she immediately knew what she wanted. Like a star hung between the blue heavens and the lake, a boat was moving toward her, slicing the lake surface and glittering like a star.

A strange young boy operating the boat flashed a smile like the brightest sunshine of the day. He said in English to Yu, "Please come on board." And so Yu boarded the craft.

Yu felt this day was the day she had desired her whole life. This young boy appeared to her to be an angel sent from heaven. He had golden hair, blue eyes, snow-white teeth, and a young and strong body that radiated vitality. His smile came straight from his heart. For the first time in her life, Yu felt no fear. She helped the young boy pull up the anchor and smiled at him as he said to her in English, "This way, like me." His eyes were so clear, nothing false or artificial. For the first time in her life, Yu smiled from her heart.

Yu felt the young boy understood her inner voice; she hoped he would give her a hug, and he did. He gently put his arms around her neck. Yu closed her eyes and let herself feel the strong and warm arms as tears welled up and streamed down her cheeks. The young boy gently wiped them away, looking at her with such pure eyes, eyes that reminded her of the first time she had met Yuanguang. Those pure eyes that could make any woman soar in the sky had indeed sent her flying. In return, Yu's eyes said to the young boy, "Why have you made me wait so long?" To which the young boy answered with his own eyes, "It's not so late." Again Yu's eyes inquired of him, "Where will you take me?"

"I don't know," he answered. "Let's follow the wind with our Noah's Ark."

"What? Noah's Ark?" Yu was startled.

"Yes. Noah's Ark." The young boy raised his strong arms to hoist the sail.

Yu now burst out in tears. "Noah's Ark? That's wonderful. Yes. It is Noah's Ark."

Yu understood this young boy was sent by heaven and was taking her to "cross over" to the other shore.

What lay on the other shore was unimportant. It was the journey itself that counted, the "crossover," a journey both enchanting and exciting! And a journey Yu hoped would never end.

CHAPTER 12

FINALE AND THE FINALISTS

1

Xiao's diary.

Four months have passed since Father entered the hospital. "No truly filial son," the old saying goes, "can spend long hours next to a sick bed." In the case of my family, forget about any filial son, even Mother was indifferent to Father's illness. I don't know what, if anything, in the world can make my mother feel pain, real heart-wrenching pain. The sound of her tired and feeble footsteps was forever imprinted in our deepest memories. But there were no memories, not a one, of our mother ever preparing a meal for us. No matter how late we came home or how hungry we were when we got there, the rickety old dinner table that has been with us for more than forty years would always be empty. When Grandma Xuanming was still alive, she had once said the old table was made of highly prized golden rosewood.

Just about anything could trigger disagreement and a fight that would entail smashing dishes and harsh language. This was a family caught in a vicious cycle that after all these years had eventually sapped the life out of Father, and we had to send him to a hospital.

"I'll die in the hospital. I'll never come home!" When he said this, his dark and withered face showed nothing but weariness, and my heart trembled as I was gripped with a feeling that this time his words might come true.

Yesterday, one of his colleagues, who had gone to see him in the hospital, came to tell us that Father had spewed some blood. "Not much, just six little mouthfuls. Maybe some hen had been pecking his throat too often," punned the colleague, obviously trying to lighten the situation. But we all panicked. Mother and I rushed to the hospital and headed straight to the office of the head physician. The doctor wasn't in and so it was left to a young nurse to relay the news to us, which she did rather casually: "Are you members of Lu Chen's family? Please hold off on discussing the growth on his lungs with him."

At that moment, Mother's hand that was holding mine turned cold.

Doctor Ke, a young recent graduate student of the medical school affiliated with this hospital, was the physician in charge of Father's case.

"This is your father's condition: since last week his coughing has gotten worse," the doctor commented, with a clearly arrogant and towering look as he knitted his refined eyebrows. "The day before yesterday, some blood was found in his phlegm, and then he spewed blood on six occasions. We immediately took measures to stop the loss of blood. We did a combined diagnosis with the radiation department. They took more than ten X-rays of his lungs from different angles and found a large growth the size of a goose egg, ten by fifteen centimeters, located on his right lung. We plan to do further tests on his . . ."

After the visit to the hospital, mother's attitude seemed to loosen up over the next few days. She started nagging us about putting up a shed in the backyard, neglecting to even mention Father. Father's illness also had the effect of temporarily putting my sister Ling and me on speaking terms again. Four months earlier, when my husband and I got into a car to take Father to the hospital, Ling had joined us and she even took the initiative in talking with me, and naturally I responded politely. My old father, weak and frail as he was, was still resolute and stubborn almost to the point of being childish; he refused my offer to help him downstairs. Supported by his cane, he staggered along, putting on a good spirit. He refused to lie down in the car, insisting instead on sitting between Ling and me. On the way to the hospital he constantly coughed up phlegm. I had prepared a stack of napkins to wipe his lips. But Ling still turned her head away to avoid seeing him drool.

My husband, Ning, and I were the image of a happily married couple until the 1990s, by which time he had become a famous photographer, and a very busy one at that. We never managed to have children, but I obtained a master's degree in English and American literature and secured a teaching position at a college. Our home was an empty nest, but I was very happy. Then it all changed when one day I accidentally came across a bunch of photographs tucked inside a book while I was tidying up Ning's things. I spread them out on a table and what I saw in all these photographs was one and the same woman, a beautiful and innocent-looking woman posed half or totally naked. I was captivated by the contrast between her seductive poses and her angelic face. It took me a while before I noticed a man in some of these photos, standing like the guardian of the photogenic star, while looking lovingly at her naked body. He was none other than my husband, Ning.

I put away the photos and said nothing, and resisted speaking to others about my sorrows. That habit I had given up long ago after the end of my first and only love affair. Over the years, I had learned to keep silent, which was why I made good progress in other areas of my life, while still carrying out my duties of cooking and washing for Ning. But I added one assignment to my daily routine and that was to prepare for the English language test required for admission to an American university. The test was held only once a year and it took three tries before I finally passed it at the age of forty, when I was accepted by a university on the West Coast. I packed up my bags, exchanged all my savings into American dollars, and took off. Three years later I moved from America to Europe, where I wrote my only letter to Ning, asking him for a divorce.

Later I learned from Yu that the angelic young woman in the photos was actually An Xiaotao, the wife of Zhulong, with whom Yu and Yadan had been madly in love. Now An Xiaotao was doing business in America.

Tonight Mother suddenly asked me: "Why not ask Yu to come back? Third daughter is your father's favorite. Now that your father is ill, she should look after her share of the duties!"

2

By the time Yushe returned to China, Lu Chen's cancer had entered the terminal stage. She was so astonished to see her father reduced to something like a mummy that she was afraid even to look at him.

But Yu held on to the belief that her father could survive. Night after night she sat next to his bed and listened attentively, hoping to hear what her whispering god would tell her. But the whisper did not come.

Yu thought of Danzhu. Lu Chen's doctor had told her that her father needed large amounts of serum albumin and antimetastasis drugs to strengthen his immune system. Yu knew only Danzhu could get these things.

Earlier, Danzhu had been transferred to a distant hospital that was guarded by a large body of security personnel. It took Yu an entire morning to finally track him down. He listened attentively, then responded quietly, "That's easy. I'll ask my father to write a note." "And then?" asked Yu. "And then, I will send the stuff over to you."

Yu scanned his face with some doubt. But this was typical Danzhu, who, as before, provided her with comfort when she least expected it. Danzhu himself never felt he was doing anything out of the ordinary to help Yu or that could even remotely be regarded as a noble deed. Yu wondered aloud how Danzhu, who was from a high-ranking family, was able to stay in touch with common people. Danzhu could only laugh at her notion and point out that he was simply acting in accord with his professional ethics. Nothing else. "But what I asked you to do is not a part of your duties," said Yu. "You are still so attentive." Danzhu smiled again and returned to his work, ignoring Yu.

For Yu, Danzhu remained an enigma. Yu once imagined he loved her, but whenever they were together, he never revealed any sign of passion. He just did what needed to be done. When Yu left and disappeared for a year without leaving a word, he seemed not to have a bit of resentment and didn't even bother to ask where she had gone. When she suddenly reappeared, he was not the least bit surprised, acting as if they had seen each other just the day before.

Within three days, Danzhu brought the serum albumin and antimetastasis drugs to the hospital where Lu Chen was under treatment. All the doctors at the hospital dropped their jaws in surprise at seeing Danzhu. Yu was somewhat taken aback by their reactions and wondered just when it was that Danzhu had become a VIP in their eyes. The director of the cancer department buttered him up with an ingratiating smile: "Doctor Danzhu, you should have just called. Why trouble yourself to come all the way here for such a trivial thing? This is all my fault . . ." The president of the hospital also came running in and insisted that Danzhu stay for lunch, and sucked up to him even more: "We didn't know that the old professor was your relative. You should have told us. Today, we'll immediately transfer him to the ward exclusively reserved for high-ranking officials and put him under special care."

All this was beyond Yu's comprehension. But of course she was very happy that her father would now receive better treatment.

In the small garden in the center of the hospital grounds, the willow trees had begun to blossom. Yu thought spring was in the air, and she and Danzhu wheeled Lu Chen to the garden. Lu Chen could no longer talk, but breathed in the spring air hungrily as tears welled up in his eyes.

"Father became so sentimental after he fell ill."

"Everyone is that way."

"Are you like this?"

"I said everyone would be like this."

"Why are the people in the hospital so awestruck in your presence?"

Danzhu looked at her and said straightforwardly, "I am now exclusively the doctor for a high-ranking official."

"Thank God, I did not know this. Otherwise, I would not have dared come to you."

Danzhu suddenly stopped and looked at her intensely. "Surely you haven't become as common as them?"

They wheeled Lu Chen into a patch of sunlight and walked toward the trees nearby.

"I am not only common . . ." Yu was trembling inside. She knew she was about to say something wrong and foolish, but as always she couldn't restrain herself. "Danzhu, I am actually very despicable. I am not fair to you . . ."

"What you want to say is that you never really loved me, right?" Danzhu said, smiling. He was surprisingly composed. "I knew it all along. So what? It's all right. You have someone in your heart and you love him dearly. You have the freedom to pursue your love. The same goes for me, too. I don't want to talk about love. That's a big word. But to me, you are very important. It's true you are very important . . . but . . ."

"But what?"

"But honestly, either me or that man you love very much—in fact, any man—would find it hard to enter your world. Actually, not just hard, but virtually impossible. No one dares to want you. To men, you are very . . . intimidating."

Yu looked at him with surprise. "Are you saying I am hopeless?"

Danzhu laughed. "Only if you undergo a lobotomy and become as foolish as the rest of us."

Had Danzhu known what would later occur in Yu's life, he would never have said that. Zhulong died young and Danzhu left. Now it is up to us to walk with Yu to the end of her life. Several years later, when the news of Yu's lobotomy would reach Danzhu, his grief was beyond belief.

Yu said good-bye to Danzhu and wheeled her father back to the ward. After an injection of serum albumin, his condition clearly improved. He could get up on his own to use the bathroom and he wanted to eat some ginseng soup. Xiao and Yu put their money together and bought some expensive wild ginseng. With a little spoon, Xiao patiently fed the slowly simmered, rich ginseng soup between Lu Chen's dark, withered lips.

At this moment Ruomu came for a visit.

Dressed in an old-fashioned light woolen coat, her body exuding a perfumed fragrance, she had written on her face a kind of melancholy look that belonged to the era of the 1940s or even earlier. Ruomu was all show. When Yu saw that look, she knew her mother's fleeting pain and regret had vanished.

Ruomu sat down looking even more melancholy. "Ah, Lu Chen. Poor me, I've been losing a lot of sleep these past days. Just now, on the way here, I almost fainted a few times." She covered her nose with a hankie, giving her face a pitiful and heavy expression. "Poor me. For all these years I've lived with you and not one day did I enjoy a good life. Now the children are finally all grown up and you fall ill. You're the one I have counted on to live out the rest of my life with. If something happens to you, who will I rely on?" Quite clearly, all of this was directed at Yu and Xiao. Xiao could only frown and say, "Mom. Why are you talking like this when Dad is so ill?" But Ruomu just ignored this and continued to wail away: "You are still alive and they treat me like this. It's good that they are taking good care of you. But am I made of iron? Don't I need some nutrition? As the old saying goes, 'Easier to see an official father die than to see a beggared widow live . . .' " Hearing this, Lu Chen choked up inside as a mist of tears rolled over his eyes.

Xiao handed a bowl of ginseng soup to Ruomu immediately and said, "Mom, I beg you not to say any more. Please let Father rest a bit." Ruomu sipped the ginseng soup and said, "Listen to the things this child is saying. I've lived with your father my whole life. How could the few things I have to say annoy him? He is here all alone, dying for someone to talk with him!" As she was talking, Ruomu cast a glance at Yu just as Yu was looking at her with eyes full of scorn and loathing.

Ruomu slammed her bowl on the table with a loud thump.

Lu Chen had a pleading look on his face, which seemed to say, "I beg all of you, stop fighting, stop fighting . . ."

But Ruomu, at age seventy and still going strong, was full of her usual self. "Look at her, look at your beloved third daughter. How does she treat me? That's right, your mother has no money, no power, you don't have to deal with me. But let's set things straight. It was I who gave birth to you. Not the other way around!!"

Yu couldn't hold back. She lowered her voice so that her father couldn't hear her, but every single word of hers was like a bullet shot out from between her clenched teeth: "Let me tell you. You make me sick!"

That hit Ruomu and hit her hard. In the never-ending war of the Lu family, once such words began to fly, the fire could not be put out. Ruomu poured out all her anger, letting loose all the foul words she had used over the past decades, except this time she was even more fierce and unstoppable. "I told you all along, this goddamn girl was going to murder someone. She murdered her own little brother. That's not enough for her. She's going to murder her own father and all her family; she's going to murder us one by one!"

Perhaps the word "murder" sounded really frightening. The doctor and the head nurse and all the other nurses ran into the ward. Ruomu switched her hollering to a pitiful weep. During her rage of yelling, Lu Chen shook his head in bitter agony. But now he quieted down; his skin color turned gray, his face sunken in, his whole body curled up like a ball, a gradually shrinking ball.

Yu walked out slowly cowering next to the wall, as her entire body had been sapped of its last ounce of strength. Her burning eyes had dried up all her tears. She realized she had not eaten or slept for five days. Now she was leaning against the chilly wall, soaked in her own cold sweat. Before she could cry out, she fell softly to the ground.

Lu Chen died that day at midnight. Before taking his last breath, his appearance remained the same. He did not leave any will or anything regarding his life's legacy. His last words to Yu a few days earlier, she recalled, were simple: "You go and get some steamed buns for yourself." There was a stand outside the hospital selling pork buns to patients' relatives when they came for a visit. During lunch hour, the smell of pork and scallions floated throughout all the wards, but the fragrance did not whet her appetite.

Lu Chen's body shrunk to a very small size but remained extremely heavy. When Xiao and the nurses had to change his clothes, they broke out in a sweat. At this point Ruomu, Ling, and Yun'er rushed into the hospital; Yadan even brought her ten-year-old son, Yangyang. The sound of wailing started up immediately. But Yu was still unconscious and caught up in a dream of her father dressed up in a Taoist robe, sitting at the side of the old master Lao Tzu, who in the sixth century B.C. had written the *Tao Te Ching*. Together they were chatting by the lake; oh yes, her childhood lake in the midst of the forest. Lu Chen's face was one of complete serenity, with no sign of the wear and tear of his real life. A deer was strolling back and forth near the two sitting men. But this fairy tale–like scene was short-lived, as suddenly bright lights appeared before her eyes as a broad movie screen appeared with a voice-over: "Professor Lu Chen will rest in peace in the green mountains and rivers." Yu woke up from the dream and was so dizzy and nauseous that she leaned out of the bed and immediately vomited. Under the bed was Ling's handbag stuffed with the ginseng Xiao and Yu had bought for their father. That sight made Yu throw up everything inside her.

"You go and get some steamed buns for yourself." She could not put these words out of her mind. Whenever she thought of them, she felt a knife slicing her heart.

3

Ling felt she had finally sunk to the bottom of her life, so much so that she developed an odd disease: a red rash covered her entire body, coupled with a low fever, night sweats, and persistent fatigue. After seeking medical treatment at a number of places, Ling was told that she had contracted a nasty skin disease known as lupus erythematosus.

Ling's reaction was to cry her heart out. No longer able to play the role of a pampered little girl after her grandmother Xuanming had passed away, for days on end Ling was unable to sleep or eat. Then, one afternoon when she was gradually dozing off, her wet nurse, Xiangqin, suddenly appeared in a dream. For some time, these two had been out of touch, but now there was a place that Ling could travel to and she immediately took up the offer. That day she bought a train ticket and for two days and one night she sat on the train as it clanked its way to the destination, a desolate corner of the country that had been recently turned into a booming tourist site named Xitan Mountain.

On meeting Xiangqin, Ling was in a state of shock. Here was Xiangqin, the woman who had breast-fed her several decades ago and who had always taken pride in her glorious, gorgeous breasts; and who, after these many years, had not changed at all. With her two gigantic breasts still standing tall and a voice that sounded like running water, Xiangqin exuded an energy and spirit that emanated from every pore of her body at the unbelievable age of sixty-seven. At first startled, Xiangqin reacted by immediately wrapping her arms around Ling, then cried, sobbing with tears and her nose both running at the same time, "My poor child. Without me, how did you get yourself in this condition?" "Poor child" was all that Ling wanted to be at age forty-seven; like a broken dam, Ling let loose a flood of uncontrollable tears. Still wearing her hair in two childlike ponytails and dressed in doll-like clothes, Ling and her supposed youthful look were long gone, as her appearance now was very unflattering.

Meeting Xiangqin, Ling now felt free to let out all her hatred. "Aunty, it's all because of that son of a bitch Wang Zhong, that bastard. He left me and my daughter for a stupid woman. He deserves a thousand cuts and a horrible death!"

"I told you he was no good. You are from a family of scholars. What is his family? Three generations of beggars! Was there ever a good beggar? Did you say he didn't want you? No. It's you who got rid of him!" Xiangqin wiped away Ling's tears and handed her a bowl of lotus flower soup with eggs and sugar.

"Aunty, I am pushing close to fifty. Who would want me now?!"

"Nonsense! There are many men whom no one wants. Never have I heard there are unwanted women. Women are treasures at all ages. Look at your aunt, I am approaching seventy. Am I in short supply of men?"

"Oh, but who can compare with you, Aunty?"

"Silly goose. All women are the same. By reading too many books you have been made foolish. Stay here with me. You'll see that in no more than a year, your aunty will fix you up nicely."

Indeed, within six months, as a result of being waited on and catered to day and night by Xiangqin, who offered excellent meals and healthy drinks, plus doses of herbal medicine that Xiangqin's grandson gathered from nearby mountains, Ling began to recover; her red rash along with the low fever gradually disappeared. One night, as usual, Xiangqin was making a lotus and lily flower soup for Ling while she sipped on a drink and sat under a dim light. She commented to Ling rather leisurely, "You just take your time and stay with me here. I have money now and am well fixed. You haven't a worry in the world. Although I have only one son, I have tons of nephews and nieces. Each of them is good to me, sending me money all the time. Now even my grandson is working. The only one I worry about is you. If you think I am still useful, let me come to you, cook and wash, and keep you company. It's better than your being all alone."

Ling knew those "nephews and nieces" must be children from her old lovers. Ling made a deep bow to Xiangqin. "Aunty, this will save my life. But what about my sisters and brothers? You have a big family to take care of."

"They were born here and grew up here. They are tough cookies and really don't need me. But you're from a highly respectable family that in the old days would have made you a candidate to become someone's precious mistress. Now that you were cheated and bullied by some worthless guy, who else other than me is going to take care of you? In the old days, my mother always informed me that she would never be able to pay back, even in her whole life, the kindness from your grandma. As my mother failed to pay back the debt, now it's my turn to make amends. You were Grandma's favorite. If the old lady were still with us, she would have cursed the death of that Wang Zhong along with all his ancestors of eighteen generations! My good girl, don't feel that you owe me anything. A woman like me, well, it was more than what I could hope for to be your wet nurse!"

Seeing that Ling was still puzzled, Xiangqin took another sip of her drink and continued: "What do you think I was? I couldn't tell you when you were little. Now I can let you in on this. I used to be a hot girl at a whorehouse where I earned more drinks than any of the other girls! Men with money and status used to fight to have me. I started at the age of fourteen to earn money to support my family. For a woman, you not only need a pretty face and a nice body, but also you've got to know how to make men desire you so that they will do anything to have you. Be coquettish! That's what you have to know. But when it comes to marriage, you must think it over. First and foremost, the two families must match. If both of your families are not on the same wavelength, sooner or later you will have to separate. You were young back then. For your marriage, the old lady almost died from shame! Now it's a good thing that it has ended . . ."

Ling looked at Xiangqin in wonder. "Aunty, you were about twenty years old when you came to nurse me. How did you get out of that place?"

"A master of a great house bought me my way out after getting me pregnant. Unfortunately, the child died from premature birth. The master still wanted to marry me and make me his second wife, but my mother refused him. Then when your mother gave birth to you but was unable to produce any milk, my mother offered me to your family. Mother had been very devoted to your grandma all her life except for the fact that she kept my past life a secret. She never told your grandma."

At that thought, Ling gasped, knowing that her willful and protective grandma would have smashed her head against a wall if she had learned that her beloved first granddaughter's wet nurse had once been a whore! Yet on second thought, Ling realized how wonderful it was that Grandma was unaware of Xiangqin's sordid past, since now her beloved granddaughter had an extra person in this world to care for her. Ling vaguely remembered the time when as a little girl she had peeped into Xiangqin's bathroom and noticed a hooligan-type guy standing in her shower. Was he one of Aunty's old lovers? She also remembered the time she had to squeeze Xiangqin's breasts to ease Aunty's pain and wondered if that little skinny kid lying next to her was her only son. She recalled that day when Xiangqin's husband then, an elementary school teacher, was on his way to a grocery store. Now remembering how that scene made Xiangqin's dangling gigantic breasts come into view, Ling knew that it was precisely the appearance of her huge breasts and nipples that awoke Ling's early desires. Now, just at the thought of them, the long-gone itchiness in the cracks of her bones all seemed to crawl back, tingling in her joints. Ling was revived.

The next day, Xiangqin took Ling to the Jinque Temple to redeem a vow to the Buddha. They saw a gray-haired old woman kneeling in front of a golden statue of Buddha and asked the monk who she was. "That's the famous Aunty Mei of Xitan Mountain! She is confessing her own deep sins and praying for her daughter." Amazed at this answer, Xiangqin asked, "But didn't Aunty Mei die a few years ago?" The monk only smiled. Running back into the main temple to take another look, Xiangqin and Ling found not a soul.

4

When it comes to knowing the true feelings of any person, words are essentially useless and powerless. And so how can we ever know what the true feelings are? In the case of Yadan, she is no longer able to write from the heart. You see, human beings are very much weird animals. When you tie them up they can't move. And when you untie them, they still cannot move because they have become so used to being tied up, their arms and legs are unable to move about freely. For someone like Yadan, the situation was even worse. When tied up, she struggled mightily and gained as a person. But once untied, she no longer had anything to engage her and her life became empty, bereft of any source of stimulation or challenge. Boredom left her incapable of producing even a modicum of creativity, so much so that even major developments in the outside world had virtually no impact on her. A huge gap now opened between herself and the outside world, particularly between herself and the opposite sex. She lived with a completely impotent man, and her resort to masturbation depleted her of any life force. It was a habit that began when she was young and actually intensified following the birth of her child, and to her surprise, her sexual desires became increasingly uncontainable. Hard as she might try, she could not put aside her sexual desire. On one occasion when she was burning with such a desire, she rode her old bicycle late at night and didn't stop until she reached the point of total exhaustion. And when standing alone on a street corner late at night, she convinced herself that if assaulted by even the worst type, she wouldn't put up a struggle, as she was so hungry for sex that she craved to be violated. If not for the words—the phony words she wrote on paper to conceal herself—our Yadan would probably have gone mad. Those phony and empty words became a spiderweb covering the once lively Yadan with the same gray color as the city she lived in.

For the longest time, Yadan had avoided looking at herself in the mirror. But escaping from our view was a different matter. Yadan, the mother of Yangyang, is now a heavyset, sloppy woman, with messy hair that has turned completely gray—a woman with no shape and no style. Her face is covered with age markings and the pores on her neck are cracked open; her skin is sapped of all color and virtually hangs from her bones in layer upon layer of wrinkles, something that one generally sees only on very old people. Her two thick legs seem to have shortened her already fat body, which made her appear from afar like a water pitcher. Old people in her neighborhood sigh at the sight of her and note that age has a way of catching up to you. If Yadan looks like this, what will become of us, they wonder. Her childhood friends, who remember Yadan as a chubby little girl with baby fat, now see someone who almost overnight turned into something ugly, something these friends find hard to accept.

Obesity is the epidemic of this century. While modern medicine has come up with various ways to halt the spread of fat, doctors seem to have forgotten one fundamental fact, and that is the life force of our bodies must grow and break forth. But when this force cannot grow and develop along its proper course, it becomes stuck inside and develops into a residue that blocks normal bodily functions. Yadan wrapped a gray spiderweb around herself and made a living by slapping words on paper, using every possible means to withdraw into herself like a turtle inside its shell. Sometimes she cried and despaired, as she was fully aware that no man would ever again express an interest in her. She and her husband, Ah Quan, had not shared a bed for six years now. Every night when she moved her heavy body with great difficulty and climbed into her cold bed under the empty blanket, she was struck by the bad odor lingering in the room, as if the loud fart from the great toothless granny on her wedding day had never dissipated. Finding it hard to get used to life here, in the dark, she would avoid touching her own body as the hot fluids inside her would drain out slowly in the form of tears, slowly trickling down from the corners of her eyes. That was her life fluid exiting her body as complete waste, while there was nothing, absolutely nothing, she could do about it except watch it waste away.

She kept fooling herself through her writing, stories in which she portrayed herself as a priceless beauty adored and loved by many men. Her novels became cheap popular chick lit, with writing that has become very formulaic and has produced nothing new. Like many writers, she sat at her desk for years dumping her own junkyard garbage onto the paper with no real feelings or emotions, the kind of writer that a few years ago she despised and hated.

Yangyang became her sole happiness, Yangyang and Yangyang alone. He is now a ten-year-old beautiful boy who reminds her of the young boy Zhulong once was. Unaware of Zhulong's death, she continued to believe for several years that Zhulong would eventually set his eyes on his flesh-and-blood son. When that time arrived, she planned to go for a face-lift, lose weight, and buy the most expensive and beautiful clothes. She would change into a different person, a different woman, an entirely outstanding woman. For his sake and his sake alone, she would accept all her sufferings, willingly. Indeed, whenever she thought of that impending day, she would feel a little better. Yadan, we know, had her naive side, believing that others shared her dream. She thought she had borne Zhulong's son, something she considered an important thing for any man. No matter what tricks An Xiaotao had up her sleeve, Zhulong would prefer Yadan. Besides, Yadan knew that Zhulong and Xiaotao were already on shaky ground. She believed single-mindedly that the day Zhulong returned would be the day they would all reunite as a happy family.

But Zhulong never returned, while An Xiaotao did.

5

At this time, expensive houses were built in the suburbs of the city, houses painted in red or white in the style of Russian mansions near a seaport. Two rows of flags flapped about from the roofs, while during festivals, colorful balloons filled the skies above the houses. Here, away from the city, the air was definitely better and the sky was very blue, with an occasional white cloud floating by. People said the color of the sky reminded them of the pristine days of the 1950s; and many of the houses had been bought by show business celebrities who would only occasionally reside there.

Not a soul believed anything could go wrong in such a paradise, until one day twenty or thirty families reported robberies of expensive jewelry and belongings that had occurred almost simultaneously. The police checked the entryways of each and every house and came away with no clues, as all had door chains that had not been broken or cut. Nor did any of the houses' windows show signs of a break-in. In the end, the police couldn't figure out how the robbers had gotten into the houses.

For a full month they staked out the area and the only clue they managed to dig up was from an old farmer who reported that he had once seen a beautiful woman coming out of an expensive car and walking into one of the houses. The police showed the old farmer a computer-generated sketch of the woman based on his description, but he could only shake his head, as even the license plate number on the car escaped his memory. The lead went nowhere.

A few months passed and the largest post office in the nearby city was also robbed. The robber wore a black mask and entered the building during lunch hour, locked the three employees in a bathroom, and ordered all the customers to lie down on the floor. The safe was opened and the thief absconded with all the cash in bundles.

Within minutes the police were on the scene and managed to seal off the place and prevent anyone from leaving, including the seven customers, four men and three women. Among them was a beautiful woman who, when the police began patting down her body, shouted: "I protest! I protest!" She promptly pulled out an identification card that indicated she was a Chinese holding an American green card. Taken into a separate room by a female police officer, she was thoroughly searched, but nothing was found.

The old police chief remembered the beautiful woman at the post office had bright eyes and long eyelashes and that when she was little she must have had the look of a baby doll. Now it was hard to tell her age, maybe thirty or as old as forty.

Nor could he imagine that in three days' time at an expensive mansion in the western part of the city, that beautiful woman whom they had searched, but found nothing on, would receive a package containing the cash stolen that day from the post office.

That woman was no doubt An Xiaotao.

Xiaotao's beauty was unchanged, and in many ways she looked even more elegant and calm than ever. Wearing a pair of red pajamas, she poured herself a drink and sat down, one leg crossed over the other, as she played with the red slipper dangling from her foot. In the background a Whitney Houston record was playing the songs she had gone crazy over after moving temporarily to America. Whenever she went out driving to "do her business," Houston's music blasted from the car, creating an atmosphere that helped her to come up with plans and which she believed brought her good luck.

An Qiang's blood ran through the veins of his daughter. There sat Xiaotao sipping on her drink with a cold smile on her face. Who would have thought that day at the post office that the woman with a heavy peasant accent from another province mailing a package was none other than the beautiful An Xiaotao! She had stuffed two shirts in the package, wrote the address of her swanky house in suburbia on it in plain handwriting, and sent it by registered mail. Then she put on makeup, covered her face with a black sock, took the cash from the safe, and reopened the package, putting in the money and resealing the package. Since the package had been handed over to the post office before the robbery took place, no one would bother to check it. Even the wily old police chief and the head of the post office overlooked this crucial detail. To her surprise, the police arrived on the scene so fast that she was unable to execute her escape, so she returned to the bathroom, removed the black mask, and flushed the tiny toy gun down the drain.

She would later recall that the old police chief asked that all the packages be examined. But all of them had been sealed with stamps before the robbery occurred and so were never opened. Under her breath, she sneered at the old bald-headed police chief, knowing she had outwitted him.

The robberies at the expensive suburban houses were, of course, also part of her extraordinary performance.

In America, she had set a remarkable record. But if there was anything from her past that could hold her back, it was the existence of Zhulong. She was attracted to him. Zhulong was special and everything about him was completely opposite to her. After Zhulong had run into trouble in China, she had gotten him out of the country. After that, there was nothing left between them; certainly nothing exciting or stimulating for her came from Zhulong, who turned into a fat, gloomy man. Xiaotao could not stand being around him, let alone consider sleeping in the same bed with him. It seemed the only thing that could stimulate her in life was picking up her old craft. Surprisingly enough, she found that people in America were not on the alert about anything, perhaps because they had never endured the class struggles that had raged all over China. She found carrying out robberies was actually a piece of cake in America. Once at an airport, she laid her eyes on a crystal necklace. She schemed in her head just how she would go about stealing it, but in the end she simply took it from the display case and walked away. It became almost routine; so easy, in fact, that she became bored. She was the daughter of An Qiang and had a natural love for intelligent and challenging games. If robbery became so easy for her, it lost all the fun.

The early death of Zhulong was expected. Such a man was bound to die young, as everyone's fate is decided prior to birth. No one could save him. She managed to get Zhulong to America, then returned to China having promised Zhulong to look for his son.

By this point we know that virtually every single member of Xuanming's family was outstanding. But they have all merged into the sea of people, making it hard for them to even recognize one another. Take the case of Xuanming's fourth sister, Xuanzhen, who was very much aware that her son had run away and ended up becoming a bandit. But how could she possibly know that her son had a daughter named An Xiaotao? Nor could Xuanming's youngest granddaughter, Yu, have any way of knowing that the clever and somewhat weird An Xiaotao was the daughter of one of her uncles. And as for Jinwu, she was the daughter of the mixed marriage of her mother, Shen Mengtang, and an American man with the name of Smith. Shen Mengtang was the daughter of Xuanming's seventh brother, Xuanyu. But among the vast sea of people, if they had happened to meet, there was no way for them to recognize each other. And yet, life is full of mysteries; and so, ultimately, this would lead them to meet and attract each other, staring at each other from various angles as if looking at themselves in a mirror. That mysterious thing of which I speak is blood ties which even in the case of a ten-thousand-to-one chance of meeting will produce a sense of mutual attraction some-how, somewhere.

Think back to the structure in our opening chapter: a network of beauti-ful trees spread out in different forms and shapes, all representing blood ties. The actual formation of blood ties is a function of chance that consolidates and spreads much like the scattering of ashes, or water pouring over stones, or even like the huge network of defense of the queen on an international chessboard. They demonstrate the art of altering formations—the spreading out of lines of defense—in a complicated but pure way, and the profound relationship between such formations and the real world.

But who can confirm the existence of this relationship? If Mengjing did not insist, who could prove that Yadan was the daughter of Tiancheng? If this were a legal case, none of the evidence would be valid, and none of the claims would stand.

The only proof would be blood.

Strangely, Yangyang's blood type is B positive, a rare type. Yadan regret-ted that she never asked Zhulong about his blood type. But she foolishly thought B positive must be a blood type for a genius. Since Zhulong was so intelligent, Yangyang, she thought, could never go wrong.

6

Yadan's current job is as a literary editor. Her office is filled with piles of manuscripts. Her boss, the editor-in-chief, asked Yadan to be the executive editor for a series of books written by foreign female writers. The editor-in-chief expected Yadan would be thrilled, but he was absolutely disappointed.

While reading the manuscripts, Yadan cursed inwardly about the lousy writing. *When Tears Run Dry*; *The Broken Spirit of Sun-Moon Lake* . . . all of these were pining and whining without cause. These female writers who write while holding their pet doggies, what do they know about suffering and misfortune? If the editor-in-chief was not in his male menopause, how could he have accepted such lousy manuscripts? There are good writers abroad, who have such good taste that they would not mingle with men like this editor-in-chief. Just like Yadan back then, they kept clean, did not touch anything dirty, and did not consort with the famous, the rich, and the authorities. Yadan would not learn or engage in the tricks others would use to achieve personal goals, and she totally despised those who did. Back then, proud Yadan thought, who needed to use tricks? The final judgment was in the writing.

In the past, Yadan, naive as she was, thought the literary critics would really read her books. When she lived in that tiny run-down room with no desk, she sat by the bed and used it for her desk, writing millions of words on it there. Every word was born from her heart, just like her child. Yadan could have become a heroine of motherhood, but instead she became a heroine of words. Every story she wrote, she meticulously designed the plot and created suspense, and secretly dreamed that someone would decode her stories and become her close friend and confidant. But no, this did not happen. Every story or novel she wrote with heart and soul, but once published, they became silent and disappeared without a trace, like a clay bullock walking into the sea. The focused heat over a good book in the 1980s was gone. The 1990s saw a pure literature, deadly boring. "Hype" was a new term in the nineties. Fat and ugly Yadan, who was afraid of seeing or being seen by people, was naturally scared of hype. Therefore, her writing career for the first time faced a crisis. Gradually fewer magazines and publishers asked her to contribute. Her income dropped dramatically. Obviously Yadan had become that kind of over-the-hill writer before she had even reached the top.

Quite fortuitously, using a pseudonym, she wrote a romance in the popular novel style. She thought it was the worst book she had ever written, and when it was done, she didn't dare to give it a final reading. She simply sent it off to a publisher. She did this because she wanted to earn some money to buy a piano for Yangyang. But the book brought her good luck. Even after several printings, the book continued to sell out. Pirated editions flooded the street vendors. The income from this book was five times more that her total income over the past several decades. Fan mail from her readers came in droves. Only then did Yadan realize: "It's like this after all!"

Yadan abandoned her old literary goals and went after the new thing, becoming a high-end romance novelist. But after the initial excitement, the inflated income did not bring her much joy. Whenever she saw the good writers she loved and read classic novels, she would feel a sharp pain in her heart. This was rather like that afternoon many years ago when she saw Zhulong walking to her house but was unwilling to see him because she felt she was ugly from the pregnancy. It was the same feeling. When she truly entered the field of popular fiction writing, she realized she had lost the two loves of her life, the two pillars supporting her life. The words she had written many years ago in the play *Q&A Behind Bars*, seemed to come through time and space to appear before her eyes again:

Life is at a crossroads.

One road is smooth, garlanded with olive branches, red-carpeted, and leads to fame, money, social status, favoritism, convenience, and a happy, cozy family. In short, one can have all the personal gains. Another road is a winding, bumpy path, overgrown with bushes; with tigers, lions, and wolves peering out of the dark, hiding somewhere along the way. This road leads to a dangerous life, endless physical pain, mental torture, unknown blacklists, shameless smearing, imprisonment, and disaster for families and descendants. On this road, no comfort, no personal happiness is in sight.

But years later, ten years or a thousand years later, history—the honorable judge—will give people a well-deserved judgment. There are always two ways to live a life: one is short, the other eternal, with the sun and moon.

Which way to go? It's time to choose.

Yadan laughed coldly, thinking that after all these years, what was bothering her now was still the same thing. Now she would choose the first option without hesitation. She would of course pick the first choice even though it would be painful to lose the second one.

The call from An Xiatao came just at that point.

Yadan picked up the phone and said hello into the receiver, and then heard the sexy voice of a woman: "Hello, is this Yadan? My name is An Xiaotao, Zhulong's wife . . . I need to meet with you. Can you arrange a time?"

The editor-in-chief walked into her office just at that moment and saw Yadan's hand shaking and her face washed over with a greenish yellow color. He cried out, "Yadan, what's wrong?"

7

Now the scene goes back to the beginning of the story.

The doors to the operating ward swung slowly open. A gurney emerged as quietly as a boat rowed over calm waters. Yushe's mother, Ruomu, for the first time shed tears as a loving mother for a daughter who had just had a lobotomy. She thought the grudges of all these years between her youngest daughter and herself had finally been all wiped out at last.

This had started at the funeral of Lu Chen. At that time, people still held wakes for the dead to let the relatives and friends come to say their farewells. The body of Lu Chen that had shrunken so small now suddenly swelled up. His face, like a slab of pork injected with water, had completely changed shape and was made up with reds and pinks. When Yu saw that face, she couldn't stop yelling, "No, no, that's not my father! No. Where did you take my father?"

At the solemn funeral of Professor Lu Chen, we saw Yushe, pale and fatigued, her messy hair all askew, break away from the grip of people, throw herself onto her father's body, lifting the red satin that covered him, and like a witch issuing a frightening chant: "My spiritual mentor, please enlighten me: this man lying here before me—is he, or is he not my father?!"

We know that since childhood, Yushe often said things like this, but she always said them silently inside. This time she let it slip out, chanting loudly in front of all.

No wonder Yu's mother lost control and started to bellow. For several decades, people at Jiaotong University had been talking about the story of the third daughter of the Lu family: she choked her baby brother to death when she was little. Later, she jumped into a lake to commit suicide, and still later she jumped from a building, damaging her liver and suffering many other bodily injuries . . . Thank God, they didn't know anything about her tattooing story. That in itself would have been enough to convince people that she was crazy.

So Ruomu's bellowing was understood by the others. Many hands reached out to grab Yu. They pulled her away from her father's body and she lost consciousness. In a daze, she felt she was pushed into a vehicle by several strong men and the vehicle sounded its siren, which reminded her of the horrible night many years ago. It was also a car with a siren and Yadan and Zhulong, who were walking ahead of her, suddenly vanished. While she was lying in the vehicle, in a daze, she thought she, too, would vanish. After that she did not remember anything.

Yushe indeed vanished. Her body was still there, but her soul, her memory, and her intelligence . . . all gone, vanished completely. After all, her mother was kind. She refused to send Yu to a mental hospital but agreed to another treatment. And that treatment would make Yu a normal person forever.

Now our leading character, Yushe, is finally a normal person. She has become very cheerful and optimistic. She gets along with everyone. Not just gets along, she likes everyone, is fond of socializing, fond of doing good deeds. She listens to her bosses and is especially filial with her mother. She nods her head to whatever her mother says. She also turns her mother's every wish and whim into realities. When her mother wanted to plant something in the backyard, she bought corn and sunflower seeds and planted them in just two hours. When her mother wanted to take a walk in a park, she peddled their worn-out tricycle and delivered her mother to the gate of the park. She was as useful and handy as a young man. Ruomu's lifestyle finally returned to what it had been before Xuanming passed away. She would sit in that old wicker chair, which had been repaired a few times, slowly picking her ears with the golden ear spoon. At mealtime, it was naturally now Yu who brought the hot dishes to the table. Yu was working at a knitting factory, specializing in handmade sweaters. Yu used to draw or paint, so she designed some floral patterns for the boss, who consequently fired his designer. Yu never demanded payment for her drawings. She was extremely popular among everyone at the factory.

A few years later, Yun'er came back from Japan. Although she looked rather tired, she was still very beautiful and was very rich. She came back home to visit only now and then. Most of the time, she stayed at five-star hotels. So Ruomu's worries all shifted from Yu to Yun'er. Every day, aside from her ear cleaning, eighty-year-old Ruomu would raise topics like, "How is Yun'er? How come she came back by herself? She is so worrisome!"

Yun'er returned around the same time as Xiaotao. That was six years after Yu's brain surgery, which is close to the end of our story.

8

The meeting of Yadan and Xiaotao seemed to have a certain historical significance. Even though Yadan had fixed herself up for the occasion, Xiaotao was still shocked at seeing this woman: old and worn-out, no looks, no flare, absolutely nothing in this woman Zhulong would find even remotely to his liking. How could Zhulong sink so low as to have a son with an old bag like this?!

Yadan was no less surprised than Xiaotao! As far as years go, Xiaotao was no more than a couple of years younger than herself. With her little girl's hairstyle and dresses, she could very easily pass herself off as a fine young lady! Yadan knew that was exactly Zhulong's type: women with a youthful look; this was precisely why he liked Yu so much. Xiaotao stood miles apart from Yu in one respect, and that was that she knew how to dress. She presented herself at one and the same time as both beautiful and pure looking, the classic lover men dream about. When Xiaotao flashed her big, bright eyes at Yadan, Yadan even forgot that she had hated this woman. But now, the hate of many years was gone instantly, like melting ice, as Yadan could only think of what a heavenly matched couple Zhulong and this young woman made.

The daughter of An Qiang possessed a first-rate ability to handle all situations. Xiaotao was stunned for just a few seconds, and then quickly extended her warm hospitality. She welcomed Yadan into her home, offering her guest a pair of soft silky slippers and a cocktail with ice, and greeted Yadan in an inviting and sexy voice: "You didn't bring Yangyang with you?"

That was enough to make Yadan feel embarrassed at her own obvious mistrust of her hostess. Awkwardly, she took out a picture and said, "For a start, here is a picture of him for you. He is in the fifth grade and has lots of homework. Next time, you come to my place and you will see him."

Not in the least offended, Xiaotao smiled. "I know you two are living on a tight budget. Zhulong misses his son all the time. He asked me to bring some money to Yangyang. It's not much, but here is a thousand U.S. dollars. At the current exchange rate, it can get you nine thousand yuan!"

Yadan was touched, and watching Xiaotao take an envelope out of her alligator handbag, she asked, "How is Zhulong's health?"

Xiaotao was startled but quickly said, "Much better than before, but he's still not up to scratch. He is too weak for any rapid cure. He has to take things easy. So when I go back, I am going to take some herbal stuff with me, like wolfberries, longan, lily bulbs, and milk vetch to make soup for him."

"I have all kinds of herbs at home. You don't have to buy them . . . Do you have a picture of Zhulong? I could take it home to let Yangyang see what his dad looks like . . ." As she said this, her reddening eyes were on the verge of tears.

Xiaotao quickly took Yadan's hands. "It's all my fault. I forgot it. I am so sorry . . . don't worry. When I return to America, I'll arrange for you to come for a visit. When you go there, you all will meet again. Yangyang is so smart that when he grows up he will go to a college in America. Then, for sure, father and son will meet. Now we have met each other and are getting along great. From now on, we are sisters. I don't want to have children of my own. So our two families can become one. We'll buy a house in America where we can all live together. That would be beautiful!" Xiaotao then kissed Yang-yang's picture. "Such a lovely child. If I have a child like him, I'll take my life as it is, even if I can't find a man the rest of my life!"

Yadan found the last words uncomfortable, so she got up to leave, but again she couldn't resist the next question: "Did Zhulong ever mention me?"

Xiaotao's smiling face immediately froze. "Of course he did. He said . . . you should take care of your health . . . taking care of a kid . . . is quite tiring . . ."

"Surely he must have said something about my writing?"

"Writing? Oh, no. He never mentioned that." Xiaotao's interest in min-gling with this ugly woman ran out. She closed her lips and watched with a certain delight as the color rose from Yadan's cheeks to her forehead.

With her sweaty hands Yadan held on to her bag tightly, as inside it was her popular romance novel. She recalled the night by the water fountain at the center of the university. Back then, she had just started her writing career and her first published short story *Buttercream Cake,* brought her overwhelming attention. All regarded her as a rising star with an immensely promising future. That night, the moon belonged to this rising star, as im-ages of their young faces floated on the water in the fountain. The silvery moonlight, like snow sent from the heavens, merged with the springwater in the fountain to create a serenity that was like music to the ear. That night, her blood and Zhulong's were flowing to the same rhythm as they were bathed in that mist of watery moonlight.

Yadan moved Yangyang and herself out of Ah Quan's house. With the money from the popular novel, she rented a two-bedroom apartment in the northern part of the city. From that day on, Yadan wanted to start a new life. In the mornings before arriving at work, she would go to a local bowling alley for some exercise. Her heavy body, like the bowling balls she was throwing, pounded hard on the shiny waxed floor, bringing a series of disgusted looks from young women nearby as they looked at this flabby old woman who managed to throw the ball into the gutter each and every time.

One night a couple of weeks later, she picked up Yangyang from his piano lesson. The piano teacher told her, "Your son is moving along very well. He has finished John Thompson's book *Teaching Little Fingers to Play*. Next week we'll start Thompson's Book One and some of Canon's songs and Beyer's piano basics. Don't forget to get the books."

It happened when Yadan was taking Yangyang across an overhead walkway. Suddenly, from afar, she heard the sound of a police car approaching, with its blaring siren coming closer. For many years, the sound of sirens had made her shiver. As she frantically hurried, she saw a masked female figure run out of a nearby building where a branch of the Bank of China occupied the ground floor. Before Yadan realized it, she felt Yangyang's warm little hand suddenly slip out of hers as he ran toward the car parked outside the bank, shouting, "Catch the rotten egg!" Yangyang's little voice sounded frail and delicate in the heavily polluted night air of the city, as if it were hopelessly enshrouded in some thick and viscous substance. Instantly, Yadan's mind went totally blank.

Yangyang fell down about fifteen feet in front of the car, just as its engine started. Yadan would have had a chance to reach the fallen Yangyang, but the police suddenly opened fire from behind. The car outside the bank took off at lightning speed. In Yadan's dying moments of consciousness, the car roared like a soaring bird whose flapping wings stirred up the filth and dust as it flew off through the still night. With the dust in her eyes, she felt the bullets from the police guns rip through her body from behind. She instinctively stretched out her hands toward her son. Upon reaching the crime scene, the police saw a heavy woman lying on her stomach with one arm stretched forward and her head raised high.

The local paper reported as follows:

YONGCHUN BRANCH OF THE BANK OF CHINA ROBBED.
POLICE FAIL TO CATCH THE THIEF.

Last night at 9:45 p.m., police received a phone call from the Yongchun Branch. They arrived at the scene quickly, but the robber had already driven away in a red car. A woman and an eleven-year-old child were caught up in the confrontation. The child was run down by the car and the woman was killed during the gunfire. The identities of the woman and child were not revealed. The child was taken to a hospital by the police and is currently still in critical condition.

9

The tragedy of Yadan and Yangyang was the biggest news on the campus of Jiaotong University. Mengjing received visitors day and night and at one point fainted from so much crying. When she came to, she continued describing to people her profound grief. But her mournful words after so many repetitions seemed to have lost all sense of relevance, even though everyone understood the sad nature of the topic. Instead, people began to draw attention to Yangyang. "You have Yangyang. You must save Yangyang." Mengjing told people tearfully that Yangyang had a rare blood type, B positive, one out of ten thousand. People fell silent. Despite Mengjing's deep sorrow, people left after only a perfunctory expression of sympathy.

Ruomu, however, seemed different from all others this time, as she seemed genuinely shocked. She returned home in silence and sat in that old broken wicker chair, lost in deep thought. Events of fifty years ago were blurring before her eyes but she remembered that Tiancheng had a rare blood type, and that if this had not been the situation, he would have been saved.

If that's the case, what Mengjing said was not a total lie. It might be true that Yadan might have been the real daughter of Tiancheng! Then Yangyang would have been Ruomu's grandnephew! Good heavens! If Xuanming were still alive, this revelation would have been a great shock to her! Xuanming, who longed for a boy all her life, would have had a great-grandson! This family clan was so short of boys but loaded with girls, too much *yin* and not enough *yang*, this would be like a spring rain falling on drought-ravaged land.

Then Ruomu remembered Xuanming's last words: "Leave the lamp to Yadan's son, Yangyang." Mother, the old brainy mother, had thought about it after all. The foolish ones were her, them, the later ones. The seeds are deteriorating. The later generations can never catch up with the older ones. This trend is set in stone, irreversible.

Ruomu remained deep in her thoughts until Yu returned from work. She stared at Yu to give her a fright. Ruomu said, "Child. Go check your blood type. Yadan is dead and Yangyang is still lying in the hospital. Poor child. If we can help, let's help them."

We have said that after Yu had her lobotomy she became very obedient and filial to her mother and her bosses. Yu immediately ran to the hospital and had her blood tested. At the dirty hospital lab, Yu stretched out her skinny bare arm.

The result, which we have already predicated, was that, indeed, Yu's blood was compatible with Yangyang's. While drawing blood, one nurse expressed some concern over the fact that this woman had a low blood platelet level and questioned whether her giving blood might cause a problem. But the chief physician could not think twice, as he was so excited to find the blood type, and he ordered the operation for the child to start right away.

Ruomu went to the hospital the afternoon the operation took place. Mengjing was very touched by her visit. Ruomu leaned over the white sheet covering the child on the gurney, staring at Yangyang for a long time. Mengjing seemed to hear Ruomu murmuring, "Poor child! . . ."

10

Yushe fell ill. She had contracted a strange disease. She didn't feel anything wrong immediately after giving blood, but by that night her whole body began to ooze out blood from her pores. Slowly, light, tiny blood bubbles seeped out through every pore. Back when Master Fa Yan was tattooing her body, her blood was very thick. But now her blood had lost color. The tiny blood drops seeped out every few minutes or few hours or few days. Every time the blood seeped out of her pores, her whole face would slowly change color, eventually becoming a frightening red. Ruomu put tissues next to her pillows, but nothing could stop the blood or wipe the pillows clean. Her blanket became permanently tinted with light blood.

These were the last moments of Yushe's life. We can say they were happy moments. She almost lived in an illusion now. She felt her mother loved her very much, something she had never felt before in her entire life. For this, she was very happy and satisfied. Yu's happiness was increased when one day at dusk (another dusk) she saw that lovely young boy push open the door to her house. It was that angel who operated Noah's Ark in America. She was so happy and so was the young boy. The young boy knelt down on one leg next to her bed and proposed to her. She said slyly, "This cannot be. I am so much older. I can be your mother." But the young boy insisted and said, "You are the most beautiful, most honest, and most lovable woman I've ever met. I must marry you." They said many more words, but Yu forgot them all. Later, Ruomu came in the room to invite the young boy to stay for dinner.

Yu remembered clearly that the young boy liked Chinese food but could not use chopsticks. So Ruomu took out a set of silvery knives and forks, the set she once used to entertain the Belgian doctor exclusively. At that moment, Yun'er came home. She grinned when she saw the young boy. She sat very close to him and told him he was very handsome. Yun'er was so natural at flirting. Yu looked at Yun'er as if she were watching a couple of beautiful young people in a film. Yu was thinking God always made people in pairs, but had left her alone without the other half. God must have run out of mud when it came to making her. So she did not have the other half and was doomed to be alone all her life.

Everything Yu saw appeared as if it were behind a thin veil and yet was still very clear. She saw Yun'er kissing the young boy and saying, "I am a hooker. Are you afraid?" Then she saw Yun'er opening her jacket to expose her two miniature breasts, then rubbing them against the young boy. As Yun'er was doing this, she picked up a piece of delicious food with her chopsticks and put it into his mouth.

Then Yu saw the two of them on the floor making love. The boy's movements were clumsy, clearly his first time. But Yun'er was like a lively little fish rolling on the floor and quickly got the young boy into the rhythm. They were turning and rolling until the young boy faced Yu. He suddenly started to yell, "Look. What's wrong with her?" Yu saw the young boy's image suddenly come out from behind the veil. His face was getting closer and closer, like a deformed shape at close range, and she suddenly realized he was not an angel. His enlarged face looked rather terrible.

11

Yushe's last illusion was very beautiful.

In a dreamy state, Yu felt she got off the bed and washed up and even put on some light makeup. She told Ruomu that she wanted to go visit the place she lived as a child. The young boy from America offered to go with her.

With him holding her hand, they walked out to a huge bird awaiting them by the door. Yu was not surprised to see the bird, as if all of this was what she had expected. It was the bird she saw many years ago. The bird looked at them with his quiet and peaceful eyes. Behind the eyes of the bird there seemed to be another pair of eyes—Zhulong's eyes. When Yu met that pair of eyes, she was filled with tranquility and peace. Slowly but surely she and the young boy climbed on the back of the huge bird. Yu thought to herself this truly felt like a fairy tale.

The bird flew steadily. The young boy said the best passenger jet in America could not be any better than this.

The bird flew above the clouds in the high, blue heavens. In that profound blueness and dancing sunshine, Yu seemed to hear the sound of water flowing down from heaven. When she turned her eyes up toward the heavens, she lit up the sky like a sun. She is Yushe—a feathered serpent, the sun of an ancient time, the sun of the *yin* world. This sun belongs only to women.

They arrived at the place where Yushe lived as a child, so fast she couldn't believe it. The place was now a newly developed scenic area. The forest and azure blue lake of her childhood were seemingly still there but at the same time not there. Their beauty, their original untouchable beauty, was gone; that one-of-a-kind beauty hidden under the covering of ghostly snow was gone. Now, day after day, they were subjected to endless streams of tourists with their unwanted comments; they had to have pictures taken with all sorts of strangers; they were inundated with their garbage and countless abuses. Their virgin purity was gone; they had opened themselves to entertain those who threw coins at them. They had long ago forgotten the secret choir of the heavens, forgotten their secret communion every day at twilight with the heavens and the clouds.

Yu sat by the lake. She felt she had returned to the time when she was six years old. Back then, Yu would stand staring out over the lake in a trancelike state, when in the dim light of dusk the many species of strange flowers along its shores would be quietly closing their petals. In those moments when sunset and moonrise shared the evening sky, these blossoms would take on darker tones, their petals becoming as translucent and fragile as glass. To Yu's ears, when squeezed between the fingers, they would emit a chaotic, tinkling sound. At such times, Yu would also see that huge mussel lying quiet and absolutely still on the bottom of the lake. One evening when there was a thunder-and-lightning storm, slipping out of the house unnoticed, Yu went down to the beach with her hair dancing in the wind like smoke, her face alternately obscure or lit up by lightning flashes. That evening, with no moon or stars, the lake was a blanket of darkness. Just as Yu was making her way through those huddles of strange flowers, a huge bolt of lightning lit up the whole lake, and she saw that huge mussel start to slowly open. It was empty; there was absolutely nothing inside. Yu bent down to get a closer look, her hair floating in the water like a pale green jellyfish. At that moment, in concert, the rolling thunder, lightning flashes, and pouring rain crushed down upon that little six-year-old girl's body. At that time, she still didn't know what fear of thunder and lightning was. All she felt was a kind of excitement, as if something was about to happen.

But after a while, the gleaming rays of a flashlight were added to the flashes of lightning. This mixture of light sources broke the images of both Yu and the lake surface into myriad facets, reminiscent of the rococo stained-glass windows of European cathedrals. At the same time, Yu began to hear her grandmother's hoarse and exhausted cries.

A lamp was slowly approaching and Yu could smell the fragrance of tea leaves.

Her ill luck perhaps all started on that day.

But now there was no lamp approaching, no fragrance of tea leaves, no grandma, no father and mother and sisters, no family members, those members of her family who hated and loved one another deeply, who opposed and at the same time were attracted to one another strongly; none of them were here with her. Only one young boy from a foreign country was sitting with her. He, who had accompanied her, was going to betray her. Today's Yu is infatuated with glittering words like "betrayal," "desert," and "subversion."

Because she understood the secret of heaven's choir.

Yu waited until twilight fell. That was her last wish in life. As the last ray of twilight appeared, she clearly heard the godly decrees that she had not heard for a long time: "What you have longed for is about to arrive." She smiled. She thought to herself that she had spent her entire life trying to understand this whispered message. She once thought that it was hatred, revenge, friendship, or even love, but it was none of these things. Only now is she beginning to get close to what the message implied.

She walked to the lake and glanced back at the young boy with a look of great disappointment and said, "That mussel is gone, gone forever."

Slowly she walked into the lake, letting the blue water swallow her up. The young boy thought she looked like a water nymph appearing in the twilight. He just waited, undisturbed, waiting for this nymph to rise again from the darkness.

12

Yushe died on an uneventful dusk.

At the time Yun'er was scanning the headlines in the newspapers:

CELL PHONE UPGRADES LIKE CHANGING SPRING CLOTHES

SPECIAL LOVE FOR YOU ONLY

COSMETICS FOR MEN—A WORLD TREND

TEN-YEAR SILENCE AFTER ENTERING THE WTO, NOW
DISHWASHER MAKES A SPLASH

TITANIC SANK IN ICY SEA BUT REEMERGED IN OCEAN
OF TRADE 86 YEARS LATER

COUNTDOWN FOR THE LAST WORLD CUP OF THE CENTURY

The day before Yushe died, her seeping blood suddenly stopped. Her skin turned as tender as a young girl's. All her body scars were healed. When the last light of day shone upon her face, her face was white and translucent, like a cup brimming over with clear water reflecting the moving shadows of clouds in the sky. That was a golden time full of dreams, gentleness, and wine. Against the backdrop of freshly painted white walls, her body was reminiscent of white silver deeply buried in the bed of a river. The two plum blossoms on her breasts also took on a white color, as if they were painted with a clear titanium white oil paint.

In this world of whiteness, Yu slowly opened her eyes. She saw her beloved mother sitting next to her. An image of a loving mother with a loving daughter had finally appeared in the closing moments of Yushe's life. Yu looked at her mother and said clearly, "Mother, what I owed you I have paid back. Are you happy now?"

The loving mother, Ruomu, once again poured out her tears: "Child. Do not mention the past. You are mother's favorite child."

Yu closed her eyes happily after hearing this. She thought she had spent her entire life working to redeem her sin. The cost was too high. Should she have a next life, she would want it to be a different life.

Ruomu saw Yu's tattoo on her back for the first time. She was stunned by its delicate design. She had had no idea what this mysterious girl had done to herself. She felt really sorry for her daughter. Ruomu felt it would be a shame to lose that beautiful design forever, so she asked Yun'er to copy it down. Yun'er thought her grandma was stupid in asking her to do this. But using a pencil, she copied the tattoo onto a sheet of paper. Ruomu was not happy with the result. She said that when it came to talent, none of them could compete with their youngest aunt, who could draw snowflakes, beautiful snowflakes, at the age of six or seven.

Then Ruomu fell into deep memories of the distant past. That snowstorm many years ago seemed to be falling on this family again. Whiteness was everywhere in her house now, glittering white rock sugar, moonlight-white bedsheets, milky white cups, pale white figurines, and a white sky outside the window. The whole world seemed to have been covered with a huge blanket of snow, of multilayered strangeness.

EPILOGUE 1

The news of Yushe's death went as unnoticed as if it had been buried under a heavy snow.

Yu's death was a kind of disappearance, a complete disappearance, just like she had never come into this world. But a year after her own death, Yadan became famous. Yadan's books were everywhere, as well as her private writings, which she had saved on her computer but had not been willing to publish. Now society talked about Yadan just as ten years earlier people talked about no one except Freud. The people who did not talk about Yadan were considered to have no culture. Readers who knew about the cold and unfair treatment Yadan suffered were very angry. "She is such a talented writer, famous for her *Buttercream Cake* ten years ago; but in order to make a living, she had to ghostwrite for other people, then started to write popular cheap novels. What a huge and true tragedy!" All the officials and critics could not raise their heads under such criticism. And those who claimed to be Yadan's friends felt proud and happy, thinking this was the best time of their lives. Ah Quan became the biggest beneficiary. Royalties flooded in endlessly from everywhere; letters from her fans poured in telling him about their sorrow. Many small-time reporters came begging for just a couple of stories about the author when she was alive. One day, the great-granny, after eating her tenderized pork shoulder and picking her toothless gums, said the ancient adage was right on the money: "An ugly wife is worth a thousand in gold." Ah Quan was deeply moved by this.

Jinwu was still vainly searching for her mother in America. But she had gotten used to living in America after all those years. She made her way into the movie world at last, playing a supporting role. But due to her age, her future in show business was limited. She started doing business and got very successful. She sent letters and faxes, but Ruomu never responded, so Jinwu still didn't know about Yu's death.

An Xiaotao's game was getting bigger by day. She is now the legal owner of a multinational company. She goes in and out of the country several times a year and has gotten to know just about everyone at airport customs. She'll make friends with anyone aboveground or in the underworld, and enjoys a high reputation as a kind of female godfather in business circles. Once in a while, she gets involved in things like liquidating her enemies. For instance, the year before last year, she helped the police crack a drug case. The daughter of An Qiang is seasoned and has surpassed her father. Just to be fair, she didn't know that night the child she ran down was Zhulong's son, Yangyang, and that the woman who died in the incident was Yadan. Of course, she will never know anything about the unusual blood tie she had with Yadan. So today, An Xiaotao lives a life free of concerns.

Lu Ling got married again five years after her divorce. The new husband is her direct boss, the son of Xiangqin and one of her old lovers. It's quite something that the oldest daughter of the Lu family became good-tempered and learned to do housework after she remarried. The second year into the marriage, the husband got promoted, so Ling quit her job and, like her own mother Ruomu in the old days, stayed home and brought Xiangqin into the house to cook for them. Xiangqin's husband died some years ago and her sons and grandsons are all in the city now. So living with Ling, her adopted daughter, tidying up the house, and cooking for them is easy. In their spare time, they all sit together and play mahjong. Life is good. For Yu's death, Ling sent a cable, which read: "Great sorrow. Take care." Many such cables were sent by Ling over the next ten years. But it was only the photo of Yun'er that left her a bit startled: "Yun'er is so pretty. She looks like me when I was young." Yun'er curled up her lips when she read that letter: "I'll be damned if I looked like her."

Today's Yun'er doesn't look up to anyone. She has money and no one knows where she gets it. She stays in a hotel, living a life like a princess. Once in a while she comes home and visits her grandma. This twenty-five-year-old is more sophisticated than fifty-two-year-olds, as no one can tell what she is thinking. She talks little, mostly just reading newspapers or fumbling in a trance with the violet-colored quartz lamp.

With Yu's death, Xiao came back from Europe. She had left her lover and lived alone. Her hair was all gray but she was in good spirits. She cried when she saw her mother. She took the copy of the tattoo when she left, saying designs like this, full of Eastern mysticism, were popular in Europe.

In the end, the old people are tougher, more resilient and enduring than the young. Like two old sisters, Ruomu and Mengjing are very close, with Yangyang as their main bond. Today Ruomu has fully accepted that Yangyang is her grandnephew, so naturally she is nice to Mengjing. But they have one problem: although Yushe saved Yangyang's life with her own blood, he was paralyzed from the neck down due to spinal damage. Yangyang is no longer the original, lovely, bouncing Yangyang. This young man, the only person in the family with this blood type who has survived, can never live a normal life.

EPILOGUE II

To leave, I leave; to stay, I stay.
To stay, I leave; to leave, I stay.

To run, I run; to stop, I stop.
To stop, I run; to run, I stop.

To stand, I stand; to sit, I sit.
To sit, I stand; to stand, I sit.

To live, I live; to die, I die.
To die, I live; to live, I die.

—SÁNDOR WEÖRES, Hungarian poet

EPILOGUE III

I don't know when I started my habit of buying pirated CDs.

This is the era of pirated CDs. Music or images are compressed and locked in with codes, but the center of a CD turns like a galloping horse. The spinning CD creates a swirl of circles, like a beautiful circle in the center of a city. Every circle has its own center, every center glitters with its own lights, just like a sunflower, when opening up its face toward the sun, creates its own heart.

One midnight when I finished watching a movie on a pirated DVD, as the computer ejected the DVD, a picture appeared on the computer screen: a wand engraved with two white serpents coiling around a black feather. The two serpents were gazing at each other without romantic feelings. In fact, they showed no emotion, but remained instead an emotionless, cold mystery.

I was startled at the appearance of this image on my computer, as I was writing a novel about a feathered serpent.

MAIN CHARACTERS

First Generation:	Lady Yang ➡➡ (Xuanming's mother)	Yang Bicheng➡ (Xuanming's aunt)			Fa Yan ↓
Second Generation:	Xuanming ➡➡ (Ruomu's mother)		Xuanzhen ➡(Xuanming's sister) ↓	Xuanyu (Xuanming's brother)	
Third Generation:	Ruomu ➡➡ (Yu's mother)	Tiancheng (Yu's uncle) ↓	An Qiang ↓	Shen Mengtang (Jinwu's mother) ↓	
Fourth Generation:	Ling➡Xiao➡ (Yu's sisters) Yu ↓	Yadan (Yu's friend) ↓	An Xiaotao (Yu's friend)	Jinwu (Yu's friend)	Yuanguang
Fifth Generation:	Yun'er (Ling's daughter)	Yangyang (Yadan's son)			

LIST OF MAIN CHARACTERS

An Qiang—An Xiaotao's father, bandit, and kidnapper of Meihua

An Xiaotao—Meihua's daughter and Zhulong's wife

Aunty Tian or Shun'er—Ruomu's maid

Danzhu—Yu's doctor

Fa Yan—Buddhist monk

Jinwu—Yu's friend

Lady Yang—Xuanming's mother

Ling—Yu's eldest sister

Lu Chen—Yu's father and Ruomu's husband

Meihua—Ruomu's maid and An Xiaotao's mother

Mengjing—Yadan's mother

Qin Heshou—Xuanming's husband

Ruomu—Yu's mother

Shen Mengtang—Jinwu's mother

Tiancheng—Xuanming's son and Ruomu's brother

Wang Zhong—Ling's husband

Wujin—a soldier and Shen Mengtang's friend

Xiangqin—Ling's wet nurse and Mrs. Peng's daughter

Xiao—Yu's second eldest sister

Xuanming—Yu's grandmother and Ruomu's mother

Yadan—Yu's friend and Mengjing's daughter

Yangyang—Yadan's son

Yuanguang or Zhulong—Yu's friend

Yun'er—Ling's daughter

Yushe or Yu—daughter of Ruomu and Lu Chen

Yuxin or Yang Bicheng—Xuanming's aunt

HISTORICAL NOTES

Time line of major events in China from the mid-nineteenth century to the close of the twentieth century, the historical period covered in this novel:

1851–64: The *Taiping Tianguo* (Heavenly Kingdom of Great Peace) Rebellion against the ruling Qing Dynasty, in which as many as 20 million people perish, swept across the nation.

1861: This year saw the rise to power of Empress Dowager Cixi, a female ruler who manipulated the government for forty-seven years and became known for her extravagance, capriciousness, and abuse of power.

1898: The Hundred Days of Reform in which attempts by the young Guangxu emperor to inaugurate moderate political, economic, and military reforms in China ended in failure at the hands of Empress Dowager Cixi.

1911: The Xinhai Revolution overthrew the Qing Dynasty (1644–1911). Dr. Sun Yat-sen was established as the president of the Republic of China in the following year but was quickly outmaneuvered by a group of powerful warlords led by Yuan Shikai.

1935: The Communist Red Army arrived in Yan'an, a small town in Shaanxi Province, after the Long March, which began in 1934. Serving as the Communist base until the outbreak of the civil war in 1946, Yan'an would also host the U.S. Army Observation Group, known as the "Dixie Mission," during World War II.

1937–45: The Sino-Japanese War that began with the Marco Polo Bridge Incident in July 1937 ended with the defeat of the Japanese empire by Allied forces, including China.

1946–49: A four-year civil war following the end of World War II led to the defeat of Nationalist forces by the People's Liberation Army of the Chinese

Communist Party and the establishment of the People's Republic of China on October 1, 1949.

1957: The "Anti-Rightist Campaign" saw the rectification and persecution of outspoken intellectuals who had been encouraged to speak out by Mao Zedong during the earlier Hundred Flowers Campaign of 1957.

1958–60: The Great Leap Forward brought radical changes in economic and agricultural policies. It was largely initiated by Mao Zedong and centered around the creation of large-scale agricultural "people's communes" and the so-called backyard steel furnaces, which were designed to overcome in short order China's economic backwardness, but which resulted, instead, in a major economic and demographic disaster.

1960–62: The "three bitter years" of famine and economic destitution that followed the Great Leap Forward and resulted in the estimated deaths of over 30 million people, mostly peasants in rural areas.

1966–76: The Great Proletarian Cultural Revolution was the seminal political event of post-1949 China, representing the personal crusade of Mao Zedong and his radical supporters, led by his wife, Jiang Qing, to purge the Chinese Communist Party of their political and ideological opponents, labeled as "capitalist roaders." Following an outbreak of violence and chaos in China's major cities, young Red Guards were expelled to remote areas of the countryside, where, known as "sent-down youth," they often worked at hard labor for years before being allowed to return home in the mid-1970s.

1976 (January): The death of Premier Zhou Enlai was followed in April of the same year by the gathering of huge crowds in Tiananmen Square in Beijing to commemorate his passing and resulted in the first mass demonstration against the authority of the Chinese Communist Party, especially its radical wing led by Jiang Qing and the so-called Gang of Four.

1976 (July): A massive earthquake in the northeastern Chinese city of Tangshan resulted in the death of an estimated 250,000 people and has been widely interpreted in traditional Chinese terms as a harbinger of major political developments. Occurring between the death of Zhou Enlai in January and the subsequent passing of Mao Zedong in September, it led many in China to label 1976 as a "year of curse."

1976 (September): Mao Zedong, chairman of the Chinese Communist Party from 1943, died, setting off a major power struggle among the leadership for political supremacy that culminated in the arrest of Jiang Qing and her radical supporters.

1978 (December): Deng Xiaoping returned to power and immediately inaugurated major economic reforms, including opening China to foreign trade and investment, along with major changes in education policy that brought the reopening of China's universities to anyone who could pass the entrance examinations.

1989 (June 4): The Tiananmen Square Incident, in which Deng Xiaoping ordered units of the People's Liberation Army to crack down on student pro-democracy demonstrators in Beijing and other major cities, drawing worldwide attention.

ABOUT THE AUTHOR

Xu Xiaobin was born in 1953 into an intellectual family in Beijing. She spent nine years in the countryside and a factory during the Cultural Revolution (1966–76). She graduated from the Central Institute of Finance and Banking and began publishing her writings in 1981. Currently, she is a staff screenplay writer at China Central Television. In China, she has published four novels, twelve novellas, and ten collections of essays and prose. *Feathered Serpent* is her first novel published in English. She lives in Beijing.

ABOUT THE TRANSLATORS

John Howard-Gibbon has done a considerable amount of translation work from Chinese, most notably Lao She's *Teahouse* and Chen Ran's *A Private Life*. He retired from teaching and presently lives in Nanaimo, on the west coast of Canada.

Joanne Wang is a literary agent with a strong focus on Chinese works. She has been a freelance translator for more than ten years. She lives in New York.